Cinder

D. N. Bryn

Contents

FOREWORD

Welcome! This story includes the traditional Grimm Brother's Cinderella content, such as familial emotional abuse and body mutilation. For a full list of content, see below:

- Familial gaslighting and emotional manipulation
- Off-screen physical abuse of side characters
- Death of an animal companion
- One scene of minor body mutilation
- Three major sexual scenes
- Chronic pain and dysphoria healed through magical surgery (own voice representation)

This book is dedicated to all the ones who hurt in secret, deep between their ribs, in ways no one ever seems to notice. May you find yourself in a time and place where that pain is so far behind you that you need no longer tiptoe around it.

And, to pigeons.

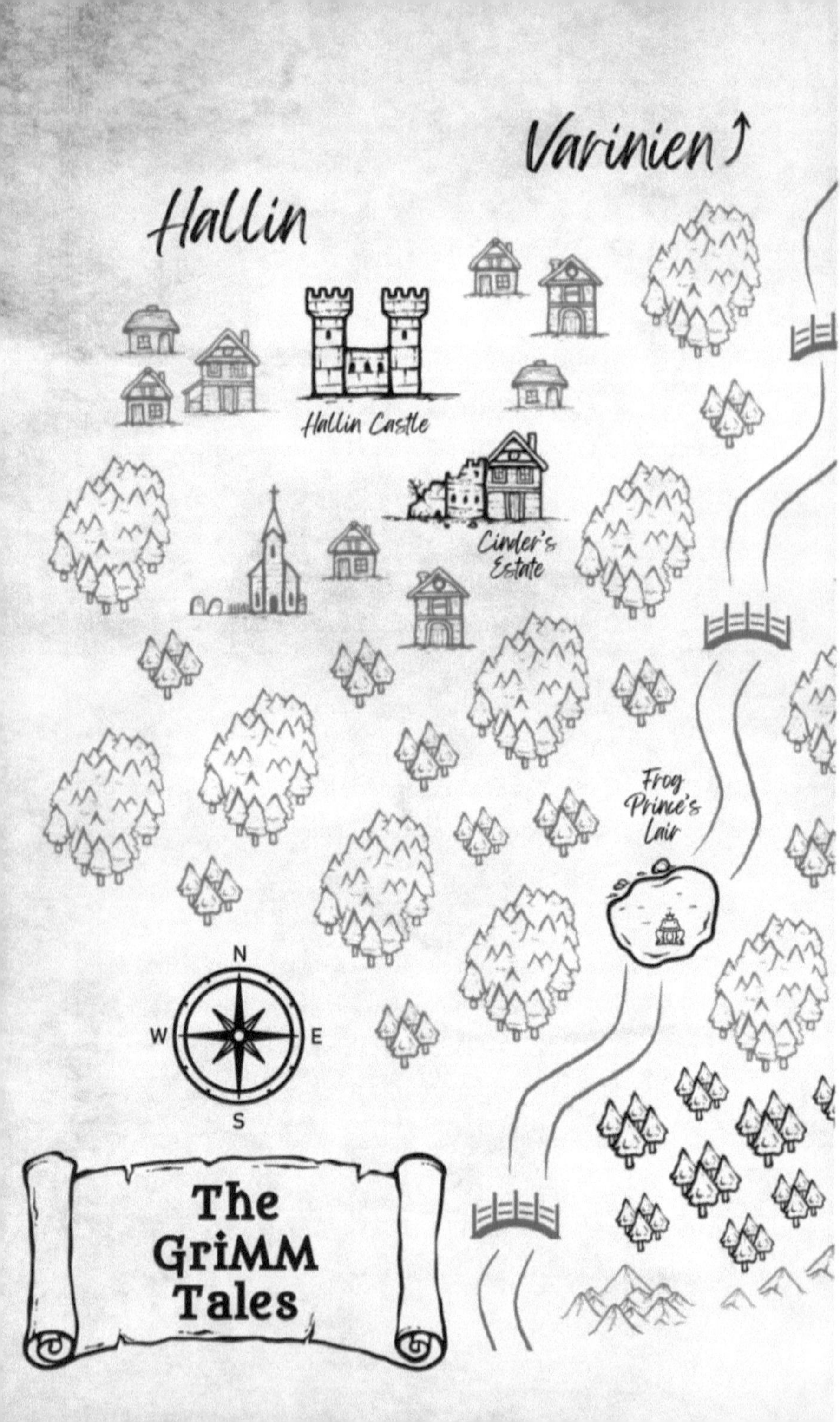

The GriMM Tales

Falchovari
Evil Queen's Castle
(Rumpelstilzchen's Haunting Grounds)
Shoemaker's Shop
Pied Pipers Music Shop
Sorcerer's Tower
Dark Forest
Miners' House
The Candy House
Old Oma's House
Mines

A rich man's wife became sick, and when she felt that her end was drawing near, she called her only daughter to her bedside and said, "Dear child, remain pious and good, and then our dear God will always protect you, and I will look down on you from heaven and be near you."

With this she closed her eyes and died.

—Brothers Grimm, Cinderella

One

C inder Szule Reinholz had not been pious, and he had certainly not been good.

He twisted his knife deeper into the back of his victim, feeling the man's heart split and tear with each struggling beat. Aldous Earhart tried to thrash free of the attack, but he was too late, the motion only gouging open a deeper wound in his flesh. He would have had a better chance had Cin not come up behind him, silent as the night as he'd plunged the blade deep between Aldous's shoulder blades, one gloved hand clamped to the man's gasping mouth. But there was no fair fight in which someone of Cin's small, slim build could have taken down a person as large as Aldous.

Besides, the justice Cin enacted was hardly ever fair, even if it was, regrettably, necessary.

Aldous gave a final cry against Cin's palm and then slowly, gracelessly, his body went limp. Cin could see little more than silhouettes in the darkness of the side street, the moon already set and the stars covering their faces with heavy clouds, as though even they could not bear to look upon the sins committed that night, but he could smell the moment Aldous' spirit left him: a sharp stink amidst the salty metallic stench of blood. The useless red liquid was already pooling around Cin's blade.

A stream of it spilled free as Cin withdrew his knife. He let Aldous's body lower, quickly stepping aside from the fresh corpse. It slumped onto the packed dirt. His hood swayed against his forehead as he shrugged back the edge of his cloak to wipe his bloody blade on its inner folds. No matter how much he scrubbed away his stains, though, Cin knew from experience that he'd feel no more clean in the end. No more like the person his birth mother had dreamed for him.

A pious child would have stayed home.

A good child would not have brought the blade.

Then, perhaps, his mother's spirit would have been there to whisper a better future into his ears and wrap the warmth of her love around his lean shoulders. If there was a heaven, Cin was certain he had no place in it. Not any longer.

As he stood over Aldous's body, two small birds swooped down on him from the darkness, angelic shadows hovering over Cin's kill. The pigeons landed one after the other on Cin's arm, their tiny talons digging into his cloak. The smaller of the two, Lacey, fluffed her gray feathers majestically, the two darker stripes along her wings invisible in the low light. Beside her, muddy-brown Ragimund nibbled at a stray string on Cin's cloak. They were two of his favorites, part of the trio of unwavering companions who'd found Cin soon after his mother's death. Other pigeons from around the town would often join them for a time, called in by the ferocity of their bizarre love for him, but these three were always with him: Cin's precious trio.

For a moment, Cin worried that perhaps their leader wasn't

among them, but he glanced toward the sky in time to spot Perdition as she spiraled toward his head, her pure-white glory creating a ghostly figure against the dark night sky. She pulled up short at the last moment, dropping onto Cin's shoulder as gracefully as an owl on the hunt. The deep coo she gave sounded almost proud.

Cin scratched the side of her small face before holding out a hand.

One by one, all three of the birds spread a wing, stripping out a feather or two each and offering it over to Cin. It was a ritual he knew well by then, having done it more and more often over the last seven years, but every time his birds gave him this small gift, it felt like a taste of forgiveness. Though never enough to satisfy the guilt that roiled ever-present inside him. That kind of absolution was for God to give, he was pretty sure. And Cin had been to their town's little cathedral just enough since his mother died to know that however much their God spoke of justice and forgiveness, he was not any more inclined to provide them than the monarchs seemed these days.

So there Cin was, with a blade and a body, its bleeding coming to a sluggish stop beneath him.

Careful not to step into its pool of red in the darkness, Cin crouched down with his feathers. He slipped them, gentle and dramatic, into the gash he'd torn through Aldous's back. His calling card's first occurrence had been as accidental as the kill that started it all, Cin's birds crowding around him as the tried frantically to stop the woman's bleeding. His impulsive swing had never been meant to end her life, only to stop the violence she'd been inflicting on her young nephew.

Cin had been barely fifteen then, his hands smaller around the weapon—not yet a blade, but a rake the woman had set aside in favor of a more intimate assault. Her nephew hadn't survived either, and that had felt like Cin's fault, too. If only he'd stepped in sooner, paid more attention on his way into their town on the far side of the capital city, not been so preoccupied by the responsibility of retrieving Louise's new dish set.

Three days later, the feathers were just as much the talk of the kingdom as the killing. They became a delicious mystery that turned the scene into more than simple brutality, and the next time, Cin made the choice to hold out a hand toward his little flock. They had answered him without hesitation.

The feathers sticking from the backs of his victims always felt a bit like mockery: as though the bastards' souls had tried to birth wings, to fly themselves to the mythical pearly gates, and failed from the start.

As Cin stood, his birds took off, vanishing into the shadow. But he could still feel their sharp eyes peering into his soul as though asking: had he done right today? Not good, not pious, but right. And he hoped he had. If not, what was the use of risking himself in this, week after week, year after year?

With the blood of twenty-two lives on his hands, it had to mean something.

Twenty-three now, Cin reminded himself. Twenty-three, and, somehow, no one the wiser, despite the all the crown's searching. It felt, sometimes, that if they'd put the same effort into protecting those whose lives were being brutally stolen, little by little, day by day, then Cin's work might have been irrelevant.

Sound echoed from up the street: the creak of a door, then the sleepy stumble of feet. Aldous's body was deep into the shadows, Cin hidden even deeper, but he still began creeping his way back along the street in the other direction. It was slow work, each step deliberate and calculated to conserve his breath beneath the tight binding around his chest. Once, he would have left it off for this—been scampering across the rooftops like a bird himself—but over the last few years his breasts had developed to a place where even the bounce of them as he climbed made his body feel wrong, stretched and skewed into something that wasn't him.

Once he could reach the street over though, there was a wall Cin could scale with enough ease to be over it and into the farmlands that came right up to the edge of this side of town. From there, he'd skirt to the east, and be home by sunrise, feet sore and ribs aching, but safe, and done. For now. Unless he found someone else to stalk. Someone else to slide his blade into three months later in the dead of night. Someone else's blood to stain his hands for eternity.

Cin rounded the corner onto the dark, empty cobbled road that connected the homes at the edge of his town, and from out of the shadows, someone reached for him. He wrenched away, his knife already in hand. Cin's body reacted on honed instincts, but still his heart beat in his ears, his lungs catching beneath their binding. How had—where had—who—

His attacker stepped back. Cin moved with them, sliding in close. Though they were nearly even in height, he could barely make an impact against the other person's bulk, and he leveraged his knife instead, slamming the hilt into the person's shoulder before wrenching the tip up under their chin, finding just the right angle to be ready to slide the blade in, one that would give them too little time to cry out, he knew, and be too sudden to hurt much, he hoped. As they lifted that chin though, their hood sliding back from their forehead, Cin caught the outline of their face and—

God, not her.

"I'm sorry," Dorthe Earhart, Aldous's wife—widow—whispered, a kitchen blade slipping from her fingers. It clattered on the street's stone, the sound so loud in the night. Beneath her hastily donned cloak, she still wore the nightgown Cin had last seen her in as he'd watched upside down through the window of her stairwell, as her husband had pulled her back into their room, her face already stained with tears. They hadn't dried yet.

Cin's fingers went clammy around his blade. His lungs felt too big for his chest, not enough air in all the space between himself and Dorthe. He couldn't hurt her. He couldn't let himself.

Cin forced his body away with a jerk. His shoe caught on the uneven stone of the street, and he felt something snap, but he righted himself quickly, keeping his hood up, his face in the shadows.

Dorthe's chest heaved once. A tremble ran through her. She looked so uncertain that it broke something deep in Cin's chest.

"Go," he hissed, hoping the raspy edge to his voice was enough of a disguise.

Dorthe snatched her fallen kitchen knife and fled.

Cin's hands shook as he watched her go, tearing back down the street in the direction of the Earharts' small town home.

Did she know? She couldn't have seen his face—not well, certainly. But maybe she didn't need to. Any little information she could give the crown's watch would be more than they had now—

and someday that more would become enough.

A terrible, monstrous little voice in the back of his mind chided: he could have just killed her. But as damned as Cin was, he didn't think he had it in him to take an innocent life, even to save himself. He could live under the weight of a great deal of sin, but not that. He'd choose to face the crown's wrath first. Or, he liked to think he would. Cin was never quite sure what lengths his body would go to when push came to shove.

It carried him forward like a thing possessed now, following his original plan to go up and over the wall into the farmland. As he walked, it became harder and harder to ignore the sharp pain between his ribs. It had started when he was young, brought on by the same endless, hacking cough that had eventually killed his birth mother, but now the ribbons of flesh ached all the deeper where his tight binding held his chest flat.

He kept each breath small and short, putting one foot in front of the other. Something on the side of his boot began to flap, peeling a little back from the shoe's sole. His ribs, at least, would feel better if he was willing to give them a week's rest, but a break in his only pair of shoes worried him. Climbing walls and creeping up behind his victims was hard enough as things stood. He did not need a broken shoe to alert the world to his presence. Or to connect his daily life to his nighttime antics.

If what Dorthe might have seen didn't ruin that for him.

Cin tried not to let his focus spiral—there was still a day ahead of him. Still a house to tend, a family to feed, a thousand things that had nothing to do with violence or justice, only stupid, ruthless monotony. His ribs would keep hurting through it all, his newly broken shoe keep catching as he went about his chores. That was where he needed his attention to rest now.

He could feel his three-pigeon flock turning to five, then ten, then dozens as the sky began to lighten.

Tucking the bloody inner fold of his threadbare cloak closer to his waistline, Cin pushed the knife strapped to his belt around to the back and slipped through the gate at the back of his family's estate. He crushed the dew-laden garden grass as he walked, mist curling around his legs. Cin's flock gave a scattered call from where they roosted in the tree that marked the grave of Cin's birth mother.

He lifted a hand to them in farewell—a thank you for being there, regardless of his deeds. The pigeons cooed, and a few of them descended to drop apples into Cin's arms. He thanked each in turn. Not a gift for him, but to cover his hide. That meant his family was awake. He had to hurry.

Cin glanced up at the back windows—curtains all drawn still. He swore though, that as he slipped into the house, one of them rustled, a dark silhouette peering down. He tucked the bloody stain on his cloak a little tighter to himself. The oversight with Dorthe was just making him nervous. His identity was safe, at least for that very moment, and that meant he had a different life to live still: one where his blade stayed locked away in its sheath at his back.

For the twenty-third time, Cin hoped to God that the Plumed Menace had killed his last.

The Reinholzes' small estate had sturdy bones and more rooms than the family should have afforded themselves when they were wealthier, much less now, with coffers waning and no marriage prospects in sight.

The wrapping hallways barely echoed from the rising of the family. Father and stepmother prepared for the morning in separate but joined rooms, ignoring each other with each grumbled breath. The eldest of Cin's siblings and their only one by blood still snored in his silken pajamas, Cin's mending of the moth-eaten fabric always far gentler than his brother's hands had ever lain on anything, or anyone. Cin could hear the apple of their Father's eye, the elder of his stepsiblings, already settling in at the upstairs piano, likely just as alert and brilliant and meticulously put-together as they had been when they finished their extensive hours of study last night. The baby of the house, as empty-headed as the clouds gathering above, shouted down the hall for Cin's help.

Cin hated them all, and hated himself for it.

He slid his muddy boots off at the door, set the apples into their bowl, and tiptoed across the cold kitchen floor, out to the main hall of the old house.

"The hearth, Cinder!" came a cry from his stepmother, her voice raised to echo down through the space.

Cin tried to make himself smaller as he walked. He collected the logs he'd stacked against the wall, ignoring the deepening ache in his side as he carried them, and spilled them into the hearth in Louise's room as quickly as he could. The ground there was just as swept of the previous night's ash as every fireplace Cin tended, yet this long-established cleanliness couldn't stop the barreling reminder of his nickname—"Covered in it! You'd think Szule slept there; the little Cinder-whore."—so firmly embedded in his family's vocabulary now.

"Cinder, child! Why are you damp?" Louise shouted from her bathing-chamber as Cin lit the hearth flame.

"I've been collecting apples, Mother!" Cin shouted back, wielding the feminine lilt of his voice to its most docile advantage. "I thought a cobbler would be nice for breakfast."

"You know that we used the last of the sugar," Louise snapped back. A grammatical inaccuracy, Cin thought—the we should have been singular.

"Yes, Mother, sorry, Mother," Cin replied, the words as familiar as the back of his own hand and as meaningless as a slap. He kept moving, up the stairs and away from his step-mother.

"Go to town for it!" Louise called.

Town. Cin tried not to let his mind flee back to the moment he'd locked eyes with Dorthe in the darkness. If she'd seen him, this way at least he'd find out sooner than later. Cin ignored the flutter of anxiety in his gut as he shouted back, "Yes, Mother."

"You can retrieve Manfred's new shoes from the cobbler while you do!" She was all but screeching now to ensure Cin heard.

He rolled his eyes as he passed Manfred's closed door—there was no use trying to get him to actually do his own chores. He wouldn't be up for hours yet, and once he was, he'd be in a foul mood until at least mid-afternoon.

"Cin-Szule!" Emma wailed from her room in a tone much too childish for a woman of nearly sixteen. "My hair's all knotty again!"

"I'm here," Cin grumbled. He paused to relight her hearth too, before taking a seat on the bed behind her. "I thought you were braiding it before you sleep, not waiting for your tossing and turning to do the job for you."

Emma made a sound of protest. "Well, you were too busy to help m— Ouch!"

"If you'd stop squirming…"

"I'm not. You're yanking," Emma snapped back, and squirmed again. The little jut of her lip was preposterous.

Sometimes Cin thought he hated her most of all, if only because he was afraid he also loved her. He slowed his motions, managing to smooth out the last of the curls in time for a knock on the side of Emma's open door. Their father stood there, one hand behind his back, looking vaguely down the hall instead of at either Cin or Emma.

"Szule, is breakfast not ready?" he asked. "I should leave for Falchovari soon, if I'm to make it through the deepest parts of the border forest by noon."

How was Cin meant to know his father was leaving again if no one had told him? He reassessed his plans; if Father was going to Falchovari, he'd take the better of their two horses, and Mother would want to keep the other home for emergencies, meaning all of Cin's excursions for the next month would be on foot. Or in the dead of night.

His father was still standing there, visibly uncomfortable.

Right, breakfast. "Can Mother start it?"

"You know we all prefer your cooking. And she has the finances to attend to."

The finances that were drowning them.

It's just water in a pot, Cin wanted to protest, but his father was already halfway down the hall, slipping away like a ghost from the home he claimed to work so hard to support. So hard that he was barely there anymore—always off on some business venture or another. Cin didn't have the heart to follow him, to catch him drinking or fucking or—worst perhaps—truly striving and failing out there much the way he failed at everything he'd ever attempted at home.

"I could help?" Emma asked, and the offer made Cin cringe, because it was everything their father had once been: willing to try, even when everyone knew how likely it was that he'd blunder the whole thing.

Cin sighed. "No, no, I've got it. Finish with your hair."

He patted his stepsister's head and left. As he walked through the halls echoing with Floy's piano music, he tried to simply enjoy the sweet melody, ignoring the spark of jealousy it stirred. If he had been better at an instrument, at a science, born first or last, more beautiful or less practical, would he have been the middle child who Louise and Penrod pushed toward arts and intellect instead of the house-keeping?

He was good at this, and there was little else he could do well that didn't involve sliding knives into unsuspecting backs, he reminded himself as he started yet another fire, placing a pot atop it.

He was good at this, and none of them were.

And he hated them for that too.

An hour later, and the food was done and served, Floy off to their painting, Emma to her daydreaming, both heads of home to the business of losing their little remaining money, and—with Manfred still gloriously asleep—Cin had a moment to breathe for the first time since sneaking out of the house late the previous night.

Reaching up under his shirt, he untied the knot on the tight wrappings around his chest. The first few loops of the bandage-like fabric loosened, but he had to work the slack through the rest of the binding until he could finally draw in the first deep lungful he'd taken in nearly a day. His ribs screamed as they shifted. The release barely felt worth the sudden feeling of his breasts slumping back into place, spilling out of him like two traitorous flaps of someone else's body.

Arms wrapped over his awkward, aching chest, Cin curled against the still-warm stones of the hearth, fighting to find a position that didn't just create more pain between his ribs. He stared into the tiny flame, imagining it spiraling upward, past the brick, into the wood of the house. In his dreams, it consumed them all.

Two

Cin's nap was fitful, haunted by dreams of the crown's watch bursting down the back door in their green and gold uniforms, the undead form of Dorthe's husband leering behind them. He woke to a pinch in his back almost as sharp as the usual ones in his sides. It was followed swiftly by a kick to the stomach. Cin winced, hissing out the pain—more severe by way of its suddenness than any actual damage.

"Cinder-whore," Manfred spat.

Cin forced himself to roll into a half-sitting position, rubbing the grit out of one eye. He instinctively checked his hands for ash. Nothing. No smears, no smudges. No outward signifier of some internal sin.

His unbound breasts hung beneath his shirt though, adding a very different kind of discomfort to his body.

"You have a fucking bed, you know," Manfred said. In his voice, it sounded like a snarl. Everything did, where Cin was concerned— Cin, or Emma, or Floy, or Father, or anyone in town he didn't deem fuckable. Not that most of them would fuck with *him* at this point. They knew him too well.

Cin stretched out the unfortunate kink in his spine, grimacing as his loosened binding slid further out of place and— Oh, he still had the knife strapped back there. No wonder it hurt. He scowled at Manfred. "I prefer to sleep somewhere it's not freezing."

It seemed as though every fall the entire family forgot how drafty Cin's room became the moment the chill set in. And every fall, Father promised he'd fix it if they got the wood, and Louise that she'd budget for supplies if someone would go to the mill two towns over with the wagon, and Manfred that he'd pick up whatever they all wanted if he got to go gambling first, and then Floy would argue that he'd only lose and if anyone were to gamble it should be someone with the intelligence to count cards. By then Cin would drag a blanket back to the kitchen hearth, where things were warm and convenient, and the whole matter was dropped in favor of just waiting for spring.

Spring came and went.

Now it was, again, fall, and just the same as everyone else in Cin's family, Manfred had forgotten Cin's original complaint.

He sneered. "That's what you always say, Cinder-whore."

Or perhaps not forgotten. He just didn't care.

"Where's breakfast?"

"Eaten by people who woke up at reasonable times," Cin responded, despite knowing he was antagonizing his brother for little gain, particularly when Cin had saved him a bowl of porridge anyway.

Manfred threw one of the leftover apples at him.

He ducked, hearing the splat of it against the hearth above his head—what a waste during yet another year of crop failures. But then, Manfred had always been a better shot with his fists than his long-throw. When he took a taunting step forward, Cin scrambled up, swiping the half-mushed apple in defense. "Check behind you, numbskull."

Manfred didn't thank him, but he turned back toward the kitchen's long wooden counters, sized for a hired cook and three maids to tend. Instead of paid hands at work, there sat one bowl with a cloth over it. Manfred sniffed its contents like they might be poisoned, before scooping out a glop on his first two fingers. He sucked on them afterwards in a way that made Cin almost wish the porridge *was* tainted.

But he knew he'd never have the stomach to follow through on that.

Manfred was a bully, not a true villain. Not worth coating the blade pressed to Cin's back with yet another layer of blood.

Cin could not seem to free himself of the knife's pressure for the rest of the day, a sickly discomfort trailing after him like the cloak that swirled in his wake. The weapon's presence was the brand of his failure to live a truly pious life; the sins that no amount of bending over backward, or forcing himself to love his family in action, if not emotion, could make up for.

Which was why, despite his family's faults, he had to support them, protect them, provide where they couldn't. He could be good and pious in that, at least. It was what his birth mother would have wanted of him—what she'd offered herself, when she'd died of the very fever she'd tended Manfred and Cin through.

It was already a mark against Cin that he wasn't sure he was prepared to actually die for them.

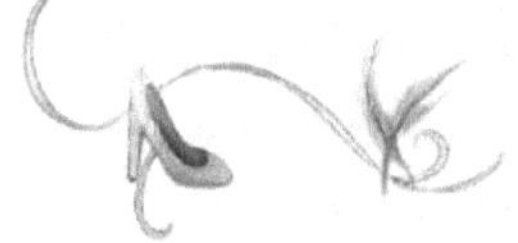

When Cin figured he'd delayed all he could, he forced himself to set off for the town despite the bundle of nerves he couldn't seem to tamp down on. If Dorthe *had* seen enough of him for the crown's watch to come anywhere near the truth, it was better to learn that news in town, firsthand, than when the guards finally appeared at his door. And if they didn't have enough to ultimately trace back to him, staying away would only look suspicious.

Besides, Louise would be on him for weeks about it, no matter what excuse he gave.

On his way, Cin stopped by the creek to wash the blood from inside his cloak. He really had to stop wiping his blades there. They had enough scraps of cloth for the menstruation cycles he and Emma underwent that bloodying one of those would cause few questions, but it wasn't as though he'd been *planning* to use his knife on Aldous Earhart, even if he *had* brought one. Watching, yes, waiting, perhaps, but not anticipating. If anything, he'd hoped for the opposite. He always hoped.

Before venturing back to the road, he stripped out of his shirt, his well-loosened bindings beginning to spiral off his chest as he did so. The deep breaths he took against the ache in his ribs felt fragile and greedy as he collected the wide strip of fabric back into a roll for reapplication. His left side was yellow and green, and he tried to ignore the curving slump of his breast as he touched the area with two fingers. A sharp pain speared deep into his chest.

Cin made a face and slowly, carefully, retied the fabric back against his ribs, tight as he could stand, before looping it around his breasts, pulling more with each wrap of the binding. As he did, he felt his inhales shift from his chest to his stomach, until his torso felt stiff and wrong. And yet right—the right *shape,* anyway.

The more he wore it, the more the pain had begun spreading between his ribs. But to allow the flesh to heal meant denying any form of tight undergarment—even those made for people who cherished their breasts. When he tried to go without the binding, much less any pressure or support, a fresh kind of distress crept into his bones, until he wanted to tear his own skin apart and become merely the bones underneath, genderless and nebulous. It felt like there was no way to skip the pain. Cin could only trade a worse evil for a lesser one.

Just like he was doing out in the world, where every salvation he offered came with a murder.

There were those, he knew, who could fix his dilemma altogether, but they traded in misery just the same as him: people in the deep parts of the woods who were more monster than human, offering magic in dark exchanges, too costly for most who sought them out. If they could be found at all. That was a path better left for the brave and the desperate; those who could throw themselves at their desires in ways that Cin's life would never allow.

His chest successfully wrapped back up, he continued on toward town, feeling far heavier than the pigeons who meandered at his side, flying from tree to barn to fence to house and back with each small estate and farm Cin passed. The closer they came to the town, the less land stretched between each home, until the gentle sounds of the outskirts became a clatter of irreverent noises.

The town center was alive—though not in a good way. Five years ago, the shops would have been crowded with wares, merchants hawking and customers laughing, children tumbling through the streets as music played from one of the pubs. Now, Cin dodged to the other side of the lane as one of those same children begged at a corner. The baker seemed to stand guard over her tired supply, and the people who could still afford to purchase daily fresh bread looked both ways when they passed an alley. Even non-food goods had begun to suffer, with stores no longer boasting the best and newest, but rather the cheap and practical, as fewer and fewer villagers could afford anything else.

The famine might have started across the forest in Falchovari, its people already strangled beneath its seemingly immortal Queen's vile hold, but it had settled in the quiet and peaceful kingdom of Hallin soon after, one crop failing, then another. Next spring, things would change, everyone said. Next spring, the fields would be full, and bellies soon after. Cin feared that would be the same *next spring* during which his father finally entered his room with a shoulder of fresh lumber to repair the drafts.

He tried not to think about his father's upcoming trip, or the way Louise had looked at Cin when she'd handed over the money for sugar, butter, and flour—like it was his fault that he couldn't make the leaves crisping to brown on the garden trees worth eating—or how, based on the sign outside the general shop, those coins would buy even less than they had last month. Cin kept his wits about him and his head down as he passed a group of the crown's watch out front, their green tunics and bright gold banding unmistakable, gave the shop's teller the little courtesies due them, and ducked aside as quickly as possible.

No one narrowed their gazes at him. No one stopped him. No one even seemed to see beyond his mask of deference to the real, living person that wore it. This was the way it always had been for him—as much a ghost in the day as in the night, ignored as thoroughly as the pigeons who surrounded him—but it felt all the weirder knowing that there was one person in town who had seen that ghost, if only in the shadows.

Cin slowed as he passed a pair of customers near the shop's door, his mind fastening onto their hushed whispers as he gave one subtle glance their way. They were Josua, the goat herder from the farm down South Hill Street, and Amelina, of all people, who had flirted unrepentantly with Josua's late aunt's husband despite his very public disinterest. Cin had watched Amelina for a week three summers ago before realizing it was all a show and the two were avidly fucking in the Muller's barn most Sundays after church.

It was a rare break from the myriad of far more distressing one-sided relationships he normally uncovered.

The knife strapped to Cin's back felt all the heavier, but neither Josua nor Amelina looked his way.

"—stabbed between the shoulder blades," Josua was saying. "They found three pigeon feathers stuffed into the wound!"

Amelina's brow went up. "That would make him the Plumed Menace's third victim this fall."

Three in the same season, when that was as many as he'd extinguish during the first three years he slid steel into flesh. With each escalation, Cin had been certain someone would catch him, even if he couldn't seem to catch himself in time to stop the killing. Now, perhaps someone finally had, though by the sound of it, that word hadn't gotten out yet.

As he stepped out onto the street once more, he tracked the dozens of pigeons lining the sills, the rooftops, the street corners—despite those around him seeming to miss the way the birds would flock to him, part of Cin would always regret that first press of their feathers into a wound. He could have been a quiet killer, not watched the price on his head go up, not kept his own legend alive. But there was part of him, he knew, the tiniest, most reckless part, that thrilled to hear his title on someone's lips. Just not that day; not with Dorthe out there, knowing or not knowing.

Cin had a final shop to stop at, but instead his feet carried him the long way around town, quiet and unobtrusive. He passed more of the crown's watch, but none of them so much as looked his way. No one noticed when he slowed near the Earharts' home.

It had been dangerous to care this fiercely in a place so close to home—in the town he moved through nearly every day—but he had not been able to ignore Dorthe, not then any more than now.

The soles of his feet ached, to run for the truth or away from it; either would be better than this. In the end, the street cleared for a moment on both sides, and Cin couldn't help himself from swinging, grocery pack and all, onto the first story overhang of the Earharts' home. It was partially connected to the house to the right of it, their little barns sharing enough of a wall that Cin had an easy route over the top. He focused on slow and steady breathing through the binding around his chest and followed the invisible steps he'd taken so many nights before, more careful than ever with the tear in his boot, along the lips of the second story windows and down to the small veranda beside the Earharts' little kitchen.

As Cin pressed his head over the side of the roofing, he picked up a faint noise. Not a sob, not a racket—two sounds he'd heard often here—but the softest of humming. Happy. Peaceful.

Joy welled inside him, and for a moment, just one single moment, he let it overcome his shame and fear. Dorthe had never sung before. How could she, when she had to know the moment her husband's shoes passed over the threshold? Even a house empty of him was not truly *free* of him.

Until now.

And for just that moment, the act of creating a living being's last breath felt almost pious.

But then Dorthe's humming faded as she moved to the other side of the house, and Cin was alone on a roof that didn't belong to him, fretting again over whether or not the widow of his victim knew him; whether she'd turn him in. The way she'd been singing, though, Cin hoped that maybe he didn't have to worry so much after all.

Slowly, carefully, he lowered himself over the edge, sliding in through the unlocked kitchen door. The torn side of his boot's sole flapped sadly against the stone floor. He listened for the distant shuffling of Dorthe's work, the same way she must have stood there and listened to her husband's for months or years, and as Cin did so, he portioned out a little of the sugar he'd just bought, leaving it in a bundle with a flower atop.

She could make herself something sweet tonight. Enjoy her new-found freedom.

Cin crept out the way he'd come, but as he climbed back up from the kitchen to the roof, the torn edge of his boot snagged on the same purchase he'd placed his weight a moment before. He slipped. His hands found the edge of the veranda, and he caught himself mid-fall, swinging there as his feet scrambled for purchase. Cin heaved his body back over the top of the veranda, his lungs burning with each chaotic breath. He lay there, gasping, for what seemed like far, far too long, a shudder more emotional than physical working its way through him.

Cin finished the route with extra care, pausing to check the street before jumping down. A watch member glanced over his shoulder at the sound of Cin's landing, but his gaze skipped right past. From the rooftop across the way, one of his pigeons cooed. Still, it felt like someone was judging him—God, or his mother, or the strangling grip of the future he was meant to have: one where he was the sort of person bright and lovely and pious enough to deserve a partner who'd carry him away from his life, instead of a family who clearly needed every ounce of usefulness he had inside him.

Three

The war-drums of Cin's heartbeat seemed to follow him all the way to the cobbler's.

He waited awkwardly while his brother's new shoes were retrieved and packaged by the old woman who'd owned the place since before Cin was born. She grunted as she handed him the final bundle, scowling down over the side of the counter.

"Your shoes look like they could use attention," she said, clearly eying the popped seam in the side of the right boot's toe.

Cin tried not to grimace. If his slip at the Earharts' was any sign, the cobbler was more right than she knew. But Louise wouldn't pay to replace Cin's boots any more often then the rest of the household, even if he left the house more... including in the middle of the night, over walls, and atop roofs. Cin had once made the mistake of letting Floy borrow his boots to go collect their science specimens, back when they were young enough that Cin still believed the two of them might be friends—the bright, curious sibling Manfred had never been for Cin—and he was fairly sure the mud he still found caked on his soles was from them. Maybe that was what had prompted the popped seam in the first place; Floy's feet *were* a size too large for comfort now. They'd have to curl their toes up against the tips if the bulk of their heel were to fit.

"I have a spare afternoon," the cobbler added. "I could get it fixed for... say a quarter of what your brother's new pair cost."

Cin laughed awkwardly, avoiding the cobbler's eyes. "If I got these repaired every time they broke, you'd never be rid of me," he joked. "It would be a feat of magic just to keep them together for long."

The cobbler huffed. "If I had *that* talent, I wouldn't be here, now would I?"

"No, ma'am, I assume not." Cin turned to go, and he felt a fresh bit of his boot tear. Before he could step out the door proper, the cobbler raised her voice.

"Heard through the guild that there's a pair of free elves setting up shop in the border forest," she called. "You could try them. They probably work on favors or some nonsense, knowing that lot."

"Thanks," Cin replied, unsure that he *was* thankful. The way she had said it sounded as though she was lumping these elves' magic in with the likes of the mythical shape-shifting Herr Candy or the illusive, bartering Frog Prince, but from what Cin knew of elves, they were a group of people more like humans than any monster of the woods. If there were magical creatures worth risking a favor to, it was likely them.

Cin had seen elves before, a time or two—occasionally they traveled through Hallin for business, though just as often these days they were moved illegally through the country in magic-dampening chains—but each time he met one felt like the first. They should not have been such a wonder, he knew. They had a country of their own to the north—a land of long winters and vibrant magic, so Cin had heard—and at one time they'd been allies and trade partners with the kingdoms of Hallin and beyond.

Now though, the danger of the Falchovari slave trade meant that most were better off keeping to themselves than risk traveling through the human kingdoms, where they might end up in a Falchovari factory if they strayed too close to the border. With their lives so restricted, these cobblers in the woods were likely more open to any kind of bartering. But there were other magical things besides elves in that forest. Cin would not be the first person to wander too far off the safety of the main road and never return. Not even the late Prince Adalwin and his assembly of guards had managed that, despite the lies that had spread of the incident later—what chance did Cin have, alone?

Louise would allow him the money to buy a new pair of boots by next summer. That would be enough. It always had been.

Arms now laden with goods, Cin made his way back through the town in the direction of home. His route took him past the main square, and he gave one hasty glance at the announcement board situated at one end. He knew what would still be hanging there— hanging in every town in Hallin within a day's ride of the nearby capital. The wanted signs were replaced each month that Cin washed the blood from his blade: reward for information accurately identifying the murderer known as the Plumed Menace of Hallin. The exact price tag rose with every few killings, as did the ferocity of country's opinions on the matter.

The Plumed Menace was a vigilante, some said, ridding the country of the scum that slid through the cracks of justice.

Or they were a serial killer, others claimed, obsessed with the joy of the hunt.

And then there were those who stated it didn't matter; that no random citizen should have the right to decide who got to live or die.

Cin thought they were the most right of the lot. Murder was murder, whether or not it had to be done. There was no goodness in killing, no piety in taking a life, only rage and justice.

From the look of the announcement, it seemed there wasn't any new information posted—though Cin couldn't be certain, his ability to read limited to the few words he'd memorized over the years. There were no attempts at a picture of him, at least, and no lengthy paragraphs of description. More confirmation that Dorthe hadn't spoken to anyone of their encounter.

As Cin left the announcement board behind, he headed for the highpoint in the square. If the day was clear enough, sometimes the peaks of the castle towers from the nearby capital city could be spotted from there. It was good luck, his birth mother had told him as a child: a chance to change their fate for the better. As she'd grown sicker, she'd begged to be brought to the square just to see it. The sight hadn't cured her, nor had it saved Cin's remaining family from their slow financial ruin, but he found himself drawn to it all the same, especially on days like these—days where he knew he'd not become the child his mother had wished for. The blood might wash out of his cloak, but the murder would not.

It was as though seeing those towers meant he was forgiven in some small way, forgiven by more than simply Dorthe.

A faint wisp of cloud cover hung low, turning the horizon to a dim gray where the farmlands connected Cin's sleepy outskirts town to the bustling capital. Cin's heart sank despite himself. It was a ridiculous superstition. But so had been the gleam in his mother's smile as she basked in this very square, giggling, *"See, my little Szule? Our God is smiling on us! Only good things will happen today."*

Still, Cin squinted through the haze to the west, hoping to prove himself wrong. As he did, Lacey and Rags landed at his side, Perdition swooping past them to drop onto Cin's shoulder. She cooed, nipping at Cin's ear.

He tried not to smile, not to roll his eyes and laugh at her—not in public, regardless of how little mind anyone seemed to pay Cin, even now—but he didn't try very hard. Perdition cooed again as Cin scratched around her little cheeks, a gleam in her bright eyes. Cin chuckled at her.

"Felon," he murmured.

Across the square, a Hallinisch solider approached the bulletin board. She wore the green uniform of the crown's watch, but her gold banding caught Cin's attention. It was delicate and embellished—a style far more elaborate than the ordinary watch members who stalked the streets after a Menace's murder. That signified a closeness to the royals themselves—a part of their personal guard, even. All the watch belonged to Queen Idonia, technically, but the bulk of them did her bidding throughout the capital, venturing into the surrounding towns and beyond when her family's need demanded it. Whatever watch work required a personal guard member had to be out of the ordinary.

The watch member pulled a fresh, rolled bulletin from her bag and began hammering it to the announcement board. The pound of her nail sent Cin's birds into the air. They circled, jabbering to each other, and landed on a nearby rooftop.

Cin's gut twisted. He had sworn the Plumed Menace's wanted poster had already been updated, the price already raised, but perhaps the crown had learned something new of him since. What if Dorthe had seen the sugar on her counter, and thought it not a gift, but some odd kind of threat? If she'd gone to the watch just then, could they have printed the new flyer by now?

Why give it to a personal guard of the royal family, though? Their hatred for the Plumed Menace ran deep, but that seemed out of the ordinary, even for them.

As Cin fought back his own panic, the watch member took a step back and proclaimed, "Behold, an announcement from King Warner and Queen Idonia!"

She did not seem inclined to stay and answer questions, but the nearest onlookers pressed eagerly in to view the nailed paper, Cin following anxiously in their wake, watching the faces of those nearest the bulletin for any sign that he was better off fleeing.

"What— Does that mean a marriage soon?" one of them whispered.

Marriage? Cin felt his relief like a bucket of cold water, crackling against his skin and sliding into his bones. It had nothing to do with the Plumed Menace, then. Which left him with a far less panicked curiosity. Cin crept through the growing crowd, listening as two of the nearby shopkeepers spoke in increasing glee.

"Every weekend? For six weeks?"

"There will be food!"

"What is it?" a child asked, grabbing hold of the shopkeeper's arm.

"A ball," he replied. Lifting his voice, he shouted out to the gathering mass as he read, "The king and queen are hosting a ball in honor of Prince Lorenz's impending declaration of marriage to a good and gentle partner, for the bettering of our heir's future ascension to the throne and to support his just leadership of our kingdom."

Heir. After growing up with the brilliant and charismatic Adalwin as Hallin's crowned prince, Cin recoiled at the words. He'd mourned Prince Adalwin's loss with the rest of the kingdom. Everyone was convinced—if not by the bloody crown, then by the long seven years since he'd last been seen—that Prince Adalwin was gone for good.

In the passing of the word *heir*, Cin felt more than just the weight of that crown. It had been found not a month after he'd killed for the second time, pigeon feathers stuck to its bloody surface. Not those of his pigeons, Cin knew, not his blade nor his rage, but the prince's death had felt personal for it nonetheless. He'd regretted, then, picking a calling card so easy for others to replicate.

It hadn't stopped him from continuing it, though.

No one Cin killed, common though they were, was worth any less than a prince. Even if that prince had been cherished as a bright and hopeful future for a kingdom who prided itself in being the gentle, kindhearted alternative to its eastern neighbor, a value which seemed to slowly be degraded with every year that passed since his disappearance. In all that time, though, there had never been an official announcement declaring in such blatant terms that his title was passing on to the couple's younger son.

A son who was getting married, no less.

"Do they have the match picked out?" someone to Cin's right asked—the wife of the local blacksmith, Cin thought.

"They would not declare a marriage without one," her friend replied.

"Then why delay the new partner's identity?"

But the shopkeeper was still reading, "This celebration will occur for the final day of every week for the upcoming six weeks, during which all are invited to the capital to partake in food and drink from the castle's reserves. There will be space in the Prince's private party reserved for eligible young—"

By then, the roar of those gathered had overwhelmed the speaker's voice. Cin caught only passing phrases, the excitement growing with each mention of food. Despite his fairly regular—if often bland—meals, Cin could feel their hunger infecting him as well. A whole banquet, for everyone. Food he didn't have to cook, didn't have to serve, food that Cin didn't have to clean up after, or shop for, or spend every waking minute working around. Maybe there would even be iced cakes or strawberry tarts, spiced veal or mutton, or even the bittersweet chocolate drink made with the legendary beans of the southern continent—all the rich and sweet food Cin hadn't tasted since before the famine set in.

And it would be a chance to glimpse beyond the tips of the towers his mother had loved so much.

Cin lifted on his tiptoes, like that would help him see through the haze to the castle that overlooked their capital. He'd been to the city many times before, walked below the walls of the massive royal estate, but the thought of going inside...

If there was anything that had the power to make God smile on

Cin again, maybe it would be that. Probably not. It was ridiculous, after all: as ridiculous as a way out of the famine and an end to the drafts in his room.

But with the blood that coated Cin's past and future, he was willing to take any chance he was given.

Four

C in had never seen his stepmother so excited—at least not over anything that had come out of *his* mouth.

She pushed back her long brown hair, half spinning in place with unbridled energy. "You mean the prince's partner has not yet been announced? And they're reserving space for eligible young people of good character in his sphere?"

Cin could have just not said anything. Was six meals really worth this? "I'm not positive. I could barely hear—"

But Louise flung herself away from him, shouting across the sitting room to where her eldest birth-child sat at the front window, ankles crossed as they read the day's newspaper—conveniently the one from the capital; Cin had memorized the nearby press's names in order to retrieve them, even if he couldn't decipher much else in print. "Floy!"

Floy's hair was perfectly arranged into coils that wrapped up and around their head, despite having very little help from anyone, even Cin, though he recognized their clean, pressed outfit of riding-style pants and a fitted vest as one he'd tended to last night just before leaving. They delicately flipped over the page they were on. "I'm not really interested, Mother."

"Not interested in becoming *queen*?"

That caught Floy's attention. They lowered the paper an inch, their sharp blue gaze and delicate brows peeking over. Cin's father had remarked once, under his breath, that Floy's eyes looked a bit like Cin's, despite their lack of blood-relation, and Cin had never been able to unsee it.

"Dear," Louise continued, "You must see the providence in this. You have all the necessary qualities."

"I would do the role justice," Floy agreed, carefully folding their paper. "I have the grace of a royal with the knowledge of an academic—I can speak all three languages of our largest trading partners." They said it as though they were talking themself into a position of leadership with each qualification. "There would be so much more to learn on the job, but it would hardly be a problem, not with my foundation."

"What if I want to be king?" Manfred cut in from the parlor entrance, his growling tone so opposite the phrasing of *good and gentle* on the announcement.

Louise looked disappointed at the thought. "Well, you can certainly try."

"And me?" Emma shouted, the volume of her voice battling with the *clunk-clunk* of her falling her way down the stairs. She emerged in the hall entrance, her hair hanging half out of her braid. Three of the buttons on her dress were popped open, despite Cin being certain he'd done them all properly this morning. "Could I marry the prince?"

"Why not!" Louise exclaimed, tossing her hands into the air.

Cin didn't offer himself as a fourth potential prince-wooer. He, at least, knew who his family was—a broken mess whose ancestors might have been somebodies, but who'd squandered all chance of that long ago. There was a reason no one Louise deemed worth their time would dream of marrying any of her children, step or otherwise. A prince would respond no better.

Cin carefully fixed Emma's buttons as she jabbered at Louise.

"Imagine living in a palace! I'd have ten rooms, and fifteen maids, and a hundred little cakes, and—"

"Yes, yes, we would be rich," Louise said, as Manfred mocked, "a thousand stupid ass thoughts all those fucking maids would have to listen to."

Floy rolled their eyes in a way that somehow made the childish action look refined.

"I'd just like to go for the food," Cin admitted, so softly he wasn't sure the rest of his family could hear him.

"You, Cinder-child?" Louise inhaled.

The chaos of the room seemed to grind to a halt.

Cin swallowed, feeling certain that he'd done something wrong, even if he couldn't place what this new sin was yet. "It's said to be a fine dinner."

Louise looked mournful. "But this party—it's at the palace, isn't it? That's a part-day's trip. With how late we'll be there, someone will need to stay here to keep to the home, prepare for our return, see to the horse when we arrive." It sounded as though it hurt her to say, and Cin wanted to believe that—wanted not to feel the pain and anger twisting terribly in his gut. "I'd ask Penrod, of course, but he's not meant to return until next month—and it's not as though you'll be going there to meet the prince, anyway."

The prince. The prince who would never have any of them—certainly not Cinder, or Emma, or Manfred. Perhaps Floy had the smallest chance… What were royals like now, anyway? Arrogant, calculated, disdainful? As a child, he would have sworn that Hallin's queen and king were nothing of the sort. They had once been kind and open rulers, like the queen's parents before them, and grandparents before that, going back for generations. They were not without their faults, but they had always connected with their people, listened and offered aid, given more than they'd taken.

Prince Adalwin's disappearance had changed that.

Rarely now did they venture beyond their own castle, sending out their watch to do their bidding, stiff and unwavering. They were not cruel, certainly, but neither were they compassionate. These balls would mark the most they'd offered their people in ages. Perhaps that was a good sign. Perhaps it meant the royal family was changing; healing.

Someone good, someone gentle, their announcement had claimed, but what was genuine and what was just for show? Whatever the case was, they certainly did not want a ragged homemaker as a future leader for their kingdom. No one would want Cin: not gentle, not regal, not brilliant, not good. None of the virtues Mother had wished from him. And if they discovered what he did in the dark… Cin could go unnoticed long enough to feast and be gone, but with the price on his head, there would never be a permanent place in the castle for him even if he possessed every one of Floy's skills and more. Not even he could hide who he was for a lifetime. His run-in with Dorthe was proof.

"Please, say you'll stay for us, dear," Louise asked.

It would be safer to agree. Gentler. Kinder. His birth mother would have. But all that seemed able to come out of Cin's mouth was, "I don't..."

Around him, the conversation had resumed between his siblings, flitting somewhere around the prince's looks and if he liked tea—that was Emma—and how well he fucked—that was Manfred—but it all felt distant. Abstract. Louise stepped in, and Cin didn't step back—couldn't step back—not as his stepmother's fingers so gently cupped the side of his face, her other hand squeezing his shoulder.

Softly, she pleaded, "You're the only one I trust for this besides Floy, and you understand that Floy must go, don't you? They have a real chance at elevating our status." Her brows knit, her thumb caressing Cin's cheek. "You wouldn't take that away from us for a bite of food, would you? Surely the royal's reserves won't be enough for all in attendance anyway. I doubt we'll get more than a few morsels at best."

It was all too much suddenly, and a rush of hot, violent emotion rolled through Cin. He jerked back, making his stepmother squeak in surprise. The moment her hands were gone, though, the fire that had overcome him turned to a void. All he wanted to do was fall into her embrace—fall and never get up.

He rubbed his hands over his arms instead, swallowing through the thickness in his throat.

Louise smiled weakly. "We'll discuss it more later." She clapped twice, pausing the chatter happening in the rest of the room. "We all have our chores to attend now, don't we?"

And one by one, they left the sitting room, as though each of them had chores indeed.

As though all chores were equal. As equal, at least, as their prospects.

Every day leading up to the weekend, Cin stopped in the square to squint at the capital, hoping for a glimpse of the palace towers.

The crown's watch had funneled back to the castle and the Plumed Menace seemed to have slipped everyone's minds, replaced by their excitement for the royal ball. It was the talk of the town, and the talk of the Reinholzes' household—even the voice inside Cin's head couldn't seem to shut up about it. He daydreamed of the food, but his desire went beyond that. This would be a night to simply enjoy himself. There hadn't been a proper party in any of the nearby towns in months, much less one he'd be invited to.

Cin wanted this one: wanted to disappear into it and, for one night, cease the constant list in his mind of everything that needed attention back home and everything he might have done wrong. To momentarily stop searching for all those who cried in the night and left their homes with inexplicable bruises. Their misery clung like ash to the edges of Cin's conscience, brittling into anger and guilt. It felt as though by setting foot into that castle, he could somehow stop being the Plumed Menace the crown was searching for. Be his mother's child instead: good, if only for a night.

Louise was never around at the right time to discuss the matter, though, and by the morning before the ball, Cin was anxious with the energy.

"Hearth, Cinder!" Louise called down the hall, a yawn in her voice. "It's gone out again!"

There wouldn't be a better chance than this. The cold wood floor seemed to creak with the ghosts of all the winters past as Cin knelt beside the hearth in Louise's room, tucking fresh firewood around the morning's embers. The flame seemed to burst to life beneath his hands before the flint could even bid it come.

"You know my fingers just can't strike a spark quite right anymore?" Louise grumbled, sliding her feet into slippers. "It's such a hassle having to rely on my children for it."

"I know, Mother." Cin pulled himself to his feet, coming over to the bedside to remake the linens the way he did for his siblings most mornings, as he asked, hesitantly, "About the ball tonight..."

"Yes, yes," Louise waved a hand in Cin's direction without looking at him. "You'll see that everything is tended here for us, won't you?"

"Actually..." Cin ignored the little flicker of fire in his gut. There was no knife strapped to his belt now. He could be good. Pious. He could. "I was thinking, it would be so nice to spend the time with you and Emma and Manfred," he lied, pretending he could want that. "I could help Floy prepare on the way—it's a long drive. Their hair and makeup may need adjusting and we both know Emma and Manfred can't handle that."

Louise's gaze slid to Cin out the corner of her eye. "I may have aches in my joints from doing the numbers for so long, but my hands are still steady enough to hold an eye-pen on occasion." But then she sighed, staring down at those very fingers. Emotion welled in her voice as she added, "Your father surely wouldn't want to see his ancestral home left untended..."

Cin didn't know what else to say, except, "Please?"

Louise shook her head, a look of gentle frustration on her face. "How do I say no to you? I suppose if, before we leave in the afternoon, the house and stable are both prepared for our return, then I'll consider it."

Cin did not know how to hate her any less in that moment, but he loved her too. "It'll be done, I promise."

Cinder Szule Reinholz was going to the ball.

Cin had not worked so tirelessly through the morning in ages. His sides ached from the lack of breaks, sharp pains slicing between his ribs, but he pushed himself forward with thoughts of the castle, as though proximity to those towers would take away every last hurt. The morning meal finished and the dishes cleaned, the laundry sorted for soaking and every hearth tended to, he had just put back his broom when Manfred trudged through the kitchen with muddied boots.

"Manfred!" Cin scolded.

He shrugged, and Cin couldn't tell whether the crook of his mouth was crueler than usual. "It's a little dirt. Or would you rather it be ashes, huh?"

Cin wanted to hit him right in the center of his sneering mug, but he could predict how well that would go. He grabbed the largest bucket from the corner instead, grimacing as his ribs screamed in protest, and shoved it into Manfred's chest before he could pass by. "I'll need more water to mop. Since you're already *filthy*, you wouldn't mind?"

There was half a chance he'd say no, and half a chance he'd cram the bucket over Cin's head and laugh, but the castle's towers must have been glinting over the horizon because this time, impossibly, Manfred just shrugged again and took it from Cin. While he was out at the well, Cin sat to portion out the beans he'd need for their lunches—not that they should have needed lunches with the ball that night, but Floy had insisted they wouldn't have time to eat a single bite while they were wooing the prince, and Louise claimed that if Cin was going to make food for Floy, then it wouldn't be much more work to just make the whole pot, now would it?

By the time Cin had it in the bowl he planned to use for soaking, there was barely any left in their stores. Which should have been as good a reason as any not to make the meal for everyone, if only good reasons were considered in the Reinholzes' household.

Manfred came sweeping in through the back kitchen door with a sloshing bucket of water. He took one too many steps, and Cin could see the direction the swagger in his step was taking him—see it but do nothing to stop it, as Manfred slammed the bucket into the table, knocking the bowl of beans to the ground. They scattered across the grimy floor with the soft *cling-cling* of Cin's hopes dashing.

He wanted to grab that bucket from Manfred—wanted to slam it down over his head, break the wood to pieces, throw them both into the flames—he wanted to—

"My God!" Louise shouted, one hand over her mouth.

"I was just trying to be helpful, Mother," Manfred said, somehow managing not to sound like he was snarling for once. "See, I brought in Cinder's water."

"After *you* muddied the floor," Cin snapped.

Louise made a sound in the back of her throat. "It's a kitchen, Cinder, the floor is never clean." She flicked her fingers anxiously. "Oh—just fix it, both of you. You know we can't waste food, not even with the ball tonight. And be more careful next time! *Both* of you." As she turned, she hissed at Cin under her breath, "You know your brother doesn't understand how to be gentle; next time take the bucket from him, for heaven's sake."

Cin *did* know, and all too well. He could have prevented this. He could have just collected the water himself. Like he usually did. And then there wouldn't be lunch all over the floor.

Louise was gone for barely a moment when Manfred laughed under his breath, backing out into the garden again with a smirk. "Whore," he mouthed as he left.

Cin just stood there. He wanted to cry—big, rage-fueled tears— and he crossed his arms over his bound chest, wishing it were flatter, if for no other reason than that way he could hug more of himself, wrap his arms all the way around his body and smother the anger seething beneath his skin. As the sounds of Louise and Manfred moved further from the kitchen and the space quieted down to the soft, tight heaving of Cin's breath, one by one his trio of pigeons appeared on the stoop of the back door.

Perdition cooed.

With one last sniffle that ached deep in his sides, Cin looked at the beans spread across the floor. "If only you could…"

He didn't even know what he was asking for. His pigeons had always been there for him, showing a level of intellect and devotion he was fairly sure not a single member of his own family possessed, but they couldn't possibly understand what had happened, what this meant to Cin.

Perdition fluttered into the kitchen, diving straight for the nearest fallen bean.

"Oh, no, that's…" But how could he take the food from her? He didn't have the heart.

As he lowered himself to the ground though, Perdition hopped her way up to him, bean still gently held within her beak. She bobbed her head… offering it… to him?

Ragimund and Lacey followed her lead, pecking up their own beans. Instead of eating them, they waited for Cin to right the bowl before depositing their gifts neatly into it. He held his breath as a flock of two dozen pigeons, doves, and more descended through the kitchen door. Each new bird collected the little morsels of food and delivered them just the same as Cin's trio had. Every bean was as clean and fresh as the moment Cin had measured them.

It was like magic.

Cin could almost believe it *was* magic, for his pigeons were always something nearly as special and peculiar. But in order for magic to happen, someone—usually with the proper talent—had to ask for it in such a way that the universe would accept, through word or ritual or a mixture of the two. And the only one who'd asked for anything was Cin, and that had been a wish more than a question.

Whatever the case, the beans were sorted nearly as soon as Cin had spoken, the flock retreating out of the room. He didn't have time to dwell on it further.

Bracing himself against the pain with each act, Cin poured part of Manfred's water onto the beans and the rest he used to mop the floor quickly before retrieving the dry laundry hanging in the garden from the day before. While he worked, Floy came to lean against the back door.

"Why, Cinder-*child*, you seem nearly finished with things already." They used Louise's nickname for Cin, despite being barely three months Cin's elder, picking absentmindedly at their nails while they spoke. "I need a selection of flying bugs and bird feathers for my current scientific exploration, but I'm clean for the ball, and Mother would hate for me to ruin that. Could you retrieve them for me? I plan to tell the *prince* of my findings tonight. I'm sure he's interested in such populations with the famine so unwavering."

Cin could feel his blood boiling, but all he said in response was, "It's been quite cold some nights. Most of the bugs are gone."

"Not all of them," Floy replied, and left.

Cin wanted to cry again, but somehow, this time, he also wanted to laugh, as his pigeons crowded down onto the laundry lines, cooing and bobbing, the other birds twittering around in the grass.

"I mean, if you insist, I'd love the help?" he asked.

He wasn't sure anything would happen, but in a flash, the birds all flew away, spreading out in every direction. Cin continued taking down the dried laundry, folding the sheets and prepping the lines to hang what he'd washed that day, and by the time he finished, the flock had brought back a dozen different specimens of flying insects, each unique and undamaged, and plucked their own feathers to add to the mix. Perfect timing, Cin realized as he passed the clock in the hall. They were set to leave on the following hour, and he had only the soaking, changing, carriage preparation, and the lunch cooking left.

The clean laundry at his hip, he took the insects and feathers to Floy, who hummed under their breath, and shooed Cin away. As he left though, Cin had an odd tug in his gut. He looked back to find his sibling staring at a specific set of pigeon feathers: one gray, one white, one mottled brown. Just as quickly, though, Floy set them down. Cin tried to breathe out. It meant nothing. And he had work to do.

Cin had had barely a moment's peace in the laundry room, the stack of clean linens sitting on the table while he added the lye to the dirtiest of Manfred's things to soak for the night, when Emma flaunted in.

"Oh! Can I help?" she asked, and before Cin could stop her, she scooped up the linen from the table and dumped it into the lye bucket.

Cin stared at it in horror as the freshly cleaned sheets sank into the water. "Emma," he said, his voice flat to cover the anger attempting to take root between his ribs. "Those were the ones that needed to go onto our beds."

"Oh." Emma watched the bucket, her eyes widening. She sniffled. Then sniffled again. Her expression broke as she threw herself over Cin's shoulders, sobbing against him. "I'm so sorry. I've ruined it, haven't I? I'm awful!"

Cin felt so, so very tired suddenly. "No, no." He bit back the rest of what he wished he could say, patting her shoulder. "It's fine, I'll just hang them to dry again, it'll... it'll work out. You were only trying to help."

She had been. Only trying to help. There was no reason for Cin to hate her for this, and yet somehow he did, deep and ugly in the worst, least pious parts of his soul. Slowly, he pushed her away.

She wiped at her tears. "Is there anything I can do...?"

"I've got this," Cin lied. "Really. Go help... Go sweep the kitchen, okay? That would save me so much time."

"It would?" Emma perked up. "I can do that—I'll go do that."

"Good," Cin said, and it was not.

He carried the now-sopping clean linens out to the garden once more, hanging them again one by one, each stretch toward the line its own tiny agony. And again, his pigeons gathered. He sighed, running a hand through the loose strands of his white-blond locks. "I don't know what you can do about this one, friends, but if you're up for it, please try..."

The flock seemed to chatter among themselves. Lacey was the first to move, sweeping down in front of the wet sheets, her wings flapping at a speed Cin had never seen from her before, moving like the shimmer on the road's horizon during the heat of summer. Slowly, the linen began to dry.

The other birds joined in a whoosh, fluttering and twirling until the whole batch of sheets were dancing lightly in their wind. Like magic. In wonder, Cin yanked them down, the fabric as dry as they'd been before Emma's disastrous help.

Cin hurried them up to the bedrooms. He avoided his family as he worked, quickly replacing linens and turning down each bed, preparing the hearths for their return that night, and jogging down the stairs two-by-two to put the lunch on the fire, running between stirring it and preparing the horse carriage. Six different apologies to their currently lonely mare later, and Cin was putting the lunch off the stove—remarkably unburnt.

He filled his siblings' bowls for them, just to be sure they didn't manage to ruin anything else in the final few moments before leaving, and quickly scrubbed the cook-bowl clean. When Louise called for them to leave, Cin piled out of the house behind Floy, Manfred, and Emma, taking an extra minute to check that everything was locked. He emerged down the front path to find Louise in the driving seat, her heavy riding cloak and gloves over her gown.

Her brows puckered as Cin approached. "Are you not dressed, child?"

He froze, still three steps from the carriage door. Of course he was dressed—simple pants tucked into his only pair of boots, and his ordinary cream tunic beneath the cloak he'd been washing blood from for the last few years. "What is wrong with this?" he asked, dreading the answer.

Louise made a sound, waving defiantly. "Have you not seen us? We are all suitable for presentation at a royal ball. You look like you've climbed out of the hearth!"

"I've been..." Fixing everyone else's problems, he wanted to say. But he could have prevented Manfred from spilling the beans, or warned Emma which linen was clean, or told Floy to find their own fucking bugs and feathers. He could have noticed that his family were all wearing their Sunday best by lunch, and he was still in the very clothes he'd spent the whole day lifting and pushing and running about in.

"Busy, yes," Louise finished for him, dryly. She sighed, shaking her head. "There's no time; we should have left half an hour ago. Next week, perhaps. We'll look through your clothes first. Find something... adequate."

Cin thought of his wardrobe—somewhat cleaner than this, but no less worn from all the work he'd done in them. He'd never bothered to save a specific outfit for anything more formal. It had seemed silly to keep an expensive piece of clothing for the sole purpose of barely wearing it.

As he stood there, the autumn sun heating his cheeks and his siblings complaining in the back of the carriage, Louise seemed to be waiting for something.

"Yes, Mother," Cin croaked out. "Next week, then."

And he watched the carriage leave.

Five

C inder ran.

He wasn't sure where he was going at first: anywhere but that damned front yard, where he'd watched his siblings and step-mother leave for a ball he'd worked so hard—so hard and yet not hard enough—to attend. His feet carried him first toward the front door, tripping over the torn edge of his shoe every few steps. Tears blurred his vision and each attempt to fit the key back into the lock grew worse as his anger rose. Finally he flung himself away, back down the front path and around toward the side of the house. He stumbled past the kitchen—also locked—and across the garden where the drying lines hung empty.

How stupid was he to sob over missing a single night of revelry? Cin sucked in a horrid breath, his ribs aching against his bindings, and wrapped both hands over his mouth like he could strangle the misery out of himself.

It wasn't the missing that felt like a boiling band in his chest, not just that, anyway, but the trying—the trying, and trying, and falling short, when two of the people in that fucking god-damned carriage hadn't had to try at all. To be born entirely mediocre—was that Cinder Szule's curse? Not good or pious, and not useless or cruel either. Something just a little stained, valuable enough to be measured but always coming up short.

Worse, too, he had seen the embarrassment in Floy's gaze, the satisfaction in Manfred's, the pity in Emma's. He hated them for it. He hated them so much it made him want to tear his own eyes out to stop seeing the memory of them driving away.

Cin tripped over a garden rock, landing on both knees in the grass and dirt. Ash-lover, dirt-wench, cinder-whore—if he could reach between his own ribs, he'd pull the names out, rip free his breasts while he was at it. Above him, a gentle chorus of coos started. Two tiny feet landed on his head, then another two on his shoulders, a final set clinging to the back of his neck as he shook.

Gracelessly, Cin came back to himself. Through the clench and release of his lungs, he managed to wipe one eye, then the next. On the ground in front of him lay his mother's gravestone. It felt only right. She might have been good and pious enough to have sacrificed for her family's sake, but she would have mourned this too. As wistful and ridiculous as Cin remembered her to be, he knew that were she alive to take on the responsibility herself, she would have wanted him at that ball, done whatever she could to get him there.

The tree that grew over her resting place rustled as more and more birds landed in its branches. Cin had planted that tree on the first anniversary of his mother's death: planted it from a stick he'd found at the base of the castle walls during a trip Father had taken him on to the city, back when his father still took any of his children on his trips. He swore it had grown into a sapling overnight, and yet no one had believed him.

"How absurd," Louise had said. "Hasn't there always been an oak there?"

"That's an ash, Mother," Floy had pointed out.

"Szule's dumb," Manfred had added, and Emma had cried in the corner as her doll's head broke off from her terrible attempts at a braid.

Maybe they had been right. For years, Cin had believed so—believed that he was delusional. Irrational as his mother, his grief and anger lying to him. But after the fantastical ways his birds had acted today, he wasn't so sure.

He stared up at the tree's branches, the dozens and dozens of birds now clustered within them, and with his throat tight and his stomach twisted, he begged: "Please..."

A breeze whistled through the tree, so slight and soft that it sounded like a song, and suddenly, all Cin's birds rose at once. They descended upon him, their wings outstretched and claws wide, a menacing cloud of tiny bodies. Cin opened his arms to them. *Please,* he thought, the word so much a part of him that it seemed to fill his chest, make his soul too large for his current form, too bright with want.

The flock twirled and tumbled around him, their claws curling back to caress Cin with the tops of their feet, a swirling mass so tight it seemed impossible that they weren't careening into each other. They took over Cin's vision, the sound of their flapping wings nearly drowning out his laughter.

As he rose up from the dirt, layers of fabric flowed around him. With one last perfect spiral, his flock seemed to collapse: a hundred eyes and a thousand feathers coming together into one sparkling form. And just like that, Cinder Szule Reinholz was ready for the ball.

The capital city was alive with joviality.

It wasn't just the palace that was hosting the ball, Cin realized as he made his way into the city: it was every open plaza, every tavern and pub, every public garden and empty warehouse. Throughout the capital, the royals had carted food and dispersed musicians, along with what seemed like hundreds of lanterns with colorful exteriors, all lighting up the areas of revelry as though the chilly fall night was the middle of spring. But Cin had only one destination in mind.

Still folded beneath the drapes of his simple brown cloak, he directed his magical steed through the crowded lanes. A normal horse would have crushed someone by now, but the delicate gray beast Cin rode upon seemed to dart and dance through the people like a flock of birds, never quite touching anyone, not even in the most overwhelmed of roads. Still, the congestion made it flick its head in annoyance. Cin slipped his shimmering gloves out from under his cloak to pat its withers.

Almost there, he wanted to tell it. Almost.

Near the castle, the party attendees grew fancier, commoners giving way to rich merchants and craftspeople, and finally the lesser nobility, all dressed in glittering gowns and fitted suits and flowing capes that gleamed as they danced in the rainbow of lantern-light. Members of the crown's watch moved between them, armed and alert, but even they seemed to be enjoying the night, chatting and laughing amongst themselves. Cin caught glimpses of the castle's high walls between the buildings, but the towers themselves always seemed hidden by one more row of fancy houses and wealthy shops. He followed the young and eligible as they climbed the path to the great arched double-door in the castles walls. Half of its metal blockade had been swung open.

More of the crown's watch meandered in and out, surveying the regular guards in their plain green uniforms as they spoke with each expectant guest. One watch member with the ornate gilding of elevated status occasionally stepped in to speak with the guards or guests, resulting in the guest's dismissal, sometimes alongside the removal of a hidden weapon. Cin felt the little knife he'd hidden in the back of his chest binding like a second spine.

He fidgeted as he waited in the line, telling himself that if the Crown had connected him in any way to their Plumed Menace, they would have come for him at his home. They had no better reason to suspect him now—except, perhaps, that he was currently covered in feathers. But the look had been fairly common among the nobles in recent decades, and few seemed to care enough about the Plumed Menace's calling card to remove such extravagances from their closets.

When Cin reached the door, though, the guards seemed to see

him little more than any strangers ever did, as though the pigeon feathers in his outfit doubled as a disguise of another sort. The guard confirmed his age and marital status, glancing at his waist and inside his cloak, before requesting he dismount. He began to relax as his steed was led off to the royal barns, and the way cleared for him to ascend the castle's steps. He took them slowly, reveling in the glory of the night and the colors that bounced across the castle's deep gray stone, its towers piercing the sky high above him.

"I'm here, Mother," he whispered. He wasn't sure that it was God smiling upon him, but this moment was still something magical; something miraculous.

Cin stepped through the entrance of the castle, and he could almost feel his whole world change. The paths of the ball-goers led him through the majestic entry-chamber, its high ceiling lit by a dozen lanterns, and past the throne room, down a spacious hall toward a sea of music and laughter. A servant took Cin's simple outer cloak, and he stepped inside.

The massive room spread out like a layered gem before him, lit by a hundred central lanterns in a mix of vibrant colors and sparkling whites, arranged to leave the edges of the room still cloaked in mystery, as though the party space might never end. Dancers twirled on the lower central floor as musicians played from a platform against the far wall, their jovial waltz seeming to hum through Cin's very bones. Along one side of the room, giant flawless windows mirrored the ball back at them, and along the other, internal balconies swept out as though they were in a theater, their shadowy occupants watching from seats or tucked behind curtains for private rendezvous. Amongst the party-goers, Cin spotted a number of castle staff serving as hosts, as well as a few of the crown's watch stationed in the shadows near the room's edges.

As Cin made his way inside, the whole world seemed to turn and look at him.

It was like being seen for the first time, a hundred gazes rolling down him, from the feathered crown braided into his white-blond hair to the sweeping length of his feathered half-cape, to the exquisite embroidery of his white and gold suit and the tall gray boots his pants tucked into. Beneath the glamorous frills, he could still feel the flaws of the clothing he'd been wearing back at the garden before his pigeons had swept around him in a spiraling tornado to leave a sparkling masterpiece in their wake, but even the tear in his shoe and the tight pressure of his chest binding seemed like they couldn't hurt him now. He was alive, and he was here, jealousy and delight on the faces of everyone who looked upon him.

This time, he was being measured, and he was the one they all wanted to be or to beat.

Lucky for them, Cin wasn't here to challenge anyone's claim on the prince.

As he thought it, he remembered to scan the room for Floy and his siblings, but they hadn't arrived yet—unlike him, they'd have to drive their carriage around to the few streets that had been cleared of pedestrians in order to make their way up to the castle. That meant he had a quarter-hour, perhaps even a half, to enjoy himself here before absconding to one of the less prestigious parties outside the castle proper.

As much as Cin wished otherwise, he had known the moment his birds descended on him that he couldn't share this glory with his family. There would be too many questions, too many demands. And Floy had already been acting suspicious with his pigeon feathers that morning…

Tonight was for him, and him alone.

Cin made a lap around the massive room just to take in the scene, letting himself wonder at the motions of the dancing guests while counting the observing watch members in the back of his head. They seemed no more interested in him than the guards out front, however, and after his second sweep through the room, he let himself breathe out the little fear he'd been harboring of them. They were here to protect the royal family and their castle, and Cin meant harm to neither. He was safe.

Safe to enjoy himself.

His initial sweep finished, Cin sampled every morsel of food presented on the long, elaborately decorated royal tables before returning for his favorites. He slipped tiny meatballs between his lips and savored the sweet burst of strawberry cakes as he sipped on a warm glass of spiced wine. He basked in the music and exchanged a few short words with other singles at the ball, mostly over the beauty of the place and the quality of the food, staying to the sidelines and avoiding any conversation where it seemed the gossip might turn to talk of the Plumed Menace.

The more he watched, the more he realized that not all the eligible individuals were there solely for the prince either. Some seemed just as distracted by their wonder as he was. Others hounded each other for conversations of business or danced as though they were committed to coming home with a partner whether the prince wanted them or not. It was beautiful and unreal and so gloriously perfect.

He only spotted the man he assumed to be the newly crowned Prince Lorenz a few times, each from a distance—once only the top of his dusky brown hair and elegant silver circlet as he danced through the bobbing crowd, and later his back, as he was walking out of the central ball-space with a guest on both arms, one of the ornamented watch members trailing dutifully behind him. It left such a sense of mystery that Cin almost wanted to see him up close before he left. He was casually scanning the room again when instead his gaze caught on the entrance: on three specific people arriving there.

His heart ricocheted, and he took a few steps back, sliding into the shadows along the room's edges. Besides the entrance, there were two great doors out to the gardens, but that would require Cin to move back through the well-lit spaces to reach them. A few other doors and spiraling stairwells led to the upper level where the shadowy, theater-style balconies were, but he had managed to find himself spaced equally far from any of them.

Maybe if he just stayed here, his siblings wouldn't notice him?

But that wasn't a chance he wanted to take.

Cin glanced to his left and right again, then up to the balcony. If he could get there without stepping through the brighter parts of the room, then none of his siblings would be able to spot him from below...

Grooves ascended along the wall where an ornamented pillar curled up under the edge of the nearest balcony. Peeling off his gloves, Cin slipped his fingers into the pillar's lines. This could do fine.

Cin gave one final look toward the watch members in view of him, but none seemed to be paying any attention to his shadowy balcony's underbelly. Taking as deep a breath as he could manage beneath his binding, he pulled himself up. The centralized lantern-light would have barely glinted off his outfit, and as he climbed, the magic overlaying him seemed to shift in color. The silvery gleams in his feathered coat went gray and the folds in the fabric flared and swirled, casting him in a ghostly haze. He slid his fingers along the curves of the balcony, tucking the sides of his toes against the frame for support, and hand over hand, Cin rose above the crowd.

As he reached the top, the tear in the side of his boot—the ordinary one, beneath the magic—snagged. He slipped, catching himself at the last moment with both hands on the banister. A sharp reminder of the state of his ribs speared through his sides as he swung himself up to the balcony's safety. He landed with the tiniest sound: the pop and tear of another stitch in his boot.

Cin grimaced. He didn't have much time to think about the repercussions this would have on his regular life, though, because the balcony wasn't as empty as it had appeared from below. And the couple already occupying it were grunting.

One of them swayed against the other with an energy far too frenzied to be following the moves of any dance, his hands on their hips as he pressed them against the wall and— Oh. They were fucking.

They might have still been fully—more or less—clothed, but they were definitely fucking.

Shit.

The couple seemed to notice Cin at the same instant he realized it. They slowed, and Cin's eyes had adjusted enough to the low lighting to make out the blush on the face of the probably-woman as she held to the lifted edge of her dress with one hand and what she could reach of the very edge of the balcony railing with the other. The probably-man pulled back just enough for Cin to catch the silhouette of his hard cock between the folds of fabric around the couple's legs—and he was a man, Cin knew, because Cin vaguely recognized him.

As the man's dark gaze settled on Cin in the low light, his eyes narrowed, scanning up Cin's body like he was devouring him, adding up every glimmering piece of Cin's facade and measuring it against his own want... and somehow, not finding Cin lacking. Not yet, at least, not draped in magic and shadows.

"Why, hello. Aren't you a pretty little dove?" Prince Lorenz smiled, the flash of teeth in the low light so similar to that of his circlet: cold and arrogant but breathtakingly beautiful. "You want in?" he asked. "I think we can make room for a third."

Six

Prince Lorenz, most eligible bachelor in the kingdom, soon to-not-be a bachelor at all, was looking at Cinder and... he was... Oh no, oh fuck, oh *fuck*.

Cin felt his mouth turn to cotton and a burn shoot across his cheeks. His head went light in a rush of nerves. It made the room spin, and suddenly Cin's legs weren't quite underneath him. The banister was, though, then empty air, then—

A pair of strong hands circled around the collar of his suit jacket, pulling him back onto the balcony with a sureness that Cin had not felt from anyone's touch in ages. The prince helped steady him, one arm slipping around Cin's waist. His breath was warm against Cin's forehead.

Cin yanked his hand off Prince Lorenz's chest as he found his footing. Had he grabbed Prince Lorenz back? The heated embarrassment in his cheeks doubled.

The little smile, so smug and dazzling, appeared back on Prince Lorenz's lips. He stepped away, shifting to take gentle hold of Cin's wrists, like he was worried if he let go entirely that Cin might launch himself back over the railing. "There now. If you wish to reject my advances, there are easier ways, you know?"

Cin's heart pounded in his ears. Should he pull away? Did he *want* to? He *had* to, he decided, just to ensure the prince understood his intentions.

But then Prince Lorenz let go instead as the woman he'd been fucking—her dress hanging back around her ankles—asked, softly, "My prince?"

He turned toward her, casually buttoning his pants back up as he did. They were well tailored, Cin noted, displaying his trim waist and toned backside and the curve of what seemed to be a still half-hard erection. "Sorry, love, I think we lost the mood," the prince said, but he reached for her as she made to leave, tucking a stray piece of her hair back with a soft, "I'll see you later though, hmm?"

She gave him a tiny bow. "It would be my honor." It genuinely sounded like she meant it.

Floy was already behind on the competition, it seemed, and this particular competitor was clearly getting a little something extra for her trouble. Cin promptly forced himself to *stop* thinking about that, because unlike the woman, Prince Lorenz had not left.

He stood beside the padded bench that filled much of their balcony's central space, casually leaning one knee against it as he fixed his elegant ruby-toned vest, realigning the delicate embroidery. His outer jacket was draped on the bench beside him, but he made no move to retrieve it, smiling over at Cin like they were conspirators in some great adventure. "You know there *are* better methods of telling a gentleman he's not your type than leaping from balconies... even if he *is* me."

"You'd call that *leaping*? Your royal highness, you humor me." Cin decided then and there that he would just stop blushing.

Enough willpower had to work, didn't it?

"Then humor *me*?" Prince Lorenz retorted, and sat onto the bench. He patted the empty space at his side.

The thought repeated in Cin's mind: could he chance saying yes? This man's family did have a price on Cin's head, even if no one had connected the Plumed Menace's actions to Cin yet. The ball had been a risk, but this...

The *Prince of Hallin*.

Attempting to leave would raise just as much suspicion, wouldn't it? There was surely the ornamented watch member just outside the balcony.

"Please, sit," Prince Lorenz repeated, tapping the bench again. Cin found his body following orders, and he wasn't sure which of his questions that answered.

The submission earned him a dazzling smile, which faded into a distant thoughtfulness—cold, not for lack of warmth, but for the depth, like looking down through the darkest water and seeing nothing shining back but a reflection.

Even in the low light, Cin could make out just enough of Prince Lorenz's face to tell that the couple of renderings Cin had seen of him were wrong: they barely did him justice, but Cin could understand why. No part of him was particularly outstanding on its own: his lips were on the thinner side, his mouth wide, his nose thick but straight, his eyes narrow and his cheekbones strong, eyebrows even stronger. But his beauty came not from any or even all of his features, but the way he used them. It was the light in his narrow gaze, the little quirk that never left his lips, the way his hair fell as though his simple, chin-length brown locks were eternally touched by a gentle breeze.

Potential Queenship or no, Cin could see why the woman had wanted to fuck him, even if Cin didn't. But Cin's problem with the fucking had nothing to do with Prince Lorenz at all, if he was being honest. That was just not a bridge he was ready to cross yet, particularly on a balcony with a royal he'd known for sixty seconds, who'd be married to someone else in a few months time. There were things he did want, could probably even want from someone like the prince, but...

Prince Lorenz broke their silence with a chuckle. "Did you really just come up over the side, or am I even more daft than previously believed?"

"No, I..." Cin hesitated. Making up an excuse would just seem all the more like he had climbed up here to spy on them. He tried not to look too guilty as he said, "There's someone down there I wanted to avoid, and this just seemed like the easiest way. I had no idea you were up here, really."

"Climbing fifteen feet of ornamented wall, in awful lighting, then over a banister, was your idea of *easy*?"

It could have been a tease, or it could have been a taunt instead—climbing ornamented walls; isn't that something thieves do?—but Cin couldn't tell beneath the cold mask that lay just under the prince's joviality. Prince Lorenz did *act* jovial, at least, so Cin decided that responding in turn was his safest option. "My other thought was to fake my own death." Cin tried out a smile as he said it. The expression felt wrong on his face. "But you saw how poorly that sort of ploy works out for me. Too many heroic princes at these kinds of parties."

Prince Lorenz laughed. He nudged Cin's shoulder with his own. "Cute *and* funny. It's a shame you won't let me fuck you."

The comment returned Cin's flush in force, his decision to stop blushing be damned, but in the back of his mind, he could not help thinking of all the times in the recent past when the people he'd been keeping tabs on—mostly feminine people, people like him in body, if not in identity—had been sneered at like that, made into a joke meant for only one side of the party, then forced to comply with the wish regardless. He didn't *think* that was Prince Lorenz's play.

But he didn't know it *wasn't*, either.

"It's not you," Cin said, choosing his words carefully. "Having sex with anyone—even you—is simply... well, it's not what I'm here for."

To Cin's relief, Prince Lorenz looked intrigued by that. "What are you here for then, my dove, if not me?"

"The ball," Cin replied simply.

"Ah, there you and I differ." Prince Lorenz leaned a little closer, and Cin could feel one of his hands resting on the bench behind Cin's ass. Not touching, just there. Waiting. "Do you want to know a secret? I found someone to fuck just to escape the party for a little while."

"But this—" Cin gestured toward the ballroom below, where music still wafted, couples dancing and laughing. "This has to be the most lovely celebration in the kingdom. And it's for *you*."

The prince snorted. "To get me hitched."

"That wasn't your idea then, I take it." He was still preposterously aware of how close Prince Lorenz was, and how Cin had continued, despite his own better judgment, to not avoid him.

"Hardly." The prince smiled, a little sharper then before. "Do I look ready to settle on a life partner? To *commit* to someone who will rule the fucking *kingdom* with me someday?" He turned slightly, and still he didn't touch Cin, but he was somehow even closer, like they were friends. Friends, or lovers. "It's not simply the sex—I could find someone who doesn't care who else I fuck—but what's life when you're bound to stay with someone regardless of the pressures or pains they place on you? I've dealt with that enough already with my family, thank you kindly."

Pressure and pains: though he didn't dare say it, Cin knew those well—far better then a pampered prince with his guards and servants, whose parents threw him lavish city-wide balls to find a partner.

"Did I overstep?" Prince Lorenz leaned back, and the shift bumped his knee into Cin's. "I find that in the dark I best preoccupy my mouth with other things, or else my tongue overtakes my better judgment."

Cin felt the heat of the prince's skin as though the layers of cloth separating their knees wasn't even there.

He didn't know whether or not to pull away. He hadn't wanted to fuck—still didn't—but perhaps just this, a touch of knees, a little flattery, was no different from the short-term relaxation and exhilaration he'd sought from the ball. *If* he knew it wouldn't lead anywhere. But he wasn't sure how to ask a question that most people seemed to know the answer to on instinct.

So, instead of moving, Cin shrugged and said, "No, no I was

merely thinking."

"Ha! You think, I talk; we make quite a pair," Prince Lorenz purred. And he looked, in the low light, like maybe he was going to do more than that. But the prince only nudged Cin with his shoulder again, soft and friendly. "What do *you* want from the ball?" When he didn't receive an immediate response, he continued, "I haven't seen you at any of my parent's other parties, though by the looks of your outfit, you're of a status to be invited into the castle without too much hassle. I don't catch any accent from you, so you're local, and yet..."

"I suppose I'm just a mystery." Cin leaned a little: not away, but toward. This was just a pleasant distraction, he told himself, noticing the instant it worked as Prince Lorenz's quick gaze dropped hotly to Cin's mouth. His heart pounded between his ribs. "An unfuckable, balcony-climbing mystery."

"You're taunting me," Prince Lorenz concluded, though he seemed entirely unaffected by the thought. The hand behind Cin shifted closer, and the prince's arm bumped Cin's, so light and momentary it might have been a mistake. "You know, it's generally considered a poor choice to be rude to a prince."

Cin tried to hide the twist that set in his gut. This was nothing but a joke, and Cin attempted to respond in kind. "Are you planning to banish me for it? I *can* go back over the balcony, if you wish."

"Heavens, no. You're far too pretty to let fall, with that cloak"— the prince motioned to Cin's shoulders, then his head—"and this hair and—" His fingers brushed one of the wisps coming off the top of Cin's headpiece. "Are these really feathers? Tell me you are *not* one of those Plumed Menace fanatics."

Those two words—Plumed Menace—made Cin feel faint, but then he put the rest of the sentence together. One of *those*.

There were *fanatics?*

That was news to Cin. Uncomfortable news, if vaguely flattering. But he still didn't want to be seen as one of them. Any connection to the Plumed Menace was one too many. "I promise, I've cared for pigeons long before the Plumed Menace emerged. These are just their feathers." With a dash of magic, Cin thought. But the prince didn't need to know that. "I keep a few of them at home."

If Prince Lorenz caught onto Cin's hesitation, he didn't show it. "How sweet! You must be quite good with them to receive such lovely gifts."

It was silly to assume the pigeons had given them to Cin directly, when so many of their lost feathers naturally ended up wherever they did, but it was the first time anyone had ever implied that Cin might be useful for more than tending the house—good at something he *enjoyed*. It made his gaze a little hazy. Prince Lorenz seemed not to notice in the low light.

"The castle has a dovecote, yet *they've* never given me a fancy cloak," he added.

"I don't think you need one. You stand out just as you are." The compliment slipped out, not in flirtation or banter, but sincerity. Cin swore he was going to blush again. He pushed back his hair, trying to give his body some distraction from the embarrassment. "I'm sure people tell you that all the time."

"Not with quite that phrasing," the prince replied, but he sounded a little off-kilter. The moment passed in a flash, his smug grin returning. "But of course I stand out. I am the prince, after all.

I have this obnoxious crown and too much power for my own good."

"The crown is a bit much," Cin agreed, though he actually kind of liked it. "Do you intend to misuse your power, then?"

Prince Lorenz smiled, and there was a bite to his baring of teeth. "Why else do you imagine my parents are looking for a gentle and good partner for me when I'm king?" The expression faded back into a smirk nearly instantly, though, and a part of Cin grieved that. There seemed something more *real* in the anger, like Cin could almost see beneath his cold, humor-masked waters into a darker, deeper place. The prince leaned in conspiratorially, raising one hand in front of them like he was painting a scene. "I was thinking: giant statues of myself—shirtless, of course—in every town, and the only holiday will be Lorenz-day, a celebration based around the thrill of an orgy with me."

Cin snorted, and despite still wishing for the sharper version of the prince, he couldn't help the quirk in his lips from the joke. "You may want to rethink the shirtless part. Too many of the young people will end up in love with you. You'll need to increase the Lorenz-days to keep up with your rising number of orgies."

"Ah, true, true." He sighed dramatically. "What a shame. I do so love an orgy."

Now, Cin was curious. "Do you actually have a lot of those?"

"Not a one." Prince Lorenz laughed. "The truth is, too many people in bed become overwhelming. Too many people..." He made a face. "I prefer one or two. Then I can really focus on them, you see? Besides, this is the most people this castle has seen in a good long time."

Cin couldn't tell if the prince was leaning in again, or if he'd just been this close already, their shoulders nearly brushing and their knees still bumping casually against each other. He could feel the prince's breath on his neck. It was as terrifying as it was exhilarating, and Cin didn't know whether to want for more or for less, his body telling him one thing while the rational center of his mind screamed for the other.

He was saved from having to make either choice by a barely human sound of triumph from behind them. "He's here!"

One of the balcony curtains was thrown aside as three people around Cin's age tried their best to sidestep the prince's personal watcher. They looked far less embarrassed by the intrusion than Cin figured they should have, considering just what Cin knew they might have found here had they been a little earlier. The prince jolted, a flash of distress crossing his face.

Cin was certain he was the only one who was close enough to catch it—another glimpse into the darkness—as it quickly transformed to a look of arrogant annoyance. "Ah, I see my esteemed guests can wait no longer." He stood, sweeping up his jacket to casually sling over one shoulder. "Perhaps one or two of us..."

But at that point, Cin could barely hear him over the sudden chatter out in the corridor. As the curtain was pushed further back, he could see a crowd of would-be suitors gathering in the better-lit area there as news spread. Through the growing throng, Cin caught sight of a familiar ornamented hat of dragonfly wings. The determined expression Floy wore beneath it was almost scary. Cin had seen Floy's commitment to their goals, and he was glad he wasn't one of the contenders standing in their way.

He was, however, still standing on the balcony.

The one Floy was currently headed towards.

Cin slid off the bench, taking a step back as he did. Prince Lorenz was still at his side—seemed to be moving with Cin, as though a part of them were attached—and Cin whispered to him, "It seems this is my time to fake that death again."

"No," Prince Lorenz turned, reaching for Cin. "Please stay; I'd rather—"

As adamant as the prince sounded, Floy was pushing closer to the balcony with each step. Cin swore Floy's eyes narrowed as they looked toward him in the shadows, and all he could think of was the way that they had stared at the feathers from his trio of pigeons, like they were looking for something. He turned, and jumped.

Cin was falling, but only for a moment. He grabbed the balcony's edge, biting his tongue against the pain the sudden motion shot through his sides, and swung down the way he'd come. As he descended the ornamentation on the ballroom wall though, the flapping piece of his torn boot caught on a curve again. He barely managed to keep hold of the wall to stop his ankle from twisting. After a moment of fiddling, grunting with each fresh ache between his ribs, another stitch popped. He dropped gracelessly to the ground.

His shoulder ached—that would surely bruise later—and every breath left a tiny agony in his side, but he picked himself up, ducking through the ballroom's revelers like a ghost in all his sparkling gray. Beneath the magical glamor, his shoe slapped the ballroom floor as he ran.

Shouting erupted behind him, and he worried that his fall had caught the watch member's attention despite the shadows, but when he looked back, he realized this commotion was worse.

Prince Lorenz was *chasing* him. He'd pulled himself over the top of the stairwell banister and was sliding down it, shouting after Cin. Every nerve in Cin's body caught fire. He slipped and skidded with each step he took on his broken boot as he sprinted through the entry halls. The bindings keeping his chest flat felt as though they were a cage around his lungs, making each breath harder than the last. The harder he pushed himself, the more he was forced to slow, his lungs burning and dark spots clouding across his vision. As he burst into the crisp night air, his sole caught on the stone steps. He stumbled, gasping, once, twice, as his muscles struggled to come back to life.

Two strong hands picked him back up. Prince Lorenz held Cin firmly, staring into his eyes with a fascination that made Cin feel naked despite all the layers of magic and lies he'd wrapped himself in.

"Are you hurt?" the prince asked, his breath short in a way Cin found stupidly sensual.

"Only my pride," Cin admitted, his head clearing as he stood there in the prince's strong hold. Surely the whole of the ball would follow them out soon, though, if the emergence of the first watch member behind Prince Lorenz was any indication. "I must go."

"Then leave me something to remember you by?"

Cin shifted on the balls of his feet. The watch seemed content to do just that, but a crowd of three people who'd recognize Cin as more than just a stranger who'd caught their prince's attention would be there any moment.

But Cin didn't want to go—the longer he stared into the prince's eyes, the more he felt like *himself*. No Plumed Menace, no homemaker frantically keeping his family afloat, but a single glowing cinder, ready to blow out or burst back into flame at a whim. He couldn't leave here and never feel that again.

"Why should I give you something if I'm to return in barely a week?" It wasn't a promise of anything sexual, but it *was* a promise of a sort.

The way that Prince Lorenz's grin grew across his face was a delight, his eyes sparkling and a breeze pushing back his dusky hair beneath the gleaming silver of his crown. He truly was gorgeous. "But my dove," he teased, "I fear a week will feel like an eternity when I'll be thinking of nothing but you."

"Then you may have this." Soft and impulsive, Cin pressed his lips to the prince's, before dashing off into the night without a second look back.

Seven

Cinder Szule Reinholz had kissed the prince of Hallin.

The magic of his outfit fell off him as he raced his steed home, each glimmering piece turning to a sparkle on the breeze, and he could not even find it in himself to worry whether the incredible clothing would return for next week's ball, because all his mind could conjure was the light brush of his lips against the prince's.

There had been power in that kiss. Not romance—not destiny or love or any of that—and perhaps not even a huge amount of sexual spark, considering the lightness and quickness of it, but power nonetheless. For Cin had wanted it, and he'd taken it. That act had felt like the inverse of his blade sliding between a bastard's shoulders: emotion and need turned to goodness instead of sin.

As he'd run from that moment, his magical mount had met him at the castle gates, seeming to know exactly what he required of it, but the instant he turned down the final road to home, it began to break apart into single birds, flapping and scattering off into the trees. It deposited him in his worn, ordinary pants, shirt, and cloak at his family's front gate. Lacey and Ragimund landed on the short fence, and Perdition took a loving swoop at Cin's head before peeling away. The other two followed.

"Thank you!" Cin called after them. The smile on his face felt right now.

He laughed and charged inside. Floy might have unwittingly driven him from the ball, but that meant the whole rest of the night was for him, alone in the house for one of the few times in recent memory. Cin locked the door behind him and pulled off his boots. As he loosened his chest binding, the ache between his ribs turned momentarily to a fire, but it slowly settled again and he let himself fall back on the sitting room's least sagging chair.

He thought of his lips against the prince's again. Of the way he'd been so close those last few minutes when they'd talked. The heat in his gaze when Cin had first pulled himself over the railing. The way Prince Lorenz had held his own dick, still slick and hard, and *looked* at Cin, like one man thirsting for another.

It was the first time he'd been so openly desired since discarding his dresses and eye-pens for a chest binding years ago, and those rare times prior had always made him feel nauseous. He'd assumed that the heat of others' attraction would always feel that way. Now though...

While Cin hadn't been able to enjoy the attention in that moment, with the comfort of hindsight and in the safety of home, the thought of the prince's lust forged a deep, fiery ache between Cin's legs. His fingers felt twitchy. He bit his lip and tipped his head back.

Slow and careful, like he was feeling for someone else's body, he slipped his fingers into the front of his pants. The gentle brush of his skin against the coarse curls that covered him there made the yearning grow, and suddenly it would have taken more effort to stop himself than it did to give in. He thought of Prince Lorenz again as he stroked himself, picturing the way the prince's body had bucked into his lover, strong muscles tight and his lips parted. What must his hair look like messed about? What did his sweat smell of? How did his fingertips feel against the skin?

Cin's pace moved from steady to rough, like he couldn't get enough of himself—just as his mind couldn't get enough of the prince. Cin bit harder into his lip and pushed himself through the spreading fire between his legs until it turned white-hot inside him, the ecstasy spilling up and through him.

He came out of it panting, shaking, and his tender sweet spot twitched. But on his lips was still that smile.

Alone in that darkness, with nothing to lose, he wished Prince Lorenz could see it.

If the Reinholz family suspected Cinder of having been anywhere besides their home, they said nothing.

Emma flounced from the carriage in a whirlwind of smiles and sighs, immediately falling into Cin's arms in a half-slumber. He listened to the rest of his siblings' chatter as he led her upstairs to undress and put to bed.

"Did you even speak with him?" Floy scoffed. "Or were you too preoccupied flirting with anything within touching distance?"

"While you lose the prince's hand to some fleeting phantom, I'm gonna get myself a pretty, rich spouse with a house that isn't caving in and cold as fuck, and never have to see your awful mug again." Manfred's snarling grew ever louder as he ascended the stairs toward his room, until it turned into a full-blown shout. "Cinder-whore! Why isn't my fucking hearth burning! I thought that was the whole damn reason you stayed home."

"I'll be there in a moment," Cin called back, instead of telling him to do it himself. It would take longer and more grumbling, and in the end Manfred would fail and make Cin finish it anyway. At least Cin had the satisfaction of knowing that Manfred had never managed to so much as greet the prince, while Cin had sat so close they'd touched and dared to end the night with a kiss.

Emma sighed again, dreamily, as Cin helped her climb into bed. "I think I'm in love, Cinny-Szule."

Cin's heart clenched, and he didn't know why. He patted her gently on the head before pulling up the blankets. "With who, Emma?"

"The prince's drinking chocolate," Emma purred. She rolled over with a yawn, snuggling the covers around her chin. "Drinking chocolate is so good..."

Cin laughed under his breath, but the tightness in his chest didn't release. If anything, the pain grew. He had the urge to kiss her forehead and tell her not to fall too deeply in love with the imported chocolate drink, but to find a nice young person who loved it as much as she did and run away with them, as far from this house as she could get. Which was absurd. She was *fine* here. She had everything she needed, and Cin to make it all happen.

And *he* certainly wasn't going anywhere.

As he left Emma's room, he caught Floy's gaze down the hall. Their eyes narrowed, but they only nodded as Cin passed.

He couldn't help but ask, "Did you get to tell the prince about your little science project?"

Floy lifted their chin. "I did indeed." They looked down at Cin with a kind of arrogance that seemed so different from Prince Lorenz's. Like Floy was keeping others out from this imagined place of betterment, while the prince was bringing them up to join him. Floy added, smirking now, "He seemed to rather appreciate it."

And Cin thought that wasn't a lie, it just wasn't the whole truth: the truth that Prince Lorenz knew how to pretend to be interested in anyone. But he hadn't pretended with Cin. He'd run after them—not for love or future partnership, of course, but from intrigue, at least. "How long did you speak for?"

"At least three and a half minutes," Floy boasted, as though they hadn't watched Prince Lorenz slide down a banister to chase after another quest. "No one else had half as much time with him."

No one but Cin.

He smiled all the way to Manfred's room. It didn't even feel like such a chore to put up with his grumbling and snarling. When Cin reemerged, Louise was waiting for him. She caught his arm.

"You know I'm so disappointed you couldn't come tonight," she said, frowning. "But I appreciate all you did for our family. It gave me such comfort to know you were here. And I'm sure your father will feel the same when he returns." She patted the arm she'd been holding—squeezing, actually; it hurt a little now that she'd let go, though Cin didn't think that was her intention—and she lowered her voice, like it was their secret. "It wasn't that grand an event, truth be told; you know your siblings are just weak for such frivolities. *I* would not even bother to return next week if they didn't require a chaperon."

It was such a blatant lie that Cin's shock almost reached his face before he managed to offer a weak smile and a nod. "Of course, Mother."

Of course. *Of course*, he said, as though he believed her, believed that the ball—that incredible, wonderful ball—had been anything less than perfection. But would he have seen through the lie if he hadn't been there? He wondered as he went through the motions of finishing out the night—now nearly sunrise. He knew Emma was easily impressed, Manfred dramatized everything, and Floy would have spoken only of how much the prince was taken with them regardless of the state of the ball itself. If Cin had not seen the ball himself, he wouldn't have known...

But he *had* been there. He had been privilege to the beauty and the joy and the prince's smug smiles, and he would be back again in seven days time. The thought made him giddy.

Bone-tired but still clinging to the embers of the night's happiness, Cinder curled up beside the kitchen hearth, and for once he didn't dream solely of its flames.

C in needed new boots. He knew the moment he slid his feet back into them mid-morning, tired and sore, the pain between his ribs barely lessened by the few hours he'd rested. The lacking state of his broken shoe was made all the more clear as he trod, exhausted, around the garden, then trekked into town. Once he had collected the short list of purchases Louise had requested that morning, he took the long way back to check on a pair of young children he'd left with only a father after watching their mother pour little doses of poison into the family's meals to force them into her care. They seemed healthy for the first time in years, the youngest giggling as she chased a new dog around the yard.

The extra walking widened the torn section of Cin's sole with every rock in his path. Somehow he made it back, only to dump an assortment of tiny pebbles out of the broken boot as he sat on the back stoop.

He contemplated arguments for Louise: it would just be a small repair; he didn't need brand new shoes; how was he meant to go to and from town like this? But the more he thought about it, the more Cin didn't want his old, battered shoes restitched. How likely would they be to break again, just as soon? If they tore on the way down a wall or slowed him as he fled a killing, what then? He was already fighting his chest binding at every turn—he could not deal with this too.

"I hear there's a pair of free elves setting up shop in the border for-est," the local shoemaker had said, but Cin had nothing to offer them. He'd *had* nothing to offer, anyway. He glanced out at his flock, not just a few pigeons now, but a whole host of birds, twitter-ing and shifting in the foliage beyond the garden.

When they dressed Cin for the ball next, he wanted to be ready to run after.

Eight

It took Cin three more days of walking with his broken boot, his foot growing increasingly more pained, bruised, and blistered, before he found a good time to slip away to the forest. Manfred had taken the money from an odd job he'd done their neighbor out to the gambling hall in the city, Emma and Louise had afternoon tea with a social group in the next town over, and Floy hadn't left their room for two days as they poured themselves into a painting they claimed was a gift for the prince. No one was even there to notice as Cin's flock formed back into the shape of a horse, whisking them away toward the east.

He followed the roads he knew, riding through the ever-deepening forest that lay between Hallin and Falchovari by way of the wide, well-traveled merchant's path that, if one went far enough, eventually connected both capital cities—both castles, even—before progressing onward toward the kingdoms beyond. All too soon, though, Cin's steed veered off on a smaller trail. He let it choose its way, the mount's magical hooves ever sure and its ears pricked as though it understood the route ahead as more than simply the looming trees and ominous rustles in the gloom that Cin could make out.

It stopped short suddenly, half a dozen of its flock members drifting off it to flit through the forest. An anxious thrill running through Cin, he dismounted to follow them. He pressed through the trees until he found the scatterings of a camp: a tent sloppily erected, fresh ash from a recent cook-fire, and tucked behind it all, a covered wagon. This couldn't be the elves... could it?

Cin stepped through the brush, but he hesitated to call out. Perdition landed on his shoulder, Rags and Lacey following, all three wary as they held tight and low against Cin's body. He proceeded with more care then, letting each step land more quietly than the last. Nothing moved but him. As he made his way around toward the wagon, he noted the lack of a horse despite the tack—ridden off into the woods by whoever had set the camp up, he wagered.

Cin flinched as three of his birds shot past him as though spooked. As they peeled upwards, their wing beats fluttered the cloth cover on the wagon. Cin caught a glimpse of something metallic inside.

Creeping closer, he leaned just enough to pull back the edge of the wagon's cover. Bile rose in his throat. *Cages.* Not a hunter's cages either—Cin had seen plenty of those as the famine strengthened— but larger, thicker versions, empty manacles dangling from the bars. Those nearest had the stain of red-brown blood.

Cin had to step back to keep the little food he'd eaten for breakfast from coming back up again. Despite all the lives he'd taken, all the pain witnessed leading up to each kill, this horror felt no less visceral, no less terrible than the worst of everything else he'd seen. Whoever this camp belonged to, they'd held elves captive in these very cages—elves who were now enslaved in some Falchovarian factory or illegally to the wealthy of Hallin.

It made Cin want to burn the wagon down, to pull every link of heated metal free from the others and leave nothing left of their magic-dampening powers behind. As much as his blood boiled, though, he knew that dismantling the enslaver's tools would not stop them for long. To put a true stop to their work, he'd have to return later.

"Remember this place," Cin whispered to Perdition.

She flared her feathers in agreement before taking off, back to the place where Cin had left his flock-creature.

The weight on his shoulders did not alleviate though, even as he mounted his steed and set back off through the woods. After a worryingly short ride, they emerged from the dense forest into a quaint little clearing. At its center, a small but sturdy log cabin had been constructed, with a large wooden shed behind it. Despite the fine craftsmanship, the set up appeared oddly sterile, empty of the homey touches that made a space feel lived in. Cin supposed they *had* just moved here, after all.

What might that make them, though: desperate or defensive? With an enslaver hunting so near to them, Cin hoped for their sakes that they were on high alert.

Beneath Cin, one bird after another peeled away from his flock-creature, gently depositing him onto the ground in a flourish of wings. Perdition landed on Cin's shoulder as the last of his mount took off into the trees behind him. His broken sole flapped awkwardly against the ground with each step toward the buildings.

Cin swallowed down the apprehension lodging in his throat and called, "Hello? I'm looking for the elvish cobblers?"

He didn't have to wait long.

An elf opened the front door of the cabin, his long, straight hair spilled over his shoulders, shining as it caught the light, but he scowled at Cin with an expression far darker than his gilded appearance.

A knot in Cin's chest released at the sight of him—no chains on his wrists, nor hunters at his back. Whoever had set up the camp nearer the main road hadn't managed to find this place yet. And now here Cin was barging in to ask for favors.

With the way the elf scowled at him, he had half a mind to apologize outright.

"How the damned did you get here?" the elf snapped.

Cin tried to put on a pleasant expression, hoping a lighter mood might rub off on the surly cobbler. He could always just leave, but then where would he be? He'd have lost a half day's work for nothing. That was a defeat worse than never having made an attempt in the first place.

"My birds led me." It would have sounded ridiculous, if not for the flock that trilled and cooed from the branches behind him, their sharp eyes alert and wings ready.

Perdition gave her feathers a tiny ruffle as though in support, clacking her beak together like a threat. It only made the disinterested elf's expression darken further.

Cin placed a hand casually over Perdition's back, pleading silently with her to back down. "I don't mean to intrude—"

As he spoke, a second elf appeared behind the first, his light hair pulled up atop his head, leaving his ears on full display. "Nonsense, you're not intruding." The newcomer shook his head, smiling gently. "We've put in place a magic that only allows those with good intentions to find this meadow. You're welcome here."

That was another relief to Cin—at least he didn't need to worry about anyone charging in on them before he had finished here.

"Elias!" The first elf hissed under his breath.

Elias looked pointedly at his scowling neighbor. "In fact," he said, enunciating each word, "I quite *miss* having visitors."

"You're only accommodating him because he's the first that's made it," the original elf grumbled.

"Don't mind Henrik." Still smiling, Elias stepped out of the house, and Henrik followed him, slower, his gaze narrowing on the birds that filled the trees behind Cin. When Elias held out his hand to Cin, Cin took it.

The kind but firm shake seemed to pull the last bit of tension out of Cin's muscles.

"I'm Elias," the friendlier elf said. He lifted his voice, calling back toward the work shed, "Johan, we have a guest!"

The shed's door opened immediately, and a large, burly human man with dark hair and a beard poked his head out. By the look of his outfit, he seemed in the middle of crafting, but he gave Cin a friendly nod and lingered in the entrance to watch after. Cin wasn't sure whether it was odd to find a human here, among the free elves, but if they had fled Falchovari together, they must have been partners of some kind.

A pang of something sharp and bitter as jealousy ran through Cin. He tried to shrug it off. Fleeing his home was the last thing a good or pious person should have found intriguing, regardless of who might go with him. His life was all he had and that was that. He should have been feeling nothing more for this trio than pity for their loss and hope for their future.

Besides, one of them was still glaring at him. "What are you here for?" Henrik asked.

"A mending, if it suits you, though I don't have another pair to wear in the meantime. All I have are these..." Cin lifted his foot, twisting his knee to reveal the dangling part of his boot's sole. "I broke it while climbing, and I'd like not to have to worry about that with the next one, if that's something you can do?" He took a breath, then added, for the hell of it, "And, if you can make them fit only my own feet, that would also be lovely."

Perhaps that would finally stop Floy from squeezing their feet into his shoes whenever they wished not to sully their own.

Elias nodded eagerly. "A new pair of such specifications shouldn't be a problem for us."

"For a price," Henrik pointed out, his tone making it clear he intended a steep one.

Cin had been prepared for this, but the thought still sent a tingle of nerves through his stomach. He had so little to offer, yet so much they could ask for when magic and favors were concerned. He'd have to suggest what he could and hope that God smiled on him.

"I don't have much in the way of payment—not traditional coins, anyway." He glanced behind him to the cooing wall of wings and beaks. "My flock is at your service though. They led me here; I think they'll oblige."

Johan had come to join the elves by then, and he loomed quietly behind them, his expression soft and thoughtful as he watched the birds.

"Done," Elias said without hesitation.

"Undone!" Henrik snapped. "He should return with coin."

Elias looked put out. "He came all this way."

"We should help him," Johan added, his deep voice so soft that it seemed like Cin wasn't meant to hear it at all.

Still, Henrik seemed unconvinced.

"My flock are good at searching the woods. They can bring you herbs, flowers, berries, or lost things from the trade road."

"What on earth are we supposed to do with a collection from the forest we *live* in?" Henrik grumbled.

Elias shot him a look. "Johan gave us a home and expected nothing in return. We've lost so much. A little more color and nature in our house will make up for your sour expressions."

Henrik's annoyance dropped at that, a guilty look replacing it. Behind him, Johan squeezed Elias's shoulder. It seemed to settle things.

Henrik shifted his sullen expression away from Cin. "This once, we'll take what your birds offer."

A tremble of exhilaration ran through Cin. He took a breath, and looked expectantly back at the woods.

For a moment, Cin's flock merely twittered amongst themselves. Perdition gave Cin's ear a nibble, then took off into the air. Every bird followed, Lacey and Ragimund taking up at the end with a final twirl around Cin's head, ruffling his hair before vanishing into the branches. Now, he had only to wait. His nerves told him to pace, but the elves and their human still watching him made that feel rude.

He turned to examining their little home instead. It gave no sign as to where they'd come from, only that they were here now, starting over in this little clearing so deep into the wood, it seemed they'd taken every precaution to stop their past life in chains from catching back up to them.

Elias cleared his throat. "Would you like some tea, while we wait?"

"Hm—yes?" Cin replied, cursing himself for getting distracted. "That would be lovely. Thank you."

The inside of the cabin was just as bare as it had appeared looking in, its plain walls and simple furnishings doing little to cozy the place up. Elias offered Cin a seat at the table and quickly put on the tea, Johan and Henrik joining as the steeping finished. Elias poured Cin a cup. Staring at the lovely brown drink, he thought of the tales where monstrous people of the woods trapped their victims with food, but this seemed so far removed from any magical terror Cin had heard tell of. The trio who sat before him were far too goodly, and yet not quite goodly enough to be monsters in disguise.

"Are you liking it here?" Cin asked, taking a sip of his tea. It was nice—no sugar or cream, but a little dab of fresh honey made up for that. "Not many visitors, I gather."

"As Henrik mentioned, you're the first," Elias confirmed. "But that's all right with us. We're enjoying our solitude. And each other."

"I'm glad you're here." Cin said, and tried to shake the lingering claws of his earlier jealousy.

His life had been easier and fairer than theirs in every way. He had no reason to want this—this tiny home deep in the woods, where his drafts would still go unfixed if he couldn't learn to repair them himself and there was no one to be ignored by since there was no town and no one to watch because there were no people to liberate from the bastards in their lives. Though he supposed there was still at least one human bastard on the prowl, even here.

Cin took a long sip of his tea before carefully broaching the topic. "On my way here, I skirted past someone in the woods—they did not appear to be the most savory fellow. Is that going to be a problem for you?"

Elias's usual smile waned, and he glanced out toward the forest. "I'm afraid she's in league with those who'd keep us enslaved."

"Here? Aren't we on the border of Hallin?" Cin had gone far enough down the trade road that it was possible he'd crossed over without realizing it, but he didn't think that was the case.

Elias shook his head. "These days there are so few safe places for our people."

"But your magic will continue to protect you?" Cin asked.

"We have no reason to think it won't."

That answer did little to curb Cin's worries—he had found their meadow using magic of his own, after all. And even if Elias and Henrik were safe, there were surely other free elves hiding somewhere in these woods. Cin felt a fierce knot of anger tighten in his gut. Maybe the offerings of his birds were all that he could officially give to these lonesome cobblers, but there was another service he'd be providing them later.

Cin drank his tea quietly after that, commenting on the nature of the meadow and inquiring about the shoe-work. As it turned out, Johan and Elias were the shoemakers, with only Henrik provid-ing the magic. It seemed to make them all happy—even Henrik, who had barely pulled himself out of his sullenness as he sipped his own tea.

All the while they talked, Cin stole glances out the window, searching for any sign of his flock. Just when he was beginning to doubt himself, one by one the birds returned.

They brought with them a collection far broader and larger than Cin could have guessed—branches of berries and nuts ripe for the taking, full herb plants that slipped seamlessly back into the soil, minerals and precious stones, unpolished but already gorgeous even in their natural state, pairs of butterfly wings and bundles of flow-ers, even a full head of glorious antler shedding carried between three large pigeons. As Cin and his hosts met them in the front of the house, they lay the most precious of the offerings directly before the stoop.

Johan and Henrik began collecting them as Elias walked Cin back the way he'd come. "Your new shoes should be ready by the end of the week."

"Thank you." Cin tipped his head, hoping all three of them could feel the sincerity of his gratitude.

As he left, his flock spinning and weaving back into its horse-like form, he glanced back to find Henrik delicately arranging a bundle of lavender from the flower selection the birds had offered. The elf looked almost happy. Cin hoped, maybe, perhaps, he'd done some-thing good for them in turn.

He needed to believe that, anyway. What he was about to do would be neither good nor pious.

C in retraced his steps with ease, random members of his flock peeling in and out of his steed as they crept like a ghost through the forest. He held only one thought in his mind: the image of Henrik and Elias, enslaved to humans once more. If not them, it would be some other elf, one who also deserved so much better than that life of subjugation.

It was not like Cin to skip from first glance to the kill, but in this case, the transgression outweighed his caution.

He found the slaver in her camp, her back turned. Cin's knife slid so easily between her shoulder blades that it felt like, this time, maybe even God had deigned to look down on him, not to smile but perhaps not to scowl either. No one else would witness Cin's deeds this time, though—the enslaver's body was too far off the road to be found by anyone who might care enough to go to the crown's watch. Cin left his feathers in her wound anyway.

Before he slipped back out of the little camp, Cin gave one last look at the wagon around the back. One by one, he unlocked the magic-blocking manacles from the cages. They were almost beautiful up close, beneath the dirt and the blood, the metal carved with interlocking patterns. He dumped them into a rotting tree and buried them in leaf litter. No elves would ever be bound by *them*, at least.

Cin hadn't given Elias and Henrik much, but this he could be proud of.

Two birds appeared with the shoes the day of the next ball. They looked just a little cleaner than Cin's pair had been, the stitching sharp and the leather tight but soft, and when he put them on, it felt as though he were walking on a road of feathers, his steps so light that he could barely make a sound even when he tried. The pair was no lavish set of slippers or delicate ball heels, but they were perfect all the same. And under the disguise of his flock's glamour, he knew they'd sparkle as brilliantly as any crystal.

Nine

Louise seemed not even to think it odd when Cin didn't push to join the family for the ball. He smiled and spouted something about responsibility and how parties were for children anyway, and his stepmother ate the idea right up. She hugged him for it, brimming with an emotion that Cin wanted to believe was pride, if it hadn't been for how readily she'd already lied to him about the previous week's ball. She climbed onto their carriage's driver box without a second look back.

Cin called his birds around him the moment his family was out of sight. Wearing his new, sure boots he sped his magical steed off across the fields to reach the main road before the carriage could. It was as much extra time as he could give himself. It would have to do.

The journey through the city was just as beautiful and festive as the first night of the ball, the lights still dazzling, and food and drink overflowing, but Cin moved all the faster through the busy streets, offering his information to the castle guards without being asked, and hurried inside. His heart pounded as he entered. His palms began to sweat. He felt absurd suddenly.

What was he even meant to do here, now? Eat the same food, admire the same decor, chat with people he would never see again, and all the while wait to be swept off his feet by the crowned—

But there he was. Prince Lorenz, strolling down the side of the dance floor, his hair lightly mussed beneath his circlet and drifting in a breeze that might have been coming off the dancers to his right, or through the open doors to the garden on his left, or from nowhere at all—just a part of the magic of his beauty. The prince exchanged words with each guest who went out of their way to catch his attention, as charming and graceful as ever.

As he worked his way through the crowd, Cin thought of the rare times he'd seen Prince Lorenz's older brother, twice during a visit to his town and once in the city, so young then that he'd been hoisted on his birth-mother's shoulders to see.

"Look at the way our future king shines with goodness! There is a man so blessed!" she'd said to Cin then.

Cin's mother wasn't alone in the feeling. He'd been just as in awe of the young royal who'd strode through the crowd as had the rest of them, taken in by the easy way Prince Adalwin greeted his people, both humbly gracious and breathtakingly regal.

Here, now, with the elder prince lost, his younger brother had made a good play at wearing that mask. He'd kept it so tight to his face that Cin would have sworn he was basking in his guests' attention, had he not seen a far more reclusive side from the prince during their time on the balcony the previous week. But somehow, the beautiful man enchanting the world before Cin was only half as interesting or desirable to him as that witty, thoughtful version he'd spent time alone with.

Cin was so eager to see *that* prince—more eager than he cared to admit.

As the prince's gaze slid his way though, Cin ducked instinctively to the side. He didn't understand why he did it, he just did, slipping into the shadows and tucking half behind a pillar for good measure. It was ridiculous, and he knew it. But it felt wrong suddenly, to want this. To want him. To want anything that wasn't for his family, for their future.

It was so unlike Cin.

Attending the ball had been one thing; of course he deserved a good meal and music and festivities as much as the rest of his family and town and kingdom. But Prince Lorenz's attention? What right had he to desire that? Especially when he was never going to be the one to wear the prince's ring, take his name, lead his kingdom.

Yet his body seemed not to recognize that fact, the tug in his gut demanding to look once more. To look, and yearn. Maybe he had no right to want this, but he did. Was it such a sin to give into himself, just this once? It would only go on for so long, after all...

When Cin glanced around the side of the pillar, though, the prince had vanished. He took a step, then another, slowly meandering toward one of the dessert tables as no princes spontaneously appeared from within the crowd. Trying not to feel as though this was God's punishment for his cowardice—or worse, his desire—he picked up a small pastry with an apple slice in the center just to give himself something to focus on. The crisp folds crumbled in his distracted hold.

"Usually, we let our teeth do that work," said a lofty voice from beside Cin. Lofty, but good-natured, and oh-so-beautifully smug.

Cin deposited the mutilated dessert onto his tongue, making a show of chewing as he turned to meet the prince's gaze. He swallowed, then deliberately licked both fingers. "Please don't tell me what to do with my mouth, Your Royal Highness."

It had sounded less like a sex-thing in his head, but for the way it made Prince Lorenz laugh, the innuendo was worth it. "You continue to mystify me, my dove," he said, shaking his head. Without warning, he pushed past Cin, and grabbed a different pastry off the table—no apple in the core of this one, but each lovely fold looked so delicate and purposeful. "Here..."

Prince Lorenz lifted the dessert up to Cin's mouth, and Cin only realized how far his lips hung open as the prince slipped the pastry between them. He held his breath at the light brush of Prince Lorenz's retreating fingers and forced himself to chew after. The crackling of the pastry and the burst of the sugar and butter made him want to moan.

"See, a more preferable experience all around," Prince Lorenz said. "You lose the full intensity of the crispness otherwise."

The surrounding guests were looking at them. Not just looking, but in some cases glaring, even if they seemed to be doing their best to hide the emotion. Someone tried to interrupt Prince Lorenz with a slight bow and a muttering of *Your Royal Highness*, but the prince acted as though he hadn't noticed, taking Cin by the arm and leading him down the rows of desserts. One of the ornamented watch members—a different individual from the previous week—followed slowly in their wake.

"So much sugar," Cin muttered, shaking his head. He'd admired it the first time, but now that this was a second night, a second round of all the most delicious of foods, it was finally sinking in.

"Pardon?" the prince asked.

"Nothing." Cin paused, blinked, and then said, "I was just thinking how lavish this all is, with still no signs the famine will end. I know the kingdom appreciates your family's generosity but..."

"Why drain our stores now?" Prince Lorenz grimaced, but the next thing out of his mouth seemed to change topic. "Do you want to see the gardens? They're not so full as they are in the spring, but it's quiet and dark."

Quiet. And dark.

Cin's mind went immediately to the things he'd told Prince Lorenz he didn't want to do last time they were in such a quiet, dark place, and nausea twisted in his stomach—not all bad, but not all good either. But the prince had, so far, always backed off when Cin had asked. At least, when he wasn't chasing Cin out the front doors.

He wrapped his arm through Prince Lorenz's, trying to ignore the flutter that simple, chaste motion birthed in his chest, and led the prince out of the ballroom.

The chill in the air felt nice after the warmth of the crowded indoors, and though a few guests poked their heads out, the prince's watch-person positioned themself in the doorway, and no one seemed anxious enough yet to try to worm their way past. Cin let go of Prince Lorenz as they reached the railing that overlooked the gardens, the great pond at its center shimmering in the light that streamed from the ballroom windows.

"I didn't ask for this," Prince Lorenz said, and Cin had a flash of confusion before he continued, "To have our reserves wasted on such a frivolous party—one in my honor, nonetheless."

"Says the man who wants shirtless statues of himself in every town square," Cin teased. But as the joke faded into the night, he tried to find the positives in this thing the prince seemed so bent against. "You must admit, these balls have lifted the spirits of the entire country. Perhaps it is frivolous. Certainly the reserves could be better distributed in a different manner. But this one is making your people happy. They feel connected to their royal family again for the first time in... years."

Prince Lorenz's brow furrowed—such an odd expression, half masked in the darkness as he stared out at the garden. "Do you really think so?"

"If the way the people in my town speak of it or the joy I see on my ride through the city is anything to go on, then yes." Cin took a breath, then let it out. "I'm certain I could critique your parent's leadership if forced—"

"No one would need *force* me," the prince muttered.

Cin logged the thought away as he continued, "—but I can't deny that this particular choice is making *me* happy."

"You..." Prince Lorenz turned to him, looking thoughtful. "You, who came here for this,"—he waved toward the ballroom—"and not for me?" There was a gleam deep in the darkness of his eyes that made Cin's heart thud. The prince lifted an eyebrow. "Or so you say, though I haven't actually seen you dance yet."

"Dancing isn't all there is to a party," Cin objected. "There's food, and music, and people, and lights."

"People and lights can be found in most places. If you're here for food and music, but not dancing or the wooing of the most eligible man in the kingdom, then you're missing half the reason for the ball."

Cin crossed his arms, looking up at the prince. "Does it count, when the most eligible man in the kingdom doesn't want to be wooed?"

There was less space between them now, but Cin didn't know which of them had moved. Prince Lorenz's smirk only grew. "I never said I don't wish to be wooed, only that I'd prefer not to accept anyone's hand in marriage," he said. He leaned his shoulders in, whispering in Cin's ear. "I, for one, love to dance."

Cin lifted his chin, feeling insufferably smug and just a little lightheaded as he replied, "Then why, pray tell, are you out here with me?"

Prince Lorenz made a sound in the back of his throat. He pulled away, both hands on his hips and his lips bunched in something very much like a pout. "Because I'm trying to get you to dance with me here, dammit. You can't be that obtuse."

Cin made a show of blinking, holding his hand over his mouth in feigned shock, but he couldn't contain the slow smile that spread across his face. "I'm not that obtuse, no. I just..." He could feel the flush from his first meeting with the prince trying to return, and he scolded himself for it, turning toward the darkness of the garden in the hopes that Prince Lorenz didn't catch it. "In truth, I don't know how to dance."

"You," the prince stated.

Cin lifted both shoulders. "Me?"

"Yes! You with your rich fabrics and your pigeons and your absurd climbing that would rival the goats on the mountain slopes to the south and you can't dance." Prince Lorenz looked very sternly at Cin and held out a hand. "Now is as good a time as any to learn.

And I've been told I'm a *very* good teacher."

Cin lifted one brow. "Have you considered that I may be a terrible student?"

"In that case," Prince Lorenz replied, "you will surely be even more impressed by my skills."

Cin's heart seemed to pound against the uncomfortable tightness of his binding, reminding him just how little effort it took for his lungs to burn and his sides to ache. But he could sacrifice for a single song. He gave the prince a stern look. "*One* dance, then."

He took the prince's hand.

He was pulled immediately closer, Prince Lorenz's other palm sliding around his waist and guiding him away from the garden patio's railing. It wasn't the closest they'd ever been, and the firm touch was so respectful it seemed less sensual than most of their other contact, but the way the prince smiled sparkled of magic, like if Cin caught his eyes at just the right angle, he might see into the depths of Prince Lorenz's soul. And, as it turned out, the prince knew how to dance well enough for the both of them. He led with a graceful command, giving instruction with both his voice and body as he stepped Cin back and forth, in and out and around and back again.

It made Cin think of the prince's body directing his in other ways, hands guiding and pressing, voice low and purposeful. The idea burned through him like a flush, and he swore his cheeks were on fire, but Prince Lorenz only smiled at him, giving him a final twirl as the music pouring from the ballroom came to a momentary close. The prince pulled Cin closer, his arm wrapping firmly around Cin's waist, and despite the subtle pain it set blooming between Cin's ribs, he couldn't make himself pull away. He'd made a promise with his lips that he had no desire to back out of—especially after a week spent daydreaming of it every chance he got.

"How do you like dancing then, my dove?" Prince Lorenz asked.

Cin gave a tiny shrug, trying to hide how breathless the constant movement had made him. "It was acceptable. For your first time with me, anyway."

The laugh that burst out the prince was beautiful in the way that he was, dark and light, odd and intriguing; a little bit magical. He tipped his head against the side of Cin's, grinning so broadly his smile seemed to consume his face. "Cheeky," he murmured, light from the ballroom cresting down his jawline.

From the ballroom windows, the other guests were watching them, the prince's personal watch member still standing guard. For all the various servants and security they'd put into place, it seemed Prince Lorenz's was the only higher ranking watcher present. It made Cin wonder... "Your parents are throwing these elaborate parties for you, but I've yet to see them?"

The prince seemed to wilt, grunting as he pulled away. Through not very far away. "They're out in the city, for once—took half the watch with them, I swear. They claimed they wanted to give me 'space' and be 'visible to the people' at the same time." He mocked them with the emphasis of his words, but his tone held an odd gentleness that Cin could not have imagined coming from himself or Floy or Manfred when they spoke poorly of their own parents. Prince Lorenz sighed. "I do believe they're truthful about wanting to be seen by the people—staying so secluded seems to take a toll on

Mother it never has on me—but space? That is not particularly of what one thinks when they contemplate being forced to choose a life partner in six weeks. Besides, they have their spies here, watching and reporting in their place, calculating how to push me into their desired match."

It wasn't that Cin hadn't known the prince's fate, but it hadn't quite sunk in before then: the misery of being pressured into a life role one didn't want for themselves. In the prince's case, a permanent one. He pressed his palm to Prince Lorenz's arm, squeeze it gently. "Are you really going to let them force this on you?"

The prince shook his head and shrugged at the same time. "How do I say no? They're my parents."

Not, *they're the king and queen*. Yet, they *were* his parents, too. Cin felt that like a sharp pinch in his chest, because he understood. Their families might have been worlds apart in power and wealth and, from the way Prince Lorenz spoke, the hatred that the Reinholzes harbored for each other was oddly lacking in the royal family, but they were still both just children of two people they didn't always want to obey, but were forced to by the world and their circumstances all the same. For the sake of a family. For the sake of a kingdom. For their own sakes.

"Let's not speak of dreadful things neither of us can change, shall we?" Prince Lorenz stepped back in a dramatic slide, thrusting his arms out as he spun. "It's a beautiful night! We have the present, and that's all we need." He lunged back in to grab Cin's hand, pulling him into a loose embrace.

Cin caved to the touch, and to the joy Prince Lorenz was putting out a little more with each second. But he realized with a growing dread that their onlookers had been accumulating. It seemed as though the gathering crowd was about to burst past the watch in the hopes of sweeping the prince away with them. Floy would be among them soon.

As Cin squinted into the sea of shifting bodies, he swore he caught a glimpse of their hat. The way his stomach churned then put every one of the little anxious flutters Prince Lorenz had imposed there to shame.

Cin turned his back on the crowd, hiding his face in the shadow as he held Prince Lorenz's hands. "Can we..."

He didn't want to be the one to suggest that he and the prince leave together, though—he didn't want to imply anything more than what he was ready to give, which was... he wasn't even sure. His mouth, perhaps. His fingertips...

But Prince Lorenz seemed even more eager to get away from the overflowing party, the dark side of his face twitching uncomfortably. "Food and music and dancing is all fine, but you said you also enjoy pigeons?" he asked, brushing his hand over Cin's cloak.

And the back of Cin's mind whispered: Plumed Menace.

But the prince only asked, "What do you say we go visit some?"

Ten

Cinder had bemoaned the size of the Reinholz home every time he carried firewood across the kitchen, down the hall, up the stairs, and through the length of the house, but that trek was simple compared to the complexities of the royal Hallinisch castle.

Prince Lorenz led Cin through the gardens, both of them laughing as they stumbled in the darkness, and back into the castle building through a side entrance, his personal watch trailing a little ways behind them. From there, they wound through a series of halls and sitting chambers, down stairs, across a bustling kitchen where the head chef threw a tomato at Prince Lorenz—he caught it, grinning, and took a bite before offering it to Cin. Three of the kitchen staff cheered. The chef waved a ladle at them, complaining good-naturedly to the prince's watch member, who only shrugged, then winked at the prince.

Cin had managed to put the danger of his vigilante activities to the back of his mind after noticing how little attention the palace guards paid him, even covered in all his feathers—or perhaps because of them, some mysterious aspect of their magic—but the casual way Prince Lorenz's personal watch interacted with him in that small moment, out of the public's eye, made Cin's insides tighten back up. He was traveling through the bowels of the castle with the prince, and that was good, joyous. But it was also dangerous.

He needed not to forget that.

Cin tried to keep the tiniest hint of that tension within him as the prince drew him into a far hall, up a stairwell. They walked down a long corridor, each tall, slim window showing a view of the front of the castle once more. A trail of arrivals made their way up the front steps. Cin hurried past, and the prince took one of the colored lanterns from the wall into a small doorway where a spiraling staircase ascended into the darkness behind.

He held his hand back toward Cin, a smug quirk to his lips. "Are you coming, dove?"

The prince's watch-person hovered somewhere behind them.

Cin glanced up into the tower's center. All the times he'd stood at the town's square and looked out at the very spot fifty feet above them, and never once had he thought he'd get to stand beneath it, much less look down from its heights. And now, he was doing so with the prince, of all people. What must he have done for God to smile upon him so? Nothing he could imagine; the price on his head agreed with him.

It made him feel all the more breathless.

Inhaling against the tightness of his chest binding, Cin took Prince Lorenz's hand for the second time that night, and up they went, leaving the prince's only guard behind.

The single lantern cast odd shadows on the tower's brick walls and tight stairs, but the prince tucked Cin close, guiding them up one flight after the next as he explained, "The dovecote has been up here since the castle was rebuilt after the fires in 1310. Old Martha

Beth takes care of it, with the help of a few apprentices. Their birds send and receive messages from all across the continent."

"Fascinating," Cin replied. "They sound far better traveled than mine."

"Oh, I'm sure after seeing their fair share of the world, they'd rather be back here, cozy with their flock."

"Like you."

"I never said that," the prince protested, weakly.

Cin laughed, a little winded by the layers of binding around his chest. His right side was beginning to ache. "No, but you mentioned the toll that sequestering yourself in the castle has had on your mother, but not on you. And I've certainly never seen you visit so much as the town next over."

"Yes, well..." Prince Lorenz slowed as they reached the top of the stairs. He paused with his hand on the doorknob. "Since my brother's disappearance, I've had good reason to keep as near the castle's walls as I can. But regardless, if I did, there'd be a thing made of it. That's so much work, you see."

That single moment of vulnerability over his brother's loss made Cin want to backtrack to it, but he knew what else lay there: who the royals still blamed for his sudden demise. Besides, the tone with which the prince continued was a clear sign to move on with humor instead. "Ah, so you're not going to christen all your shirtless statues in person, then?"

"I can't begin to imagine what form that christening would entail," the prince replied, grinning like he was picturing *exactly* how he might perform such a ceremony in his hypothetical orgy world. With a wink, he pushed open the dovecote door.

A flutter of wings and coos greeted them as the pigeons shifted in the nooks tucked across the circular wall between tiny windows. Two of the birds swooped out to land on Cin's head and shoulder, then a third, and a fourth, giving him playful nips and nuzzles. He laughed, scratching them behind their little downy heads.

Prince Lorenz—who remained completely untouched by the birds—whistled under his breath. "You truly are a pigeon-whisperer."

Cin made a noncommittal noise, though inside he felt himself beaming. "I suppose we have similar souls, them and I."

As he spoke, he scooped one of the birds up on his finger and transferred it to the prince's shoulder. It hopped forward, nuzzled the side of his neck, then gave a happy coo. Instantly half a dozen other birds joined it.

Prince Lorenz grinned, and Cin swore a slight flush came over his cheeks as he tried his best to awkwardly support the birds as they inspected him. "You're also are gorgeous, curious, good-natured, intelligent, and far too accepting of me, you mean?"

Cin snorted. "Shows how little you know me."

He could feel his own cheeks heating for certain now. Had he really come off like that, or was the prince merely flattering him? Perhaps the glamorous clothes distracted from his sharp, pale features, and he *had* been curious enough to sit down with the prince that first night—not that anyone else at the party would have refused—but good-natured and intelligent? Accepting... He supposed he could see that, so long as one knew nothing of all the bodies he'd left in his wake.

"Just don't take it as a sign that I like you," he added, trying to lighten the mood with a half-grin and a nudge in Prince Lorenz's shoulder.

"Hardly. People only abscond to quiet dovecotes with those they *despise*." The prince winked. He held one of the birds up to his face to give it the tiniest kiss on the beak. "Tell me, then, why would *you* say you're like these little beasties?"

That felt too raw a place for Cin to venture, but swathed in the gentle coos of the pigeons, and the darkness broken only by their single lantern, with the prince's strange smugness inviting Cin to join in some kind of absurd reality where the world conformed to them both, he decided to try.

"I'd say, not beautiful, but functional. Not intelligent, but reasonable. Not good-natured, but..." He held the thought in for a moment, attempting to transform it from a huge integral piece of himself into simple speakable words. "Trying, I suppose, not to put more bitterness into the world than I take in. To exist in the background, in anyone's way but my own, yet letting nothing stop me from doing my duty."

As he spoke, all but one of the pigeons fluttered their way back into their nooks. Prince Lorenz watched Cin, his brow tight. Softly, he said, "That sounds good for the world, perhaps, but taxing for you."

Cin chose not to acknowledge the quiet accusation. He lifted the final bird that had lingered on his shoulder up to its nook. It gave a coo, and hopped in. "And," Cin said, "I also always know my way home."

However much he hated that home, he knew it: knew its hearth and its routines, its pains and its fears, knew it like it was a part of him. Ugly, but stable.

"Where might that be?" Prince Lorenz asked. He glanced out the nearest window. "Where is this town I should have been visiting?"

Cin had to look through a couple of different windows before he found the smudge of it on the horizon. Despite the clear autumn night, the lights of his little town were nearly masked by all the lanterns in the city. He pointed in its direction. "There."

Prince Lorenz slipped in beside him, and Cin was about to move when the prince's arm wrapped around his waist, casually holding him as they gazed out. "It looks lovely."

"It looks like a scattering of random lights," Cin protested.

The prince scoffed. "Most scatterings of lights do appear beautiful at a distance."

"Clodpate." Cin should not have been able to call his own prince an idiot to his face, but as soon as the endearing insult had left his lips, he found he could. He could deny Prince Lorenz, and dance with him, and tease him. He could kiss him, once.

Maybe, even, he could do so again.

But a catch in his chest stopped him. There was something festering beneath their friendship, even if the prince wasn't aware of it. But the longer they stretched this out, the more Cin knew that he couldn't just set the other pieces of himself to the side for one more night, even if that release had gotten him here in the first place.

Casually as he could, he swept a pigeon's lost feather off the sill beside them, twirling it between his fingers. It was indistinguishable from half the gray-toned selection within his own cloak. There was no delicate way to bridge the gap, but he had to try.

"When we first met, you thought I might be a fanatic of the

Plumed Menace." Cin asked. "Are those really a thing?" It wasn't the question he needed answered, but perhaps it would get them there.

So far as he could tell, the prince didn't think the question odd. They *were* in a dovecote, Cin supposed. "So I've heard. One of my watch—Gisela—she claims her brother wears a necklace with feathers in support of the Menace. He was in the watch himself, at its founding. Thinks they should be doing more of what the Plumed Menace does. Hunting the kind of people he claims the Menace is killing, instead of the Menace."

"And you disagree?"

The prince watched Cin through tight eyes. "What do *you* have to say on the matter?"

Cin felt his stomach tumble in on itself. His thoughts of his darker self were no more outright flattering than the ones he'd already shared with the prince, but he doubted they aligned with the prince's—not when his parents had put such a high price on the Menace's head.

Prince Lorenz softened at Cin's hesitation. He pressed a hand to Cin's shoulder. "I don't want your opinions hidden simply because we might view the world differently," he said. "I want the chance to see what you see, too."

What Cin *saw* was blood, pooling as his victim's heart beat its last. But what he *thought* of the matter was a different thing, one he could perhaps explain in a way the prince would understand. "I think the people Plumed Menace kills—any who are truly bastards, anyway—deserve to be brought to justice, and the watch isn't doing that." Under the warmth of Prince Lorenz's gaze, admitting his own struggle to parse his beliefs felt far easier than he'd expected. "I don't think the solution is to praise the Menace though, or to make the watch more like them. I just know something is wrong, and we should be doing more to confront that, whatever that doing may be."

All Cin knew was how to climb the fences that bastards used to hide their sins and slide a blade into flesh. To become a sinner for the sake of others. With every body that dropped to his feet, he knew it wasn't the solution. But it was *a* solution.

Maybe that was why he kept tucking the blade into his belt, kept stalking the cruel and the greedy until they proved their atrocities to him. Or maybe he just couldn't feel safe himself without it. Cin could never decide.

The prince nodded, slowly, his gaze distant and deep, iced over in a way that Cin couldn't read. But as he spoke, he sounded thoughtful, not judgmental. "I certainly would not praise the Plumed Menace either. What they are doing is wrong—I can see no way around that—*but* the watch clearly isn't helping in that. They would never make it outside the capital if not for their investigations of the Menace's killings. Perhaps my family has benefited from the extra guard. They are no more useful to the kingdom then the Menace is."

It was the *but* that Cin clung to, hiding it deep inside his chest. Perhaps the prince held no love for the blood on Cin's hidden blade, but he too knew the system they had now was no good. Someday, it would be him who had to deal with that. Him and his future partner.

Carefully, Cin asked, "Do you think they'll ever catch the Menace?"

The prince's expression soured, though perhaps it was the flickering of the light and the tipping away of his face that just made it appear so, because his voice was steady when he answered. "I don't have much hope for that." He shrugged, like he was pushing the idea away, trying to keep it at arm's length. "It's my parent's obsession, anyway. They're the ones who have to believe the Menace took my brother from us. They need someone to fight, someone to blame. Otherwise, it's them who let him go on that diplomatic journey in the first place, and they can't bear to doubt themselves like that." The weak smile he gave was more like a grimace. "They are the king and queen, after all."

"You don't need to be the rulers of a country to cling to your own reasoning over the truth," Cin muttered, thinking of the times his blade had been unsheathed because someone couldn't let go of their own folly at the cost of the flesh and bones of those they had once loved. "But you're not as certain as them?"

"No." Prince Lorenz shook his head, quick and sharp, and his hand went to the center of his chest, his fingers curling against his heart. "His disappearance doesn't fit the Plumed Menace's pattern. Every other victim has been of middling or lower status, the body unmoved from the place they were killed." He sounded pained but distant, as though he were looking through the endless pool of his own gaze to see that loss, instead of living it himself. "Parts of the forest between Hallin and Falchovari are dark places—who knows what one might stumble across there... What might follow you out, if you're not careful."

Cin pressed his hand to the prince's arm. "Thank you for telling me."

Prince Lorenz gave him a weak smile, shallow and a little haunted. "It's not something I'd like shared around, if you please."

"Your secrets are always safe with me," Cin promised. He smiled back, hoping to offer a little joy back into the conversation. "Who else would I even tell them to? The birds?"

"See, that I cannot possibly believe," the prince said, but he sounded more teasing, the somber tension fading from his voice. "How do you not have a line of suitors—friends, if you'd rather—trailing us down the steps?"

"People don't usually notice me." Cin shrugged, but the motion shifted his feathered cape and he chuckled. "I'm not often dressed like this, though."

"I'd notice you dressed in anything. Or nothing." Prince Lorenz smirked. "Nothing *would* be preferable."

It was such a ridiculous line that Cin couldn't help snorting a laugh. "But why?"

"Well..." Prince Lorenz wrapped one arm around Cin's shoulders. As he spoke, he trailed his fingers across Cin's back, along his neck and through his hair, the touch so soft that it should not have left such a fire in its wake. "You know when someone just calls to you? Their body, their bones—it's like magic. It's a magic that makes me want to see inside you and be inside you all at once, and I could give you a thousand reasons why, but they'd all be insufficient."

Cin tried to fight back the yearning that feathery caress had left in his core, to focus on the words instead—words that worried him.

"That sounds suspiciously like love, Your Royal Highness."

"Oh, bah! I've never been in *that* kind of love." Prince Lorenz scoffed, his arm slipping down and around Cin's waist. "My heart has never fluttered for anyone. I'm not swooning over you—no offense. Whoever I end up with, I won't swoon over them either. It's simply not in me."

Cin took that in slowly, thoughtfully, trying to find the differences between his own experience and the prince's, and those portrayed by the great lovers of the world. But he'd witnessed—if only in passing—the existence of both great sexual partnerships and deep friendships amongst those living in his town, and who was he to count them as something more or less than any romance? Besides, knowing the prince would not accidentally fall for him was better for them both.

"Heart flutters are for the weak," Cin said. The prince's honesty made it easy to keep talking, slowly unraveling a part of himself he'd never had someone to share with before. "I'm not certain I've ever felt one either. Though I suppose I've had far less opportunity than you to discover what swooning is like. I just know enough to be aware that it isn't this."

"This is a different kind of spark," Prince Lorenz agreed, pulling Cin closer. He licked his lips, purposeful in a way that was excruciating to watch. "But I do make you feel *something*, too?"

"You make me feel many a fiery thing," Cin murmured, one hand pressed to the prince's arm. Slowly, purposefully, he lifted himself, onto the tips of his toes and—

Prince Lorenz caught Cin's mouth with his in an instant, both arms suddenly around Cin's back as he pulled him closer. Cin could feel so much of the prince, his fingers grasping muscles, the press of jewelry or armor—or some other metal—over his heart beneath his jacket, his hips ground against Cin, one of his thighs wrapping around the side of Cin's leg, his nose tucking against Cin's cheek, and his mouth—his *mouth*. Their first kiss had been a simple brush of lips, but this was an act of devouring, teeth and tongue and reckless flurries of nerves so aggressive that Cin barely knew what to do with it but to moan and melt into the attention, letting Prince Lorenz take a small portion of what he had been asking for since the moment they met. It should have hurt more than it did—Cin's ribs already aching, his binding cutting off his breath—but the spark deep inside him seemed to rage over the pain, pushing it aside, for better or for worse.

Quietly, gently, as to not be intrusive, Cin brushed one hand up into Prince Lorenz's hair, gliding his fingers through the soft strands as the prince sucked on his lower lip so hard that the place between his legs seemed to catch fire. He swore he could feel the bundle of his want solidifying just as he caught the very obvious rise of the prince's—hard and long and bringing flashes of when Prince Lorenz had held it in his own hand last week on the balcony.

"I want to touch you," Prince Lorenz whispered, and it was a plea, but it was more than that: dark and low and heavy with lust.

"You want to do what?" Cin taunted, barely getting the words out into the crook of the prince's shoulder as he sucked gloriously on Cin's neck.

"I want," Prince Lorenz growled this time, his hand grabbing Cin's ass as he pulled Cin against him, rocking his hard bulge into the taut and ready point between Cin's legs in a way that birthed fire deep inside Cin. "I want to press my fingers between your... folds? Do you have folds, or—"

"Yes," Cin cut him off, laughing and groaning at the same time.

"I want to run my nails over the tenderest parts of you until you scream. I want to feel you come around my fingers and beg for more after." He ground against Cin as he said it. Cin's lashes fluttered and his hands grabbed the prince's clothes on instinct, needing something, anything, to keep himself stable against the desire wracking through him.

"Yes," Cin said again, and again as Prince Lorenz popped open the front buttons of Cin's pants and pressed in his hand, rubbing downward with such purpose that Cin's hips bucked into him, and again when he found Cin's sweet spot with his thumb, rolling it as he sucked on Cin's neck.

Then, Cin could say nothing at all, everything that came out of his mouth a torrent of emotion and need too sharp for words. He bit down on the prince's shoulder, rocking into the prince's hand as those fingers seemed to turn him inside out. It was like neither of the mediocre times he'd tried such things in town as a teen, with hints of the rush and fire he'd felt at home while thinking of the prince's mouth, but this—this was hotter and heavier and fuller and rougher and better in every way, unpredictable and perfect.

The swell came between his legs with such sudden burning bliss that he had to bury his scream in Lorenz's shoulder, his eyes rolling back as he came. He went nearly limp with panting after, clinging to the prince for support. His sweet spot tingled, leaving him with little, awkward sobs of pleasure as Prince Lorenz carefully withdrew his hand.

Cin knew, in the back of his mind, that he should be offering to return the favor—even if he didn't know how to give anyone half of what Prince Lorenz had just given him—but the pain between his ribs was sliding back into being, harsher and more jagged than before. It was all he could do to hold to the wall with one hand and the prince with the other and pretend he hadn't come out of that magical bliss into agony.

As he tried to pull himself together, the prince drew his hard dick out of his pants and began rubbing his own saliva aggressively up and down its length. One of his knees quavered and he leaned against the pigeonry wall. Almost immediately, he stiffened with a groan. Cum spilled over his fingers. He released a shaky breath.

They'd both finished.

It was over.

Cin found himself strangely disappointed—not in anything they'd done, but in that their moment of pleasure had come and gone so quickly, a spark of heaven followed by the hell that was forming in Cin's sides. He knew he had no right to feel such loss over the speed of it all; whatever this was between them would never be meant for anything more than a kiss and a quick fuck. But at the thought of their evening foray coming to an end, Cin already found himself missing Prince Lorenz: his easy banter, his generous nature, his way of bringing Cin into the joke. And now his lips. And his tongue. And his fingers.

The prince cleared his throat, and Cin found he was staring at those very fingers. He turned his gaze out the nearest window— down to the castle entrance. His stomach dropped.

Below, Manfred and Emma were leaving.

Floy wasn't with them, but it didn't matter—if anyone reached their home to find Cin gone, his ruse would be up. No more ball nights, prince or no prince.

Cin gave a stiff bow to Prince Lorenz, feeling naked as he stepped toward the door, as though with each stride the prince might notice his pain and worry. "This was lovely, but I—"

"You're leaving?" He said it with such sadness that Cin's heart leaped.

The prince truly did like him—wanted to be here, with Cin, in this lucky tower, whether God smiled upon them or not. It made Cin want to kiss him again. But that wouldn't stop his siblings from leaving the ball. "I'll be back next week."

"There's so much left of the night!" Prince Lorenz made a show of looking Cin's body up and down, a little quirk to his lips. "There's so much left of you, as well."

"I know," Cin smiled. "Some day, perhaps you'll earn that rest of me."

"Cheeky!" the prince protested. He followed Cin out of the dovecote and down the towers steps, laughing as they went. "You want me and yet you deny us both! How cruel is that?"

The prince's watch-person stepped to the side as Cin reached the bottom of the tower, and he tried to ignore them as they moved back down the hallway to give Cin and the prince their space. He pecked Prince Lorenz on the lips. "Perhaps I want you to work for it."

"What kind of work is this?" The prince snorted. He grabbed Cin playfully, kissing his head and neck, and teased, "Usually, I need only ask for things and they're brought to me!"

Through the tall windows along the hallway, Cin could see Emma and Manfred pulling away in their carriage. As much as it hurt to let go, Cin slipped free of Prince Lorenz's embrace. He waggled his eyebrows. "You might just have to come get this one."

The prince's smug grin grew, and he reached for Cin again, but Cin was ready. He twisted beneath the prince's searching grip and strode across the hall. Throwing open the nearest of the tall windows, he clutched its pane as the glass swung out like a door. He dropped his feet down to the stone wall beneath, holding his breath to see whether the magic in his new elvish shoes would truly support him. His boots held him despite the lack of footholds, and he reveled in their stability as he clung to the wall outside the window, half his body still inside the building's threshold.

Cin smiled, a thrill running through him. He would have Prince Lorenz's lips again—his tongue, his hands, and more perhaps. "Find me next week, and you can claim me then."

The prince leaned both hands against the sill, his face an inch from Cin's as he replied, "All of you?"

The thought came with a tiny spark of fear and a far larger blaze of excited anticipation, threatening to roar Cin's desire right back to life again. "Anything you want."

Then, he swung to the story below, along the arch of the main door and down to the ground, and as swift and sure as the birds who'd granted him their magic, he was gone.

Eleven

C in had just dissipated the last of his flock's magic and locked the kitchen door behind him when Emma and Manfred pounded on the front entrance, Louise calling around the side of the house for the carriage to be retrieved.

What relief Cin felt turned quickly to annoyance, then exhaustion as his siblings bickered and protested over irrelevant nonsense. The moment they made their way to bed, their mother proceeded to describe just how Floy had taken it upon themself to stay at the ball longer, how honorable a sacrifice it had been, and how of course she'd left money for their travel home at the city's carriage-house. Once Louise finally finished her dramatic speech and turned in, however, it left Cin with another hour of work and nothing to preoccupy him but his growing fatigue, the effervescent pain in his sides, and the thought of Floy still at the ball.

The ball, to which Prince Lorenz had surely returned, giving his attention to guests who could actually accept his hand in marriage, and all that would follow such a union. One of those guests might even be Floy. Imagining that—Floy dancing with the prince, holding him, whispering of their perfect life and wooing him with the many talents they'd honed—made Cin sick to his stomach.

But when he tried to picture himself there instead, a part of that crowd seeking the prince's lifelong partnership, all he could think of was the price the crown had rightfully levied on his head, the watch stationed around every turn of the ballroom, and then, the way Emma would call for him after a bad dream or a hard fall, like Cin was the only thing keeping her together.

No, his place was here. With her, with his family, being the only bit of good and pious he could manage.

Even when he hated it.

The next morning, Cin took one look at the mirror in the hall and froze. Slowly, he lifted his fingers to the round, tender bruise on his neck. It sat just where the prince's mouth had been. Cin's stomach fluttered. A part of him almost wanted his siblings to see it—to know he, the Cinder-whore, had someone willing to mark their affection upon his skin. But that would lead to more questions, and when he didn't answer them, to more scrutiny.

Grabbing his scarf from the kitchen, he wrapped it carefully around his neck and tucked the ends into his shirt. They made lumps against his chest binding. The tight wrapping seemed to pinch especially hard around his ribs as Cin struggled through his work, tired and sore and daydreaming of the prince. His trio of pigeons sat nearby whenever he was outside, and when he moved into the house, they perched by the windows and hopped across the kitchen stoop. The sight of them got him through the grumbles and snaps of his family, until Louise finally demanded Cin pick her up a new ledger book from town.

"Ribbons!" Emma added, throwing herself dramatically over the back of the couch where her mother sat. "I want a pair of ribbons for my dress! Blue and white, to match my gloves. Please, please?"

"I need a new hat," Manfred added.

Cin swore Floy muttered under their breath, "What you need is a new brain…"

Then the room broke into shouting as Emma and Manfred argued with Louise over who deserved what most. Cin slipped out the back. He could feel Floy's eyes on him as he left, prickling against his neck like they could see straight through the weathered fabric of his scarf.

By the time he reached town, he was winded inside his binder and had to loosen his scarf twice. He rested in the square, the hustle and bustle moving around him, and stared in newfound wonder at the towers glinting on the horizon. He had been there—toured through one of those very towers with none other than the Prince of Hallin himself—and he wanted to shout it to every passing townsperson who seemed bent on ignoring him. After so many eyes on him the previous night, it felt odd, suddenly, to be delegated to the background once more.

Out in the open, and yet no one to actually see him, for *him*. Not that there would ever be anyone to see him in his entirety. He could be the Plumed Menace, or the good and pious sibling, or the man who'd bantered and danced and come on the prince's fingertips, but not all three. Not for anyone but himself.

A hand clasped onto Cin's shoulder from behind. He inhaled, spinning to face the stranger. His throat caught at the sight of her. "Mrs. Earhart?"

Widow Dorthe Earhart was dressed in a short blue frock and trousers, her hair neatly done up and a single black ribbon of mourning at her throat. Her cheeks glowed with color. "I'm sorry; I didn't mean to startle you." She smiled at Cin, and quieter she added, "I just... wanted to thank you."

Cin's stomach still dropped out from under him. She'd known. All this time? It had been two weeks—two weeks since he'd come face to face with her in the darkness, her late husband's corpse cooling down the street and his blood still staining the inside of Cin's cloak.

But maybe, maybe it wasn't that—or she was pressing on purpose, hoping he'd acknowledge it? Cin's gaze went instantly to the street corners and shop fronts around them, searching for any sign of the crown's watch hiding in wait. Setting him up seemed too cruel for what he knew of Dorthe, but he couldn't risk discounting it entirely, even if the square itself seemed as quiet and peaceful as she did.

Cin tucked his scarf tighter and tried to look confused instead of terrified. "Thank me for what?"

"The sugar, of course." She pushed her hair behind her ear, and her gaze dropped. "And you know, everything else."

Everything else.

But there was only one other thing Cin had ever done for her. His heart ached at the thought that this was real, that he *had* done something right—something right for Dorthe, anyway. It couldn't wash the blood from his hands, but there was a peace in that, at least.

Hoarse and still a little wary, he replied, "You're welcome. For the sugar, I mean."

A flush spread across Dorthe's cheeks. She was quite pretty, Cin realized, now that she had the space to be herself: lightly plump, with soft hair and long lashes, perhaps five or six years Cin's senior—around the prince's age, Cin figured.

"Good. I, um, thank you." She laughed awkwardly—so sweet and embarrassed that Cin felt bad even thinking she had been trying to set him up, even if he hadn't quite managed to pull his attention away from the space around them. "I suppose I just said that."

"Yes, well, it's no problem," Cin replied. He tried to smile for her, and thought he almost managed it. "I'm just happy that you're safe."

"Thank you." Dorthe bobbed her head, and turned away—nearly—shifting half back a moment later, not quite making eye contact with Cin. "You know," she said, even more softly, "Once it's appropriate, I'd like to pursue someone new." The flush in her cheeks strengthened. "I'd be honored if you'd consider me."

The thought hit Cin like a blow to the head: a dizzying, breathless rush as a blur of imagery poured with it. He tried to see himself moving out of the family house, slipping into a home where Dorthe's soft singing filled every room, waking up to her smile and laughing as they made their dinner, never afraid that she wouldn't know the whole him. Perhaps he'd take over the position the late Mr. Earhart had vacated at their local inn—learn the trade well enough to open a place himself, with Dorthe at his side and a couple of adopted children underfoot.

It felt like a good life—a *great* life.

Just not *Cin's* life.

"I mostly like men," he managed, awkwardly, tugging at his scarf again. It was an excuse. Maybe he could be attracted to Dorthe, or maybe he couldn't, but hers was likely one of the best offers he'd receive. She was beautiful, in her way, and Cin knew regardless of his own attractions that he could find it in himself to give her anything she needed, if he could find it in himself to give her anything at all.

But that was the problem: he couldn't. He couldn't be hers. He already belonged to the Reinholzes, didn't he? His family needed him, and the house, if it was to stay warm, and the garden, if it was to grow anything good, and this just wasn't the right time to leave them, if there was a time at all. He had to be good in this, as good as his birth mother had wished for him, and leaving his family for anyone, even Dorthe Earhart, was as selfish an act as strapping his blade to his back when he'd left to follow her husband that night.

Dorthe must have picked up on Cin's emotions, because her blush deepened, though it seemed with a different kind of embarrassment this time. "I'm so sorry. Please forget I suggested it." She turned to go.

Cin wasn't sure what came over him, but in that moment he couldn't let her leave feeling unwanted. He grabbed her arm gently, slipping in front of her. "Dorthe?"

She looked a little haunted, but she paused for him.

"You deserve someone amazing," Cin said. "You'll find that person. It's not me, but they're out there."

A hint of Dorthe's smile returned. She placed her hand over

Cin's and squeezed. This time as she walked away, she held her head up and her shoulders back. She would be okay... because of Cin. It didn't make his murders right, but it was something, at least. Something good.

Though a small part of him still worried over her knowing his identity—even with no malicious intent on her part, there were so many ways this could go wrong—it was almost worth it just to have someone, anyone, see who he was. It almost made him want to run after her, not to accept her offer, but to counter it with friendship. The longer he thought of it, though, the harder it seemed to get his feet to move or his voice to call out.

He'd already given in to his desire for the ball, for the prince— and those, at least, would be short-term. What time did he have to selfishly waste on a friendship with Dorthe? What right did he have to ask that of a woman who'd already been through so much? She deserved the space to find herself an amazing partner. If he could not bear to give that to Prince Lorenz, at least he could give it to her.

Cin pulled his emotions back together and forced himself to move along.

The local shop had not replenished their last stock of ledger books, but the shopkeeper directed Cin to another in the town over where their supply was likely better. It would be a bit of a trek for a simple book, but he had no particular interest in being home at the moment. Before he left, he bought one of the cheaper blue ribbons in the tailor's shop. Louise would complain, but the joy that would come over Emma's face was worth the trouble.

Cin followed the north road through the scattered farms, houses, and woods that out-skirted most towns in the region, his binder aching against his ribs. The sound of a man's shouting and a woman's crying caught his attention. He thought of Dorthe—her smile, her blush—and before he could stop himself, he was slipping through the trees, perfectly quiet in his magical shoes.

The home was barely off the path, a four-room structure with the back door open to the well. A middle-aged woman fled through it as she sobbed. She crumpled on the far side of the well, her hands over her eyes. The sleeves of her dress slipped down, revealing a series of purple bruises like claw-marks.

Cin could still hear the man inside the house, slamming and clattering. He seemed done with her for now, at least. Cin made a vow to come back, though—perhaps this was a rare occurrence—perhaps there was some explanation Cin wasn't seeing. By the darkness of those bruises though, he doubted it.

And next time, he'd have his knife with him.

The home off the north road was quiet the next few times Cin visited that week, but his own house made up for it with the chaos that seemed to erupt at every turn. The high of the ball that weekend turned to a low of arguments, Manfred going so far as to hit Floy in the jawline, which they blamed—rightfully—on Cin because he'd dodged a similar blow minutes before, after the breakfast had been eaten without saving any for Manfred. It hardly seemed to matter that it was boiled duck eggs and bread, which even Manfred could manage on his own.

Somehow, Cin made it to the next ball-night without murdering any of his family members, forcing a fake smile as he waved them off in the carriage. The moment they were out of sight, he whirled around and sprinted for the garden. He swore his magical steed had never run so fast.

When Cin arrived at the castle, the line for the entrance appeared longer than usual, but as he waited in it, he realized it was simply moving slower. The guards—all a part of the crown's watch now—scanned through a series of papers as they spoke with each participant before determining which to allow in and which to deny. As Cin counted, it seemed at least half of those who'd been deemed acceptable before were being turned away.

His stomach twisted and he could feel his nerves transfer to his mount as it danced from foot to foot in line. He told himself that with so many barred from entry, it could not have anything to do with the Plumed Menace. But if not their sins, what would the attendees be judged on? Perhaps the only the most elite families were being admitted. Perhaps the most beautiful. Perhaps the most good. Cin fit none of those.

When he reached the front, the watch member barely glanced at him.

"Full name and hometown?" they asked.

Cin swallowed down the lump in his throat. "Cin—Szule Reinholz, from the village of Darmburg."

The watch member scanned through their papers, pausing for

longer in a few places, before shaking their head. "Unfortunately you've not been included in the reservations for this gathering."

Cin felt as though the world were caving in around him.

# Twelve

"You are free to attend any other public celebration for the remaining weeks of the ball." The crown's watch continued, but Cin could barely focus on their words after their initial rejection.

It was like being hit by Dorthe's proposal, with none of the bittersweetness, only the pain and the loss. This had been the one part of his future he had allowed himself to want, to take selfishly for his own, with no blades or blood involved. And now he'd been denied even that.

Cin had to believe it wasn't the prince's doing—not purposefully. He hadn't known Cin's name. He'd never asked. Perhaps he'd been saddened when he'd realized it, or perhaps it had never even occurred to him when the list had been compiled. Maybe it would have made no difference anyway; Cin was likely as much a passing fancy to Prince Lorenz as he was to Cin.

Cin had seen the castle, had danced with the prince—there were other parties with food and music all across the city. He could enjoy those. They wouldn't have Prince Lorenz at them, but... he could find a way to appreciate them regardless.

The watch member looked as though they were about to transition from the considerate dismissal to something with more bite. Cin forced himself to nod at them, trying not to look entirely devastated by the news, and stepped out of the line. Each stride away from the gates felt worse than the last. He wanted to scoff at himself.

Cin had not come here for the prince, had not even initially cared to meet him at all. If anything, staying away from the man whose parents had put a price on the Plumed Menace's head was probably for the best. But the further he walked from the castle's front entrance, the more Cin was certain: he didn't *want* to leave Prince Lorenz behind yet.

Their brief time together had been a light in Cin's grim, gray life, and there would only be a little time left to bask in that glow before the prince had his future stolen away with an exchanging of rings, and things returned to normal for Cin. Cin was not about to see that time cut short. If Prince Lorenz didn't want to see him again, then the wonderful, arrogant rake could tell him to his face.

Cin glanced back at the front gate, where the crown's watch were firmly directing a crying young woman away. He might have been able to slip under their notice so far, but he was fairly certain that causing a scene would just get him kicked out of the city or, worse, arrested. There were ways to get through a wall that didn't involve gates, however...

After walking his mount a short way down the length of the castle's wall, the high, gray stone skirted by shops and houses on this side of the city, Cin found a decent enough place where the nearby party lanterns didn't quite reach and the buildings on either side of the bare wall were dark. They were just a bit too far off from the wall itself to be worth jumping between. Cinder brushed his fingers along the old, worn brick of the wall and nodded to himself. This would do.

This would do just fine.

His steed dissolved into a flurry of birds as Cin crimped his fingers in between the castle stones and began to climb. Without the magic of his shoes and the gentle guiding lift of his flock, the ascent would have been a ghastly thing, dangerous and torturous, but as things stood, he reached the top with barely a scrape to his finger calluses. He pulled himself over the parapets, dropping onto the top of the wall like a shadow. Perdition landed on his shoulder.

Cin scratched the back of her head, whispering in her ear, "Let's find ourselves a prince, shall we?"

She cooed in response, giving him a nip of encouragement as though to say, *get on with it, then*.

"Impatient!" Cin laughed.

Someone—soldier or staff, Cin didn't know—approached from farther along the wall, and Cin slipped across it before they could come close enough to spot his silhouette in the darkness. He held his breath, and leaped over the far edge. As he fell, his flock spiraled around him. He hit the ground silent and soft, birds zipping out across the grass to either side of him.

Cin found himself at the back of the castle gardens—a better position than he'd expected, so near to the ball but still hidden in the darkness. Despite the joyous noise of the ongoing party though, Cin's attention caught on a more distant sound from back down the wall, toward the front gate. Something like shouting. If he wasn't mistaken, it sounded like Prince Lorenz's voice, raised and twisted with frustration.

He crept in the direction of the upheaval, avoiding the plethora of crown's watch that seemed to be on guard nearer the ballroom and staying to the shadows as he wove around a garden house and a few small structures build off the side of the castle wall, ending up near the edge of the main building's lavish central entrance. From there, he could just make out the conversation happening at the gates. The watch member Cin had spoken with stared at their feet while a man, larger than life in his elegant green and gray jacket, his dusky brown hair fluttering from beneath his circlet and his firm chin held high, snapped at them.

The sight of him caught in Cin's throat. A part of him begged to rush out and demand the prince's attention, but the larger part did not know just how to do that—had never forced his body through those motions before, never wanted something badly enough to demand it out loud. So, he watched.

"And you sent him *away*?!" Prince Lorenz shouted, his tone incredulous.

The guard continued to look down, and Cin could barely hear their steady but quiet response. "His name was not on the list, Your Royal Highness."

"I gave you a perfectly clear description! Dashing, long hair nearly white, striking blue eyes, more feathers than the Plumed Menace themself? None of this rings a bell?"

Prince Lorenz was talking about *Cin*.

He felt as though, like the magic of his outfit, he'd wished it into being, but hearing that description still plucked at a place in Cin's chest that he hadn't been paying attention to. Cin had scaled a wall for the prince's affections, and here Prince Lorenz was, shouting for the loss of his: like two pieces of a puzzle that slid properly together, even if they were meant only for the moment.

That made it far less dangerous to step out of the shadows, but now Cin's curiosity had gotten the better of him. He wanted to see where this would go… What kind of man the next ruler of Hallin truly was, when he didn't have Cin with him to impress.

"My apologies, Your Royal Highness," the watch member said. "It won't happen again."

"No, it certainly won't," Prince Lorenz seemed to threaten, but then he continued, "Because *he* won't be *back* here again, since *someone* told him to *leave*." He groaned, not like he was speaking to his lesser but to an annoying sibling. "God, do you remember his name at least?"

The watch member grimaced, clearly thinking back and coming up short. "It might have been… Cinder-Ella? Or something of that nature?"

"Cinder-Ella isn't even a name, *Berit.*" Prince Lorenz said the watcher's as though it proved just what was and wasn't one. He ran a hand down his face and groaned, before waving toward the awkwardly waiting guests. "What's done is done. See to the line, I suppose." His voice lifted, the jovial, arrogant tone Cin was accustomed to returning to it. "My apologies to you all—I hope to see you inside." He seemed to pick a man out of the crowd in a way he made seem not so random by the purposeful slide of his gaze, and winked, "You especially."

The speed with which his flirtatious expression dropped the moment his back was turned to his guests made Cin think otherwise.

Behind him, the watch member returned to their duties. They looked mildly embarrassed, chastened, but not the least bit upset or nervous.

By the time Prince Lorenz made it to the castle's entrance, his gait stormy as his expression, Cin was leaning against the wall just inside the door, his arms crossed. He lifted a purposeful brow. "You don't even know my name? I'm insulted."

"My—" The prince jerked in surprise, his curse half swallowed by a sharp inhale. Then a single, soft laugh left him as he reached for Cin. He grabbed Cin's shoulder with one hand and cupped Cin's chin in his other, like he had to ensure that Cin was really there. "God, did you just witness all that?"

"It was quite a display." Cin gave a half-grin. "Someone might have almost gotten the impression that you *wanted* to see me."

"I was not aware my parents were cutting down the guest list until they asked for the names of those I'd actually been conversing with most. You have, to be fair, never offered me yours."

"Cinder-Ella will do."

"Surely that's not actually your—"

"It's close enough." Cin winked, hoping to move the conversation along.

In truth, he didn't want to offer a true name, less because he feared the prince might hunt him down, and more because he wasn't sure what he *would* give. When was the last time Cin had introduced himself to a stranger who might actually care—might actually remember? He was not Szule—had not been clothed in dresses and hope and his birth-mother's love in so long; he wasn't certain anymore that the Szule in his mind had ever been real. But he was not merely Cinder either, not simply that word thrust upon him in spite.

Cin was the house he tended, each decrepit ash-gray mote of dust that he cleaned from it, and the wings of the birds who'd carried him here, and the knife tucked at his back. He did not know how to put all of that into a single name.

"Well, *Cinder-Ella*," the prince said, his pronunciation playfully mocking, "I'm sorry to have disrupted your night so. Berit is a fool, but they have a good heart, I swear."

"Do you know all the guard's names?"

"I know everyone's name but *yours* apparently. Cinder-Ella," he repeated with a little laugh, before winking. "*My dove* has a better ring."

With the line now moving again, a new guest had begun ascending the steps behind them. In that smooth way of his, the prince slipped his arm through Cin's and walked them both down the hall toward the ballroom. One of the nearer watch members broke off to follow quietly, but Prince Lorenz paid them no more heed than he had any of the previous nights.

He leaned toward Cin, his breath on Cin's ear as he whispered, "How, pray tell, *did* you get in here, if not through the gate?"

Cin turned his face, letting their noses brush. "Couldn't you guess?"

Prince Lorenz's eyes scanned languidly down Cin's body, then back up, as though he could possibly have found his answer there. "Did you trespass? You menace!"

It was not a reference to any plumed murderers, but Cin still had to quiet the sudden jump in his heart rate, swallowing down his tension to keep focusing on the prince he'd climbed a castle wall for. The prince who'd been riled by Cin's exclusion. But what did any of that actually mean for them both?

Cin stopped Prince Lorenz before he could walk them into the ballroom, pulling him back and to the side, until they were both half-hidden by the decor of the elegant hall. The prince took it with a little more passion then Cin had intended, pushing Cin up against the wall, one hand already on Cin's hip and his other in Cin's hair.

"Wait," Cin insisted, and touched a finger to the prince's lips before he could lean in for the kiss.

He pressed his mouth to Cin's finger instead, taking Cin's hand in one of his. "All right, I'm waiting," he teased, watching Cin though half-hooded lashes as he peppered Cin's hand in kisses.

"Rake," Cin grumbled, but he couldn't keep the smile off his face. This was exactly the attention he'd yearned for the entire walk away from the castle's front gates. It was also exactly the attention that would distract him from the conversation they needed to have. Cin cupped the side of the prince's face in his hand, holding him momentarily still. "Your Royal Highness, what are we?"

"Humans, last I checked," the prince replied, "Though you're as radiant as any mythical fae and devilishly handsome as any demon sorcerer."

"You know what I mean." Cin leveled him a stern look. "I'm not going to marry you—you still know that, right?"

Prince Lorenz looked minutely less cheeky as he answered, "I am aware, yes."

"And you're not going to grow attached to me and ask for my

hand anyway, or something idiotic?"

The prince gave the tiniest eye roll at that, before returning to kissing Cin's fingers between his words. "I'm not going to fall in love with you, or with anyone, remember? I don't *do* that."

"I don't mean *in* love, I mean... just *love*. Platonic affection, or partnership, or whatever you wish to call it," Cin clarified. "I can't become *that* for you either."

"We're just here to enjoy each other for the moment, that it all." Prince Lorenz lifted an eyebrow. "Satisfied?"

"But you do need to marry someone. And when that happens, I also can't—I *won't* be slinking around the castle interrupting your new partnership"—Cin could see the protest in the prince's gaze, and silenced it with a scowl—"regardless of what your partner agrees to." Just imagining the scrutiny, the time he'd need to get to the prince and back, not knowing when it might come to an end— Cin could not have withstood that, even if the price on the Plumed Menace's head was not in play. "Tell me you understand that, too?"

"I understand," Prince Lorenz said, purposeful as he stared into Cin's eyes. "This is not my first fling, you know."

That made Cin flush slightly. "Well, perhaps it's mine," he admitted. "I just want neither of us to be hurt after this." And he meant that, not merely for himself. He didn't want to break Prince Lorenz's heart any more than bear that pain himself.

Before the prince could answer, though, someone pushed aside the planter Cin had hidden them behind, nearly knocking over the statue at its side in the process. Fear and anger tore through Cin in equal proportions, so strongly he had to stop himself from reaching for the blade tucked against his back when he realized their assailant was none other than an overstrung crown's watch, complete with the gold brocading of the royal family's personal watchers.

"Your Royal Highness?" he gasped, one hand still on his hilt despite his worry having loosened at the sight of a Cin in the place he seemed to have half expected to find the Plumed Menace. "I turned around and you were—"

"I'm fine, Wilhelm," Prince Lorenz chided, sounding just a touch exasperated. "Lieselotte left the gate to stalk me here—she's down the hall. Go tell her you've returned." When Wilhelm blinked at him, the prince lifted his brow. "The only risk here is a good fucking. Unless you're joining, I suggest you leave?"

Wilhelm coughed in embarrassment. "Right, my apologies."

By the time he stepped back though, it was already too late. It seemed like half the remaining guest list had spotted Cin and the prince, two dozen suitors flooding down the hall expectantly. A look as mournful as the one in Cin's chest passed over the prince's face, there and gone in a flash.

As slowly and carefully as time allowed, Prince Lorenz took Cin's hand, squeezing it as he stepped back, into the light. "As for *your* worries, never fear, my dove. This prince's heart is locked away as tightly as his future."

And Cin, despite his usually better judgment, found himself believing it of them both.

After the watch member's interruption, it felt to Cin as though he had far too little time to spend with the prince before Floy's arrival cut them short, forcing Cin to slip out to the gardens and back over the wall—though by the looks of the other guests, every second Cin stole of Prince Lorenz's attention was a moment too long. Even Floy—the only one of Cin's siblings to make it past the gate—remarked on it the next day, grumbling haughtily about a guest in a feathered cloak whom everyone claimed was becoming the favorite.

"But Prince Lorenz did not look for him for another moment after I appeared," Floy added. "We'll have to arrive earlier next week. I want his eyes on *me* the *entire* night."

Cin was confident that Floy was overestimating the amount the prince actually cared to speak with them. Confident, but not *certain*. By the way that Louise pampered Floy for their selection as a continued attendee, it seemed that, in the Reinholz house at least, Floy was destined for future Queen-hood.

At least Manfred and Emma were not put out by the prince's dismissal of them—Manfred, because he'd realized it was easier to convince someone to fuck him if they weren't seeking the attention of another man, and Emma simply because she was Emma. Very little held her attention for long, even rejection. It was one of the few positives of her scatterbrained disposition, and the longer Cin had to listen to Floy flaunt their place in the continued lineup while Manfred grossly detailed his list of exploits, the more Cin wished his other two siblings were a little more like her.

When Cin arrived for the next ball, he found the guest list had been cut again, and to his great humor, that he'd been added to the top of the list as simply *The Cinder-Ella*—ten lines up from Floy Reinholz, he noticed with disdain. With the new reduction, there was no one left in attendance who preferred the sidelines, no one kissing on the balconies or flirting in the stairwell. Everyone wanted their moment with the prince, and there was nowhere left for him to run.

The last moments they'd had together lingered in Cin's mind, leaving Cin wanting for more. More of Prince Lorenz's touch, more of his heat. More of him, just pressed there beside Cin, laughing and teasing and making Cin feel as though there was nothing beyond that moment, no home to return to or family to cater for. Just him.

Cin could not shake the feeling that they were wasting their precious time together.

He tried to tell himself that the prince needed to see the other attendees—to know them well enough to chose one as his future partner. But then, if he really wished to, Prince Lorenz could visit any of them during the week. Cin had only these few nights and nothing else.

For once in his life, he wanted to *choose* someone. To be brave enough. To make that first move, even if it was the only one he planned *to* make.

He played his fingers across the stem of his cup and watched Prince Lorenz flirt with a beautiful young man whose family possessed ten times the Reinholzes' holdings and half of their arrogance. In the next break in their conversation, Cin managed to slip in, brushing his fingers to the back of the prince's hand as, for once, it was him who leaned in first.

"Take me back to the dovecote," Cin whispered, and what he

meant was *take me back to that moment*: just *take me.*

The Crowned Prince of Hallin held out his hand to Cin. "As you wish, my Cinder-Ella."

Thirteen

Cin led Prince Lorenz halfway through the gardens, following the route he'd taken the last time, before the prince pulled Cin to a stop. The pigeon trio that had been trailing above them all took roost, their dark eyes watchful in the night.

Prince Lorenz looked back toward the celebration still setting the night alight. At least three—no, four—attendees were making their way out of the ballroom to trail after him, the prince's nightly personal watcher splitting her attention between the prince and them. Prince Lorenz grimaced.

"What if I don't want to take you to the dovecote," he said. He wove his fingers through Cin's, squeezing gently. "What if we could go somewhere else instead?"

"Somewhere better than a tiny room smelling of pigeon droppings?" Cin snorted, whispering to the sky after, "No offense, darlings." One of his trio cooed—deep and low; that would be Rags, the sweet boy. "You'd be hard pressed to find a lovelier getaway than that, but do tell."

Prince Lorenz hesitated, his attention drifting back toward the guests and guards now lingering around in the garden walkways nearest the ballroom, the former looking as though they hoped they might slip into the conversation unnoticed. For a moment, a flash of distress passed over Prince Lorenz's features, but between the shadows and the quick mask of his usual congenial arrogance, Cin nearly missed it. His voice still held a faint tremble though, as he said, "Anywhere but here." His grin returned in full force, sparkling and devious. "Show me your little bundle of lights up close. Let me see this town I've spent all my life just beyond."

Cin almost choked on the thought. "It's *your* ball you'd be leaving."

"And I don't want to be a part of it." The smile didn't fade from Prince Lorenz's face, and for all the other guests, Cin supposed they must be seeing only the same charm and arrogance as ever—but only because that mask was eternally hiding something more. Some depth even Cin didn't think he'd truly seen yet.

And maybe this was a path to discovering whatever lay beneath it?

"Is it safe?" Cin asked, narrowing his eyes at the prince. "Will we be taking your watcher?"

If not for Prince Adalwin's disappearance, he did not think he would have worried so. The elder prince was said to have vanished despite having his entire entourage with him, though, and he had been even farther outside the capital, where the trees were left to grow tall. The forests between Hallin and Falchovari boasted their own monsters, their own princes—ones of swamps and forgotten castles. But Cin did not know any that went out of their way to frame the local murderers.

People were, often, their own kind of terrifying that no monster could outdo.

"My parents would demand I take at least two dozen." Prince Lorenz looked none-too-thrilled at the thought. His disgruntled expression turned playful, though, as he leaned toward Cin, looping one arm around Cin's waist. "You tell me. If the Plumed Menace appears, will you protect me?"

A little shiver ran through Cin, and he didn't know if it was from the prince's nearness or the mention of the menace. At least he knew his own blade had never come near Prince Lorenz's brother. "With my life, Your Royal Highness."

"Then what need have I of anyone else?"

That statement was delicious and terrible all at once. The prince *would* need someone else very soon: someone whose finger he could place a ring on. "I do warn you, my town is not much," Cin insisted. "The dovecote is likely the more interesting of the two."

"For you, perhaps," Prince Lorenz agreed. Then he leaned a little closer, his lips brushing the curve of Cin's ear in a way that made Cin's whole body catch fire. Everyone else in their line of sight seemed to be catching something far greener. "I could make it worth your while."

Cin breathed in. "Done." He turned his head, letting his nose brush the prince's as he added, "But we're taking *my* horse."

It was the coolest night yet that fall, but the feathers of Cin's cloak seemed to hold in the heat as they rode at a breakneck speed down the main road out of the city. No one had overcome their shock fast enough to stop them—no one could have, with the way Cin's steed could dive and dart through a crowd with ease. Watching the wonder that spread across Prince Lorenz's face the moment they left the city's farthest walls, it seemed *he* was the one more in awe of their figurative escape than Cin. It made Cin want to glance back at him all the more for it.

The prince sat behind Cin's saddle, his arms wrapped tightly around Cin's waist and his breath hot on the back of Cin's neck. His lower body moved in time with Cin's, both of them gliding to the rhythm of their mount's strides, though he seemed to be leaning back some—giving Cin space. Not that he needed it.

Cin did not slow until he was certain that no one would try to follow them.

Prince Lorenz gave a breathless whoop that turned quickly to laughter, his fingers pinching fondly into Cin's hips. "Ah, this is brilliant! Are you certain you're not a horse-whisperer as well as one of pigeons?"

"You were the one who first called me that." Cin gave him a little elbow in the ribs, teasing but still sharp.

He oophed out air, but his voice still sounded like he was grinning from ear to ear. "But I wasn't wrong, was I?"

Cin didn't validate that with a response. He pulled his mount to the side of the road as a carriage passed—not his family's, he made sure to note. Despite everyone who seemed to be out in the city celebrating, there were somehow still people on the roads making their way to the ball. Few lights seemed left on in the homes they were quickly coming upon.

"This is where you were raised, was it?"

"Yes," Cin admitted. Before the prince could come up with another question, he asked, "And you've really never been here in your youth? I know your parents visited on occasion. Even your brother had..."

It was clearly the wrong topic, because Prince Lorenz went stiff against Cin's back, his hold on Cin tenuous suddenly. But still, he answered, "Yes, Alwin certainly would have."

Alwin—*Prince Adalwin*: the new heir to the crown said his brother's nickname with such tender ferocity that it felt like a whole new depth of him had been flashed before Cin.

The prince snorted under his breath. "He actually *enjoyed* the diplomacy of it all, my dear brother."

The laughter, the smiles, the flirting—what was that, if not also a kind of diplomacy? "But you seem so good at managing the ball guests?"

"Skill does not equate to desire," the prince objected. "I *desire* to retreat to balconies and gardens, to frolic and fuck, and never, ever have the future of my kingdom depend on whether I can say the right words at the right time in the right way to the right person. I learned to act the charismatic prince well enough to escape it, because I watched Alwin succeed at the real thing for so long. But the crown—it was always supposed to be *his*."

The way the prince spoke of it made the whole ordeal sound painful. For all of Cin's annoyance over his lot in life, at least he was the most capable at his work of anyone in his family. Nor did he particularly want Manfred's gambling lifestyle, or Emma's ditsy failures, or Floy's obsessive arts and sciences. The one thing Cin did love was his birds, and while he had no proper dovecote of his own, at least they were always nearby; Perdition herself was circling above them now, her white feathers nearly glowing in the starlight. "What would you have been, had you not been this?"

"I..." The prince paused, and seemed to genuinely think on it, before humming. "I don't really know. I was never planning to be anything, besides his younger brother." He laughed. "And rich." His arms wrapped snugly across Cin's stomach and he nuzzled into the side of Cin's neck.

God, did that feel good. With the houses growing closer and closer together, Cin hoped no one inside noticed them.

"I suppose you won't teach me to whisper to pigeons?" the prince asked, his voice light and teasing in Cin's ear.

"Since pigeon-whispering is not actually a skill, no."

"Cruel."

"Reasonable."

"You abuse me." It sounded as though the prince was rolling his eyes, and his voice dropped as he added, "My brother would have approved of you, at least." After a pause, he asked. "Do you have siblings?"

"Yes. Three."

"And?"

Cin scoffed a laugh. "What more is there to say? They are thorns in my side whether I like them or not."

One of the prince's hands unwrapped from Cin's waist and he

could feel it drift between them, clutched near to Prince Lorenz's heart as he whispered, "I suppose I knew how that felt." And he sounded pained, certainly. Pained, but something else as well.

Empty, Cin thought. Would his heart break that same way if he lost Manfred and Floy? If he lost *Emma*?

Cin recalled the way she'd told him that she'd been excluded from the castle's inner circle, pouting one moment and sighing wistfully of the city the next, as though being dismissed by the prince merely meant that the rest of the world had opened up to her. Then, she'd daydreamed herself off the bottom step of the stairs that Cin had been trying to urge her up and nearly sprained her ankle.

Idiot child.

"Family is family," Cin said.

The prince grimaced. "Family is family, and then that family makes you choose someone new to join them as a permanent thorn in your side, and they give you six weeks to do it in."

"Any front-runners, yet?" It was the same complaint Prince Lorenz brought up every night, and yet so far he hadn't seemed willing to offer over any ideas as to who he might choose. With the pot dwindling and Floy still in the running, Cin was more and more anxious to know his thoughts. But he also didn't think he could force them out of the prince.

Prince Lorenz gave a dramatic groan and buried his face back into Cin's neck. "I'd rather be stabbed through the heart."

"Just be sure to wait until I'm far gone, so I'm not implicated in it." Some masochistic part of Cin's mind imagined for a terrible, fleeting moment what it would be like to press a set of feathers into Prince Lorenz's bleeding heart, but the horror of it made him so nauseous that he blocked the vision out.

"God damn; I was hoping you would help," the prince grumbled, a teasing edge to his voice.

"I could not bear the thought! I'll defend myself against villains if need be, but while you're clearly a scoundrel, I don't think you have a malevolent bone in your body." As Cin said it, he realized just how very true it felt. Even if he couldn't see beneath the layers of darkness in the prince's soul, he knew at the bottom was a good man. A slightly arrogant, possibly lazy, definitely lustful man, but a kind one, nonetheless.

Prince Lorenz chuckled. "You think too highly of me. If I am not even a little bit malevolent, it is for lack of skill, not effort."

Cin elbowed him in the ribs in response. Before he could recover, Cin turned their steed into the town square. "Welcome to Darmburg."

They dismounted, and Cin escorted Prince Lorenz through a jovial tour of the dark, empty space, even less populated than on a normal night, with most of the townsfolk having gone into the city for the festivities. Cin pointed out the shops he most often frequented and places where memorable town events had taken place, like the spontaneous and scandalous marriage of a local lady to her maidservant, or the time five men had failed to catch a pig for nearly three hours. As he did, he ignored the direction of Dorthe's home and the time four years before that he'd stalked a man through the square before sliding a blade into his back three streets down the following week, though they felt so much a part of him in that moment that he swore Prince Lorenz would see the truth of him even without the words.

"And this is where your statue should stand," Cin concluded, dramatically motioning to the center of the square, where currently a simple flowerbed sat. "Then, my pigeons can gather upon it whenever I visit, and grace your bare chest with their droppings."

As though to demonstrate, Lacey and Rags both swooped low, spinning around each other before shooting off into the night again.

Prince Lorenz nodded, holding his chin as though deep in thought. "I agree, that will greatly improve the scene."

Cin shoved him in the shoulder. He shoved Cin back with a laugh.

His attention wandered, and he meandered away from Cin. It took Cin a moment to realize where he was heading: the announcements board. In the darkness, all but the largest words were too small to properly make out, but Cin's gaze still caught on the flyer of the Plumed Menace. Perhaps he should have felt uneasy standing beside the man whose very parents had put that price on Cin's head, but between the prince's utter lack of suspicion and the unfortunate fact that Cin would only be seeing him for a few more weeks, it seemed pointless to worry.

The prince didn't even glance at the flyer, immediately singling out his own ball's announcement.

Snorting, he tugged the paper down. "I think enough of Hallin knows I'm to be married, don't you?"

"Perhaps your *one true love* will wander forth from the forest next week, read the announcement, and rush to the ball?"

"*Love?*" the prince scoffed, so softly Cin might have heard him wrong. He stared at the paper in his hands, stared as though seeing right through it. "There's only one love of my life who I'd like to wander in from the forest, and he's the ass who left me in this predicament." With a bitter sniffle, he crumbled the paper, letting it fall from his fingers after. "But *he* is never coming back."

Cin hesitated to respond, uncertain whether the banter and lust of their friendship allowed for this level of comfort. But he wanted to be that support for Prince Lorenz—even if it was only for the night. And that was enough.

He slipped his arm through the prince's, embracing him gently. The prince leaned into the touch, breathing out a trembling sigh. Neither of them spoke, but it seemed slowly, cautiously better.

They kept wandering, arm in arm in the quiet of the night. As they approached the highest point in the square, Cin slowed their pace. He let his head fall against the prince's shoulder and stared out toward the shining of the capital, where the castle's towers were a clear glimmer against the stars.

"When she was alive, my birth mother used to boost me onto her shoulders and make me look for the castle towers." He didn't know he was going to say it until he did, but the words came so easy in the dark, with Prince Lorenz. Everything was easy like this. "She said it was lucky to see them."

Cin could feel the prince's lips in his hair, pressing little kisses to his head. "Well, now you're here with me. Is that not luck?"

"Luck," Cin whispered, "or magic," knowing it was both. "When I was standing here earlier today, a woman from town asked me nearly to marry her."

Prince Lorenz pulled away so suddenly that Cin stumbled, and the prince grabbed him by both shoulders, staring at him in confusion. "You were proposed to? You have— Are you— But we—" He seemed to be trying desperately to put together a puzzle that was making less and less sense to him with each moment, and Cin stopped him before he could twist himself into knots in the confusion.

"I'm not engaged, and she hadn't been dating me," he clarified. "Her husband died recently. I believe the idea was more of a business arrangement, but with the potential to grow into more."

"Oh," Prince Lorenz responded, still looking confused. He nodded slowly, and pulled Cin closer once more. "All right then."

Cin narrowed his eyes at the prince. "Why? Do you think no one could possibly be in love with me?" It seemed simultaneously like the truth of the world and also a thing that Prince Lorenz was unlikely to think of anyone.

The prince snorted, and the edge of his lips quirked. "I think it would be impossible for anyone to know you and not love you, if they were presently capable of the feeling." He said it in such a way that seemed to imply *he* wasn't, but Cin didn't have time to press him about that before he continued, "I merely suspect you are not one to be in a serious relationship while letting the prince of the realm finger you in a dovecote. By which I mean, you would be just as terrible at orgies as I am."

Cin felt himself flush. "I do think I might be made for one person at a time... if any." He looked back out toward the distant gleam of the castle lights. "I understand why you don't want to marry. How can anyone decide to end one life and begin a new, a new person, a new future, when they can't know what will come of it? What they'll lose in the process?" He did not add, "what will fall apart the moment they're gone from that old existence?" But he felt it, just as strongly as the moment Dorthe had asked for his hand.

Prince Lorenz said nothing. He looked out toward the castle, his face unreadable in the starlight. Soon, the prince would have to accept a vow of partnership with someone whether he wanted to or not. And Cin's life would go back to what it had been.

The ache that left in his heart was too unbearable to sit with.

He wrapped his arm through Prince Lorenz and tugged gently. "Where should we go now?"

The tiny pull seemed to drag the prince out of his stupor, and his expression transformed from darkness to light, grin sharp and eyes sparkling. "Can I see your home?"

Panic shot through Cin, and then he realized, with a dry humor, *what did it matter?*

The state of their home wouldn't change the prince's desire to suck on Cin's lower lip or get off on the feel of Cin's swollen nether regions. He wasn't going to marry Cin, no matter how much money the Reinholz family had, or had lost.

"Why not?" Cin laughed. "I've seen yours."

"Not all of it." The prince smirked, and swept back up onto Cin's mount, this time planting himself in the saddle. He reached a hand out to help Cin up.

Cin crossed his arms. "Do you know where you're going?"

The prince only grinned wider. "You'll tell me if I'm offtrack."

"Now that's cruel." Cin took his hand.

Prince Lorenz pulled him up. "Reasonable, I'd say."

As Cin wrapped his arms around the prince's waist, pressing his face to the places the prince had done with him, he could only smile and hold on while they raced out of town.

There was surely no way this could go wrong.

Fourteen

T he darkness hid much of the Reinholz estate, particularly its flaws, for which Cin was grateful. It looked mildly imposing in the night, its long main building of two stories—three in the center—surrounded on one side by the garden and the other by the carriage house and the barely used barn and storeroom. Compared to Prince Lorenz's castle, it was a hovel, but the prince—who was not marrying Cin—was also not marrying for money. Nor fucking for it. Cin wondered what he *was* truly marrying for, other than the gentle goodness his parents had advertised, but then Lorenz dismounted and strode toward the manor's front door, and Cin was distracted by following him.

"It's locked—there's no one home," Cin warned him, realizing only too late how many bells that would set off.

Prince Lorenz turned, lifting a brow. "You let all your servants attend each ball night? That's very good of your family." He sounded genuinely proud, which made Cin feel all the worse.

"It's... well, it's only us now. The famine has hit us particularly hard"—*there* was a lie, at least; the famine hadn't helped, but their family's fortunes had been flailing for years prior—"and Mother let the staff go. We've been getting along all right on our own, though."

This seemed to confuse Prince Lorenz. "You don't even have a cook, then?"

"I do the cooking." Cin shrugged. "It's come fairly easy to me and I enjoy it."

The prince looked like he was trying to fit that into his idea of the Cin he'd known so far—the wealthy, chaotic gentleman who raised a royal dovecote's worth of pigeons. It didn't seem, at least, that he was finding it distasteful, only odd. "And who tends the horses, then?" he asked. "And the gardens? Your family does that alone as well?"

"I do most of it, but I don't mind," Cin reassured him. "It's actually rather relaxing when you're in the mood. We only have two horses, and the crops have been small, so it's less work than you'd think."

By the look on the prince's face, any amount of gardening seemed to be more work than he'd ever imagined *himself* doing. "And you all do the cleaning, for the whole estate? And launder? Tend the hearths? Fetch the shopping? Patch the drafts? That must be enough work for a dozen servants."

"It's not *that* big a house, really." Though it certainly felt that way on dusting days, or any time the wind whipped through the damaged ceiling, which was most days in the winter. Cin cringed despite himself. "It does get drafty, though. Father says he'll patch the roof, but he's off on business most months of the year, so it tends to be forgotten."

Prince Lorenz shuddered visibly. "How hideous—no offense." He narrowed his eyes at Cin. "And the rest? Does your father help with any of that?"

"Not generally." Cin looked aside, like that would make the whole line of questioning go away. Each new inquiry was beginning to feel like a small barb beneath his ribs. "He runs the business, and Mother does the finances, and I care for the estate."

"I thought you had three siblings?"

Cin snorted. "Useless ones."

Now Prince Lorenz was folding his arms as well, practically scowling. "Still, they should be helping you! If not them, *someone*."

"What if I do clean, and launder, and tend the hearths, and fetch the shopping? They are the tasks that need doing, and I've the skill to do them. If I can keep my family home from falling into ruin then it's my responsibility to do what I can. No one else will. No one else can!" Cin had to survive these frustrations every day. He didn't want to relive them now, during the one time he had for himself and his own desires. But now that he was, he found himself scowling, the pain inside him turning to something sharp between his lips. "The world isn't like your pretty castle. Life isn't as easy for us as smiles and balls and marriages. Some of us must work to live; not everything in our lives is handed to us on a platter."

A wave of embarrassment flooded the prince's expression. "I know," Prince Lorenz whispered, and he looked so vulnerable in that moment that it broke Cin's flash of anger into a thousand pieces, stunning him free.

He breathed out, slipping his fingers against the prince's arm, encouragingly.

"I'm being selfish and arrogant," Prince Lorenz said. "And not just in this, but in my life. I know I need to put my cares aside for the sake of my people and my family—and that's what I'll be doing.

It's what I've been trying to do." Cin couldn't see much of the prince's face from that angle, the sliver of a moon rising behind the prince's head, but he could feel the gentleness in the prince's touch as he caught Cin by the shoulders. "But you—you have no reason to torment yourself to keep your family afloat! You had a proposal of partnership just today. *You* could choose a new life, a better one."

That life—the life with Dorthe—flashed before Cin's eyes again, and this time, he wanted it. Just for the tiniest second, he *wanted* it. Then, the weight of the rest of his life settled back down, and he didn't have the energy to want any longer. "Your *Royal Highness*," Cin begged: not a title but a soft, aching thing. My *love*, it sounded like, though for the life of him, he didn't know why.

Prince Lorenz's hands shifting, sliding up Cin's shoulders and cupping tenderly around his neck, one thumb caressing his cheek. "Does your family make you happy? Does this estate?"

Cin thought, oddly, not of his birth mother's esteemed virtues for him, but of Emma. Kind, ignorant Emma, watching everything she touched fall to pieces the same way their family's fortune had fallen apart under their father.

In the silence, the prince's voice felt like a beacon, his words a lighthouse. "The thorns in your side should be from the roses that sweeten your life. If they are not, pull them out."

Cin closed his eyes and felt nothing but the prince's fingertips. "If only I could pull you out," he grumbled, knowing as he said it that what he meant was the exact opposite. "But it's not that easy for me. I can't leave my family to suffer. I can't be that selfish. Just like you, and your parent's future for this kingdom—I can't simply walk away."

The prince opened his mouth like he was going to protest, but as he stared at Cin in the darkness, all he ended up with was, "Please do what you can then, for yourself?"

"Only if you make the same promise," Cin whispered.

A small, wistful smile graced Prince Lorenz's beautiful mouth. "What else do you think I'm doing here, with you, if not that?"

He brushed back a stray wisp of Cin's hair, and it felt suddenly as though they were both trapped within a cage, together but apart all at once. They were both living the lives that they had been given, and they'd known from the beginning that those lives were only aligning for a short time.

Who were they, to think they had the right to change each other?

Cin leaned into the pressure of Prince Lorenz's palm as it drifted up to cup his cheek. At least they were not entirely alone, even now. Their short time was not yet up.

"Have I ruined our outing?" Cin whispered. Then, more dramatically, pushing out his lower lip slightly. "Are you not going to kiss me, now?"

The prince's laugh seemed to emerge like a light from the darkness. "Of course I'm going to kiss you, dove," he whispered back.

And then he did.

Prince Lorenz wrapped one arm around Cin's waist and pulled him close, mouth hungry but more contained now, kissing Cin like he was taking a deep drag from the well of life.

When he finished, Cin's knees were shaky, his lips tingling, and he leaned against Prince Lorenz, playing with the edges of his prince's jacket. "You are so good at that."

Cin could feel Prince Lorenz's smirk against his forehead, and hear it in his low voice. "You are infuriating."

"A thorn, yes," Cin agreed. "Acquaintances you tease and fuck can be thorns, correct?"

"If they are you?" Prince Lorenz chuckled. "Most certainly."

He kissed Cin again, and it seemed as though he was searching through Cin's mouth, stealing his breath away before moving on to Cin's jawline and the soft space behind Cin's ear. Cin laughed at the sensation, playing with the prince's hair as the prince kissed his skin.

"There," he said, pulling Cin against him. "Was that a kiss?"

"It was at least *three* kisses, I think." Cin pressed his lips to Prince Lorenz's once more, quick and soft, then lay his head on the prince's shoulder. They stood like that, holding each other.

The yard felt almost lovely like this. There was something deep in Cin's bones that he hadn't realized usually prickled in this place, until he lingered there in the prince's arms, and felt it gone. Momentarily banished, at least—unable to return so long as Prince Lorenz was holding Cin up.

The prince's fingers trailed up and down Cin's back, and after a while he asked, "Did you grow up in this place?"

Part of Cin lamented losing the quiet, but he nodded. "Yes—it was my father's mother's estate once. My birth mother is buried in the garden..."

"And you really love it here?" Prince Lorenz seemed merely curious this time. Unless he was simply hiding his judgment better now.

"It's my family home," Cin said, and hoped the prince understood that as an answer. It was the only one he could give. "It's got no dovecote, though. An irreparable failing, if you ask me."

"Where *are* those pigeons of yours, hm?" A smile came into his voice. "I haven't seen those birds that keep following you around since we arrived."

"It's late. They do sleep, you know," Cin grumbled, teasingly. "But I think they may also be giving us space."

"Ah." The prince's hands slid down Cin's sides, cupping his waist. "Well, I can see one benefit to there being no servants in your house."

"What is that?"

His palms glided lower, fingers wrapping around Cin's ass as he whispered in Cin's ear, "We have the whole place to ourselves." He squeezed, sending a flurry of desire through Cin, but then those glorious hands were gone, motioning to the back door. "Shall we?"

The thought instantly turned Cin off. "Let's go around the back instead." It was, oddly, not as cold as it should have been, and Cin suspected there was something magical about that. "Too many less-than-sexy memories inside."

The prince took the redirection in stride, shrugging as he extended a hand to Cin. "Far be it from me to make my pleasure anywhere ordinary."

"Have beds ever factored into your many endeavors?" Cin asked, guiding Prince Lorenz around to the garden, deliberately circumventing his birth mother's grave. If anything, he thought she'd be proud of him for managing to get frisky with the prince—but they could still put some distance between them and her.

"Only when it's someone *else's* bed," the prince answered, and it sounded like he was, oddly, telling the truth.

Cin unwrapped his feathered cloak, settling it over the grass. He wasn't sure what they were *doing* yet—wasn't actually sure how much he felt comfortable with—but it seemed right. "Your royal mattress is probably too plush anyway. Your partner would end up asleep instead."

Prince Lorenz—now just visible enough in the moonlight to see the details of his expression—made a face. "As though I'd ever be such a boring partner as to let that happen."

He helped Cin settle onto the cloak, half on top of him as he knelt to catch the back of Cin's head in his hand and brush his fingertips over Cin's lips.

"Prove it," Cin whispered.

The prince kissed Cin yet again, but this time the slow, seeking gentleness was gone. He kissed like he had back at the castle dovecote weeks ago, with fire and lust, as though already dreaming of the place this would take them. Cin moaned into Prince Lorenz's mouth between gulps of air, one of his hands finding its way onto the prince's chest as he supported himself with the other. He dragged it down, feeling the prince's taut flesh beneath the fabric until his thumb brushed something hard as metal hidden beneath.

Before Cin could distinguish the shape, Prince Lorenz scooped that hand up, pushing Cin back and onto the ground without breaking the kiss. The moment Cin settled, he felt the strain of his chest binding all too keenly. His breath came shallower, but he couldn't seem to stop, stars spotting his vision as he kissed the prince back.

Before too long, Prince Lorenz broke away from Cin's mouth, leaving Cin to gasp as the prince sucked on his neck. One of his hands put rolling pressure between Cin's legs, and Cin swayed into it, moaning. When the prince shifted his face downward, though, his fingers already working open the front of Cin's pants, Cin forced himself to sit up.

He caught Prince Lorenz's chin in his hand. "Wait."

Worry flashed in the prince's gaze, so selfless it made Cin ache.

He took a breath, solidifying for himself that this was what he truly wanted, before he continued. "Please, I want to do you first. Let me make you come."

Fifteen

Cin had never done this before.

Fingers, yes, but never his mouth.

As he settled between Prince Lorenz's legs, an anxious exhilaration threatened to dislodge his stomach. The prince was accustomed to much better service—would he even enjoy the work of an amateur?

"You don't have to," Prince Lorenz said, seeming to pick up on Cin's uncertainty. "Just watching you gets me off."

Somehow, the option to back out made Cin even more determined. "Then be sure to keep your eyes on me," Cin challenged.

He ignored the pinching of pain between his ribs as he lowered toward the prince's stomach, unbuttoning him the way he'd started for Cin. His cock pressed free with little urging, already half-hard and just as thick as Cin remembered. It wasn't beautiful—Cin didn't think a cock could quite qualify as that—but the sight of it and the way the prince shuddered as Cin drew his fingertips down its length made Cin imagine the pressure and fullness of it sliding deep inside himself, leaving a wanting deep in his core.

He didn't think he was ready for the reality of that quite yet, but just the vision, aching through him, made it so easy to press his lips to the head of the prince's cock. He licked, then sucked, sliding Prince Lorenz further into his mouth as he wrapped his hand around the cock's base. The prince's eyes were still on Cin, his cheeks flushed as his lower lip quivered.

"Damn, you're the most handsome thing I've ever seen," he whispered as he caught Cin checking on him. "Keep— Keep doing that. A little faster, if you wish, a little deep— *Ahh.*" The prince's words turned to a ragged moan as the tip of his cock brushed up against the back of Cin's throat.

Cin nearly gagged, but he focused on the growing want between his legs, empty and hungry, and sucked harder, adding just a little teeth as he bobbed back. Prince Lorenz responded to that with another sound, deeper and even more desperate.

"You are doing brilliantly," he said, his voice breathless and a mess with hitches, "Oh you gorgeous, ingenious creature, how do you fuck me up like this, I don't—"

Cin used his teeth against the prince's shaft again and pressed the tip of the prince's cock against the back of his throat with intention this time, squeezing around its base.

Prince Lorenz bucked toward Cin, cursing and grabbing onto Cin's hair with one hand, and then suddenly he was coming, warm and tangy into the back of Cin's mouth. Cin almost choked again, then swallowed, and swallowed a second time before gently releasing Prince Lorenz's cock from his mouth. It was softer and smaller now that he'd come, but the giddiness of doing that, of seeing the prince melted on his cloak on the grass, flushed and grinning at Cin, was enough to keep Cin just as desperate as ever.

He didn't know how to ask for what he wanted—but it turned

out that didn't matter, as the prince scooted back, motioning for Cin to lay down in his place. It took Cin a little more effort than his lover to open the front of his pants and undergarments enough to give Prince Lorenz room, but just the sight of that small part of him laid bare seemed to give the prince great pleasure. He brushed his fingertips through Cin's lower hair, stirring up fresh tingles of desire with each drag of his nails.

"Still the most handsome thing I've seen," he murmured, and dropped his head between Cin's legs.

Cin found he couldn't watch after that, not for lack of wanting, but for the way his chest tightened and his lashes fluttered with each deft stroke of the prince's tongue. Every inch of him felt on fire, the blaze gathering in his most tender of places as Prince Lorenz skillfully used his mouth to stoke, licking and sucking and scraping his teeth in such perfect rhythm that every time Cin thought he could take no more of it—no more without either sliding out of his skin or coming in a conflagration—the prince switched.

Before long, Cin found his fingers in Prince Lorenz's hair, little noises escaping him that sounded ridiculously like pleas. "Oh God, oh God, oh God," he whispered.

Those towers had to be magic after all.

As the prince settled in on the nub of Cin's pleasure point, Cin could feel he was a goner. He held his breath to the rush of burning bliss, white hot through him as his body strained to take it all in, feasting upon the ecstasy the way the prince feasted between Cin's legs. He trembled out of it, gasping into his contractions.

As they faded into a sloppy, fizzling happiness, Cin couldn't help but grin. He stared up at the night sky, at the prince, at the soft touches of light and dark, long shadows between, and everything felt suddenly beautiful. Still beaming, Cin tipped his head back, and laughed.

Prince Lorenz settled beside him. He chuckled as well, brushing stray hairs out of Cin's face. "What is it, my dove?"

"You," Cin snorted. His smile felt so real, so right. "You're too perfect." He turned toward Prince Lorenz, curling into his space. "I don't think you should get married, because there's no one good enough for you."

"No one good enough for selfish little me in my perfect royal life?" the prince teased, and there was no bite to his voice, and only a little sadness.

Cin brushed a strand off his forehead in turn. "I was wrong about that—or, misdirecting, at least. You can't help the life you've been given, and despite your stupid, beautiful castle and all your servants and parties and power, it wasn't easy to lose your brother like you did; having to suddenly step into his shoes."

"You're right, it wasn't." He tugged at the front of his shirt as he said it, seeming mindlessly to probe at the skin below. "But I— I've made do." There seemed to be more there, beneath the darkness of his gaze, but the prince only quirked his mouth in a half-smile and kissed Cin on the forehead. "Thank you for this."

Cin almost rolled his eyes. "I'm sure you've had better sexual partners."

Prince Lorenz opened his mouth like he was going to protest, but instead he looked confused with himself, his brow tight and his gaze distant, as though working through a difficult problem. "More skilled sexual partners, perhaps," he said, finally, "But not... you."

The prince's odd phrasing pinched in Cin's chest, and he chose to save them both from the awkwardness, sitting himself up—oh, God, did his sides hurt beneath his chest binding—and hold out a hand to the prince. "You should head back."

"You have the only horse," Prince Lorenz put in. He accepted the help, and collected Cin's cloak after, patting it off and helping Cin secure it back onto his shoulders. The garden was cold suddenly. Like it knew they were leaving. "And my parents will be all the more peeved at me if I don't at least return to the castle *with* someone I've conceivably wooed. You know, if I play my cards right, you could even stay the night."

The thought made Cin strangely sad. He smiled through it. "I have to be here in the morning."

"Tragic," the prince complained.

"How much trouble will you be in for all this?"

"Oh, heaps, certainly. But what can they really do to me? Take the crown I've never wanted in the first place?" Prince Lorenz shrugged. "My parents will lecture me and I'll be roped into the very most boring meetings around the castle for the rest of the week with three guards trailing my every step." He wrapped his fingers through Cin's and squeezed. "It'll be an annoyance well worth the night."

"In that case, I won't pity you even a little."

The prince looked absolutely cheeky. "Not even enough to ride me back?"

Cin had backed himself into a corner, it seemed, but the only way around it was to send the prince off with Cin's flock-creature, and hope it didn't vanish out from under him the moment it left

Cin's sight. "If you insist. I can't linger, though. It's getting late."

Prince Lorenz joined Cin on his steed out front without further protest, Rags and Lacey fluttering from their perch on the flock-creature's withers as they mounted. His arms around Cin's waist felt different now, as though he were holding on for something more than support and deeper than touch. Something Cin wondered if even he knew how to describe, much less to give in return.

Many of the parties throughout the capital city had waned dramatically by the time Cin and the prince arrived. Even the crown's watch was mostly absent—or, just as likely, out in the surrounding towns, looking for their prince. Pockets of music and laughter still persisted though, where it seemed that personal drink had been brought out after all the palace had provided for the night was finished off. Cin didn't blame them. When there was so little joy or richness in the kingdom during recent years, it felt necessary to take what small comforts were available and hold tight for as long as possible.

Cin wrapped his hand over the prince's where he held to Cin's waist, and squeezed gently.

Though he could hardly know what it meant to Cin, Prince Lorenz still slipped his fingers through Cin's and squeezed back. Held on. And for the first time, Cin felt himself not just weep inside, but rage at the knowledge that he'd have to let go.

As they rode, he watched for any sign of his family's carriage, but he saw nothing yet. With the prince suddenly vanishing from the ball, there was a good chance that Floy was determined to stay until his return. Cin wanted, more than ever, to ask Prince Lorenz his thoughts on them, but he still dreaded the possibility that the prince might actually be considering them for his future partner.

He knew Prince Lorenz's marriage would not be for love, would likely become little more than a business arrangement with how the prince currently spoke of the ordeal, but the thought of Floy having access to him—calling him by his given name, siting across from him at dinner, holding his arm as he walked behind the king and queen—made Cin feel sick with something a little like hatred. But Prince Lorenz was no fool. He might have been keeping Floy around for their intellect and persistence, but there were likely far better options among the remaining castle attendees.

Attendees who Prince Lorenz had spent the entire night away from.

As Cin and the prince traveled closer to the palace, the buildings grew in size and scale. Tightly packed, gorgeous town homes surrounded fancy squares of wealthy shops where pockets of partying continued. From down the road, away from the echoes of joy and life, came a sound like a scream.

Cin straightened up, hoping he was wrong, but all three of his trio also went alert from their positions on the surrounding buildings, Perdition swooping to land on Cin's shoulder. Then there it was again—Cin was certain. Soft, and distant, but definitely a sound of terror and pain. He'd conditioned himself to notice such things, to pull them from the woodwork when no one else would. And here he was, yet again, perhaps the only one who had.

The prince didn't seem to hear the cry.

It would be better for Cin to ignore it. Saving someone here, so deep in the wealthy parts of the city with the prince at his side, was far different than the work the Plumed Menace had taken on—even *if* he had no intention to kill here. Whatever he did could put a spotlight on his existence at the balls, his friendship with the prince.

Cin's mount shifted beneath them, Perdition ruffled her feathers in anticipation on his shoulder, and in the moment of silence that followed, he found he couldn't ignore the ache in his bones nor the pull in his chest. If he *was* the only one who could help, then he had to do so, consequences be damned.

"Did you hear that?" Cin asked. "Down the road. I swear someone screamed."

Prince Lorenz's brow shot up. He didn't question Cin, didn't even pause to try to hear the sound for himself. Simply trusted. "What are we waiting for?"

His unquestioning determination to help made him all the more handsome.

As though they had one mind, Cin's steed took off, charging in the direction of the sound. They had to turn down a side street, then a wide, paved alley between the rows of fancy houses. The clop of hooves should have overwhelmed the now fainter, muffled sobs, but whatever magic the transformed birds possessed let them practically fly, soundless through the night, Cin's trio of tiny feathered angels guiding their way from above.

They emerged around a corner into the small gardened yard of a wealthy town home, and Cin found the person in an instant—spotted the man hulking over-top them, anyway. He'd pinned his much smaller victim onto the stoop of the dark back porch. By the muffled anguish to their whimpering, he was clearly holding one hand over their mouth, and the nature of their weak struggling made it easy to imagine the scene hidden by the shadows. Easy, because Cin had witnessed it so many times before.

His chest tightened, the blood that pounded through his veins turning to a war drum in his ears. He slid off his mount without a thought, throwing himself at the large man, grabbing into his clothes, twisting, then yanking. His great size barely budged under Cin's exertion, but then a second pair of hands joined Cin's and together they pulled.

As they ripped the man back, his victim scrambled, falling over themself to get away. They seemed too breathless to thank anyone, too panicked still as they tried, desperately, to tuck the pieces of their simple servant's clothing back around themself, their hat sliding off their head in the rush.

Despite the hands gripping his lavish shirt and shoulders, the man dove at his victim again, bellowing under his breath, "Come back here, you fucking—"

The man's victim wavered, and Cin had the sickening realization that they must be their attacker's hired help, caught between the job that provided them food and board and the horror of what their privileged employer was trying to take from them. But there was no real choice here, not after all the times Cin had seen something like this play out.

They took a few more steps, crossing through a pocket of moon-light, and Cin caught a better glimpse of them—bruised skin, long hair, and, free now of their hat, the tips of two pointed ears. An *elf*, here, in the city. Cin could see only one of their wrists, a flash of skin as they struggled to slide the rest of the way into their shirt, but he recognized the manacle clamped there.

All the nausea he'd felt when he'd first seen the elf-holding cages back on that wagon in the woods rose bitter and rancid in Cin's stomach, but this time his anger overwhelmed it. "Go!" he shouted at the elf. "Now!"

Finally, the elf ran.

"You fucking—" The man spun sluggishly, landing heavy on one foot. His breath stank of drink and his expensive jacket hung rum-pled, half off him. "I paid good money for that elf." His gaze seemed to slide right over Cin and lock on Prince Lorenz, gorgeous even now, in the low light and the panicked anger. His fists balled. "You'll wanna take their place, huh?"

He lunged at the prince.

Fear shot through Cin, then rage. He could see the future that would play out—the pain, the loss. There was no God to smile on Prince Lorenz here, just as there'd been none to help every other elf who'd been enslaved by a rich Hallinisch bastard. Only Cin. Only ever Cin.

Before the thought had finished, he was already moving, his feathered cape sweeping out behind him.

This man, this bastard, this villain, had bought an enslaved elf, not even simply for the status or their magic, but to violently extract every piece of them—soul and body—he could. And he thought he could take the same from Cin's prince. Would take the same, next time he could, from whoever he could.

Cin's body knew itself even in his ludicrous glamor, this false pretense of regality and goodness, and his hands found the small blade that he'd tucked against his back that morning. He had it free in an instant. As though he possessed the very wings his feathered coat implied, he all but flew onto the man's back, blade poised. A little voice, soft and mothering, told him *no*.

Be good, be pious.

But the man beneath his grip had not been, over and over and over, and no one else had stopped him. He was doing it again, despite Cin clamped to his back, one fist slamming into the prince's stomach as he grabbed him with the other. No one else *would* stop him. No one else, but Cin.

So he rammed his little knife into the side of the man's neck. Flesh gave way beneath his blade as he tore, like cutting the wrong way through a freshly plucked chicken.

As though his puppet's cord had snapped, the man lurched to a stop. He reeled once, his hands trying to reach for Cin. He grasped unsuccessfully at his neck, at his own blood, but as Cin wrenched free his blade, its sharp edges were what he found first, hand clamping down only to recoil with a howl. Then the blood started pouring. It spurted, hot and sticky over Cin's fingers, and the man sank to his knees.

This time it was easy, the knife going back into that serrated muscle so smooth and sure. Cin drove it until the tip hit bone, and twisted up. The man's growling and scrambling dissolved into a choke, then nothing.

Cin dismounted as he crumpled across the pavement.

Hands shaking, Cin stood there. Perdition dropped onto his shoulder. She nuzzled into the side of his neck, and somewhere above, behind, around, were Ragimund and Lacey's gentle coos, too soft and melancholic for anything but a funeral. The fire that had fueled Cin—the surety so deep in his bones that reason couldn't touch—drained away. His chest felt empty. Nausea turned in his stomach.

Yet again—yet again. How many times was this now? How many bodies...

Yet again, not pious, not good.

But this time, it wasn't the corpse at his feet that disturbed him most. Not the stench of the dead man's blood still dripping sticky and hot from Cin's arms, nor the weight of the knife in his hands. It was the prince's gaze, so aghast that Cin could feel the shock, each tiny, sharp breath he took before he spoke a miniature dagger to Cin's chest.

"Did you—you just—you—" Prince Lorenz barely managed the words as he straightened, one arm wrapped around his bruised side.

And so awkwardly he seemed not to even know what he was doing, the prince took a step away from Cin.

Sixteen

With that single step back the prince took, Cin felt like his whole world was falling away from him. How had their blissful night turned into *this*? He'd murdered someone—murdered with the rage of the Plumed Menace. Murdered someone in front of the third most powerful person in the kingdom, the man whose parents already had a price on his head.

Murdered someone in front of the only person who'd sought Cin out, tried to see him for who he was.

And now Prince Lorenz was clearly seeing something else entirely.

Cin reached for him instinctively, bloody knife still in hand. "Your Royal Highness—"

"Don't," Prince Lorenz warned.

Cin froze. What could he say now? What could he do? He could run—back to the house he'd just brought Prince Lorenz to. The royal guards would be there by the morning. But he couldn't just leave his home, either. He couldn't—

The prince took a deep breath, in then out, in then out again. He looked through the darkness, from Cin to the corpse and back, his hand clenched again his heart, fingers digging into the fabric. What he said was not what Cin expected; it was somehow worse. "You don't even care..."

Cin felt his insides turn in on themselves. His skin burned, like God was here after all, that infrequent smile turned to a fatal glare.

"You don't even care that you..." The prince repeated, a vague wave toward the dead man the best he seemed able to conjure.

He was attacking you, Cin should have said, or *he'd been assaulting that elf*, or better yet, *he said he* owned *them*, but what came out was the excruciating endpoint of all those, small and soft but not the least bit timid: "Not this time."

It was the wrong thing to say.

Wrong in every way.

"Not *this* time?" The prince gave a tiny half-laugh, desperate and delirious. He ran both hands through his hair turning away, then back. "You've done this before?"

Cin carefully tucked the little knife against his chest. He could barely see through the panic rearing up inside him. Could barely think. "Not like this?"

Prince Lorenz began to pace, his arms trembling as he cupped the back of his head. "My God," he whispered. "My *God*. He's *dead*."

"He was hurting you." It came out so much softer than it felt in Cin's head, almost like a whimper. A plea.

The prince's gaze flashed back toward Cin, and while his expression was shadowed in the darkness, Cin could see the drop and fall of his Adam's apple as he swallowed. "With his fists! I can take a few punches. There were two of us, and one of him, and we have the horse."

It sounded so logical the way he said it, so unambiguous, but Cin could still feel every emotion of that moment as though it were happening over and over again inside him: fear, anger, hatred, and the pain—the pain that would keep coming, whenever the man chose it, like it surely had so many times before, until someone else stopped him.

The pain of watching Prince Lorenz be the one who hurt for it.

Something hot and tight tore through Cin's chest, so much like anger and yet when it burst forth, it brought with it a blubber and a choked, "I'm sorry."

His knees felt useless suddenly, the binding around his chest so tight that he couldn't breathe. Hadn't *been* breathing. More than just his sides hurt, as though his ribs were curling inward, cutting him up from the inside. Then, he was sinking.

Prince Lorenz didn't catch him. That hurt more than the ground, more than the endless ache beneath his bindings or the bite of his small knife into his own skin as he held it too tight.

"I'm sorry," Cin cried, softly, so very softly for how large the scream inside him felt, for how desperately his soul seemed to want to tear off the mortal folds of his own skin and explode into a thousand unseen pieces, everywhere and nowhere all at once. "He'd been hurting someone. He was hurting you." Just like the others. So much violence. So much pain. "I couldn't let him." Cin stared at his darkly coated hands, at his knife, as capable of as much death as any larger, stronger weapon, and said what he knew, "I just couldn't let him."

He wasn't even sure the prince was still there—couldn't bring himself to check—until, so softly, an unbloodied hand wrapped around his, then another. Prince Lorenz uncurled Cin's fingers from the blade, taking it away. He tucked it into his belt. "You do care, after all," he whispered. "That's good."

As the prince crouched there in front of Cin, he seemed to take more of Cin in, a dawning creeping over him. "If you've killed others like this... like him..." Prince Lorenz swallowed, and it felt as though he was eating Cin's heart with each word, tearing into it with his teeth to find the feathers beneath. "You've killed..." He swallowed again. "How many? How many, *Cinder-Ella*."

It echoed in Cin's ears like a very different word.

Menace.

"Only the times there's been a body." Cin had heard Prince Lorenz claim with his own lips that he didn't believe the Plumed Menace was guilty for his brother's disappearance, but he still prayed to the God he'd so defiled that the prince saw the truth in him. "I swear on my life, on everything, that I had nothing to do with your brother's disappearance or the feathers on his crown, none of it. If I knew what happened to him—" Cin choked back a sob, and it seemed the only sound he could make for a moment. When he continued, his voice was brittle and terrible. "I *wish* I knew that. If I did, I'd give you that peace—I'd give you anything."

Prince Lorenz's fingers fastened around Cin's shirt, grabbing his cloak and collar with one hand, his other digging into his own chest the way he always did when he spoke of Adalwin. It was nothing like the times he'd grabbed Cin in the past: no protection, only purpose. "You swear it? You swear it wasn't the Plumed Menace who killed him?"

"I swear," Cin sobbed, the emotion unleashing inside him, so furious it seemed his soul was trying to force its way free of his body. If only he could rip off his skin and escape the awful purpose he'd chosen, or been chosen for—Cin didn't know the difference anymore. "I would never have touched him. Every time, I've known my victims were terrible beforehand, known they bring only pain to the people closest them, and still I regret what I do. If there was another way..." Between his tears, he managed to lift his face towards the prince's, and Cin couldn't see him through the blur of his world, but he hoped—prayed—that Prince Lorenz could, at least, see him. "I don't ever want to kill them. I don't want to be *this*, this *menace*."

The last word barreled out of him in a hiss, and the sharp edges of it seemed to tear through him. He cried all the harder.

Prince Lorenz crouched there, not a movement, not a sound. But Cin could feel that tension still in him, the war between his desire to help the Cin he'd kissed in the garden tonight and to renounce the Plumed Menace his parents had put a price on. The latter seemed to be winning.

"Then *why* be the Plumed Menace?" Prince Lorenz asked, finally.

"I'm not strong; I've no power," he choked out. "How else do I stop them? How else do I save anyone..."

"I don't know," the prince whispered. "But it shouldn't be this, right?"

Cin sniffled. "It's all I have."

"It's... wrong."

Cin wiped at his cheeks, then his nose. He could feel the stain of the blood left on his face after. Marking him. "I never claimed to be good. Or gentle." He barked, a sharp, short sound. "I told you, I didn't come to marry a prince."

He could feel Prince Lorenz's gaze on him, cold and deep as the heart of a lake in winter. "But you *did* come," he said, finally, and Cin could not for the life of him decide what that meant. The prince stood. He did not pull Cin up with him. "If we just leave him here..."

Cin shook his head. "I killed him. I deserve to take responsibility."

"This will not look good, you know." Prince Lorenz stated it so bluntly, like he didn't know how to feel about it. Or, perhaps, like he felt nothing. "A man of wealth, so near to the castle—it'll bring back the rumors of my brother's disappearance, founded or not."

"I am aware," Cin said, but he didn't mean it. As much as he tried desperately to hold onto the weight of the situation as he stepped back, pulling three feathers off his cloak—he'd have no reason to wear it again—he could think of nothing but the nauseous shock of losing Prince Lorenz like this.

It was only two weeks before their time would already have been up, he told himself.

But moving on like this: leaving himself as a bitter taste in the mouth of the man he'd so enjoyed, even cared for...

It made Cin sick in the worst way. He forced himself to move, his body reacting sluggishly, and he could barely feel his fingertips as he pressed the feathers he'd pulled into the side of the dead man's neck. There: it was done.

He turned his full attention back on Prince Lorenz, and wished suddenly there was more light—that he could see every wrinkle and depth to the prince's face. Every pain, even if that pain was caused by Cin. "Will you tell anyone?"

Prince Lorenz didn't answer—didn't answer fast enough anyway.

And Cin added, "I'd have no way to stop you."

A future as a criminal on the run flashed through his mind as he said it: his current life abandoned; his home and family suffering for it. And he'd gain nothing. Yet a part of him, tight and hot, felt more compelled by that than the idea of a marriage and the happy ever after with it.

What was wrong with him?

"I don't think I will," the prince said, finally, then corrected it to: "I have no *desire* to. I know the consequences that will befall you for that and I wouldn't wish them on you, regardless of your actions."

Cin could do nothing but nod. He had to leave—not just because of the body cooling at his feet, but the carriage likely heading back for his home at that moment. If the prince chose to keep this a secret, then Cin still had other woes to worry over.

There was one last thing to be said, though. "They were an enslaved elf. Here, in Hallin. So close to the castle…"

"I know." The prince sounded bitter as poison as he said it. "Elves do not belong bound to anyone, least of all to the likes of *these*. Hallin's stance on that will not change."

"A stance did not stop this," Cin muttered.

He didn't know what he wanted from the recently crowned heir—to do better? He was not king yet. Besides, he'd seen his own mother establish a watch for the crown only for this to continue while they walked but streets away, their attention elsewhere. Never where it was needed; even, ironically, the time the prince their system protected was *here*. Perhaps this was larger than them both.

But looking down at the rich bastard's cooling body, he knew that wasn't entirely true. Cin had access to one thing, certainly: a sharp blade and the wrath to use it. Again, and again, as many times as it took.

Cin tipped his head. "I have to go."

"I know," the prince said again.

He offered no hand to help Cin mount, no kiss goodbye, no reassurance. Even a look of pity, if he had one to give, was stolen away in the darkness.

So, with three birds clutching to his shoulders and blood drying on his hands, Cinder-Szule left.

Cin felt sick to his bones for the full ride home, so lost in thought and anxiety that even Rags' soft nestling against his chest and Lacey's motherly plucking at his hair could do nothing for him.

His time with Prince Lorenz had been cut so short. There was still the rest of his life, of course—if the prince didn't turn Cin in. If no one happened to ask him about it. If he never let anything slip by accident. But then and there, it seemed as though the rest of his life might as well not happen.

He could go back to Dorthe, he supposed; she understood what he was already, and might be willing to run with him to Falchovari to start a new life there, under the long shadow of their terrible queen. But he knew without a thought that he'd compare any future with a partner to those beautiful moments he'd spent with the prince. Every smile to his smile, every laugh to his laugh, every soul to the way his always seemed fuller and more mystifying, the final depth of him always further down. Cin had no desire to put Dorthe through a lifetime of always coming up a little short in Cin's heart.

As though his anger and grief were a predator at his back, Cin pushed his steed faster, then faster still, letting the pain in his ribs overrun his mind until the magical horse nearly vibrated itself apart as it flew across the countryside and the two of his trio who'd been trying to comfort him were forced to release him and fly alongside their stoic white shadow instead.

Cin's emotional turmoil turned to panic as he caught sight of an all-too-familiar carriage making the final turn towards his home. Even if every distress of the night was erased, he still had much left to lose if Louise and his siblings realized he'd been outright lying to them for weeks.

He directed his mount through the forest in a mad dash that would have ended with him thrown into a trunk or his brain knocked out by a thick branch if not for the magic that carried him. If it were a month later, he knew, the trees would have cast off their golden leaves, exposing his silhouette as he cut through the foliage and rounded the back of the house. His steed vanished beneath him into a swarm of birds, their fleeing bodies seeming to pull the last of

Cin's outfit glamor with it.

It left him wearing what felt like rags in comparison. Rags, and a dead man's blood.

Cin could hear his siblings' voices as they spilled out of the carriage, Floy in a huff, Manfred complaining, Emma as lost in her beautiful daydreams as ever. Cin fumbled the house key, grabbing it a second time to shove it into the lock, and somehow—somehow—it turned. His heart seemed to throw itself against his ribcage with each frantic step he took through the house. His sides ached from it.

He could hear his family's knocking already.

"Cinder-Szule?"

"Cinder!"

"Fucking Cinder-whore."

A little voice in the back of his mind screamed that a knife could end this. End them, end him, he didn't know. But the prince had kept Cin's blade, by accident or on purpose—he didn't know that either.

The knocking and shouting continued.

Cin almost bolted for the door, before remembering his bare skin was still covered in blood. He'd left a water bucket in the laundry after last laundering-day. Cin ran for it. He plunged his hands in first, rubbing, rubbing, then splashing it onto his face—careful not to drench his hair. He had nothing but the inside of his own thin underthings to wipe over it all, but he did, and—

They were banging now, Louise calling with such fury that Cin swore it had been years since he'd heard her like that. He scrambled down the hall, messing up his hair with his hands—fuck, still damp, how were they damp—as he ran. At least his clothing was already a disaster.

Cin nearly slammed into the front door in his flight, yanking it open so fast that Louise's fist flew through the space. She stumbled into him with a gasp. For a moment, her gaze went too wide, too knowing. Then she huffed, straightening her outfit and scowling at Cin. "My God, this is a level of irresponsibility I expect from Emma, even Manfred, but never—"

"I'm sorry," Cin didn't even have to pretend—the bite of Louise's words hit home. He'd known better, known he was out too long, known that accompanying the prince back to the city was a bad idea, and he'd—but he couldn't dwell on that now. He'd already washed the blood off. Lamely, he added, "I fell asleep."

Louise only scowled harder. As she pushed past Cin, she grumbled, "Be sure it doesn't happen next time."

Manfred pushed past after her, markedly harder than Louise had. "Bet you were fingering yourself in the ashes," he spat.

Floy followed him, their nose in the air. They seemed to have no time for Cin, but he caught their muttering, "We should have stayed. I *told* Mother he was merely testing us..."

Last came Emma, throwing herself against Cin's chest in a dramatic sigh. He sucked in a pained breath, but she didn't seem to notice.

"I still think you're the best," she said. Her brow furrowed, and she touched the edge of Cin's cheek tenderly.

Blood, Cin realized. He hadn't fully cleaned it after all.

Instead of accusations, Emma said only, "I'm sorry you're hurt."

For a moment, Cin hated them all a little less.

But then Floy stopped in the doorway to the hall, turning back. Their eyes narrowed. And Cin felt like they had been the one he'd killed in front of.

F loy seemed no less suspicious of Cin the next morning, but they said nothing to him, slinking around the house during their usual morning piano hour as though searching for something—across the floors, the walls, the back garden. Cin wasn't sure what they were looking for, only what they stood to find if he'd been any sloppier coming home.

Cin tried not to let it terrify him.

He didn't quite trust when Floy seemed to turn back into their normal self, spending the better half of the day complaining that they'd left the ball too soon. According to the gossip, the prince had shown up in the final hour, twice as flamboyant as ever, and danced with every attendee who remained. And, to hear Floy tell it, the worst tragedy of their century was the fact that Floy had not been there. It would have made Cin smile, if not for the fact that he was just as hurt, deep down.

Prince Lorenz had witnessed Cin kill a man and gone back to flirt his heart out. It didn't help that it was what he was *meant* to do, what Cin had always expected of him. He had to choose a partner, and Cin had taken him away from that, out on an adventure that ended in tragedy. The fact that he had managed to pull himself together enough to act the princely rake was incredible.

And, if Cin had any sense, he'd be more worried about what the prince could have said to those who'd planned the party than to those attending it.

By midday, word had already spread throughout the kingdom that the Plumed Menace had struck again—this time at the kingdom's heart. It turned out that Cin's victim had been a lower aristocrat, already partially disgraced by his many unsavory habits, but to hear some tell it, he was the prince's truest friend, closer than the elder brother who inevitably came up a minute into every gossiped conversation. Was this, they asked, a return to origin for the Plumed Menace; a sign that they truly had killed Prince Adalwin?

Worse though, were the other brand of whispered rumors, circulated by the Menace's fanatics: that if the Plumed Menace truly was content to kill aristocracy if they were deemed terrible enough, then that must mean Prince Adalwin had been one such villain. Cin felt sick at the thought of Prince Lorenz hearing such nonsense, even if he would, technically, know better. Know better, yet be holding all that knowledge inside himself, to protect Cin.

As one day turned to the next, Cin wanted to trust that if the prince had not spilled his secret yet, then he had no plans to. But he had felt his blade sever through muscle and tendon, seen the look on Prince Lorenz's face after, felt the blood on his hands, and he could only trust so much.

Cin ran spirals around the thought, working himself into a panic before forcing his mind elsewhere. The way he kept himself sane was to focus on what justice he had brought—could bring—as the

Plumed Menace. The little spots of good he'd sacrificed his right-eousness for. He went out more and more, feeling a rush every time he spotted a member of the crown's watch in town, an empty hollow after.

On his way home, he'd visit the woman he'd last seen sobbing behind her farmhouse well—not introducing himself, of course, always keeping to the brush and the roofs—but still he felt the more he saw of her, the closer to her he became. He knew her now, knew how much she loved the cats that lounged in her garden, feeding them even when her husband disapproved, how she could read, and read well, and would take a break for a book at exactly noon every day, her choices so varied that Cin swore she must have a library hidden somewhere in her tiny house. And how outside of those two joys, she was terribly unhappy.

Her sobbing behind the well was far from the last of her breakdowns.

By the end of the week, Cin made it there in time to catch the preamble to one, sitting on the couple's roof as the fight crescendoed into screams.

"Get rid of her!" The husband shouted, moving through the kitchen after his wife. Cin couldn't make out the rest of his lecture, until he was poised on the other side of the house, leaning out above their front window. "Your family is *nothing* to us anymore. Nothing."

Cin's stomach sank. Cutting her off from her family—that was what her husband was asking. *Family*. Security. Home.

It made Cin cling to the hilt of the kitchen blade he'd placed in his knife's empty sheath.

But he didn't go down. He thought of Prince Lorenz's face, the horror and shock, and he crouched there, motionless, as the woman ran through the house, out to her place behind the well, and sobbed again.

Chest binding tight against his heart, Cin sobbed with her.

Seventeen

The day of the next ball came, and the watch had not come for Cin.

That should have made him feel better—his safety intact, his identity a secret. His role as the Plumed Menace could continue, just as it always had, and he with it. Yet the more certain that future became, the more pointless it all felt to Cin.

He had been meant to lose Prince Lorenz someday. Cin reminded himself of that as the afternoon pressed on and the rest of his family piled into their carriage. Still, Cin lingered in the kitchen, scrubbing the same pot he'd been working on throughout the day— a tricky burnt spot of beans caked to the bottom after Manfred had failed to let Cin know when their dinner last night had come to a boil. Every shove of the brush against the caked burn spot left Cin more restless.

He had denied that loss's premature arrival before. He'd ascended the castle wall the night he'd been left off the prince's list, and asked to go away with him when the party seemed bent on cutting their time together short. He'd had the courage, the fire, to go after what he'd wanted then. For once in his life, it had seemed so easy, so right.

Had seemed like it wouldn't end this way: angry, and empty.

Cin dropped the half-cleaned pot with more force than necessary, sweeping out the back door without a thought to where he was going, only that he had to move.

He had to know whether the prince would live the rest of his life despising Cin.

He had to—

But he couldn't look Prince Lorenz in the face and see the same haunted, disgusted expression he had the week before. Cin knew, without a doubt, that he wouldn't survive that again. If nothing changed, though, he didn't think he could survive this either.

His legs ached to carry him back down the road, through town—to the well woman's husband, or any other bastard. He needed to see the red drip down his hands again, and know that he deserved this. That the sin was worth the justice, his pain worth their healing.

Cin understood, though, deep within himself, that to rush through another killing was the wrong choice too, and instead he turned and turned, his feet on a track as chaotic as his thoughts as he paced back and forth, marking a trail through the garden. With a cry of desperation, he collapsed to his knees on his mother's grave, dropping his head to the wet grass.

"I saw your towers," he hissed at the dirt, wishing he could feel his voice resonate inside her bones. "I danced with the prince. I climbed over those goddamn walls for him. I brought him *home* with me. What more do I *need?*" Hot, wet tears slid down his nose.

He'd done so much, let himself *want* so very much, and yet just like that, their relationship had meant nothing.

Cin could sense one of his pigeons at his side, feel the gust of a wing and hear the soft shifting of the grass. The deep, fond coo was Ragimund. Cin twisted his head to watch the fluffy brown and white bird. Gently, Rags nibbled on Cin's nose. Cin sniffled.

The thought of not going, of kneeling there at his mother's grave for the rest of the night, pathetic and miserable... He could already sense the desolation of inaction curling around his heart, trying to drag him down into the grass, into the dirt. Into nothingness; just a blade and a body to collect blood and ash for the rest of his life. Just what he'd always been, before Prince Lorenz.

As Cin sat himself up, Lacey landed on his shoulder like a tiny angelic being, her gray feathers so soft as she rubbed against his neck. Then, she fit her beak around his earlobe and *pulled*.

"Hey!" Cin chided her.

She hopped, pulling again, and Rags joined her on Cin's other shoulder, running his little brown head into the side of Cin's as he squawked. As though that wasn't enough, Perdition hurled herself at Cin like a battering ram, driving him to his feet and toward the front of the garden. More birds swooped with her, creating a guiding stream around Cin.

"All right, all right," Cin grumbled, giving in to their pressure. "You know *he* left *me*, don't you?"

But that wasn't entirely accurate. Prince Lorenz had left, but he hadn't said he never wanted to see Cin again. He'd been distant, condemning even, but not once had he told Cin not to come back. It was a pathetic hope, so ridiculous that Cin nearly dismissed it. Being ridiculous had gotten him there, though: dreaming, and wanting, and *taking*. There were still two ball nights left up for grabs. So Cin took again, one step toward the castle.

His birds continued to swoop and the patterns of Cin's ball glamor folded out from his ordinary clothes. He tried to remove his feathered cloak, but it spilled immediately back into place, the magic transferring it from the ground to his shoulders like a wisp of shadow: real, then not, then real again.

The whole outfit boasted the same feathers that Cin had left in his victim last week. Someone would notice... or they wouldn't. He supposed that was the cost of his sins, after all: he had to choose now, to be safe or to *be*.

And to keep *being*, he had to see Prince Lorenz in person, speak with him, even if it was for the last time, and know whether there was anything left between them to salvage.

The wind whipped like needles against Cin's face as his magical steed tore down the road. He fixed his gaze on the glimmer of the castle's towers, ignoring the dark trees and farms around him as they were replaced by lights and music, every party he could have attended blocked out of his mind in favor of one thing: one piece of information. It was later than ever before by the time he made it to the gates, no line remaining with the list so cut down. Only one of the doors had been opened, a single primary watch member guarding it from in front, though Cin could glimpse a far greater number beyond. Extra security would be reasonable after a murder so near the castle the previous ball-night, Cin told himself.

He recognized the main guard, and—unlike the week when Cin had been forced to scale the castle walls—Berit also seemed to recognize Cin.

Their face paled slightly, and Cin held his breath.

"Apologies, Cinder-Ella, but you've not been included in the general castle attendance this week," they said, an awkward tremble to the words.

Cin felt the weight of all his hope crash back into him. Everything inside him felt wrong: twisted. This world blurred around him as he told himself to breathe, just breathe. This was the answer he'd expected. It was better than nothing, but as he sat there, his limbs numb around his steed and Perdition nuzzling his jawline, it wasn't *enough*.

Berit had stepped closer, and they were still speaking, slightly hushed, but it took Cin an extra moment for their words to even register. "You should leave—"

"I have to see him," Cin said, growing more insistent with each word, more desperate. He could feel himself falling apart at the thought of leaving, the kind of falling that would land him back on his mother's grave so hard he was unsure whether he'd rise again.

Berit looked nervous, shaking their head. "I'm sorry—"

"Just for a minute." Cin clenched his reins, staring out past Berit's head, down the path toward the castle. "Please, Berit. I know he's your friend—"

The watch member shook their head all the harder, pushing against Cin's mount as he hissed. "You don't understand, you must *go*! Leave—leave the *city*; it's not safe for you here!"

Not... *safe*?

But no one had come for Cin. The prince would have told his parents where Cin lived if he meant to turn Cin in, wouldn't he? Cin had no time to dwell on the matter, though. As Berit continued their attempt to steer Cin's mount away, a commotion set in behind them. Servants and crown's watch scampered aside for half a dozen watch members who Cin could only classify as soldiers, each uniform utterly practical and every belt weighed down with a different weapon.

Cin's flock-creature pranced beneath him, but as his mind screamed to turn and run, his heart held tight to what he wanted—what he was going to take, watch or not, soldiers or not, Prince Lorenz be damned. With a nudge of his heels, he urged his steed into a gallop straight through the castle gates. Berit stumbled back with a cry of surprise, and none of the mounted soldiers had time to react before Cin was charging through their midsts, his flock-creature's magic carrying him between their flesh-and-blood horses like a ghost.

"Prince Lorenz!" Cin screamed. His steed's fantastical hooves threw sparkles of light against the stone of the pathway as he ascended the stairs toward the castle's entrance, aimed to shoot like an arrow straight through the main hallway.

A servant waiting near the front dashed for cover, but two of the watch newly stationed at either side grabbed the metal gates and pulled them. They shut just as Cin reached the top step. His mount tossed its head as it came up so short that he had to grip into its feathery mane and sink his hips to keep in the saddle. Each of his ribs seemed to scream out in unison.

The flock-creature dancing back into motion beneath him, Cin frantically searched for a new plan between the hollowing pain in his sides.

Around the back: through the gardens?

But two more soldiers were coming up from that direction—that was where all the crown's watch were congregated, after all, with the ball in full force. If Cin could get somewhere less exposed though, climb up and through a window, perhaps—

It was enough of a plan to pressure him into motion as a crossbow bolt shot over the side of his mount's rear and clattered into the metal of the castle's gate. Cin took off around the far side of the castle from the ball. It was darker in that direction, barns and storehouses and orchards instead of royal gardens. Two more crossbow bolts whizzed by his head, so close his hands shook as he turned out of sight of the castle's entrance.

It thundered behind him like a thousand watch members were chasing him.

Panic welled in Cin's chest, pressing up against the pain that shot between his ribs. His mount clattered down smaller steps, past a muddle of buildings, around a tiny, enclosed garden, under a row of apple trees, but it all seemed like a blur, a nothing—nothing that could help him. He had to get to Prince Lorenz. It was the only thing that felt real.

Cin's world tunneled again, but the blackness didn't dissipate, clinging to the edges of his vision, of himself, tight and unrelenting. The path curved suddenly, right up against the castle wall. He pulled his steed up short, his heart thrust into his throat. His breath came faster. He could still hear the castle soldiers clattering behind him.

Suppressing the growing terror in his chest, Cin leaped off his mount.

All he had to do was climb—and that was something Cin had plenty of experience in. As he fit his fingertips into the bricks of the wall, though, the magic of his shoes letting him stick to the side like a spider, his head grew light. Cin tried to take a deeper breath, but his chest caught on the binding he'd reapplied before leaving home. The presence of it—always an annoyance—felt ruthlessly constricting now. He'd climbed with it plenty of times, he told himself.

But those times were never with this speed, never this fear.

As he pulled himself farther up the side of the wall, it felt as though each breath provided only half of what he needed. Perdition swooped at his back, like her single small body could lift him up— and maybe if the whole flock joined her, it could work, but as Cin thought that, the castle soldiers came whipping around the corner and into the alley. Still in their horse-mimicking form, the flock-creature bolted at them. It startled the soldier's mounts, giving Cin another few seconds.

A few seconds he desperately needed.

As Cin climbed past the second story, stars danced across his vision. The ache in his sides sharpened with each grab and pull of his arms. He pushed himself harder for it. He was so close, he could feel it, Perdition cooing in his ear and beating against his backside in a vain attempt to support him, his feet stable with the aid of the elvish magic.

Below him, the castle soldiers shouted—to each other, to him, he couldn't tell. He just needed one more hand in front of the other. One more tight, terrible breath against the screaming of his ribs. One more...

Cin's fingertips missed the next brick's edge. He tried to shift his feet to balance his weight. The world seemed to tunnel in, a flurry of darkness. He grabbed again, fingertips skidding against stone.

He fell.

The only thing Cin could think as it happened, was that it

couldn't *be* happening—he hadn't fallen, not in years, not since his flock had first taken to him—but that flock was now dispersing from its creature form far below, only Perdition left to pathetically tug at his clothes. The rest made it to him only as he neared the ground, their little bodies battering into his, slowing his fall until—

A pair of strong arms caught Cin.

His mind went, hopelessly, to Prince Lorenz, but then hands clamped down, four, then six, latching onto his arms and legs— then suddenly he was dangling between two of the soldiers, another tying his arms behind him. Some alarming part of his brain screamed at him to squirm, but too much of his body had already shut down with horror. This was it. The Plumed Menace had killed a man. The crown had figured it out. He had run, and they caught him.

This was it.

And Prince Lorenz wasn't even here.

Cin's body went numb as the soldiers shoved him forward— back the way they'd come.

Perdition swooped down at them, her tiny feet outstretched as she dove for the nearest soldier's eyes. The soldier ducked her assault the first time, but then they drew the long wooden stave from their back. Cin's heart stopped as they swung. The sound of Perdition's body colliding with the wood shot through him like a bullet, seeming to tear him apart as it went. Her body fell into the darkness, and then they were moving, and she was gone. Just... gone.

Cin craned his neck as though that could bring her back, as panic set deep into his bones. She had to be all right; she was knocked aside, that was all. That *had* to be all. But every second that neither

Perdition, nor any of his flock, reappeared lodged a fresh blade in Cin's chest.

He sank into misery as the soldiers dragged a hood over his head. It felt excessive—what was he going to do now? Break his bonds and fly away?

The thought sent a terrible silent bark of laughter through him, threatening to turn immediately to a sob. The ground beneath Cin turned from the path, to the dust of the yard, to a stone cold enough for the chill to seep through his shoes. The path sloped down—underground. His treatment seemed to roughen with each step, the soldiers shoving and growling at him.

Lights flickered beyond Cin's rough-spun hood, growing bright enough that Cin could see the imprint of each orange glow through the fabric. The soldiers shoved him to the side, then down, forcing him onto a stool. They yanked his bound wrists and when Cin leaned, he could feel them tied to something behind him. One of the watch pulled his hood off.

The full musk of the room assaulted Cin's senses. He gagged from the combination of the stench—filth and sewage—and the dampness that clogged his nose and throat. His eyes adjusted to the lighting immediately, the five lanterns filling the small stone chamber to the green crust between the near-black blocks. In his peripheral vision, he could just make out the bars his wrists had been tied to: the bars of a cell. His future. The fear that slithered through him at that thought made him wish the soldiers hadn't broken his fall after all.

They stood around him, half of them staring him down while the others watched the doorway. Through it, he could hear the near scuffle of footsteps, and the far gurgle of an underground river, and something else beneath it all—a moan, he thought. Or a dozen of them, crying in unison. How many others were down here? How long did they last before God forgot their souls entirely, and their bones grew the same mold of the walls, every sparkle of magic and life they'd once known caving into aching hollows of empty want?

Someone was clearly coming to condemn him to that now; if not God, then a mere mortal. Perhaps Cin had lost the privilege not only of a divine smile, but of a scowl as well.

The soldiers straightened fully to alert as the last of them led a shorter, thin figure into the room. It took Cin a moment to recognize them, piecing together the points of their ears and the uncertainty in their eyes. They wrapped their fingers around their wrists one after another, twisting as though to reassure themself that nothing remained there to tie them to their old enslaver. As the elf lifted their gaze towards Cin, they flinched.

Cin's heart caught in his throat. He wanted to plead with them: *look at me, I saved you. Now save me.*

But how could he ask that of them, when their troubles had been of none of their doing, and his had been all his own? He had not needed to kill the elf's enslaver in that moment. Cin had simply... wanted to.

He'd *wanted* to stop the pain the man had already caused from spreading. But as Cin hunched there, his wrists bound behind him and the elf he'd saved shifting nervously in front of him, he could feel the desire twisting deep in his gut. He'd wanted that man dead from the moment he'd heard the elf's scream.

Just as he'd wanted to see Dorthe's late husband bleeding out across the town's cobblestones. Just as he'd wanted to plunge a knife into the throat of the man whose partner ran to cry behind the well after the fight, cradling bruised wrists and raw cheeks. And because of that desire, he'd never get the chance again.

Someone was finally, finally, going to stop him.

The elf met Cin's gaze for just a moment, before nodding to the soldier at their side. "He's the one."

They left without another word.

That was it, then, truly. Sitting there, listening to the elf's footsteps fade out, Cin thought of the prince: a small, half-hearted imagining of the ball proceeding somewhere far upstairs. It was the most he could let in without breaking. Because either Prince Lorenz had made this all happen, or if it had happened despite him, and Cin... Cin might never know which. He had been betrayed, or he was the betrayal, and either version hurt.

As the sound of the elf vanished, Cin expected the soldiers around him to leave or to act, but they continued to stand at attention. Waiting. Dread built in Cin's chest with each breath that passed. He could still hear the moaning in the quiet, no longer human, but the divine cry of a thousand-eyed angelic being weeping through a hundred mouths stolen from those who could no longer gnash their pulverized teeth. He wished desperately that he could have seen Perdition one last time—to know she was safe. Even to know if she wasn't.

Finally, a new set of footsteps approached. They seemed to take the whole span of the night to reach Cin's chamber, slow but steady: an impending executioner's blade. And as the small group finally entered the chamber, Cin's brain seemed to shut down. Those on the outside wore what looked as though the ornamentation on the castle's gate guard had been transferred onto the soldier's practical uniform: beautiful but deadly. And as Cin's mind finally caught up with reality, he realized why.

In the center of the pack of guards walked two people Cin had only ever seen at a distance: figureheads shining in the light of their own regal lineage, all the poise and beauty and arrogance of their son, but none of the playfulness.

Standing in the center of the dungeon chamber, prepared to condemn Cin personally, were the queen and king of Hallin.

Eighteen

Cin sat, bound, before the royal couple of Hallin and he swore they could discern every sin he'd ever committed.

Queen Idonia was the first to step forward, and for an instant Cin saw his sibling in her place. Her dark hair was perfectly arranged, chin held high, and manicured brows lifted ever so slightly like she was judging the world with each slow movement of her thick lashes. She wore a deep green half-dress as ornamental as Prince Lorenz's usual outfits, cut open in the front to reveal her billowing pants and tall boots, their rims now smudged in the grime of the underground chambers. Her crown for the evening looked made of the thinnest silver strands, twirled together around a maze of diamonds.

King Warner stood just behind her, as aloof as his partner. He'd dressed in teals and golds, his jacket so long it was nearly a dress itself, and his own crown—slim and silver—sat over brown hair that reminded Cin of his son's, short but thick and seeming to move in a breeze that didn't exist. He had his son's plump nose too, but there the similarity stopped; the king's lips were full and his eyes far wider, almost shifty in their motion.

As both the monarchs focused in on Cin, he felt like one of

Floy's bugs under a microscope. He tried his best to bow his head to them, hoping, praying, that the respect could still gain him some favor—a quick death, a last meal, something. He could feel the blood leaving his cheeks as he straightened. His voice came out weak and cracking. "Your Royal Majesties."

"He is so young," the king murmured to his wife. What Cin could hear of his tone sounded anything but sympathetic, a hint of disgust entangling his words.

"Old enough." Queen Idonia sharpened her gaze on Cin. "You would be wise to tell us the truth," she said, and she seemed closer suddenly, as though she could invade Cin's space with her voice alone. Low and dark, she asked, "What did you do to him?"

A chill ran through Cin, completely unrelated to the cold in the room, as though the distant moaning creature of his imagination was sinking its claws into his shoulders in preparation for dragging him to the hellish depths. He could see the wealthy man's blood spilling down, could feel it seeping through the wrinkles in his hands, clinging there like a brand. *What did you do to him?*

Sinner.

Cin attempted to swallow the saliva collecting in the back of his throat, but he choked instead. *What did you do to him?* Killed him, of course. But there was something in Cin's chest screaming that he was getting this wrong. It was the wrong question, the wrong answer.

The queen pressed forward. "Why did you kill our son?"

Cin's world went dark and bright all at once, everything and nothing as his chest caved in. "Lorenz?" What had happened to Prince Lorenz? How had he not—

"Adalwin."

Cin cursed the miserable panic that was turning his thoughts to chaos. Prince Adalwin, of course. The queen and king wouldn't be here for a random aristocrat, and if something had happened to Prince Lorenz in the last week, they would have turned the kingdom upside down the way they had for their eldest son before they found his bloody crown, pigeon feathers stuck like ornamentation to the dried red crust.

Cin felt the blood drain from his face. He shook his head, tiny short motions, as though the more times he could deny it, the more likely they were to believe him. "I had nothing to do with that, I sw—"

"You *are* this killer they call the Plumed Menace," Queen Idonia insisted. "We know what you did to Brando Von Achenbach. Had you intended to take Ren from us, too?"

Fueled by Cin's already growing panic, flashes of such an end for the prince whirled through Cin's mind: the blade slipping, tearing into Prince Lorenz's chest, his blood welling over Cin's hands to cover the stains of every other murder—to replace them tenfold. Cin felt sick. He needed to see Lorenz; needed to pull him close with soft hands and feel that he was still in one piece, that no terrible imagining on Cin's part could hurt him.

But the queen and king were here instead. "Do you deny it?" Queen Idonia asked.

"I could never harm the prince," Cin cried, though everything in his chest screamed yes, he might, who was he to claim piety? Cinderwhore, Cinder-freak. Cinder. Sinner. "I would never—to either of them! I'm not..."

The sentence choked him before he could finish, a sob clamping down his lungs. He curled forward. The tension between his muscles and bones was so strong that it seemed all he could do to keep his skin from splitting open.

"I'm not..." he managed again, and nothing more.

"Don't lie to us." Queen Idonia stalked toward Cin. Her guards took a step as well, as though they might try to stop her, but the ferocity in her charge must have scared them off, because they all simply watched as she grabbed Cin by the hair, snarling like a warrior queen from days long past. "Tell me *why*."

Cin could feel the bite of her nails and the heat of her breath and yet all he could focus on was the speck in her eyes, one twinkle of the brightest green in the sea of brown, the same hue he'd seen before in Prince Lorenz's. In her son's.

This wasn't merely the queen. She was Prince Lorenz's *mother*: a woman who had pointed him toward distant goals and told him to be good and prayed to see him live on when it finally came time for her to slip away. And all she wanted was to know that the villain who'd taken her eldest child away from her could no longer take her youngest.

Cin felt for her; felt for her son. And somewhere, deep beneath that, he felt jealous, too. But it was an afterthought, that ache pressing down beneath the sight of her pain; the same pain Cin had seen in Prince Lorenz. He couldn't let that fester. Couldn't let it consume her. Couldn't let it hurt anyone else. "I'm sorry," he choked out. If he was going to be condemned either way, perhaps he could at least save her from this. "Adalwin—"

"—didn't die by his hand." The prince's voice seemed to come from nowhere and everywhere, slipping out of Cin's imagination in a tantrum of emotion. He stole the attention of the small, packed room as he surged through it, and then he was there, pressing himself between Cin and the queen, one hand on his mother's shoulder. "Mother..."

He was so soft with her, so purposeful and focused, that just seeing it, seeing him in all his gentleness, his love, emerge here only to reach for someone, someone that wasn't Cin—it hurt.

It hurt.

"We both miss Alwin, but this is not the way..." the prince whispered, pulling her from Cin and into his arms. He clutched at his heart, looking lost as she broke against him, and Cin could see the fear reverting from anger back to its original state: to grief. King Warner joined them, his arms cradling under his weeping wife's as he drew her in.

Cin wanted to grieve with them. He could have at least taken the blame to give them peace, if he was to be condemned anyway. But Prince Lorenz hadn't asked. He barely seemed to see Cin.

Sagging forward, Cin closed his eyes against the sight of a love he would never have, even should they call his own family in for a final farewell. Perhaps Emma would come for him. Perhaps.

Through the haze of his misery, fingers traced up his cheek and cupped his head, a voice murmuring in his ear, "Oh, my dove, what have they done to you..."

And suddenly, Prince Lorenz's arms were wrapped around Cin instead, holding him. There, present, caring. For him.

Cin released a sob.

He curled into the embrace. It seemed at first only to open a deep gash in his chest—the feeling that this was what he *needed*. What he'd always needed, every time his soul sought to implode. This was the cure.

This was everything.

Then Prince Lorenz stumbled and pulled back as two of the crown's guards tried to push in between them. Behind the prince, Queen Idonia shouted, "Ren!" Her voice clear and sharp once more. "Get away from him."

"No!" Prince Lorenz shot back, just as fierce as his mother. "You've made a mistake." He pushed off his family's watch, and while he didn't drop down to his knees again, he stood his ground before Cin, looking as regal as Cin had ever seen him.

Queen Idonia did not seem cowed by her son's display. "I know you may think you care for this man, but he has much blood on his hands."

The prince held up his hands in protest. "I will not have this conversation with them in it," the prince snapped, waving his hand at the guards still flanking him.

Somewhere between the queen and king's arrival and now, the original watch members who had captured Cin had left the room, but four of the crown's personal watch remained, their weapons as fine as the ornamentation on their green uniforms and their tension clear in their stances.

Queen Idonia scowled, but the prince snorted at her as though the expression alone was one side of a silent conversation. "He's bound to the cell and weaponless—how much safer could I be? Remember, I've ridden out of the city with him."

A look passed between his parents, but the queen nodded to one of the watch members after. They bowed their heads and left. The crumbling wooden door creaked on their way out.

It had barely settled before the queen was back at it. "This man you've been spending so very much *time* with is the one they call the *Plumed Menace.*"

"On what evidence do you suggest such a thing?" Prince Lorenz demanded, like he hadn't seen Cin commit murder just a week prior. As he said it, he whirled toward Cin and dropped back to his knees, his arms around Cin's waist. This time, his hands worked diligently at the bonds that held Cin to the cell bars.

Cin drew in a little sob, pressing the side of his face to the prince's neck in thanks. He tried to hold his hope at arm's reach—this was not safety. This was Prince Lorenz, yes, but even if he were to plead for Cin's freedom, his parents still had to accept.

King Warner coughed in protest of his son's actions, and the queen stormed right up to them both, her arms crossed and her expression twisting in the lantern light.

"He was at the scene of the crime," she retorted, "identified by a witness just this hour."

The bonds snapped free of Cin's wrists entirely and Prince Lorenz turned to glare at his parents. "Did this witness identify *me* as well?"

"You..." His mother's eyes widened.

"Of course I was there!" The prince shot to his feet once more, one hand coming to rest against the back of Cin's head, cradling. His voice welled with all the emotion of that night. "I stood there and watched as Von Achenbach lunged for us, and..."

Cin could feel every last one of Prince Lorenz's aches deep in his own chest as he awaited the inevitable. Perhaps from the prince, at least, he would sound heroic, though Cin knew that to be a lie. There was the slightest of chances that he had saved a person that night, but undeniably he had killed one.

Queen Idonia stared at her son, her face pale in the flickering lantern light. "Then you saw what, my son?"

The prince cleared his throat, and while his horror and misery remained, his confidence returned to stabilize it. "I saw my friend in peril, and a knife at his belt, and I could not..." He shook his head, wiping aside a bit of moisture that clung beneath his eye. "I acted without a thought."

The implication of his statement pieced together slowly, tenderly, each word leaving an ache deep inside Cin. It hurt in the best way, terrible yet lovely. Even after seeing what he had done, who he *was*, the prince was protecting Cin. By taking that blame on himself. It was so much more than Cin had expected; more than he could have believed anyone would do for him, much less this man who'd been utterly distressed by the sight of the blood on Cin's hands.

Prince Lorenz looked so mournful—so *guilty*—too, that Cin could only believe that the emotion came from a place of understanding. That between the murder and now, the prince had put himself in Cin's shoes. "I'm sorry I did not have the heart to tell you," he said. "I was panicked and I had remembered the feathers in Cinder-Ella's cloak and I thought, if the Plumed Menace had killed such terrible people as Brando Von Achenbach in the past, what would be one more to their name? I did not imagine it would spark... all this."

Cin felt himself tremble, flashes of cold and heat coursing

through him. It seemed the wrong reaction to such commitment, so negative in light of the prince's offer of salvation. But that was just it—the offer; the salvation. It wasn't divine, but it was more than anyone had ever deemed Cin worth. Even if, by the expressions of Prince Lorenz's parents, he would serve a far lighter sentence for Cin's crimes than Cin would have.

The queen stared at her son with a sudden wave of compassion and calculation, as though already conceiving of a dozen ways to save him from this revelation.

The reaction from the prince's father was more surprising, simply for the stoic distance he'd maintained thus far, now shattering as his eyes welled with tears. "Oh, son," he whispered, one hand on his heart.

Queen Idonia's gaze snapped between Cin and her son. "Perhaps he didn't kill Von Achenbach, but are you certain he's not still the Menace? His feathered cloak, and his regal attire with no title— No one had seen him before these balls—" she said in a staccato jumble, jumping from one reasoning to the next.

The prince responded with impeccable calm. "I've been to his home; I've seen his mother's grave. He is just a humble son of a once-wealthy family who jumped at the chance to attend a royal ball. Was that not the reason we invited everyone? You wished for me to build relationships amongst all the classes—as you had with Father. Those were *your* words, were they not?"

Queen Idonia glanced at her husband, her mouth tight and something oddly like a blush peppering the edges of her cheeks. Cin could almost see them both as younger people, a regal, bold princess turned soft and curious over a local carpenter's son who sat by the castle wall to write poetry in his free time. Somehow, between then and now, they had become this: grief-stricken and harsh, trying to strong-arm their kingdom's future at the expense of their son's current happiness.

"The soldiers believe he has magic," King Warner said. His voice was softer than Cin would have thought, delicate and musical, but the words themselves were like a stake in Cin's chest.

The whole family looked at him, even Prince Lorenz. A flash of worry crossed his face, and his fingers lifted, tucking awkwardly against his heart. When he spoke, his voice was hoarse. "Magic?"

Cin gave a sharp little shake to his head. "There is magic I benefit from, but it is not mine. I traded for my shoes with a pair of free elves near the border, and my steed, while more agile and intelligent than a regular horse,"—he could not say they were secretly a flock of pigeons, not now—"is a docile creature. But I am certainly no wizard."

He tried to balance his innocence with confidence, but the flurries of emotion that had already passed through him in the last few minutes still tore up pieces of his insides, and he was fairly certain he just came across as desperate. Desperate though, he could lean into.

"Your Royal Majesties," Cin added, "if I had any strong magic to speak of, I hope I'd be halfway to Falchovari by now."

Prince Lorenz had begun nodding slowly, releasing the grip he'd taken on his own chest, but the queen looked unconvinced. "You ran from our soldiers," she snapped. "Can you explain that?"

"I believe having five armed soldiers rush you on horseback

would frighten most people into running." It was a risk to be so blatant, Cin knew, but he felt the conversation already tearing away from him, and he could not give it up without a final fight. "And I mean no disrespect, Your Royal Majesty, but would you have been more inclined to listen to me had I come quietly?"

"I'm certain I would have," Queen Idonia insisted, but she looked less so by the second.

Still staring down his mother, Prince Lorenz took one of Cin's hands in his and squeezed it. "I promise, Cinder-Ella is not the villain you're searching for. I know him, and I trust him. He has a—a good heart."

A *good heart*. It seemed like a mistake. Like he'd stumbled, then picked the word he knew his parents would accept.

Queen Idonia still looked concerned, but something else crept into her voice. "Ren," she asked, almost hesitantly, "You truly do care very deeply about this man?"

"I do indeed; well enough to know that he is not the villain you want," the prince repeated.

"He convinced you to leave the castle, and I hear the *city*, even, without your watch! And you—" She lowered her voice. "You *killed* a man. This *Cinder-Ella*—if that is even his name—may not be the Plumed Menace, but he is not"—she looked almost ashamed now to say it in the same room as Cin as she finished under her breath—"an appropriate *partner*."

"That is fine, then," Prince Lorenz snapped, "because I'm certainly not *marrying* him."

Cin's chest ached at the words. It was just the way it was said—the sureness, like any other outcome would be preferable. Cin had always insisted he was not there for the prince. But the prince had been here for him just moments before, and now...

It was nothing.

Cin was not marrying *Prince Lorenz*, anyway.

"But you *are* marrying," Queen Idonia snapped.

"You need someone at your side," his father added, gentler, setting a hand on his wife's shoulder as he said it. Some of her frustration slipped away beneath his touch, though a renewed determination seemed to compensate for it.

"So you say!" The prince looked one wrong step away from exploding, not in anger but something more miserable, dark and suffering.

As much as Cin's heart continued to hurt for whatever senseless, useless reason, he still wanted to reach for Prince Lorenz, to take the prince in his arms and tell him that he could have all he wished from life—nothing more and nothing less. But he was the last person who could offer that to anyone, particularly not if the queen and king were bent on denying it.

Prince Lorenz seemed to work through enough of his emotions on his own, though, lifting his chin to meet his parents' gaze head on. "I will promise you this, then—if you allow me friendship with whomever I wish, then you can pick my partner at the end of next week's ball. Choose any candidate you think suits this country. I don't care. I'll marry them. But leave Cinder-Ella, and my affection for him, alone. He's been through enough. He deserves not to lose anything more."

In a little huff, the queen turned to her husband. King Warner muttered something to her under his breath, and it seemed they were continuing a conversation they'd had many times. Finally, the queen shook her head dismissively.

"We'll continue to discuss your partnership later," she said.

Prince Lorenz looked away.

Cin's chest ached for him. His arms felt strangely empty—empty, like his heart.

"Until then, you may have this friendship of yours, so long as it *stays* within the castle walls," Queen Idonia told her son. "Your father and I do not leave here without someone else to wield the blade, and neither will you. There will not be a repeat of your impulses, regardless of the circumstances. A king's duty is to the protection of his people's lives, never the taking of them."

They could not know that their son had done just that by taking the blame for Cin.

As Prince Lorenz's mother passed him with a pat on his shoulder, her gaze fixed on Cin. Behind her, King Warner chided the prince softly, but Cin could focus on nothing but the queen as she stopped before him, her grandeur dimmed only by a hint of shame.

"Our apologies for the ordeal we've subjected you to," she said, and Cin couldn't tell whether she was genuine, but perhaps her sincerity was less important than the words themselves, and their offer of a truce. "We felt the evidence of your involvement was too strong to deny, but it appears we had only part of the story." She glanced back at her son warily. "It seems that impulsive protective measures run in our family."

"You thought you might learn what happened to your son. That's not a sin." No more than anything Cin had done, anyway. He found, despite the terror of her treatment, that he could not blame her for it. Least of all because she *had* found the Plumed Menace—he just hadn't been the one responsible for her eldest's demise.

The queen nodded. "We thank you for your understanding. *And* for your silence in all that has transpired in this room."

"I assure you," Cin replied, "I would bleed my last drop for your son before I let him feel the wrath of the world." It was a risk, but by the tilt of appreciation in the queen's chin, Cin thought he'd judged well.

"As you should," she said.

"He's a good man." Cin believed that. "He'll be a good king." He believed that too. Whether the prince wanted the role or not, he'd take care of the kingdom, though the work might make him miserable in the process.

Even the king smiled faintly from Prince Lorenz's side as his wife replied, "We know he will."

And her tone was clear: they knew—knew how much he didn't want this. And wished, too, that he had another choice. But the man they'd all expected to lead after them was gone now. All they had left was Lorenz, forced into shoes he couldn't fit by people who understood just how great a mismatch this would always be. Perhaps that was why they were pushing so hard for him to take a partner? They thought that if he had someone at his side who wanted to do the work, he'd feel relief.

"Enjoy the remainder of the ball," the queen said, giving her son a final narrow-eyed look as she left, and Cin was pretty sure that meant: *don't spend all your time with him.*

If he wasn't marrying Cin, the prince had to marry someone, after all.

The king nodded to Cin, and left behind his wife. Cin could hear the footsteps of their guards pick up partway down the hall, then begin to fade into the distance. The bubble of the underground waterway replaced their sound, and it was just Cin and Prince Lorenz, watching each other from what seemed like a hundred miles apart.

Nineteen

In the shadowy, dank space, with everyone but Cin and the prince now gone from sight and sound, the room seemed hollowed out, each sway of the lantern light creating new caverns between the grimy dark stone blocks of the walls.

Cin broke first, the tiniest sniffle yanking him back to the present.

Then suddenly Prince Lorenz's arms were wrapped around him again, scooping him up in a hold so perfect that Cin couldn't even care that his ribs still ached in sharp rhythmic intervals. He could feel the soft trembling of the prince's breath, and for the first time, he realized how scared Prince Lorenz had been. Scared, for *Cin*.

"I am sorry I was not here sooner, my dove," he whispered, lips pressing into Cin's hair and neck. "When I learned tonight that my parents were planning something for you should you arrive, I didn't know what to do but turn you away at the gate and hope..."

It was everything Cin had wished to hear and more. He drew his fingers along the prince's jawline, gently pressing his head back until their eyes could meet. "You took the blame for my actions."

"I couldn't let them condemn you without hearing your side or seeking to understand why." Prince Lorenz cringed, turning his face away. "All week, I've made myself dwell on that night—and not simply the way it ended, but all that you shared with me. And don't misunderstand; I still hate what you've done. But in drawing back from the emotion, I have realized that I am not you. I've not lived your life. I cannot say that I wouldn't have made those exact choices were I walking the world in your shoes instead of my own. And so, too, I can't judge you without knowing more."

The sheer compassion in the prince's voice felt like a balm on a wound Cin hadn't realized went so fiercely deep. He was seeing Cin, not simply from the outside—a feat many had already failed— but searching for the soul behind his actions, recognizing that Cin had his own well, his own depths, contradictory and indefinite. Who had ever sought them out before? And here was this man, this *prince*, acknowledging the complexity of Cin, even if he could not understand every last hidden crevice.

Being willing to sacrifice for that unknowable, nameless soul.

"I came in the hopes of telling you anything—everything," Cin said. "Just ask."

Prince Lorenz swallowed visibly, "What you said back when you killed Von Achenbach, it was that you had to, to stop him from hurting me, because you're not... strong enough to fight him?"

When Cin slowed and thought back through his memory of the night, he could see how the prince had come to that conclusion. He shook his head. "It wasn't just to protect you, though that was part of it. Every time I kill, it's to protect someone, but also to protect *everyone*—everyone who would be harmed by them in the future. I did it to prevent further pain for you in that moment, but also the next elf he would get his hands on. I'm not strong enough to fight, you're right. But if I could simply beat these bastards up, it would still be wrong, and it might not save anyone—or it would only protect them so long as I was there."

"So you want to prevent the future pain as well…" Prince Lorenz's brow knit. "But we have the watch. If you or I had subdued Von Achenbach, we could have brought him to them, to be dealt with justly, both for the harm he'd caused me and the violation of our kingdom's law against elvish enslavement."

"Yes." Each breath felt like inhaling through a pincushion now that Cin's terror had passed, the pain his climb had ignited between his ribs excruciating. "I didn't— It didn't occur to me, then. It's not normally like that, with the people I kill."

"Like what? That they've committed provable harm? Because you just said that you kill the guilty—"

"Guilty isn't a word I used," Cin protested, tugging mindlessly at his shirt, like that might stop the agony between his ribs. What right did he have to profess guilt or innocence, when he was guilty himself? Pain was his expertise, not piety. "But regardless of what they do, the crown's watch doesn't come to the villages unless there's something in it for the crown."

Prince Lorenz snorted. "They would, surely. If they were asked."

"Should we *need* to ask?"

"Well… no," the prince concluded, shaking his head. "No, you're right, you should not. Not from your leaders, nor their watch. But that justifies a fight not with these villains you kill, but rather with *us*."

That made Cin laugh, somehow, a tight, awkward sound strained by the searing ache between his ribs, but a laugh all the same. "Would you *like* to be stabbed, Your Royal Highness?"

"Perhaps that depends on the weapon in use." Prince Lorenz sounded almost jovial himself, a tiny smirk peeking at his lips, but the good humor faded with a sigh as he cupped the side of Cin's face. "Would you consider letting the Plumed Menace be the one who dies next?" He ran his thumb over Cin's cheekbone, down the corner of his mouth, his gaze so deep, and yet soft beneath, as though a fall there could break nothing. "You could let him go and just... be you? This burden should not be yours to bear."

Cin choked on a lump in the back of his throat, and tried to look away, but he found he couldn't. He could only fall. "I don't think I get to make that choice," he whispered, not sure how else to put it. "I know I'm doing this all wrong. I'm not a hero, nor a judge, nor a god. I have no right to decide who lives or dies. My hands are covered in more blood than can ever be washed clean. I'm a bastard just as much as anyone I kill, but I—I can't just walk by what I see and do nothing, even if that means I am worthy only of the same pain."

"My dove," the prince said, so tenderly it hurt, "life is complicated, and there's no way to be just good or just gentle, but that means that sometimes our victims aren't good or gentle either, and their villains are complicated."

Cin traced the prince's hand upon his own face, and all he could manage through the wave of his emotions was a soft, "Complicated, like me?"

"You're not a villain. But you are complicated." Prince Lorenz met Cin's gaze once more, this time fierce in every way he'd been tender before. "And you *are* good. Perhaps not all your actions are such, but they're a manifestation of you, and you are *good*, my Cin-der-Ella."

How could that be the thing he saw in the depths of Cin? Amidst so many shadowy monsters, the prince picked a ghost. "I'm afraid you're wrong," Cin admitted. "But I thank you for saying it."

"May time prove me right, then," he said. The corner of his mouth quirked up. "You still have one last week to stab me through the heart."

"If it means you don't trade your choice of partner away to your parents, perhaps I will."

"Oh please." Prince Lorenz snorted. "Have you seen the shallow and power-hungry bastards who fill my ball? If I'm to be cursed with one of them, at least I can guarantee a little more time with you before then."

It sounded like such a romantic notion for a man so determined not to marry Cin. He fought back the ache from his earlier rejection with the same sad fact: Cin could not marry Prince Lorenz anymore than the prince could transform his lust for Cin—or any other—into romantic desire. Cin had been the one to tell him they'd need to part ways eventually. The one to ask for this momentary arrangement.

"A little more time," he whispered back.

"Unless... I can ask for more?"

Cin's heart leaped at the thought. His soul seemed to cry out, raging inside his chest, and everything in him screamed past the pain of his ribs that this—this—was what he needed: more time with Prince Lorenz, with his only and best friend, this wonderful man who could know him, all of him, and think him not a villain for it.

But the world had not changed since he'd first told the prince they would have to part ways after the balls. There was still no way for him to leave his home regularly to visit the castle. No way for them to spend time together regularly that wouldn't eventually bring his identity into it.

"You knew what this relationship was to be, ending and all," Cin said.

And damn, did he hate himself for it.

A flash of pain crossed the prince's face, but then his hand went to his chest, and his expression turned as charming as any moment on the dance floor. "Well, I had to at least try. You did say I could ask you anything."

"True." Cin nodded, then cringed, when somehow even that hurt his sides. "If you're satisfied though, I must leave. One of my pigeons was hit during the chase. I need to find her."

If not her, then her cold, broken body, but Cin couldn't bring himself to admit that possibility out loud. He didn't have room in his chest for those emotions yet, should they be necessary.

For now, he had to believe she was all right out there somewhere.

"Of course," Prince Lorenz said. Before Cin could stand, the prince's arms shifted around him, one of them slipping under Cin's knees and the other at his back.

He swept Cin up and carried him toward the door.

Cin's position put extra strain on his chest binding, and the sharp pain beneath it, but the thought of trading the prince's embrace for the ability to breathe or to think seemed silly after a week of believing he'd never get to touch Prince Lorenz one last time, kiss him goodbye like their separate futures didn't matter.

As they passed a few other open cells, the sounds of the underground river fading behind them, Cin realized his angelic chorus of moans had always been the echoes of the water. Every other chamber in the decaying dungeon was empty. Perhaps it was not the only place in the palace where prisoners could be kept, but at least it seemed the crown did not regularly deem anyone worthy of this terrible treatment. Cin wasn't sure whether to be insulted or honored by that.

Was its emptiness the reason so many bastards roamed the streets? This form of justice seemed no more desirable than a blade, though.

Prince Lorenz finally set Cin down at the top of the dungeon's stairwell, where the musky, dark tunnels turned to the clean and well-lit hallways of what appeared to be the castle's guard wing, though of the few guards who passed by them, none stopped to intrude on the situation. Word must have already spread that Cin's name had been cleared, even if the reason behind it would remain a secret.

As Cin tried to step away though, Prince Lorenz took his hand. "You won't be questioned if I'm here."

Cin couldn't argue with that, nor with the warmth of the prince's hand, nor the way his presence made Cin stronger as he forced himself to journey back around the castle toward the darker side of the estate. As they walked, birds gathered along the eaves of the buildings, dozens upon dozens of them flooding down from the dovecote above. Guiding his way.

He followed them.

Cin's binding seemed to be growing tighter with each step, but he didn't bother to take the time to stop and loosen it. There would be no soldiers chasing him now, at least. No rooftops to fall from. Once he found Perdition, it wouldn't matter if the pain brought him to his knees.

He gritted his teeth at the memory of his capture, and for what felt like the hundredth time, he wished he had been born slimmer in the chest, with a form that didn't require any pressure placed upon its tender sides for him to feel at peace with his own body. Since they'd arrived, the mere sight of his own breasts left him wanting to slip backwards out of his skin with such aggression that the pain had always seemed worth the price... but now...

And if the shortcomings of his body had somehow led to Perdition's death...

Cin didn't want to even consider that. But the closer he came to where he'd been caught, the more the gathered birds seemed like a funeral procession, their heads bowed and their silence unnerving for such a large flock. He held the prince's hand all the tighter.

Together, they walked through the darkness.

Twenty

At the base of the castle wall, Cin found his magical steed, its legs folded under it as it laid on the stone street. From a distance, its body looked wrong, and it took Cin nearly reaching it in the dim lighting to make out the layers of feathers and wings sprouting from it, as though the mass of birds that created it were only half-transformed. Its eyes met Cin's as he approached, and instead of the usual dark horse irises were dozens of tiny bird one, collected together, blinking in their own time, with their own tiny lids.

Prince Lorenz startled to a halt, but Cin could sense the chaotic beast's acceptance of them instantly. The flock-creature lifted its head and cooed, motioning Cin closer with all its jumbled wings. Letting go of the prince's hand, he came to it, stroking along its feathered neck. Despite his best attempts, he could already feel the tears pooling in his eyes.

Between the flock-creature's delicate front legs lay a small heap of white.

Cin pressed his hand to his mouth. Prince Lorenz's arm wrapped around his shoulders, easing him down as he knelt at his flock-creature's side, carefully stretching one hand toward Perdition's huddled body. Her tiny back raised and lowered. He choked on a sob of relief.

As gently as he could, he scooped her up. One of her eyes opened a sliver and her wings twitched as though in an effort to rearrange them. Cin pressed her to his chest, petting a single thumb over the top of her head as the tears slipped, unbidden down his cheeks. She cooed.

Alive. Injured, but alive. It was the best Cin could have hoped for.

Prince Lorenz said nothing, simply stroking Cin's back, and for that he was grateful. This didn't seem the time for words.

He set Perdition between his legs as he reached beneath his shirt to unwrap his chest binding. As the fabric loosened, his body instinctively took a deep breath for what felt like the first time in ages, the inhalation shooting pain between his ribs like just filling his lungs was enough to tear his flesh apart. Before his disgust could stop him, he pulled the binding free. The immediate weight of his breasts made him cringe, but he tried his best to ignore it as he wrapped Perdition up in his chest binding and tied the little sling of her to his sternum. She nuzzled into his skin, then went quiet.

"Will she be all right?" Prince Lorenz whispered.

Cin cupped his hand over Perdition's sleeping form, cradled her against his pained ribs. His heart beat against hers beneath their seemingly eternal binding. As he closed his eyes, he could feel the answer building soft and strong in her little body.

"She will, with time."

For him, *through* him, Perdition would live. But because of him—because of his damned chest—she nearly hadn't. That was not something he was willing to risk again. Not if there was any way around it.

Prince Lorenz slipped two fingers under Cin's chin, lifting it back up until their gazes met. He seemed to look into Cin's soul, taking in all of his complexity with a gentle hunger. "Will *you* be?"

The question caught Cin so off-guard that he could feel the confusion shift across his own features before it occurred to him how odd it was to have anyone care for his wellbeing in this way. "Why do you ask?"

"You're hurt," Prince Lorenz stated, nodding downward. Somehow, he had noticed Cin awkwardly adjusting around it.

Cin grimaced. "It's an old injury. My chest binding aggravates it, as does any pressure or support for my chest, but it's growing worse and worse these last few months."

"Is there anything that can be done?"

The thought of the prince of Hallin trying to fix Cin's troubles felt so impossibly unreal, yet here he was, as thoughtful and kind in this as with every other piece of Cin's being.

"Only a powerful magic, beyond what most elves or mortals could conjure," Cin told him, stupidly, selfishness, just a little hopeful, "I've been too... too complacent to search for a source, but I think now I have to. I can't go on like this, not as the Menace, but not as myself either."

Prince Lorenz's hand drifted to his chest, resting against his heart so subtly that Cin would have thought nothing of it, had he not seen the same motion time and time again. The prince's fingers dropped as soon Cin took notice, though, his gaze moving away, growing harder—more distant.

Cin reached for him. "If you know of—"

The prince shook his head sharply, and though he didn't seem to move away, Cin's fingers didn't quite make contact. "That type of magic is dangerous, and dark more often than not. It requires something of yourself in return."

"Some things are worth the sacrifice, if it makes you more yourself in the long run."

A faint smile crossed Prince Lorenz's lips. "That's a rare find, my dove. But I... I trust you." His fingers twitched, and he glanced out toward the castle's front, then back to Cin. "Were you planning to leave now? You could always stay the night, you know. I can commandeer you a room here."

"You are already in enough trouble, Your Royal Highness." And there was a pinch building behind Cin's heart that wouldn't let go, a gut feeling that to stay would sacrifice more than just his family's compassion. This night he was called to other things. He squeezed the prince's fingers. "But I will be back next week. As early as I can get away."

"I will be waiting." Prince Lorenz lifted both of Cin's hands to his lips one after the other, before dropping them so slowly it seemed he was trying to memorize every curve and wrinkle and callus of Cin's fingers in the process. He leaned in after, his mouth brushing Cin's ear as he whispered, "Stay safe, my Menace."

And despite the pain those words fashioned in Cin's chest, he couldn't help but smile.

N o one stopped Cin on his way out.

It was eerie to go from being sought out to purposefully ignored, but with how worn out Cin found himself, he was glad to return to his usual invisibility. The lively city atmosphere had faded—a bad sign if Cin had any hope of getting home before his family—and as he rode onward, the gathered castle birds slowly began to peel away, until there was only Lacey and Ragimund left to follow him out into the farmland, keeping a watchful distance as though they were two tiny scouts in the darkness.

With Perdition strapped to his chest, Cin could not bring himself to urge his once more horse-shaped steed into the sprint he'd been taking from the city to home, but he could spot no carriage lights before or behind him, so it probably wouldn't matter. Whatever he did, he would not make it home in time to keep his family's ire at bay. That thought should have brought him panic. Instead, Cin found the tug toward a steely determination, the *want* becoming an overwhelming pressure against the pain that still sizzled between his ribs.

Magic, he'd told Prince Lorenz. Magic Cin had never had the courage to seek out, nor the necessity to push him toward that sacrifice. But with Perdition's battered body tucked against his heart, cradled between two unwanted lumps of flesh, over the top of an ache it seemed he'd never be rid of, he could not dream of a world where he failed her again. Where he failed himself.

When he finally approached the Reinholzes' estate, he could see that the door was open—so at least one of them had been insightful enough to look for the key they kept in the barn. Cin could not bring himself to turn off the road, not even to stop his flock-creature as it walked onward. As though sensing Cin's desires, it stayed its course.

Cin glanced back at the house, and then simply watched. As his steed walked on, the forest on the far side of his family's estate slowly blocked his sight of it. Cin's mount kept moving. His heart tightened, hope and fear battling for space. His flock had taken him to the elves before. If they could sense magic, could know what he needed...

"You'll take me where I need to go?" he asked into the sky, breathless and low.

Above him, Lacey and Rags called in unison. It was enough. Enough to trust them. To trust himself.

Cin's flock-creature didn't stop. They passed home after farm after forest after home, the moon sinking lower and lower in the sky. Just as the night turned cold enough that Cin began to shiver, two large owls swooped out of the trees, their bodies transforming to a lush robe of silvery feathers that wrapped around Cin. His steed kept on walking.

They passed one town, then another, both dark and quiet in the early morning hours. By the time the sky began to lighten, the depths of Hallin's eastern forest surrounded them. Only then did Cin consider asking his steed to turn back—at this rate, they'd leave the south-east border of the kingdom by lunchtime—but his flock seemed more confident than ever, its ears pricked forward and its gait purposeful.

Cin had come this far on trust and hope and desire. He feared turning back now would leave a gap in his soul forever.

As they neared the border river, Cin's flock-creature strode confidently off the path, into the forest depths. Despite the deepening woods, no branches hit him. Bugs and birds twittered, and in the distance he caught the howl of a lone wolf. The forest drew darker and thicker still. Just as Cin worried he'd lost track of time and the night was setting in, the branches thinned and the light pierced back through. The rush of a far-off river resounded, the melody to nearer bursts of frog-song.

Despite the chill of fall, the air turned summer-thick, muggy against Cin's skin and dense in his lungs, and Cin's flock-creature broke free, stepping into a spotty swamp. At its center rose a stairway to the hulking outline of an ancient, crumbling structure. Stone spilled from high walls and the lush tops of craggy trees sprouted within half-toppled rooms. It was as gorgeous as it was eerie, a haunting fixture that loomed over the dark pools of the surrounding swamplands.

This was a place of magic, if Cin had ever seen one. A shudder ran across Cin's shoulders. He could still turn back. But whatever the cost, he'd committed to this—to trusting his flock. To trusting in magic.

Hopefully that magic would provide him deliverance, not destruction.

The chorus of croaking frogs died down as his flock-creature walked purposefully toward the ruined structure. Cin twisted his fingers into its mane and held there, watching, waiting, trying to calm the anxiety fluttering through his chest with each slow breath he took. When his mount stopped near the edge of the ancient building and stamped a hoof, he carefully slid off.

His skin prickled. His knees felt weak, his head light and his ribs still aching, and he grabbed onto the vine-strewn well at the stair's base as he ascended the first step. Somewhere, or everywhere, a frog croaked. Cin's heart skipped a beat. The world went eerily quiet again.

There had to be someone—or something—here. A sorcerer, a witch, a korn demon; this far west, perhaps even Herr Candy of Falchovari, using his shapeshifting magics to lure in his prey before devouring them. His flock's endorsement did not necessarily equate to safety, only the possibility of something worth the risk.

Cin cleared his throat, and with one hand tucked behind his back, wrapped around the hilt of his knife—for whatever good it might do him against the magic of this place's keeper—he called out, "Hello? I come seeking the inhabitant of this castle."

Cin's voice echoed, leaving a quiet behind it as though he had carved through the sounds of the frogs and the babble of the water and cast them away. Deep within the crumbling structure, he swore something shifted.

"Hello?" Cin repeated, half-hoping amidst the anxious flurry in his gut that no one would respond at all.

Just as he was about to release his breath and turn back, a scratchy masculine voice replied, sliding through the air like it was as thick and sultry as the swamp, impossible and inhuman. "And here I was thinking I'd have a peaceful day," the creature said, "free of *annoyances*."

Cin shivered at the sound, and with the way the words grasped at him, he had a feeling that, one way or another, he was not getting out of there until the ruler of this putrid place had finished with him... whatever that entailed.

Twenty-One

C in swallowed against the fear gathering at the back of his throat. He glanced from the gaps in the castle's crumbling walls to its hollow windows and the long gash of its front entrance, to the dark water surrounding it on all sides but the one he'd come down, yet he could find nothing in the shadows: no menacing silhouette or sparkle of magic that might give him a hint as to who he was speaking with. Worse, he couldn't tell where the voice had even come from.

Keeping his flock-creature at his back, he decided to hope for the best; his birds would not have brought him here had they thought this swamp creature would be the death of him.

Carefully, Cin answered, "I can leave, if you wish."

"Would you really?" It was hard to tell from the way the voice creaked and echoed—so inhuman—but Cin thought he was being laughed at. Mocked. "And here I'd thought you'd come for a reason."

Cin pushed back the flood of shame that accusation birthed. He had not wasted all this time, left his family to fend for themselves, only to leave at the first sign of struggle. If he was going to be here, then he was going to be here for himself. He would have what he'd come for, whatever the cost.

For once, his sacrifices were going toward something selfish.

Cin felt every hope for his body blooming beneath his too-present breasts. Tears pricked at his eyes. He cleared his throat, trying not to look as though he was still a heartbeat and a half away from fleeing, and stated, "I have. I seek your magic."

The swamp creature seemed to scoff at him, the sound echoing like a flurry of bullfrog croaks. "What do you have to offer me in return?"

It was the same question the elves had asked him, but as with them, he still had very little he could give. His flock's humble offerings had been enough for kind-hearted Elias. Cin wasn't so certain they would work on such a creature as this shadowy king of the swamps.

But he had to try.

"I have magic of my own—my flock, who brought me here, to you. Our services are at your disposal."

"At my disposal, are they?" The growl rumbled through the space, everywhere and nowhere at once. "What good are birds to a lonely prince such as myself? There are creatures small and large aplenty here, and many are already mine."

As the swamp dweller spoke, the water around them swelled. Cin took an instinctive step further up the stairs as a hundred eyes pressed out of the dark water—frogs, staring up at him. They leaped along the side of the well below and the empty brick sills of windows above, their eyes as sharp as Cin's pigeons'. Not the mythical Herr Candy, not a sorcerer, not even a demon—Cin should have guessed from the swamp alone, but the hundreds of frogs finally slid the last of the puzzle into place.

This was the realm of the one they called the Frog Prince, the elusive, young monster born in the last decade. He was said to spy through every pond, his powerful magic requiring an equally powerful sacrifice.

Cin had to find something he desired. Something worth the magic Cin wanted more than air—had wanted since the day he first cut the binding around his chest.

"My blade, then?" he shouted, glancing from one of the crumbling castle's many gaps to the next, wishing he might catch a glimpse of the creature he was bargaining with through the foliage and the shadows. "If you have enemies, I can do my best to deal with them."

"What enemies of mine do you think can catch me here?" The frog prince seemed bored by the very thought.

"Please, I came all this way." Cin tried not to sound as desperate as he felt. "There must be something you can take from me in trade." They were dangerous words, but now that he was here, now that he'd admitted to himself what he wanted, even if the creature of the swamp didn't yet know, he found he couldn't leave without giving it his all. Even if his all turned out to be everything.

"And some have come farther for more," the frog prince replied. Something within the castle's main entrance shifted, a glint of green and then a sliding shadow, before the gloomy interior settled again. When the voice came again it still echoed from everywhere. "What are you here for, Pigeon Prince? Wealth? Power?"

"What would I do with either of those?" Cin asked. His family had been wealthy once, and squandered that perfectly fine the first time. They'd been powerful once too, and now they were all but forgotten. Even princes—the regular, mortal ones—like Adalwin could be vanished or killed in an instant despite everything they had, or sometimes because of it.

Still, the frog prince made a sound of disbelief. "Easier said than lived."

"The whole of the eligible kingdom is fighting for the prince's hand like he's worth nothing more than his privileges," Cin replied. "I have sought neither from him, even if he might have offered them to me."

A moment of silence stretched, even the frogs hushing as though with an intake of breath, and Cin worried he'd said something wrong. When the monster of the swamp spoke again, it was softer, a bristling hush to his voice. "What do you know of the Hallinisch Prince?"

Cin could feel a sparkle of magic in the air, like the tension before a great storm. It felt like a test. One he could not risk losing.

Yet, he could not lie to the Frog Prince either.

"I know that Prince Lorenz is kinder than he appears, as thoughtful as he is witty and as empathetic as he is flirtatious. He is so much more sensitive than his persona would imply. Where others are concerned, he is far braver than anyone notices, yet he's not selfish enough to stand up for what he deserves," Cin said, hoping with every word that Lorenz knew it. "He's worth more than any of those power-hungry bastards vying for his hand. He should be able to choose a partner in his own time, and not one right for the kingdom, but one right for him."

Just as quiet and strained as before, the frog prince asked, "And you think that should be you?"

The thought was a spear between Cin's ribs, running deeper and more miserable than any physical pain his own chest could produce. "He wouldn't—"

The frog prince cut him short. "So, you're not here for power or wealth. You're here for love."

"I would never force him to love me." Cin shook his head, a shudder crawling up his spine. "I know he won't care for me as more than a friend, but I wouldn't ask him to feel anything that isn't in his nature. He deserves better than to be bound by magic into something he's not. I would never ask that of him."

"You are truly his friend." The strain seemed to break partway through the frog prince's statement, turning gentle with a croak and a snap. A shadow swayed within the castle's main entrance.

For a moment, Cin imagined he could see the swamp's monster, rotting away in this dying place. Alone. Whatever happened, Cin prayed that never became the case for him. "I am," he said, and wished it could always be the truth.

"What, then, do you want, Pigeon Prince?" It sounded less like a demand now, and more a question, simple and solid.

"I wish for my body to feel like a home, instead of a house." Cin took a breath, dwelling in the unwanted weight of his breasts, the pain between his ribs, the wrongness of it all. "Have you ever felt that? That there's some part of you that isn't right for you to inhabit? But you're forced to bear it anyway, by some ruthless twist of fate, to be reminded every minute of every day that you are a foreigner to your own flesh?"

The shadow moved again, and this time, Cin could make out a

silhouette against the darkness: long, gangly legs and spindly fingers, his head and torso hidden by the foliage. The frog prince's voice, as inhuman as it was, sounded pained as he spoke. "How do you know this new you will feel right?"

Cin closed his eyes, and imagined everything he wanted coming to pass. He felt, as always, so many, many things. And as always, one of them was fear. Fear he didn't want to admit to; fear that regardless of what he did, nothing could make this right. That it was an affliction trapped deep in his bones and it would just come back again.

He knew this present, its pains and its flaws, and there was comfort in that.

But not enough comfort.

"I don't know whether it will be right for me," Cin said, finally, and the fear drained with each word. "But it can't be more wrong than this. So I have to try."

He had to try—to try for a better him, a better future, one he wanted. If it was a sin to be selfish in this, then damn him. Cin would find what was right for himself, one way or another.

"Then take this." The shadow shifted once more, and from within the castle a small, round object rolled forth. Dirt and moss slipped from its sides as Cin hesitantly retrieved it. Beneath the grime, he was met with a shimmer of golden magic.

Another test?

"Drop it into the well," the frog prince commanded.

A test, or a trick. Cin had little hope for anything else. But that little hope was bright in his chest, pulled taut between his own wants and the way this mysterious monster had reacted to them, as he too knew what it was like to be something he was not, and Cin clung to that. "What will I owe you?"

The shadow of the swamp's monster shifted again. "From you, I will ask only that you continue to care for that prince of yours," he said. "Prove that he is worth all that you say."

Cin's body for... his continued befriending of the prince?

Cin wasn't sure he could parse out the why of it, but he was too afraid that if he asked, the kind offer would be revoked. He'd touched something inside this lonely swamp monster, and that monster had responded in turn. Cin's throat caught at the thought of it: everything he'd wanted, but saw no way to take, in exchange for everything else he needed. To continue his relationship with Prince Lorenz would be so easy, so perfectly, terribly easy, and yet so very very hard at the same time.

Whether he knew it or not, the monster of the swamp was asking Cin to abandon his family—little by little, over months and years— and trade his time with them for that with the prince. They would hate him for it, question him, demand things of him that he couldn't give. And yet...

The more Cin allowed himself to imagine it, laughing with Prince Lorenz, lying in the grass beside him, watching his face as he teased and flirted and cursed in the heat of passion, taking care of him when he hurt and listening to him the way he'd done for Cin that night—that seemed worth any pain his family could inflict. And besides, he'd have a body that didn't pain him for it.

He had come all this way.

Cin carefully unbound Perdition from his chest, and Rags and Lacey carried her sling back to the safety of his mount. They all waited there, watching him. He gripped the magic orb tighter as he stepped back down the steps and leaned over the side of the well. With one last, deep, pained breath, he dropped it in.

No sound came—no sign that it had slid into the dark water below—but a shimmer of light burst forth, pushing Cin back. Stars swarmed his vision. His limbs went numb, then tingled back to life as the world swayed back into place around him.

He could barely breathe—could barely think. His body—it felt wrong, and that—

That felt right, somehow.

Cin crept his hands around his chest, expecting still, despite everything, to be wrong. But his chest was flat beneath his palms, as flat as it had ever been with the tightened bindings that took his breath away, only now he was coming to himself enough to open his lungs... and open they did. Cin inhaled, deep and strong, meeting no pain, no resistance, just the soft pressure of his lighter chest.

A sob slipped out of him, but unlike all the other tears that day, this held only joy. He could feel himself smiling, his cheeks pinched and the edges of his eyes pressed together, but he couldn't help himself. This was real. This was him.

And somehow, the monster from the swamps had given it to him.

Cin scrambled back to the base of the steps, grinning into the shadows as he clutched at his chest, just to prove to himself it was still right, still so perfect. "Thank you!"

"Remember your end of the bargain." The frog prince's voice grew distant as he spoke, and Cin caught only the glint of green eyes before he vanished into the ruins.

He knew the monster was gone, could feel it, somehow. The deal was done. Cin had a new task to be completed, a new price to be paid.

And all that it entailed was everything he'd always wanted. It was equal in cost; Cin could spend his life caring for Prince Lorenz, and never have it be enough. But the problem was, Cin didn't know *how* to have a life with Prince Lorenz.

Right now, all he knew he could claim with confidence was a week.

Twenty-Two

The journey home seemed to take a thousand hours, each stride of Cin's mount feeling as though it brought them one step back for every two forward. All the while, he could think of only two things: the feel of his chest in that very moment, flat yet unrestricted, and the equal parts hope and dread of his future. At this rate, by the time he returned home, he would have been missing for nearly twenty-four hours, so far as his family knew.

He wasn't certain how much he could push his mount—it was, despite its magic, still a beast made from living creatures, creatures who could tire, and then who knew what would happen to their magical form—so he let it choose its own pace, slower and slower as the day went on. Not that it mattered, he told himself. His stepmother would already be furious. He could imagine Manfred storming around, demanding of his siblings everything that Cin regularly provided, which Floy would refuse while Emma tried to step up, only to make matters worse instead of better.

Cin decided that if the house was still in one piece by the time he arrived, he'd be grateful. Louise could levy whatever anger she wanted on him—he'd take it all in exchange for the flatness of his new chest. Every time he remembered the slide of his hands across it, he felt giddy all over again. The moment he'd been free of the dark depths of the forest, he'd paused. With cautious fingers, he'd pressed at the spaces between his ribs.

No pain.

Not a spear, not even an ache, not even as he'd taken his fullest, deepest breath in years, laughing it back out with hands wrapped against his sides. It was a state he hadn't felt in years. His cackle had ended in a sob of joy, and he'd quickly stripped off his layers.

Beneath his undershirt, fresh, pale skin lay perfectly draped over two masculine curves of muscle; the nipples he'd once despised for their size and protrusion now sat perfect to each side of his chest, smaller and taut. He was *handsome*. It hadn't been important in the moment—he'd have accepted anything he'd been offered so long as he could climb and run and not worry about a binding igniting his latent pain, but this—this was a chest he'd be excited to show off to someone.

To someone in particular.

In his sleep-deprived delirium, Cin felt himself flush at the thought. Everything they'd done together had been hasty and clothed, but any entanglement where Cin stripped to the point of revealing that much of his bare skin would imply something more than fingers and mouths. Two weeks ago, that would have scared him—*yesterday*, that would have scared him, too, though he'd never have even imagined it possible.

But he'd been in Prince Lorenz's arms, had the prince give up more for him than Cin had any right to accept, and that kindness, that sacrifice, made the idea of opening his body for the prince— not simply in his fantasies, but in reality too—exhilarating instead of terrifying. Even if it meant nothing but a moment of pleasure...

That thought hurt, and Cin forced himself to push past it. Even if his deal—and his desire—kept him at the prince's side, he'd be no more destined for a partnership with Prince Lorenz than he had the night prior, or the weeks before that. The prince would marry, and it would not be to Cin.

It would be for the best. Cin would be carving out space for Prince Lorenz, pulling himself away from the family who was missing his presence at that very moment. His was already not a good or pious life, even without that selfishness.

He tried not to dwell on that as he passed out of the border forest, back though the strange towns and into those more and more familiar. By the time the Reinholz estate appeared on the horizon, the sun was twinkling its last. Cin's stomach groaned, reminding him just how many, *many* hours it had been since his last meal. God, he hoped *someone* had put food on for dinner.

His flock-creature shivered out of from beneath him, shaky and abrupt. He stumbled onto the path, barely finding his balance as his flock headed for the nearest trees: for the same sleep and food that Cin desperately needed. Only Lacey and Ragimund stayed, just long enough to nuzzle against Cin's neck before weakly flying off to join the others.

"Thank you," Cin whispered in their wake. Beneath his transformed bosom, his heart ached from joy. He could feel Perdition's little body still warm against his chest. She cooed softly, but when he tried to let her join the others, she barely managed to stand from within her sling, so he tucked her back against his chest and pulled his cloak over her.

Cin steeled himself and walked around to the back door.

The kitchen was dark. So dark, and cold, in fact, that at first it seemed as though no one had touched it since the night before. As Cin crept across the chilled stone, though, he passed by the hearth. A tiny whirl of ash streamed up from its edges. Cin stopped to press his fingers into the thin layer of soot and no pain sparked in his sides. There *had* been a fire here, one which must have consumed the remaining wood Cin had left the night prior, but no one had bothered to clean the remains after.

He turned, and his foot hit the solid side of the cook pot—left haphazardly on the ground. Cin grimaced. They had certainly *tried* to cook something in it, though by the coarse grim layered on the bottom, it hadn't gone well. No one had even bothered to soak it, either.

As he moved through the kitchen, it was like stepping into a haunted version of his life; into a house not quite his own, inhabited by a family he could recognize the shapes of, but not the faces. Grime on the counters, an apple core tossed to the floor, every surface cold and careless in the darkness. At this time of evening, the space would usually have been alive with Cin's post-meal preparations, a crackling fire dancing off his busy hands as he cleaned and prepped for the coming day.

Instead, there was a ghostly version of his home, disrespected and distressed.

At least they had tried, he wanted to tell himself. He wanted to, but somehow—somehow he couldn't. Not yet, not while his heart burned like a tiny fire had been born under it and his bones trembled from deep within. Right now, he was angry. Irrationally, uselessly angry.

Cin held his breath and moved into the house proper. Beneath the creak of the old wood, he could hear a whisper of his family's voices, growing ever clearer. Ever harsher. Making his way down the hall, he caught the flicker of very low flame reflecting from within the second parlor, and the haunting murmurs turned fully to frustrated hisses.

"You were the one who dropped it last!" Floy said.

Manfred managed to grind out his words in a snarl even worse on the ears than his usual. "And *I* put it *out*."

Somehow Louise matched him in tone and emotion without losing an ounce of her usual conceit. "Not before it burned a hole in my floor."

"I can—" Emma tried to insert, but every other voice snapped back a harsh *no*, in varying levels of anger and dismay.

The flickers of the hearth's tiny fire in the parlor sputtered to the sound of curses, then steadied. It had to be nearing embers now.

For one fleeting second, hope swelled in Cin's heart. Maybe now, now they understood how much Cin was worth. Not in Louise's back-handed way, but with genuine respect. He *was* holding their family together. They'd all known it to some degree, but now, perhaps, it had sunk in just how much effort and care and skill it took for Cin to do what he did for them. And if they could understand that *now*, then later, when he spent a little time each week at the castle...

But Cin stepped into the room and reality rushed back in.

"Cinder-Szule!" Louise's dramatic gasp of both Cin's given

names might have been mistaken for joyous surprise in the moment it took her face to transform. "Where in God's green earth have you *been*, child?"

Cin opened his mouth as Floy and Manfred both began to insert their own frustrations, but Louise wasn't finished. She spoke over them all, storming toward Cin with her skirt lifted in one white-knuckled fist, the flickering embers in the hearth casting eerie shadows across her features.

"You were given a responsibility! One you *claimed* you could be trusted to *handle*. Yet we return from the city to find the house locked, the fires dying—your poor brother had to break into our own home! Because you chose to go dallying somewhere!"

"He broke the window frame," Floy added, and Cin couldn't tell if it was a taunt at him or at Manfred.

It felt like neither, like nothing. Cin was just so tired of it all. Deep inside him, he knew his bones were trembling, his heart surging in a panicked rhythm, but his mind was elsewhere, untethered and... not unbothered, but one step removed from the bothers of his own body, like a nerve had been snapped from between them.

"I didn't intend to be gone so long," he said, and somehow he sounded the right amount of distressed, despite the slow, steady drone of his own inner voice. "I went to the woods, to see about magic for my chest and— And I got it. But it just took longer than I thought." A white lie, he realized, only after the words were out. But it was as close to the truth as his family was likely to understand.

"You left for magic?" Louise made a sound almost like a laugh. "Just thought, well, today seems a good day to run into the woods alone, without a word, and leave my siblings and parents to suffer!"

She stamped her foot.

From the darkness of the chair in the far corner, something shifted—not something, but someone, rising from the shadows, still half a ghost himself as he cleared his throat in a dry, swallow sound. "You could have died out there, been tricked into enslavement, or worse, and we'd not have known. Szule, my dear, were you not raised better than that?"

The weakness of his father's voice hit Cin first, not simply soft or uncertain, but tired and empty in a way Cin had not witnessed since his mother's death. As though he'd given up: given up on Cin.

Cin's throat twisted suddenly, a lump forming so thick and ugly he couldn't swallow it down. "I'm sorry," he whispered, and he was, truly—not for leaving, perhaps, but for *something*. He felt sorry: for the lives his family lived, for the desolate state of their hearts, for his own existence within their pointless little world. He wished things were different. For all of them, no matter how much he'd hated them for so long.

But for himself especially.

Louise scowled, pulling at her own fingers. "Not sorry enough yet."

With that, she raised her hand.

Cin felt the jolt before he registered the slap, and he stumbled, just slightly, just enough to feel like a fool for it. The sting spread across his cheek moments after, starting with a prickle and turning quickly to a burn. His jaw ached. He breathed in, trying to right himself, not simply physically, but mentally.

Louise held her hand like touching Cin had laid a curse on it. The whole room was watching him: Floy, their brow lifted, and

Manfred, smug as he'd have been if he'd landed the slap himself, and Father, his gaze so vacant he seemed not be there at all. Emma looked away, her cheeks nearly as red as Cin's must have been.

"Now," Louise said, pressing her shoulders back, her chin up. A serene expression cloaked her previous rage. "You will proceed to the kitchen for dinner, as all of us have yet to eat for the evening."

"The fire—" Manfred protested, but Louise cut him off with a hard look that made Cin wonder if this wasn't the first time some-one had been slapped that night.

"There will be a fire in everyone's hearth by the end of the night," she said, soft but unwavering. "You can have patience." She took one look around the room, at the staring eyes of her family, and clapped her hands. "Now!" she shouted, as though she'd given any-one a task to do but Cin.

As though the last twenty-four hours hadn't made it clear that no one but Cin was capable of any reasonable household task any-way.

He took a step back, but drew a breath, and before he could stop himself, he said, "They could come help me in the kitchen. Maybe if they were taught—"

"Then what?" Louise snapped. "We suffer through their incom-petence in the meantime? Do you *want* us to starve tonight?" She snorted. "You had your magic adventure; you're done. There's no reason you'll need to go tromping through the woods again."

Cin's hand went to his chest—his perfect, flat chest. The magic that had gone on there seemed like anything but some "tromp through the woods". Anything but worthy of dismissal. Anything but *this*. "Mother," Cin started to say, and he didn't know where the sentence was going—to beg, to plead, or to demand—but then it didn't matter.

Louise hit him again.

This time, Cin lost his balance entirely. The jolt, the pain—fresh on old—sent him stumbling to his hands and knees, his palms on the cold, hard wood of the parlor where its ruined rugs had been pulled back. He inhaled, half sob, half something worse. His fingers gripped at the floor, and the first two of his right hand dug in. The wood there was gritty. Dark. Ashen.

It must have been where Manfred had dropped the ember earlier. And now it was Cin whose skin it stained.

He could hear Louise hovering over him, her voice so low it seemed meant only for him.

"I should think now, of all times, you'd be inclined to listen more than you speak," she hissed. "You have no marriage arrangements, no apprenticeships, no money, no skill outside this house. There is nowhere for you to go but here."

Cin could not bear to lift his face toward her, lest he see something worse than his stepmother's wrath—his father, standing silently behind her, confused and disappointed.

Louise was right. Cin had no job or income, no offers of marriage—save for Dorthe's, and it did not feel right to bind her to himself merely to be free from his family. But he had one thing she still knew nothing about. He had the friendship of Prince Lorenz. And for one fiery second he almost spat that fact into her face.

But even if he stayed the prince's friend, that relationship would eventually be eclipsed by Lorenz's future partnership, his co-leader.

So Cin drew himself quietly to his feet, his head bowed, his eyes pressed closed to keep the misery from seeping out of them in liquid form. Tight and low he said, "I'll get the food ready."

His body strained with so much tension that he felt like one wrong move would snap him in half as he made his way back through the house. He seemed to have stood in the center of the dark kitchen for a thousand heartbeats before his mind flew back to him at the sound of timid footsteps behind him. For a second, his heart twisted—Father? But he knew it wasn't before he even turned.

Emma stood before him, her body so slight in the beam of moonlight that spilled in through the single kitchen window behind her. She stared at Cin, and he thought her throat bobbed, her eyes almost glistening. Waiting for *him* to reach out to *her*?

When Cin couldn't muster up the nerve, his baby sister shrugged, her lips twisting.

"You have a little..." She bundled the edge of her sleeve over her hand and wiped at the slapped side of Cin's face. A long smudge of darkness came off.

Cin shivered. So many years since he'd been the Cinder-child, covered in ash, made to do the same chores until he could show he was capable, responsible, only to have that responsibility trap him into them, and here he was, still stained in the soot of the hearths that kept him warm.

Still just Cinder-Szule.

He wanted to cry.

He wanted to watch his knife slip, unhindered, into flesh.

He wanted his only friend there with him as he did both.

He wanted...

He *wanted*.

Twenty-Three

Despite Cin's anger and grief, the grumbling in his stomach pushed him to keep moving.

He stoked a fire in the hearth. As he waited for the stove coals to heat, he peeled the final bundle of potatoes he'd harvested from the fading garden a few days prior, pulling them up by their black, frost-bitten stems to find barely-edible tubers beneath. When they were cooked through, he fed a few of the pieces to Perdition, who cooed her thanks before letting him tuck her back against his heart. It was still a wonder not to feel the sharp pain shooting through his ribs at every turn.

His chest: it was *his* chest, and there was not a moment since he'd taken his first breath against it that he worried it wouldn't be there for the next. But the lack of ache in his sides felt different. Like his body still expected to hurt, every motion prepared for a compromise with the pain.

Cin had not realized just how cautious every action he took had become: the energy he'd dedicated to approaching things from the right angle. Holding and cutting, pushing and pulling—everything felt different now, like he could be careless after so many years of not realizing he was caring in the first place.

He threw the basil and garlic into the pot whole and sliced the onion in quarters, nearly taking his finger off with it as he sped up the motions beyond what his ribs would normally permit. The end result wasn't fit for a prince, or even the original inhabitants of the Reinholz estate, but it would fill their stomachs just fine.

It filled Cin's, at least, and only Floy grumbled about the flavor of the broth, Emma and Manfred both slurping down their entire bowls in a feverish haze while Louise snapped at them for their manners and Cin's father diligently stared into his own soup between every slow bite. They left Cin to clean the dishes after, yawning their way back into the now-cold second parlor. Cin yawned too as he moved the soup off the stove.

From down the hall, Floy shouted at him to tend their hearth.

One of his hands slipped. The towels that padded them shifted as he struggled to catch the large pot, shoving it back into place. The side of his thumb stung, and he shoved it absently against his tongue. The taste of ash filled his mouth.

"Any time now!" Louise called, echoing the demands of the rest of Cin's family.

His hands shook as he lit one hearth after another, each fire taking longer to coax into something capable of warding against the late autumn chill. His hands felt raw by the end. It was all he could do to drag himself to the kitchen hearth. The room was snug now, at least, the embers still hot. He was too tired to wipe the ash that had crept forth from the fire as he bundled his cloak and lay across the warm stone.

A foot immediately prodded him in the side.

"Cinder," Louise snapped, no "child" tagged gently onto the end to soften the blow. "You have a room of your own! One not covered in *ashes*."

Cin sat up groggily. "There's still a draft."

Louise only gave him a firm kick in the thigh. "How do you think we lived while you were off gallivanting on your little adventure? At least *you'll* have a fire. Go!" She kicked again.

Cin grunted as he stood. His attention slipped over the embers, still bright and hot in the hearth, and he thought of what it might be like to see one spill out of its stone home, to watch as their world went up in flame. But that would take Cin with it. If he was going to burn his world to the ground, he refused to go up in the inferno. Not now that he had something to live for.

"Fine," he muttered to Louise, and stumbled miserably toward the hall, his cloak bunched in his arms.

She called after him, "And clean yourself tomorrow before you tend the chores! You're as filthy as a damn whore."

The rest of the week went little better. If Cin had any hope that his family would get over his absence quickly, it was dashed with each new demand and pointless badgering. Only Emma didn't harass Cin. Whenever the rest of their family grew too restless and aggressive, she seemed to vanish, sneaking away in her nightgown for hours at a time, her hair a mess and her knuckles raw with cold.

Caring for her every inadequacy had always annoyed Cin, but somehow this was far worse. It felt as though the only light in his home life had been extinguished, turning to a ghostly presence that fled from the horrors that surrounded him. And, when Cin had the courage to admit it to himself, being abandoned by Emma hurt. It wasn't as though she'd have been able to change the rest of their family's treatment, but he had not realized how much having her tiny spark of affection had made everything else feel bearable. Like he could be doing this all for her.

He *had* been doing it all for her.

Cin choked on the thought through the end of the week, and all Saturday morning as he tromped across the house trying desperately to get enough done that he could run into town before his family left for the final ball. Louise claimed that Father would be attending with her, despite how little interest he seemed to show in it. He seemed already to be plotting his next trip in his mind.

He'd sat at the table that morning long after breakfast had been cleared, staring out the window into the distance. Every attempt Cin had made to speak with him had ended with one word: not sharp, not short, just detached.

Was he still hungry?—*No*, soft, unconcerned.

What had he heard of the balls?—A shrug, his gaze unmoving.

Was his trip successful?—*Enough*, spoken as though he was dreaming of living it again.

For once, Cin almost—*almost*—didn't blame him. He didn't want to be there any more than his father did. But unlike his father, Cin had no easy way out, not for any longer than a half a day at least.

The one good sign of the week was watching Perdition heal.

She seemed more chipper by the day, hopping around Cin's drafty room, where a crack he'd left in the window allowed her flock-mates access. They brought her bugs and seeds to complement the vegetable and boiled potatoes that Cin had been sneaking her from his own meals, and she'd made a little nest for herself in the fabric of his old binding. Despite her improved energy and enthusiasm, she had not attempted to fly again, one of her wings tucked in awkwardly even when she made a point to stretch and flap the other.

He worried at what that meant—both now and for her future—but regardless of whether the wing healed, Cin was determined to be there for her, just as her little flock had been there for him.

When he left with one of the horses on Saturday morning, he turned east to loop around, past the home of the woman he'd watched cry behind her well far too many times already, whispering an apology to Prince Lorenz's kind heart as he did. However much he hated it, he was still this: still a menace, turning the villains into victims.

He found the house dark, though—both front and back doors locked and the horse and wagon gone from the barn. He hoped that meant the woman had left for good, but more likely the couple were just out visiting friends or family for the day. If her husband still gave her that decency.

In town, Cin tried his best to ignore the ball gossip. Everyone had a favorite for the prince's hand—none of them knowing yet that it wouldn't be his choice at all. Few truly thought their future queen might be Floy, though every mention of his sibling's name still made

Cin's stomach twist. Worse though, were those who were placing all their bets on the mysterious feathered seducer. There were so many—too many—and Cin swore he heard whispers of the Plumed Menace within some of their giddy conversations.

At least none of them seemed to notice him, not as the prince's friend, much less as their notorious killer. Dorthe waved to him when he passed her on the street, but most of the town couldn't even seem to place him as Cinder-Szule, even when they should have, when he'd seen them every week for years, knew their names and lives and loves. Or maybe they did recognize him, and they simply didn't care to know him beyond that. No one had ever seemed to.

Except Emma.

And Lorenz.

Somehow, he seemed doomed to lose one for the other.

By the time he'd finished his rounds, the supply pack he'd mounted on the horse was barely any heavier. A little flour, a block of cheese, a few of the vegetables he'd traded for their potatoes, a couple of jars of jam that would have to last them half the winter if Father's next venture didn't bring in something more substantial, and an embroidery needle for Floy, to replace the one Manfred had broken earlier that week—whether by accident or purposefully, Cin still wasn't sure.

The only reason Cin was picking up the new one at all was because Floy had insisted there was no way they could go without the needle for another Sunday. Which made Cin particularly confused when, on his way through the main square, he spotted Floy across the street. Confused, then *annoyed,* then confused again as Floy glanced both ways before slipping down the alley past the town's main chapel, the buildings now constructed so tightly around it that its little graveyard out back barely saw the sun.

Cin had meant to pause in the square's high place for his usual glimpse at the castle's towers—even having visited them couldn't remove the superstition—but he sent up a hasty prayer for God not to frown on him as he redirected toward the chapel instead.

He kept his distance as he followed Floy around the far side of the chapel, turning right, then left, then right again. When he came back out onto the next main road though, they had vanished. Into a house? Down a side street? He couldn't know for certain.

Why Floy had come to town in the first place... Cin wasn't sure what to make of it. He didn't have much time to dwell on that, though, as someone barged out of the house around the corner in front of him.

He recognized her instantly, tears streaming down her cheeks with the same ferocity as they had on all the days she'd hid behind her well. Her husband stormed after her. Cin's hand went to the knife at his back, instinct driving the motion before he could even piece together a useful thought, and he shifted his mount into the shadows of the home's outer wall where it met the empty city street.

Before Cin could act, a second woman stormed after them both.

The husband turned to her, his voice low and sharp. "Olinda has had enough of your cruelty."

"She was our sister before she was ever your wife!" the new woman snapped back. She shoved around him and grabbed onto Olinda, her hand clamping onto her sister's wrist. "Do not listen to him. We told you not to marry a damned Falchovarian! Can't you see how he's trying to turn you against us—against your own *family*."

The words seemed so tender, so caring, but Cin could see the way they tore into Olinda, just as the woman's fingernails tore into Olinda's wrist—tore the same cruel lines Cin had attributed to her husband.

Cin's understanding of the situation shifted rapidly, recounting everything he'd seen in a new light. The man he'd assumed was the villain stood to one side awkwardly, anxiously, looking like he wanted to pull his wife and her sister apart, but didn't think he had the right. He'd already said all he could to try to convince Olinda not to keep coming back here—perhaps too loudly and messily, but out of love nonetheless. The way he was watching Olinda then, Cin could see that affection coursing through his being.

"Linny," he begged, offering her a hand, as though by taking it, he could finally free her from this burden.

Olinda's fingers twitched toward his, but her sister grabbed her other hand too, yanking at her.

"You cannot leave me here to care for Father alone," she hissed. "We are your *blood*."

She had barely spoken when Olinda jerked back, tearing her wrists free. "No!"

By the shock on her sister's face, it seemed it was the first time she'd ever done so. "No..?"

"I don't *care* what you say." Olinda took a step back, then away, gripping onto her husband's hands, but her ire stayed fixed on her sister. "You and Father have needed too much of me, for too long, and I— I need Theobold now. He built me a garden, he gives me space to read, he leaves me be when I need it. He did not turn me against you. You did that all yourself."

Her sister sputtered, her cheeks reddening, but Olinda finally turned her attention to her husband as he whispered, "Can we go home?"

"Please," she replied.

Together, they turned away from the fuming sister.

Her face contorted. She spun and stormed back into the house. But she didn't close the door.

Cin's gut twisted. He dismounted, one hand still on the hilt of his blade, and when the woman barreled back out of her home with a butcher's knife in hand, he was already there, slipping in behind her. But for once, he couldn't bring himself to drive metal into flesh, couldn't bear to watch the blood pool over his hands.

His mind rang with a voice, calling him to be *good*. This time it wasn't his mother's, though; it was Prince Lorenz, cupping the side of his face, telling him he already was. Cin still couldn't believe that, but he knew what he did believe: that sometimes the victims weren't good or gentle and their villains were complicated. And that meant so too was their justice.

A blade speared deep in this villain—*his victim's*—throat would be too simple.

Cin pressed it there heavily instead, holding her from behind.

"I would not do that if I were you," he hissed. "You are not worthy to be her sister. Forget about her. Or I will not forget about you."

Olinda and her husband did not once look back.

For a heartbeat, Cin wanted the happy couple to be him with his prince so badly he thought he might trade the whole world for it. Reality pulled him from the dream, though, as the back of his neck prickled with a tense, anxious sensation unlike anything he'd felt in town before. It was so akin to what he'd felt stepping into a monster's lair that it took him a moment to recognize it as the feeling of being watched.

But when he glanced behind him, no one was there.

Twenty-Four

When Cin reached home, Floy had already returned, the family's other horse resting in the barn, and from what Cin could tell, it seemed everyone was preparing for the ball.

He should have been preparing as well—prepping the carriage, setting up the hearths for his quick return, finishing the midday meal—but he was distracted, mind and body, by visions of Olinda. There was a yearning behind the thoughts, not sexual or romantic or even platonic, but deep and terrible and beautiful. She ran through his thoughts again and again: the way she'd pulled back from her sister's clutches and the determination in her voice when she'd denied their grip on her, not simply the physical hold her sister had taken, but the nails she'd dug into Olinda's very life and love. The sight of her walking away, hand in hand with her husband.

Free.

Not free from turmoil, not free from work—there was plenty of that at their own home, Cin knew, and Theobold was not perfect, despite his obvious love for his wife—but free to take on those tasks with dignity and joy. Life was difficult outside Prince Lorenz's beautiful castle, more than ever amidst the hardships of their seemingly endless famine; Cin hadn't lied to him about that when he'd stood in this same place, staring down his home. But there had still been a lie in there somewhere... He could feel it now, deep in his soul.

He just didn't know what to do with it yet.

Slowly, thoughtfully, he set to work in the kitchen, letting himself linger in the freedom he did have: the lack of pain between his ribs. Already he felt he was forgetting what it had been like to live around that tension, his body quickly sliding back into rhythms he thought he'd forgotten now that he'd had time to adjust. Louise seemed not to notice in the slightest when she bustled into the kitchen, snapping for Cin to help with her hair.

As he slid in the final pin, she dusted herself off, like Cin's nearness might have left her ashen. "You'll have the hearths lit upon our arrival this time?" she said, more accusation than question.

It would be easy to say yes. To wait for his family to leave, and race past them. Spend his little allotment of time with the prince while still pretending to be the good and pious child.

But Cin wanted to be Olinda. He wanted to hold the hand of the man he loved and walk away from everything else, every cruel word and responsibility. That wasn't an option for him, not so long as he would be juggling caring for Emma, upholding the commitment his mother had placed on him, with his affection for Lorenz. He could still take something of Olinda's courage, though. Possibly, he could take *enough*.

"I thought Father could stay in my place," Cin said, feeling every muscle in his body tighten for the fight. "He has no interest in the ball, and might appreciate an evening by the fire."

Louise's expression wrinkled like she'd tasted something sour.

"You father has been on the road making the coin we need to eat, not flouncing off in the woods. He deserves to enjoy this ball far more than someone who abandoned their responsibilities and family for *days*."

"*A* day," Cin corrected, his heart slamming into his ribs even as the dagger of a rebuttal snapped out of him. "I was gone *one* day. This estate should be able to survive without me for far longer."

As Cin spoke, Floy slipped into the room, leaning against the wall with their eyes half-closed, watching Cin and Louise coolly. They must have inferred the context of the argument, because they interjected a scoff. "What would *you* do at a ball, Cinder?"

Cin tipped his chin up and looked them dead in the eye. "Dance with the prince."

Floy looked unamused. They lifted an eyebrow. "You? You can't dance."

"You're right, I couldn't," Cin admitted, heat growing inside his chest, "because I'm the one always here, always caring for the house while you and Manfred and Emma run off to live your lives." He could feel his lips curl in an expression so unlike him. "But I *can* dance now. Prince Lorenz taught me."

Floy stared at Cin, blinking as though putting together a series of facts in their head, but Louise merely barged back into the conversation. "Don't lie to us—"

"You take long enough in your carriage that it has been easy to slip around you." He'd thought confessing it would mean giving something up, but instead it felt like taking something that was rightfully his. Louise may have thought she was successfully lying to Cin's face, telling him that the ball wasn't worth it, that he could never possibly do the housework and still enjoy the night out, yet here he'd been the one keeping secrets from her, stealing back all that she'd tried to hide away from him.

"You really danced with the prince?" Floy asked, softly, the jealousy clear on their face, and their mind seemed to be tearing through the possibilities, landing on the truth they'd nearly stumbled upon time and again.

Cin leaned toward them, lowering his voice to a whisper, and he could feel the smirk spreading across his face. This face the prince had kissed. "I danced with him in the ballroom, and I fucked him in the dovecote."

The resentful fury that took over Floy's expression was priceless.

Louise spun around in a frantic flurry, charging into the hall with her skirt in one hand. "Penrod! Tell your child how preposterous he is being!" She continued shouting as she rushed down the hall to where Cin's father sat in the first parlor, Cin following sharp on her heels. "All the times I told you the house was being cared for by Cinder, he has been lying, sneaking about, willfully abandoning his responsibilities—"

"Don't you see, I can tend the house and still go to the ball—I've done it most nights already!" If anyone could understand, make Louise see sense, surely—

But Cin's father didn't even look up from the newspaper he'd borrowed from Floy. "Listen to your mother, Szule."

"See," Louise snapped, looking like that was enough to win the argument. It always would have been before, the flat distance of Penrod's tone pulling up Cin's grief, his birth mother's words echoing in his mind behind every one of his stepmother's: *be good, be pious.*

But goodness was more complicated than Cin had assumed, and piety ineffectual. He scowled, meeting Louise's gaze with barely a flinch before his spine turned steely. "I am not yours to command. I am going to that ball tonight, and if you'd like all of your personal hearths lit when I return, you'd best not try to stop me."

Louise gasped. "You are most certainly not!" she sputtered, lunging toward Cin like she was going to grab him. She was larger than Cin—though certainly not stronger—and Cin stepped back quicker than she could adjust, slipping out of her way to grab the doorknob of the front door.

Floy leaned in the doorway to the parlor, their arms crossed, glaring daggers. Manfred peered curiously over their shoulder. Cin ignored them both, opening the door and walking out into the yard. A shiver ran through him, his limbs light and his heart pounding, pounding like it always had been, only he could finally feel it. His flock swarmed around him, scooping him up from below and carrying him forward, toward his prince.

Behind him, Louise shouted at Manfred and Floy to stop Cin, but they were both too slow. Cin galloped his flock-creature out of the yard, leaving his family behind.

God's smile, wherever it might be hiding from Cin, was nothing compared to the grin on his own face.

At the front gates of the castle, the watch members barely glanced at Cin before waving him in. No soldiers came tearing around the corner to arrest him, though a fair number of the crown's watch still manned an absurd number of posts, one person standing every three strides down the whole length of the castle's entrance, as if they feared the prince himself might try to flee down it. They outnumbered the guests three to one now. It seemed, whether by Prince Lorenz's request or his parents', that the list had been cut down to the final few. Or, the final few plus Cin, anyway.

He'd glanced at the list as he passed, skimming just long enough to spot Floy's name near the bottom. A short list, but still not lacking the one person Cin wished least to see. At least the rest of his family would be absent, and with the plethora of watch members lingering about, there was little harm Floy could cause to Cin's person that wouldn't be noticed and dealt with immediately.

To accommodate the change in attendance, the sides of the ballroom had been filled with other eccentricities, among them couches and potted plants, birdcages, a fountain that had to be magic.

It was easy for him to spot Prince Lorenz amongst the dozen or so remaining guests, his bright smile and gentle laughter lighting up the space all around him more clearly now that there wasn't a throng of onlookers to drown him out. Cin thought he recognized a few of the remaining contenders for the prince's hand: a shallow but kind lord a decade older than Prince Lorenz, the studious son of a wealthy business man, a pair of twins whose genders and identities Cin couldn't tell apart but who seemed equally sharp-witted and rational, and the woman who had been fucking the prince the day Cin met him—an esteemed poet, he'd learned since.

They were all logical choices for the new co-ruler of Hallin. Cin didn't—couldn't—hate them for being here, for being selected as the best-of-the-best. They *were* the best-of-the-best, after all. But that didn't mean Cin wanted to stand to the side for the rest of Prince Lorenz's life, watching them take over his time, his energy, his bed.

What made it all the worse, though, was that neither, it seemed, did his prince.

As he drew closer, Cin could see the shift in Prince Lorenz's attention, the slipping away of the chivalry and arrogance and poise into a soft, bright smile. His eyes seemed to twinkle as he broke away from his conversation with the other guests to meet Cin halfway, both his arms outstretched towards him. He was such a joy to look at that Cin almost didn't catch the frustrated and jealous glances from the guests Prince Lorenz had abandoned.

"My dove," the prince whispered, taking both of Cin's hands in his. "I'm glad you're here. After you spoke of magic last week..."

It felt as though a flush went through Cin's chest at the idea of Prince Lorenz thinking of him at the very moment he'd stood before the frog prince. He pulled Prince Lorenz a little closer, smiling as he teased, "Did you worry for me?"

"I..." Prince Lorenz's gaze dropped, and he released one of Cin's hands, his fingers pressing against his heart in a now-familiar way. Cautiously, Cin lifted his own fingers to set them atop the back of the prince's hand.

"What is it?" Cin asked.

Prince Lorenz shook his head, his smile flashing back into place.

"As I said, I'm just glad you're here." He pulled Cin to him, maneuvering them both into the small dancing space that remained in the large ballroom. The musicians rolled into a new song just for them.

Already, Cin could feel the other guests' eyes boring into him, and the hour was still early enough that new additions were coming through the doors as they danced. He took a deep breath, reminding himself of what it felt like to have sought after what he wanted, what he knew was right for him—no pain, no fear. In its place was the joy that had touched him at the Frog Prince's request: to care for his Lorenz.

He wanted *that*, too.

Cin inhaled again, and when he released it, he let himself say the words. "I could always keep being here? I know the parameters I dictated at the beginning of this, but I'd like to continue seeing you, after tonight, in whatever capacity you'll have me. I don't want you to become a distant memory."

The prince's face lit up, whatever tension his original smile had masked fading away so quickly that it felt unreal after. "Yes!" He laughed. "I will do whatever you need—make a space for you here, or come to you in Darmburg—anything. Our friendship is the most important part of my life."

Friendship. That was all it would be. All it could be. Even if there was a world where the kind of friendship they had, deep and true and lustful, could be forged into a partnership—even a marriage—there would still be no place at Prince Lorenz's side for the Plumed Menace. And the idea of being a king of Hallin someday... Cin wasn't sure he could even envision that, much less live it. Part of him was still thinking of the tasks he'd need to complete when he returned home.

The prince spun Cin around before pulling him back in close. His breath on Cin's ear was delicious. "I must ask, though," he said, his voice beaming with delight, "what changed?"

Cin could have told him of the Frog Prince's bargain, but now, basking in the prince's joy and the lightness of his own heart, he knew that had merely been the crack he'd needed to open himself up to the idea, not the reason for it. "I'd always yearned to," he admitted, heat pooling in his cheeks despite everything he'd done to stand up for himself already that day. "But my family wouldn't have approved it. They never wanted me here. All this time, they've thought that I've been home, tending the house, while they're in the city for the weekly balls. When I finally told them I'd been here, all along..."

It broke my stepmother's heart, Cin might have once said, and to some degree he'd have believed it, even if that heartbreak was purely selfish, pushing Cin to prove his own dependability and trust tenfold. But now what he saw in his memories was not Louise's devastation or his father's empty sadness or his siblings' jealousy, but wrath. Reassertions of control. Hands on wrists. Nails and slaps and deep, unhealing wounds.

Cin hadn't wished for his family to see him here, because he hadn't wished for his family to see *him*.

If wedding rings could not go on invisible hands, perhaps neither could chains.

Horror hollowed out Prince Lorenz's expression, and he seemed to miss a beat in the dance, barely picking it back up in time to swing

Cin into the next move. "After all the work you do for them, they wouldn't even let you…" He made a choking noise. "My dove, my— my Cinder-Ella, that is tyrannical! Abominable! You deserve admiration, respect, *love* for all you do for them, not… Not *this*."

"I believed they only wanted me at home because no one else can tend it well," Cin said, and stopped as a fresh kind of pain spread through his chest, not the deep hurt he'd lived with for years, but a fire, hot and angry.

There was so much more to their mistreatment—Cin had seen it first-hand, as Louise refused to even consider the thought that Cin could both enjoy the ball and tend the house, or that he could teach any one of his siblings to help. Perhaps not born of outright malevolence—if Manfred or Emma had been a little more skilled and Cin a little less, perhaps it would have truly been one of them in his place, always pushed into the work, always expected to carry the burden. But it hadn't been.

It had been Cin. The Cinder-whore, with the ashes of his family's sins smeared across his cheek.

How the hell had he never seen this?

Cin hadn't realized a tear had slipped free from the corner of his eye until Prince Lorenz wiped it aside, cupping Cin's cheek after, his gaze so soft for such an enraged expression. His thumb ran across the very place where soot had smeared six days prior. "If they don't treat you as you deserve, you need never return there. You have a home here, a family here, whenever you need it."

It was the kindest offer Cin had ever been given, and he wanted to cry all the more for it—for the beautiful gesture as much as his inability to ever accept. Because regardless of whether the prince knew what he was asking, for Cin to live with him, in the castle, sur-rounded by the crown's watch, he'd have to give up the Plumed Menace, settle for a quiet, secluded life, watching the prince live out his with someone else.

Cin thought that would kill him just as surely as living under his family's thumb was.

"Thank you," he whispered, trying to keep the sadness out of his voice. "You know one of my siblings is still in the running for your hand? They'll likely be here soon."

"Which one are they?" Prince Lorenz all but demanded. "I'll tell the guards to cross them out!"

The thought made Cin momentarily happy, but he did have to return home after this, still. He shook his head. "Don't. It'll be just as delicious to see their face when they watch you and I dance."

"Then dance the whole night we shall." The prince laughed, add-ing an extra flourish into his next move. "But please do tell me their name. If they are one of my parent's favored..."

Cin wanted to sink into the floor as he said, "Floy Reinholz."

Prince Lorenz breathed out a sigh so relieved that Cin's anxiety instantly lifted. "They've not even been brought up," the prince said. "I think they've only remained on the list this week to give the impression that we've included those from beyond the city so that it seems less inevitable when they select a candidate they've known for years. As valiant as their intentions were in inviting the whole of the kingdom to my coerced marriage, they still fear the thought of a stranger within their home."

That meant Cin had never been an option either. It hurt more than it should have—but exactly as much as he knew it would. More and more, the thought of someone else with his prince was sharply painful where it had been more an aching frustration before.

"Floy, though?" Prince Lorenz made a face. "My God, aren't they nearly intolerable!"

Cin suspected that the prince was dramatizing things for Cin's pleasure, but he smiled anyway. "Truly the worst. Though I imagine they put on a decent mask for you."

"How much of a mask can you don if your only conversation starter is scientific classifications of flying animals?" Prince Lorenz shook his head in mock disgust, though after a moment he looked sheepish, the impenetrable depths of his gaze seeming to part for Cin to view the full breadth of his curious emotions. "It was actually an interesting topic, I can't lie." His lips quirked. "If only Floy talked more about pigeons, I might have been seduced."

Cin slid his arms around the prince's waist, his gaze landing pointedly on Prince Lorenz's mouth. "Is that the only reason you're here with me, then? It's all down to the pigeons..."

"You do know a fair bit about one particular winged fowl," the prince confirmed, leaning closer as he wrapped the arm on Cin's hip firmly around his back. His lips brushed Cin's, but instead of kissing, he spoke, ever so gently. "It's one of the many, many aspects of you which fascinate me."

Prince Lorenz pulled Cin's upper lip between his, then Cin's lower, breathing into them between his gentle sucking. Cin could manage nothing but to release that air in a sigh, cradling the prince's lower back in one hand. There were people watching, he knew, people jealous of him, hating him for this, even, but somehow that made it all the more delicious.

For once, Cin was the one whose life everyone else wanted.

He lay his head onto the prince's shoulder after, swaying absent-mindedly to the music.

"Truly, though," the prince said, solemn and soft, "if my parents lose their minds and select Floy as my partner, I swear on my cold and bound heart that I will throw myself off the dovecote tower before I submit to marrying them. I would never subject you to such a thing."

Strangely, the thought of watching anyone marry the prince felt just as terrible in that moment, but Cin covered his flash of despair with a snort. "Don't you dare subject me to your untimely demise either." He kissed the prince gently on the cheek before snuggling back against him. "At least, not unless you're taking me with you."

Prince Lorenz hummed sadly. "How tragic that would be..."

The two of them together was already tragic, though, Cin knew—whether it had hit Lorenz or not, Cin was certain he'd not emerge from the highs of their free-falling relationship unscathed. And perhaps a part of him wanted no one in their vicinity to be un-touched by that. He drew back, both hands finding Prince Lorenz's, and held on tightly.

Through the entrance hall, Floy emerged, their stance tight and their expression already clouded by jealousy, yet somehow the sight of them couldn't dampen Cin's desires in the slightest. "Though we'll still see each other, this may be our last night like... like this," Cin told the prince. "I want to go out in a blaze of glory with you. Before you give your hand to another, I want them all to know it was me you chose first."

"Well, isn't that serendipitous?" The prince outright simpered.

"Because I want the entire kingdom to know that you are the most magnificent creature to ever breathe."

For what felt like hours, Cin was barely ever out of the prince's reach, not from the delicacies they slipped each other, to the turns Prince Lorenz took Cin in across the dance floor. It was all things they had done during previous ball weeks, but it felt different this time. No longer a first, but something better. Something fuller. Where an unfathomable man had been six weeks before, there was now a friend and lover; sometimes still mysterious, but just as often Cin found he could spot the emotion beneath the prince's mask of charm, and predict his responses in seamless rhythm. They flowed together, enthralled still, but now also in tune.

And the whole room noticed.

Where there had been rumors before, now there were facts: jealousy and defeat, some guests turning angry while others slipped out or faded into the corners. The woman Prince Lorenz had been with on the balcony the first ball night tried to steal him away for a dance, only to be graciously turned down. Her neck reddened from the strength of her blush and she stormed off into the garden. One of the twins left to console her.

All the while that Cin and the prince moved through the room, amusing themselves in every way they could think to, he kept an eye on his sibling. Floy was watchful as well, their gaze always turned toward Prince Lorenz. Toward Cin. He could only spot their resentment in the tiniest of twitches and the way they kept pushing forward to try to speak with the prince, only to be ignored as he wrapped his arm around Cin and laughed at some joke he pretended Cin had whispered to him. Their growing frustration was enough to make Cin giddy, though.

It served Floy right to feel less desired, for once. Less esteemed, and exalted. Without their mother to hoist them onto a pedestal, perhaps they were realizing that they were just a person, like any other—no more or less above the drudgeries of life. Cin had as much right to a beautiful party and an attentive lover as they did.

And Floy was not the only one upset by that.

Who does this arrogant seducer think he is? the other guests whispered. *Lower class, is he? But then it has to be magic that makes his outfit so fine... Would Prince Lorenz truly put his kingdom in this stranger's hands? The prince is a rake, surely, but regardless of who he sleeps with, he'll choose a competent marriage partner, right?* Even Floy was saying it.

Cin was certain they all knew he could hear them; they simply didn't care anymore. There was no hiding their frustration every time Prince Lorenz leaned in to kiss Cin's neck, or whisper in his ear, or wrap his hands around Cin's back.

As the night grew long and it seemed there was no intention to bring the ball to a close, Cin could feel Prince Lorenz's presence more and more keenly. Every touch, every whisper, every laugh—it left Cin more and more breathless. And as the time ticked away, he began to think less and less of those around them, one of whom was destined to spend the rest of their life with the prince, and more of all that he hadn't gotten to do with Lorenz. His Lorenz. His prince.

Whatever the dawn might alter for their continued friendship, he was not leaving here without knowing every last mystery that Prince Lorenz had to offer him. He needed, too, to know when and where and how they'd keep seeing each other.

With the last step of a minuet coming to a close, Cin slid closer to his prince, letting his hand wander down to the small of the prince's back. "This has been lovely, Your Highness, but a proper blaze burns beyond the ballroom, does it not?"

Prince Lorenz glanced at the guests around them, then the servants and guards beyond that. "With the announcement of my partner impending, we may need to get creative in our absconding." His expression grew smug and he leaned in. "It's a good thing I'm acquainted with a man who can climb just about anything."

Cin mirrored his look. "I certainly can." Most especially now, with his chest freed of the bindings it had once demanded and his ribs released of the pain that had infiltrated even their former intimacy. He wove his fingers through the prince's, and squeezed. "Let's go climbing then, shall we?"

And as Cin walked away from the dance floor, hand in hand with the prince, he pretended for a moment that he could be just like Olinda.

Twenty-Five

As Prince Lorenz drew Cin toward the gardens, three of the other guests tried their best to interject, even the reluctant academic pressing forward to wave awkwardly for attention, but Cin's prince gave them all a devilish smile.

With his free hand, he snatched the nearest guest's, kissing it quickly then all but pushing her away as he shouted, "Patience! I'll see one of you in bed for the rest of your days!"

The statement stung, but then the mask of flirtation with which Prince Lorenz said it dropped off the prince's face the moment he turned toward the darkness of the garden, and Cin felt pained for them both.

The prince looked to Cin worriedly, "You know I don't mean that?"

"You're a rake, what can I expect?" Cin teased, but when it landed no better for Prince Lorenz than his own heart, he gave the prince's hand a reassuring squeeze. "Tell me when we're free of them."

Prince Lorenz looked relieved. How peculiar, that a man so brazen with his philandering would be so desirous of a chance to explain himself. He had been the one to choose this mask for himself, and yet…

Cin put the thought aside for the moment as Prince Lorenz pulled him to the right edge of the patio where it surpassed the bounds of the ballroom within, up against the castle where a bench pressed to the wall. Just above them to their left, the room had a tiny balcony.

Guests were already flowing out of the garden doors, a steady stream of crown's watch casually slipping along the outside of their mass. Cin could see a few more along the garden's periphery, servants walking between. It seemed the whole space was slowly being lit. They'd have to hurry.

Prince Lorenz glanced to the tiny balcony. "Can you?"

Cin didn't wait for him to finish. He scurried up the wall, the magic of his shoes adding support as he paused halfway, holding to the balcony with one hand and pulling the prince up with the other. It was sloppy work, but Prince Lorenz managed to slot his foot atop Cin's for long enough to use Cin's body as an extra handhold, dragging himself onto the balcony. Cin followed with far more ease.

The prince was panting, but he smiled as he stumbled through the balcony doors. "Those magic shoes of yours, they don't also give you that strength, do they?"

"They're sturdy, I suppose, and they won't size to anyone else's feet, but that is where their magic ends, I'm afraid." He felt proud of himself as he said it. It was an odd sensation—the satisfaction in sharing something he'd used thus far in ways meant never to be known by anyone. But here his prince was, knowing them. Knowing Cin. And admiring. Cin grinned. "I climbed the ballroom balcony the first night without them."

"You're a wonder," Prince Lorenz said, and kissed him.

It was a fleeting peck, and he took Cin's hand again just after, guiding him quickly through the room—a parlor of sorts—and out, down the hall, moving away from the ballroom. Cin could hear commotion coming from elsewhere in the castle, but Prince Lorenz seemed adept at avoiding it, taking Cin through servant corridors and into barely touched rooms that seemed they'd once been elegant before their contents had been stripped out. It seemed even the royalty were not unaffected by the ongoing famine, whatever their current series of balls tried to claim.

As they moved, Cin finally broached the question the prince had seemed to so want to answer in the garden. "Why do you flirt with them?"

Prince Lorenz grimaced. "I don't know," he said, then groaned. "It's who I'm supposed to be—the rake. I suppose it's the one skill I truly possess? I can't lead, and I can't negotiate for peace, and I can't give grand speeches that inspire a kingdom, but I can look one person—or two or three—in the eye and tell them what they want to hear about themselves. Make them trust me, trust that I'll please them in the moment, at least, and then... well, usually I *do* that. Only now that feels like it would be a betrayal to you." He looked lost, his gaze distant.

Cin wished he could tell the prince that it wouldn't be a betrayal when he finally jumped in bed with his future partner. He should do his best to love them, if he was to be trapped with them for the rest of his life. Cin would still be there, loving him in the ways that he could. They could both be happy.

But Cin didn't believe that.

"If I cared at all for my country," Prince Lorenz continued, shaking his head, "I should be at my own ball, using the skills I do have to find the person who can govern in my place, and I cannot even manage that."

Cin raised his brow. "Are you so certain you need someone? Leading, negotiating, inspiring—none of those sound far off from what you're already doing."

The prince scoffed, but he looked a little less distraught after. "Are you saying I should hold an orgy with the whole kingdom?"

"If you wanted to scandalize us all, that would be better served by making your shirtless statues also trouserless." Cin smirked.

"You know actually, I like that idea. I'll have a special one placed just across the road from your bedroom window..."

"You're still dodging the point," Cin reminded him.

"The point of what? That I should be as capable as my brother and parents, and yet my only decent quality is getting myself into people's pants?"

"You get people to look at you, to trust you. You connect with them." He could see the prince already opening his mouth, but Cin cut him off, "And not *just* those you sleep with. You have rapport with those who serve in the castle and guard it—don't deny that."

"Why would I?" Prince Lorenz held up one hand. "They're lovely people. I'm honored to call so many of them friends. But I cannot lead by making friends with the whole of Hallin."

"And," Cin continued as if he hadn't objected, "you convinced your parents to let me go free, to let us stay friends, even."

"They're my *parents*."

"They are the *queen and king* of Hallin."

Prince Lorenz scoffed. As he did, the sound of annoyed voices echoed from further down the hallway, and he pulled Cin to the side, through a door into an unused suite with sheets draping the furniture. By the sprawling room set up and attached servant chamber, Cin guessed they were nearing the living quarters of the royals themselves. Prince Lorenz seemed not to care, pacing the length of the room almost mindlessly before Cin caught up to him, sliding an arm through his to pull him to a stop.

"Why does it hurt you to think you might be able to put the same skill you employ with your sexual conquests to use in other ways? Or that you already are?"

The prince shook his head, but he looked away. His voice was low when he finally spoke again, his soul seeming adrift on a sea of confusion. "As punishment for last week, my parents assigned me to meet with the locals in council—to hear grievances that we may address widely through better governance."

Cin cupped the prince's neck gingerly. "How did it go?"

Prince Lorenz shrugged. "It felt good to meet with the people— not to party with them or give speeches or act as ambassador on their behalf, but to simply sit with one or two and listen to their troubles. Perhaps I even managed to help a few of them." His shoulders shifted like he was trying to shimmy his way out of a shrug. "It's nice to believe so, anyway."

"I'm certain you did. You have a gift for making people's lives better," Cin said, smiling softly. "You first saw me, awkward and alone, and despite my refusal to give you anything, you took it upon yourself to turn my night into something spectacular."

Prince Lorenz snorted. "You were very handsome."

"True. But there were plenty of other beautiful people in attendance."

"How odd." The prince's voice shifted, going low and heavy. "Because all I see tonight is you."

Cin's heart jumped and fell, all at once. He wanted to say, suddenly, *but you would never* choose *me for the rest of your nights*, like a barb tearing out of his throat from the rose he'd so desperately swallowed these past weeks. Instead, Cin put on a weak smile, and as gently as he could manage, he replied, "You'll have to be a little less blind by the end of the night. It will be very hard to put a ring on the finger of your future partner if you are looking at me."

Despite all of Cin's efforts, the prince still looked like he'd been slapped. "You know that I don't want—" he started, but the energy seemed to rush out of him, and he turned his face away, sighing.

Gently, Cin asked, "What *do* you want?"

"I don't know." He looked so lost.

"Don't you?" Cin tucked back a strand of the loose locks of the prince's hair beneath his royal circlet. *I'm right here*, he wanted to scream, *take my hand and walk away with me. Run if you have to.* "If you could go anywhere, live any life, where would it be?"

"Before Alwin..." Prince Lorenz's fingers constricted against his chest, as though he was clutching into the flesh itself. Pain tore across his face. He seemed to shake it off with a quick, sharp twitch of his head. "This *is* my life. I can't be dreaming of another."

It was an expression so familiar to Cin, ugly and demanding and, from what he could now see, mostly a lie. "But you could have so much more."

Prince Lorenz only shook his head again and took a step back, falling out of Cin's reach.

Cin followed him, cautiously. "Your Highness…"

"You don't need to *Your Highness* me," the prince grumbled, still not meeting Cin's gaze. "I have a name, you know."

"Prince *Lorenz*." There was a little bite to his voice, and it seemed to snap the prince back to himself, if only partially.

"Ren," he said, almost meeting Cin's gaze for once. "My closest friends call me Ren."

Closest. The word stung in ways that it shouldn't have been allowed to: like there were others who shared this intimacy—who would continue to, someday, when Cin was no longer needed. He tried to duck in front of his prince, look up at him properly in the hopes of seeing through whatever terrible distance had come over him, and he wasn't sure why he said it, because he knew it couldn't end well. Yet he did anyway. "Is that what I am, Ren? One of your closest?"

"Of course." Prince Lorenz's fingertips twitched against his chest, digging in deeper after. "You mean as much to me as anyone has these days."

Cin cupped the back of his hand, looking at him—looking into him and hoping that would be enough to make him understand. "These days?"

The prince looked confused, then slowly distress began to creep onto his face. "My dove, you know what our relationship has to be."

"Why? What if I wanted more?" Cin pleaded. "Not romance—I don't need you to feel differently for me—but I want to be deeper with you. I want to be *yours*. Not one of, but your *one*."

Prince Lorenz flinched like he'd been struck. "It sounds lovely, but—my dove—I must marry someone, rule a *kingdom*."

"I'm not demanding you give up that." As much as a part of him wished he could, wanted nothing more than to pull Lorenz away into the night and never look back, that would be a battle Cin didn't have much hope in winning. "I'm asking you to *choose* me. Even if you have to choose a partner, too, even if I'll hate them for stealing parts of you away from me, even if this can't be forever, I still want to be your everything."

There was an emptiness on the prince's face that spoke louder than his own voice. "If I could, I would, but I…"

"You don't want me that way." Each word felt as though it was a piece of flesh torn from the fabric of Cin's throat, gritty and rough. In the dimness of the room, the world swayed.

"It's not about want, or— Or I'd have you in a heartbeat." Prince Lorenz sounded so imploring, taking both of Cin's hands in his own. "But you knew what this was, all it could be, when we agreed to it. That hasn't— It *can't* change."

"I *know* what I agreed to." Cin did. He'd known, and he'd been stupid enough to believe that was enough. "But when I agreed to it, I didn't think I'd end up loving you."

No, but that was wrong. He hadn't *thought* any of this, but deep down, beneath the denial, Cin had figured, not that there was no chance he'd grow to love Prince Lorenz, but that in any amazing, miraculous world where that impossibility came true, that in those futures, there was none where Prince Lorenz didn't love him back, in his own way. No world where Cin got this far only to find that he was alone; not simply a tragedy, but a tragedy of one.

"Oh, my dove." The prince looked on the edge of falling apart.

"It's not that I don't care for you—"

"But you don't care enough," Cin whispered, pulling free of the prince's loose cradling of his hands. He watched, waiting for the flash beneath the prince's cloudy eyes that told him there was more, that he was wrong. But he could see everything of Prince Lorenz's emotions on his face and what he saw was a man who'd already lost the only battle he'd had the strength to fight.

"I'm afraid I'm sorely lacking in that area," the prince said, so soft that the words seemed empty, empty of emotion, conviction— of everything.

But that emptiness from Prince Lorenz was the encouragement Cin needed to feel everything raging within him. To take in the full extent of his pain, and accept what it meant: he was in love with Lorenz. Madly, stupidly, perhaps even romantically, a soft, giddy warmth having sprung to life inside him over his weeks of seeing Lorenz's heart unfold, of deepening their friendship until Lorenz no longer felt like a friend. He felt like everything Cin had every needed; the only thing he ever wanted.

And Cin could not bear to let that love take root in an empty chest, unrequited and useless. He knew he couldn't abandon the prince forever, but he needed space now. Space to let go.

Cin turned towards the door, but moving through the castle on his own felt too vulnerable, so he moved to the suite's largest set of windows instead, managing to push back the curtains before Prince Lorenz set after him.

"My dove, wait—" The prince's voice sounded frantic.

"I can't." Cin made to throw open the window. The latch caught. God-damned—

"Cinder— Cinder-Ella!" Lorenz begged.

Cin could feel tears burning in the back of his eyes, but what came up was pure venom, all his pain flashing to anger. "That's not even my name, *Ren!*"

"I'm sorry," the prince scrambled, like he could place himself between Cin and the window if he tried hard enough. "Don't." He pulled his jacket off, the elaborate fabric falling to the floor. "Don't leave, please." His fingers went frantically to the collar of his shirt, pulling that back too. Was he stripping?

"Ren!" Cin couldn't— He couldn't be here anymore. He couldn't deal with this—whatever this was. He yanked at the window latch again. This time it budged.

"Please, I—" Lorenz pleaded, dragging open the front buttons of his undershirt. "This will make sense, if I can show you..."

The latch came free under Cin's fingers, but as he pushed the window open, Prince Lorenz caught him by the wrist, thrusting Cin's palm against the center of his bared chest. But where Cin's fingers should have met with skin, something else protruded in and out of the flesh. Metal. Circles of it, wrapping deep into muscle and between bone, a cage in the center of Prince Lorenz's chest.

"My dearest dove, I don't command the depth of affection you deserve for a life with me, not because I don't wish for it," Cin's prince sobbed, "but because I *can't.*"

Twenty-Six

C in stared at the mangled flesh beneath his fingers, shivering at the contrast between the warmth of the prince's skin and the unnatural cold of the metal around his heart. The bands were scarred and jagged, like they'd been flayed apart from a larger circlet, and deep scarlet stained the golden metal that might have once been blood. Hesitantly, Cin drew two fingers over one of the rough bars, watching as the prince's chest shuddered beneath. Cin could feel the gentle thud of a heart beating within its cage.

"You're not the only one with a bit of magic," Lorenz teased, though the joke came out strained and sad.

Cin could feel the tears beginning to slip down his cheeks, but he couldn't help it. All his anger and heartbreak were still there, but now it seemed they'd turned themselves inside out, or perhaps just right-side up. What hellish dark sorcery was this, that someone had locked the prince's heart away, left him to suffer a life without love? "Does it hurt?"

Lorenz wouldn't meet Cin's gaze as, quietly, he answered, "Not so much as it once did, but now the more I think of you—the more I care for you—the pain returns."

For that, Cin wanted to kiss the spot above his prince's heart, to feel it beat against his lips. But he couldn't. So he thumbed the metal instead, letting the rough edges scrape into his skin. "You could have told me sooner..."

And Cin imagined, briefly, if he had—had told Cin long before he'd had the chance to fall in love with Lorenz. Had stopped the ache in Cin's chest before it had even begun.

The thought made Cin nauseous.

Lorenz grimaced. Beneath his touch, Cin could feel the prince's body start to shake, whether from cold or anxiety or both. "I wasn't certain how to," he admitted, sounding ashamed. "I never sharing my peers' dreamy moods as a teenager, and while not all of them understood how intensively I could love despite that, I was always content with who I was, and how I felt. It made little difference in my life whether what I shared with the people I cared for was born of romantic passion or a more solemn love of trust and devotion. But to suddenly have the love I did feel slip through my fingers..." Lorenz shuddered harder. "I've told no one of this, not ever. Not my parents, nor the servants, not even my lovers—I never let anyone strip me of my undershirt." He gave a bitter laugh. "There will never be any bare-chested statues of me."

Cin's chest ached with a pain that felt as though metal were being wound around his own heart. He cupped Lorenz's cheek, tracing it with his thumb. "But you've told *me*, and I'm grateful." He drew in a deep breath, looking Lorenz in the eyes as he said, "Now, tell me the name of the bastard who did this to you, so I might dig out their heart and put it in a cage of my own."

That brought almost a smile to his prince's face, the soft twitch of his lips offset by the sadness in his eyes. "I am that bastard, my dove."

Cin blinked. Confusion knotted his gut, then alarm. "You…?"

Lorenz sighed, stepped back—but not far. "Sit with me. I'll tell you everything."

Cin followed Lorenz through the suite, but from somewhere beyond the doors, someone shouted. Another voice responded, just as frustrated.

Lorenz cringed. "On second thought, they'll probably check these rooms soon. Would you care to go back to mine? I'm sure someone has been there by now; we'll have more time." A larger shudder ran through him, and beneath it the little shivers still raged. "Also, a well-stocked hearth."

"Let us, yes." Cin let go of his prince, finally, collecting up Lorenz's things from the floor, and they set off again.

They kept to the servant entrances and side halls again, darting on soft feet across the ornate rugs in the main chambers when they could not avoid them, but it was barely three turns later when Lorenz led Cin through a servants' door into an elaborate suite much like the one they'd just been in. Unlike those rooms, however, these ones were clearly lived in.

Books and stray papers were piled across most raised flat surfaces, three foreign-looking plants sitting on perches at the large windows, a violin discarded on one couch and a set of pillows and blankets forming something like a nest near the large hearth. Wood had been stacked inside it, though it currently lay unlit.

Cin felt instantly awkward just standing there, in a royal's personal chambers, much less those of the man he loved. Instinctively, he moved toward the hearth. "I'll provide us some warmth."

Lorenz scrambled past him. "Oh, allow me. You surely do this all the time."

Cin's brow lifted. *"You* can light a fire?"

"After our night in your garden, I made my attendant, Felix, teach me." He sounded satisfied with himself, and Cin decided to let him have that pride. It was cute, and Cin loved him just a little bit for trying. The warm glow in Cin's heart twisted jarringly at the thought of the cage in Lorenz's own chest, trying to lock out the affection that came so easily for Cin.

But at least Lorenz *was* there, offering what he could, Cin consoled himself as his prince struck the fire to life. He'd donned his undershirt again for the journey there, but the top two buttons were still open, and the fabric hung as he leaned forward. Cin could just glimpse the metal beneath.

This had all been so complicated already, and now it was even more so. A part of Cin still wanted to flee and be done with it—at least for the night—because at least that way, he'd know there was no hope of forging anything deeper. But if that meant hurting Lorenz in the process, he didn't think he was capable of that—not when he'd clearly been hurt so badly already.

As the fire crackled to life, Cin watched the flames dance and spread, sitting beside Lorenz on the bundle of blankets. They didn't touch, but that seemed right for the moment. There was a kind of emptiness in the air, and Cin didn't know how to break that.

Lorenz brushed his fingers over his heart, bunching and straightening the fabric that lay there, tracing the metal beneath it.

"To understand this, you have to know how fiercely I loved him..." His voice was weak, each word strained, stolen from some dark and distant place.

"Him?" Cin whispered.

Lorenz seemed almost to startle, blinking, then nodding. "Alwin—my brother."

It seemed contrary to the ways Lorenz had spoken of him, with mild awe and hints of jealousy, like a distant thing, always to be compared to. But then, Cin supposed his own relationship with Emma was not any less complex, yet his own heart had ached all week at her dismissals and avoidance. The opposite of love was apathy, after all.

The prince's gaze had been trapped by the fire again, but now Cin watched his face as he spoke, little pinches and tightenings moving through it as though everything he was feeling was hidden beneath a layer, not of a mask, but of... magic. "We were inseparable as youths; every game he devised I would rush into headfirst, every worry I would console, and every wonder I'd appreciate. As we grew up, and grew different, that somehow never truly changed." His words sounded a little too clinical for the context, despite how low and heavy his voice stayed. "At times, I wished I could be more like him, but I knew, too, that he had the weight of the world on his shoulders, and I never envied him that. I would not have traded our places for anything... except perhaps, to bring him back."

So soft was that final line, that Cin would not have caught it had he not watched Lorenz's mouth move. Slowly, carefully, he slid his hand over his prince's. Lorenz did not pull away. "It must have been terrible to hear of his disappearance," Cin whispered.

Lorenz nodded, still staring into the flames. "I'm aware that at the time, it felt like more than I could bear," he said, hoarsely. His eyes shone, just a little, a wisp of emotion breaking through whatever magic so callously bound his heart. "If we had only known for certain that he had perished with his entourage in the forest, perhaps that would have been different, but having only his bloody circlet as proof—it was horrid. I watched my parents swing from hope to grief to desperation and back with each morning, and I slipped slowly toward something darker."

"Oh, Ren." Cin squeezed his hand, feeling the waves of the emotions Lorenz described flood through him in turns. He'd felt them all just that day—not for a sibling, perhaps, but for an entire future. At least he had the ability to affect his, though. Lorenz had been powerless. But for one thing...

"I took his circlet—the same one that was feathered to frame your Plumed Menace—and absconded to the forest, alone." He breathed in, then out, and the shadows seemed to dance menacingly across his face. "When our soldiers found me, I told them I'd been looking for Alwin—my parents even believed me, though they forbade me from leaving the castle alone again. But I... I think I was looking to die with him."

That was such love, such terrible excruciating love, that it made Cin feel hollow, setting a yearning in his soul for something so ruthless as to be deadly. It seemed wrong to want such a thing, but Cin could find no sin in it. Maybe *that* was how God smiled: with an existential merging of joy and tragedy.

"I lost myself in that forest," Lorenz continued. "I recall only snatches, sobbing and breaking, praying to God and the trees and the fairy creatures that the grief be taken away." He fingered the cage around his heart, his eyes closing as he traced along the top band where its ragged edge was revealed. "Finally, I stopped praying, and I demanded," he said, flatly. "It was that or death."

"You conducted dark magic?" Cin whispered.

"I don't know for certain, but that was how it felt. In the center of a fairy circle, I tore my brother's circlet apart with my bare hands, ripping long strips of metal like they were the bark of a tree, and plunged them into my chest. I cannot imagine there was any light magic in a feat like that."

Cin edged closer, removing his hand from Lorenz's in order to rub his back, their shoulders pressed together. "If you were the one who placed the bonds, could you not take them away again?"

"It was all a haze. I've tried to pull against them, to wish them away, even. After I left you the night we killed Brando Von Achenbach, I took a pair of tools to them for leverage. It's only drawn blood." Lorenz shook his head. "To remove them myself now, I think would kill me."

To remove them *himself*, he said, and Cin believed him.

But perhaps, someone else?

A flicker of hope sparkled in Cin's chest, so small that he feared accepting it. Lorenz could not return to that place of grief that had allowed him to force the magic to his will the first time, but Cin had magic of his own, even if it was of a far different sort.

"What if someone else might..." Cin stumbled over the suggestion, not sure how they'd go about it, but certain there had to be something worth trying—anything for Lorenz. "I've found better, lighter magics, in my life, in the woods even..."

"You did go after all, didn't you?" Lorenz seemed to really look at Cin then, perhaps for the first time since they'd absconded from the ball. A quirk came into his lips, cautious but optimistic. "You seem different."

That brought a smile to Cin's face, sad though it was in the midst of Lorenz's pain. "My chest is not quite so lumpy now."

Lorenz's nose wrinkled. "No—well, yes—but in other ways," he said, like he was still working it out as he spoke. "You're less tense. You don't flinch or brace. Your smile is softer. You're... no longer in pain?"

Cin nodded, not sure he could put to words everything that meant to him. It was all that the prince had said and so, so much more. But just as he didn't know how to share the full bliss of his transformation, neither could he grant that joy to Lorenz, and the knowledge hurt just as much as his pain had. He touched gently along the edge of his prince's metal binding. "If I could give this magic to you..."

Lorenz's expression melted from awe to misery. His throat bobbed harshly, bitterness in his voice. "I had that chance, and look what I did with it."

Cin tucked his hand over his prince's. "Don't hold it against yourself, Ren. You did nothing wrong."

Lorenz grimaced. "But you did everything right!"

"I was lucky," Cin insisted, gentle as he could manage. "My flock guided me to the Frog Prince, who understood my plight and granted me a trade far kinder than I could have dreamed. It was nothing I earned, and nothing I could possibly repeat."

Slowly, Lorenz seemed to force himself to nod. Still, he looked worried. "What *did* you give up, my dove?"

"Nothing," Cin reassured him. "I promised to continue caring, was all." Specifically for the prince, but if he revealed that, Lorenz would want to know why—why was he so important, why would this monster in the woods care whether *he* was loved? And the answer that had been creeping around Cin's heart was still too wild and whimsical to dare speak aloud. "It was a boon, really. He gave me permission to—to love the people I love."

Lorenz wrapped his arm around Cin's, squeezing him gently. "It is everything you deserve."

"But this is not what you deserve." Cin leaned against him, feeling every shudder and breath shared flesh to flesh. "What can I do to help you?"

"Find me that Frog Prince?" Lorenz gave a sad laugh, so broken that it made Cin's heart ache.

Perhaps it might be that simple, Cin suspected, in ways Lorenz could not even fathom, but if it were, then this prince of the swamp was not simple in the slightest...

Cin tucked the thought away. There would be time for it in the morning, when the sun lit the land and monsters and magic felt a little less dangerous. Right now, he had a different prince to focus on.

Lorenz turned his face toward Cin's, pressing his mouth to the top of Cin's forehead. "When I'm with you, I can feel something awakening inside me, and its grown so strong that often it bleeds through the bonds. When we talk, when we touch, this curse begins to shatter for a moment. It's painful, but it's wonderful too." He breathed out a shaky, hollow breath. "Then the moment you're gone, I'm empty again. It's why I can't devote my life to you, you understand? Who would I be to pull you into a future where the one person who is meant to be there for you, profoundly and un-conditionally, forgets he cares for you the moment you leave his sight?"

"I would still love you," Cin whispered, almost pleading.

But it was a naive hope, he understood. Lorenz was doing for him what he had done for Dorthe just weeks earlier: stepped aside, knowing he couldn't give her the fullness of what she deserved. He might not have agreed with Lorenz that it was what he needed, but he doubted that would reassure his prince nearly enough to convince him to be selfish in this—not *his* prince: his good, kind, just prince, already more loving and lovely as a man devoid of the emotion than anyone who possessed it. Lorenz would let Cin go and think it mercy.

Unless Cin could end the need for that mercy in the first place.

"You say it's better when I'm here, when we talk and touch?" Cin's voice came hoarse, but he pushed onward. "That means there's hope then, does it not?"

A tear slid down Cin's cheek, and he sniffled in surprise. When he reached to brush it away though, it was Lorenz's eyes that were wet and red.

"While you're with me, I can believe that."

Cin pressed his thumb under his prince's eyes, one after the other, and smiled despite himself. "Then I should never leave," he said, knowing it was ridiculous, knowing it would never work, knowing they were still, despite all their hope and comfort, bound for the same tragedy that had caught Cin the moment he'd fallen for Lorenz.

His prince smiled back at him. "Well, this is certainly a different tone than I had imagined for our last evening."

Cin's laugh was small but somehow, weirdly content. "You did bring me back to your chambers. I think for you, that means we can't be intimate here."

"Now, now." Lorenz narrowed his eyes mischievously. "I said that I never sleep with people in my bed. This, if I'm not mistaken, is what we in the most prestigious classes call a *floor*."

"Cheeky." Snorting, Cin gave him a little shove, and when Lorenz returned the favor, Cin flopped backward across the blankets. He tried to stretch his arms above his head and snuggle into the nest of comforts. The magic of his clothing was clearly not as in tune to his needs as it should have been, because his fancy jacket cut the motion short, pinching in his shoulders and armpits. He lay there awkwardly instead, lifting his brow at Lorenz. "Do you do anything in that great big bed of yours?"

Lorenz leaned over Cin, and one by one he began popping open the buttons on Cin's jacket. "I do sleep there. Occasionally. But it's so downy that my back feels better here, and besides, here is warm."

"You privileged little prince," Cin teased.

He grinned down at Cin. "Guilty as charged." But through the dangling collar of his shirt, Cin could see the shadow of his bound heart, and he knew that no life was so simple.

Cin felt his own expression soften, stupidly, the ache in his chest rearing its head, but in its claws was a joy so unlike anything he'd known. "I'm glad you tried to fuck me that first night."

"Oh?" Lorenz pushed Cin's jacket over his shoulders, and Cin sat up enough to let his lover—his love, if only in part, in half—pull the fabric free and strip it off. "Wishing now you'd said yes, hmm?"

"No." Cin laughed, sitting up further, until his legs were tangled in Lorenz's, their faces close again, breaths shared. "I have very much enjoyed knowing *you* more, the more I *know* you."

"Sounds pretentious." But Lorenz seemed a little bit in awe as he said it. He gave a tug to the collar of Cin's shirt. "I've shown you mine..."

The flush that spread over Cin's cheeks and down his neck wasn't unexpected, but it still felt like an announcement that he'd never done anything quite like this before. But Lorenz had. And he trusted his prince with his body—even with his heart, despite everything. Or perhaps, weirdly, more because of it. "I suppose it's only fair."

Lorenz's grin sparkled in his eyes. He didn't hesitate, flipping through each of Cin's vest and shirt buttons like his fingers knew their forms already, setting Cin's knife and sheath off to the side with reverence, and when he got to Cin's undershirt, he stripped it up and over Cin's head like a thirsty man trying to dig water out of the desert. The little exhale that left him after brought a mist to Cin's eyes.

"You're the first to see it," he said, feeling a bit like he was babbling, but he needed to fill the silence while Lorenz took him in.

Lorenz gave a low whistle. His eyes lifted, creasing at the corners. "I'm going to touch you now, my dove. If you don't want any part of my lust, then tell me outright, because otherwise, I will take you for everything you are worth. Every piece of you will be mine, and I will say no to nothing."

Yes, Cin wanted to plead, to shout, to tear between Lorenz's ribs and convince his poor, strangled heart that it could be free again, with him. But the little twist in his gut stopped him. He could feel the burn in his cheeks as he ducked his head. "Everything, except... I don't mind my more feminine bits being down there, but I don't want you inside them, if that makes sense?" He'd never had anything in his other hole either, but he knew that was a way it was often done, and it sounded more pleasant, at least in his mind.

"You make sense," Lorenz said, and it was everything Cin didn't know he needed to hear. He fingers crept around Cin's hips. "Now, if that's all..."

Fuck, this was going to kill Cin, wasn't it? But, well, he could accept that. He breathed in, then out, and whispered, "Take me."

"As you wish," Lorenz whispered back.

Twenty-Seven

Cin's heart beat faster as Lorenz pulled him closer and pressed him down. One of his hands fisted into Cin's hair and he searched out Cin's face and neck with his lips, nibbling and sucking and tugging at Cin's skin as he fit Cin against the blankets. It was so much, so sudden, that every little sensation welled to bursting inside Cin, pressing back against his skin as though Cin's soul was shifting to meet with Lorenz's mouth. He searched the ceiling without really seeing it, tearing into his lower lip with his teeth. Slowly he worked up the confidence to lift his hands. He placed one on Lorenz's hip.

The little moan that Lorenz made had to be dramatized, but it gave Cin the confidence to slide his other hand into place, drawing them both up and under the back of Lorenz's shirt. His skin felt so perfectly smooth, muscles strong and tight beneath. With each touch, everything seemed even more right.

Then, Lorenz found Cin's freshly transformed nipple.

It wasn't the same sensation that he'd had before the magic shifted his chest, but it was better somehow—righter. He sunk into the feeling without the shimmy of discomfort beneath his skin that had always accompanied anyone—himself included—touching those tender places in the past. As Lorenz's teeth sunk into him, sudden and sharp, Cin arched back, and over the top of his trousers, two fingers found the sweet spot between his legs so fast he thought they were his *own* for a second, before they began to move. He moaned, and he wanted it suddenly to be his fingers, but his fingers inside Lorenz, to know how to do *this* to the person he loved. A wave of heat rushed him at the thought.

"That's it," Lorenz cooed, teasing at Cin's sweet spot. "Tell me you want me."

The thought dragged a flush through Cin's whole body, but he said it anyway, aching against Lorenz's touch. "I want you."

"Tell me you need me."

"I need you." Cin felt like he was begging, but he couldn't put into words how true that was, now and forever, his fingers and his affection and his support.

Lorenz lifted himself up just enough that Cin could see the smirk on his lips. "Then touch me, my dove."

Cin groaned. Still, his hands didn't seem to know how to reach for Lorenz. He tugged awkwardly at his prince's trousers. "Can I..."

"I will say no to nothing, remember."

Cin did remember, but that didn't make it any easier. Between that and the ache spreading beneath Cin's skin, the yearning for touch or to *make* touch, to make *love*, he pushed himself forward. He had the prince's trousers off in no time, his own somehow coming with them, and then Cin had his own mouth on Lorenz's body, kissing his way down Lorenz's stomach as he fiddled with his lower undergarments.

Lorenz stumbled the rest of the way onto his back and Cin

pulled those free. His prince laughed, his elbows propping him up, his bent legs wide, and his cock so stiff it made Cin feel jealous. He looked awkward and disheveled and beautiful.

And Cin *wanted* him.

The lopsided grin on Lorenz's face grew as he said, "You're the first person to see this much of me in..." he shrugged. "Well, since before we lost Alwin, surely."

The knowledge landed hot between Cin's legs and that warmth seemed to travel quickly to his heart. What they had was still special, even with the cage around Lorenz's heart. Lorenz had made that clear time and time again. He reached for Cin, but Cin put two fingers to his chest. "I'm not done looking."

Lorenz settled back into place, his head tipped to one side. "You find me to your liking then, I take it?"

"Of course I do." Cin snorted, but he couldn't keep the smile off his lips as he slowly lowered his mouth to the inside of Lorenz's knee. "Now hold still."

"As you wish."

Cin kissed his prince's skin again, moving up his inner thigh. With each press of his mouth, Lorenz's smugness melted into pleasure, his body relaxing into Cin's touch. Somehow, Cin had not expected that—not expected, either, how sweet it would feel. This was different than their previous times together, no less desperate, necessarily, but that want was made softer by their unspoken desire to stretch things out, to pleasure each other as deeply and fully as possible before this night and its beauties were taken away.

If he could, Cin was going to remember every inch of Lorenz's body, draw forth every song of bliss his prince's lips could produce, brand his fingerprints across so much of his lover's skin that no touch could ever replace his.

And so he did, one tender kiss at a time, lips moving to tongue and then to teeth as Lorenz moaned, until finally Cin was between Lorenz's legs, teasing his hard cock with the softest of sucking. As he did, he plucked the feathers trapped in his hair clip to flutter them across his prince's family jewels before exposing the head of his cock to trace them across the especially sensitive skin there.

Lorenz seemed to be fighting back little bucks of his hips as he whimpered. He shifted his shoulders, his hands opening and closing at his sides like he wasn't sure if he wanted to pull Cin's mouth closer or push him back into the blankets and take him fully. "Are you not going to let me have my fun too, dove?"

"If I must." Cin smiled, and let Lorenz's cock free. Instead of surrendering, though, he climbed over top of his prince to kiss him properly. He groaned as Lorenz gripped his ass, and wove a hand through Lorenz's hair beneath the ring of his circlet.

"We can take that off," Lorenz grumbled between Cin's lips. He reached to remove the crown, but Cin shooed his hand away.

"I like it."

"Then it stays." Lorenz gave Cin's still-clothed ass a squeeze that seemed to tingle its way deeper into him, tightening his hole with a greedy ache. "But these underthings *must* go."

"You did promise to take me for everything I'm worth," Cin reminded him.

Those words seemed just enough to unleash the restraints Lorenz had been putting on himself. He pushed Cin back, settling him onto the blankets—still soft, still slow, but his want clearly bundled beneath as he drew Cin's undergarments off him, gazing at Cin's bare form with unbridled lust, and something more—not love, perhaps, but pride, and joy, and awe.

With no fabric to cover him, Cin could feel his wetness leaking through the barrier of his curls. Lorenz took full advantage of it, slipping his fingers in and dragging them up. When he hit Cin's sweet spot, Cin's hips jerked against him.

Lorenz looked devilish, his eyes alight and his hair shifting in that magical breeze that seemed always upon him. "Now, now, not *yet*. I did say I'd have *all* of you."

This time when he cupped through Cin's wetness, he pulled his fingers back entirely. Cin couldn't see what he was doing, and for a split second his confusion overwhelmed his desire, until suddenly Lorenz's fingers brushed over the delicate, tightened skin of Cin's asshole.

Even though he'd only touched Cin from the outside, that single swipe brought a flash of want with it, and a desire that Cin couldn't explain—a sensation of emptiness and the need to be filled, to have Lorenz spread him apart then and there and push into him just to see what would happen, what it would feel like. Before Cin could fully make sense of the desire, Lorenz's fingers returned with more of his silky wetness, massaging the slick substance against Cin's opening. Cin arched back, wanting almost to moan, but his breath caught in his lungs instead.

"You like that, my dove?" Lorenz teased.

Cin felt his blush as though it had struck between his legs as well as across his face, hot and tingling. When Lorenz pushed his thighs a little farther apart, he had to stop himself from whimpering. Lorenz seemed committed to cleaning him out and soaking every last drop of that slickness into his other hole, but Cin could feel himself only growing more wet with each touch, his lower regions heavy and swollen with need.

As Lorenz worked the outer ridge of his hole again, he said, "I asked, do you like this, dove..."

"Yes," Cin moaned, and the end of the word was dragged out of him as Lorenz ran a finger in, then out, and in then out again. Cin inhaled so sharply it felt like a sob. The ache inside him thickened, burning deeper, like if Lorenz only pushed a little more, a little more, he'd light a spark all the way through Cin.

"Do you know how handsome you look?" Lorenz whispered as he pushed further in, enough to make Cin want for more and more again.

He arched, burning with need. He didn't feel handsome—he felt desperate and undone, small and hungry and a little frustrated in the very best way. "Do I?"

"I can show you..." Lorenz said.

And Cin wasn't quite sure what he could mean by that, until he scooted back, enough for Cin to see between Lorenz's legs again. He lifted two fingers drenched in Cin's wetness, grinning, then brought them to his own hole. As he pressed into himself, his princely arrogance shattered into whimpers of need. To watch him spread himself open, Cin felt raw.

A part of him begged to reach forward, to push Lorenz's fingers farther and make him gasp and groan and writhe, but he was still too frozen, locked in his own feelings as Lorenz repeated the motion, thrice over, until he had three fingers inside himself, Cin's wetness dripping between the crack of his ass. Lorenz's cock twitched as he pulled out.

A sloppy smile on his face, he struggled to his feet, and Cin could do nothing but blink at him.

"I may not do much intimate entertaining here," he said, opening a chest against the foot of his bed. "But I do store a couple of fun things I've collected over the years. I've been waiting for the right person for this one..."

He drew a wrapped package forth, unbuckling the fabric around it as he sat, clearly delicate for the sake of his hard cock and wet hole. It took Cin a moment to understand the contraption he pulled free. Part of it was in the form of a cock—a fine one at that—but then the piece curved around, cupping downward from where the member would normally sit, only to rise back up in a small, bulbous— *oh*. Heat flashed through Cin and his asshole tightened around the wetness still coated there as he realized: were the cock to be held between his legs, the end would have to be pressed up *into* him.

Cin should not have loved the thought of that so, having so little experience with how it might feel, but then everything in him was screaming that he did know, that he *needed* to know.

"You don't have to," Lorenz said, "if you aren't—"

Cin cut him off. "If you put that inside me, I swear I am going to fuck you so hard that you'll trade your kingdom to come."

The little flash of powerless desperation that slid across Lorenz's face was worth that entire kingdom and more. Lorenz dragged a bit more of Cin's wetness over the bulb of the piece before lowering it between Cin's legs.

Anxiety flared through Cin as the bulb pressed against his opening, clearly bigger that Lorenz's fingers had been. He held his breath, trying to focus on his earlier want, on the thought of it already inside him, pressing against him, making him wide and full and—

Cin breathed out, and so gently he barely realized it, Lorenz forced him open. His lashes fluttered as the sensation caught up to him—not pain, but something that sat between it and pleasure, sharp and rough but blissful too. A moan slipped out of him, his inhales shaky as the bulb settled into place.

Lorenz pressed a little farther, and Cin could feel the piece's curved length fitting beneath his folds, the nub at the end of its imitation of a cock sliding up to rub against Cin's sweet spot. It felt good, in an intrusive, delirious way, and it felt, too, of magic. When Lorenz let go, it clung to Cin like magic too, the little nub against his clit humming subtly. He closed his eyes and let the feeling tingle through him, as though his body were a different shape, stretched and pressed until his senses were all a beautiful mess.

"Look at yourself," Lorenz whispered.

Cin almost didn't want to. He didn't want to be disappointed. But the way Lorenz cupped the side of his face, their thighs brushing, breathes intermingling, made it worth the risk.

When he opened his eyes, be found the carved piece between his legs, long and hard and lovely.

A thought flashed through his mind: he could have had this—the real thing, anyway. When he'd gone to the woods, met with the monster there, he could have asked for more than his chest to be reborn. But as he shifted up, helping Lorenz spread his legs, angling his hips until his wet, tight hole was there for the taking, Cin decided he'd made the right choice. What he wanted, what he craved, wasn't a cock between his legs—it was the ability to make his prince weak for him and see him writhe and beg as he was fucked, and now he had that.

Cin had everything he wanted.

From the physical, at least. With Lorenz on his back, Cin could see the outline of the cage around his heart where his shirt fabric draped across it. The fire danced shadows over it, and Cin reached up. He could feel the way his ornamental cock bumped Lorenz's flesh one as he unlaced Lorenz's undershirt further, then further still, until it hung beneath the metal. Lorenz shivered. His gaze met Cin's.

"Fuck me," he whispered. "Please."

Cin hovered over him, his skin inches away from his prince's, and he felt like one half of a pair of magnets, his body wanting nothing more than to collide with Lorenz's. Still, he whispered back, slow and silky, "Are you asking *me*?"

"Yes, my dove," Lorenz pleaded. "My Royal Highness, my l—" His body seemed to swallow the last word for him, misery crossing his face, and Cin took pity on him.

Using one hand to help—he didn't want to get this wrong—he found Lorenz's hole with the tip of the ornamental cock, and pushed. That first pressure was almost too much against his clit, a taunting vibration spilling through the front of the magical fuck-piece and down along his tender, swollen skin. But then the shudder ended up in his ass, and Cin could not help but buck into Lorenz.

They both moaned together, sloppy and tense.

"Please," Lorenz said, his voice hoarse with want.

Cin's smugness tried to work its way onto his face, but he wasn't sure whether it would make it between his moans and gasps as he pulled back and pushed in again, feeling the same wave of pleasure rush through his lower regions. The final thrum of it spurred him faster, harder. Lorenz released a sound like a sob, his head tipping back.

Cin tried a slightly different angle, and this time Lorenz's response was a gasp and a tremble.

He couldn't tell if that was right or not. "Where is the best—"

"I don't want the best." Lorenz breathed, grabbing Cin by the wrist and holding on, holding tight through Cin's next thrust, and the one after, as he kept talking. "I want your worst. I want you to keep—just keep—until I come apart." He seemed to be doing just that, his fingers curling and his neck arching. "Don't let me walk back into that ballroom," he pleaded. "Make me yours."

So Cin did. He focused only on the ragged speed of his thrusts, bucking into Lorenz like he was trying to widen the space between his love's legs permanently. Lorenz screamed and writhed, but between his pointed sobs were mumbled sounds of *yes* and *please* and *oh God*, until he was tense and shaking, and Cin was shaking with him.

Each pressure into Lorenz sent a fresh rush through Cin, growing until not even the moments he took to draw back would let his body rest. As they began to overlap, his wetness contracted in bursts of ecstasy, turning his motions even more erratic and forceful. He pushed through them, biting his lower lip while a white hot burn of need grew steadily between his legs.

Lorenz seized so suddenly it caught Cin off guard, this scream different from his others as his body went stiff and his cock emptied in a splatter of white. The sudden tightening pressed Cin's magical fuck-piece against him harder, its vibration writhing through him. A shock of bliss followed it, starting from his sweet spot and rolling through his pelvis, settling deep in his ass as every muscle between pulsed in pleasure. He seemed suspended there for so long that he thought he'd break apart, his consciousness sliding into a heavenly state.

Then, suddenly, the rush subsided.

Cin pulled back with a gasp, slumping against Lorenz's hips, barely holding himself up with one hand. His worn nether regions twitched and thrummed as he slowly pulled Lorenz's magical fuck-piece out of himself. He set it to the side, and leaned against Lorenz.

They were both still breathing hard, and Lorenz was staring at him, so many emotions tight across his face that Cin could somehow see them all, yet distinguish none. So gently that it felt more like a breeze than a touch, Lorenz ran his thumb across Cin's cheek.

"My dove," he whispered.

Cin stared back. Something wet and terrible slid across his vision, and he didn't know why. He tried to smile through it, and it just pushed free a single tear. "Yes, Ren?"

"Thank you," he said, softly, smiling back at Cin through shining eyes. "For more than the pleasure, I mean. Thank you for seeing me, for listening, for staying with me regardless of whether I can keep you, whether I can love—" He drew in a sob, looking away.

Cin cupped the side of his face and a single tear to match Cin's own spilled out. Before Cin could comfort him though, Lorenz kept speaking.

"You are so very perfect. How— How are you everything I could ever want and I still can't—" He cut himself off in a hiss, and his fingers flew to the metal exposed in his chest.

Magic sparked through the air.

Hope seemed to collide with Cin's heart like the impact of a hammer, taking the breath out of him. He watched, more desperate than he had been in all the needy, lustful minutes before. In his head, he begged—the magic, God, Lorenz—*please, let it work, let this have been enough.*

Lorenz pulled at the bonds jutting from his skin, heaving with each breath. Tears streamed down his face. But the metal didn't budge. With each frantic failure, the ragged edges of it cut into Lorenz's fingers, leaving bloody smears across his hands.

Cin's heart caught. He rushed to stop Lorenz's tugging, shushing gently. Between Lorenz's sobs, the spark of magic still hung in the air though. Waiting. Anticipating.

"Please," Cin whispered, and wrapped his own fingers through the bonds.

The metal pinched his skin as he pulled. He felt something move and, bracing himself, he tugged harder.

Lorenz cried out in pain and he grabbed at Cin's wrists. "Stop!"

Blood trickled from around the sides of the bonds.

Cin sniffled, then sobbed. He let Lorenz scoop up his fingers, squeezing tightly as they both cried, forehead to forehead until it seemed that all the love in the world had to be soaked in salt.

Twenty-Eight

The cage still bound Lorenz's heart.

Cin felt as though the world had dropped out from under him a second time. It was not as though all hope had been lost—there were no rules to the magic that had been inflicted on Lorenz, no reason to believe that their intimacy would give either of them the strength to remove it. But there had been magic in the air...

Cin didn't think he'd imagined that.

As he and Lorenz walked through the halls of the castle, their clothes fit snugly back into place, he wasn't so sure. What Cin did know though, was that the ache in his *heart* was real. That deep, fierce pressure that told him he could—he would—do anything for Lorenz, if it would keep his prince safe, make him happy. It felt so good and true and right, that every time Cin looked back at the ways he felt for his family, he cringed inside.

Emma, perhaps, he did love—even if that love was a bit distorted at the moment—but as for the rest? What were they to Cin, really? After all their years of cornering him into being the person who was most useful for their needs, he could not dream of a reality where losing them broke him the way Alwin's loss had broken Lorenz.

And Emma...

Cin's heart caught, but he pushed himself through the ache with a long breath. She'd shown that she cared more for keeping in their family's good graces than for reciprocating Cin's lifetime of affection when he needed it most. And perhaps that was not her fault—she'd grown up with these people who cared as little for her as they did for Cin—but it was still her choice. If Cin had to return to that house, where she avoided him and the rest of his family saw him only for the pieces of himself they could use, could he truly force himself to keep living through that?

There was a better future out there waiting for him, he was certain of it.

Such a revelation should have hit harder, burned brighter, but instead it was a tiny anxious ache in his gut. Lorenz's fingertips brushed his, and Cin's stomach fluttered. Whatever Lorenz's fears for his caged heart, he was still the one thing on Cin's horizon that he truly wanted. He just had to hope Lorenz could understand that.

As they stepped through one of the castle's exterior doors, the candle light behind them, Cin drew Lorenz around by the hand, taking his other as well. "I know what you think you're saving me from, but I want a life with you, whether we can remove your bonds or not."

The soft light in Lorenz's eyes made Cin feel weak and warm, but the prince swallowed and took a breath, asking with all solemnity, "Would you give up the Plumed Menace for it? Come live at the castle? Marry me and take the throne at my side?"

In the heat of their emotions and passion, Cin had nearly forgotten the blood on his hands—the blood in his future. Unless he chose to stop. It had been the only thing that held him together during the week alone with his family, but if he had Lorenz, maybe...

Where would that put him though, in a castle, as a king?

His whole body still revolted at the idea.

Lorenz didn't want that life either, though. And Cin could tell himself that meant they would be suffering through it together, but there was a better way, a way for them both to be happy. A future worth walking toward, hand in hand.

"I won't give up on creating justice, but we can find a different way, together... if you come away with me." Cin felt like he was sliding into a well, reaching out and asking the love of his life to fall in after him, but he kept on anyway. "We could go wherever we wished, be responsible only to each other. It would be a good life."

And it would be. It would be spectacular.

In the silence that followed, Cin could hear the sounds of celebration from the direction of the main gardens, music and laughter and a kind of tension that was palpable even from there. But it all seemed meaningless compared to the war that shadowed across Lorenz's face.

Cin couldn't tell what emotion was winning, but with each second that passed, he knew, with a terrible onslaught of dread, that their relationship was losing.

"I..." A shine came over Prince Lorenz's eyes.

Cin wanted to shove him away and wanted, too, to pull him so close and never let him go.

"When I look at you, I *want* to be with you, more than anything," Lorenz finally managed. "But my parents and my kingdom have both already been abandoned by one prince. No matter how much happier it would make me to run off with you into the sunset, I have a people who have given me and my family everything, and I can't ignore that, certainly not while I still bear my brother's crown in my chest."

Cin's throat caught. This all rested on Adalwin, on a man who'd vanished so many years ago, but after what Cin had seen in the forest last week...

It wasn't a strong enough hope to be worth clouding Lorenz's judgment, not as uncertain as Cin still was, but there was a chance, if he could lead the prince back there, that perhaps they'd find out together—could fix everything with the snap of monster's fingers.

"What if you gave them something different in return?" Cin lifted Lorenz's hands to his chest, clutching them there. "We could search for what happened to your brother. My flock can guide us through the forest, and you will know what to look for—we have a better chance together than the crown's watch ever did. And perhaps even, along the way, we'll be able to pull that broken crown out of your heart, even if it's one small piece at a time."

"I would love that." The words Lorenz spoke said yes, but everything about him contradicted that, from the misery in his voice to the desperation in his gaze. He would love it, in any sense he was capable, that was true. But he still wouldn't let himself.

From around the bend of the castle, towards the gardens, a distinct trumpet tune sounded: the signal for the arrival of the queen and king of Hallin.

"My parents," Lorenz said, as though everyone in the kingdom didn't know—and love—that sound. But right now, Cin hated it.

"You have to go back to them, don't you?" he forced himself to say. It felt, suddenly, stupidly, like it had always been the only option, and with each word, Cin's dread turned to something worse, wrenching at his insides as though trying to tear him apart piece by piece. He wanted to cling to Lorenz even harder. *But what if I need you more than they do*, he wanted to cry. Cin had been *needed* all his life though, and need was not always a good thing.

Lorenz gave Cin's fingers a squeeze. "Just for now. Let me think on your offer."

Cin's heart sank. "But when you step back into your castle tonight, won't you stop caring for me? Your parents will have announced you a partner. You'll have a whole new life ahead of you."

"That's why I have to think on it." Lorenz smiled sadly. "I have to know that I can make the choice to leave my position, my future, even when I'm not with you, or I'll cause us both pain in the end."

"All right." It was the hardest thing Cin had ever said. But if Lorenz needed this... If Cin had to let go before he could hold on... He tried to smile back. "You'll know where to find me."

They walked, hand in hand, but it was not into the future. Not yet.

Instead, they emerged into a garden full of light and sound. The change in atmosphere was blinding, Cin's emotions flaring like they could shield him from the festivities. Lights had been lit throughout the meandering walkways, the chill of the night pushed out by bonfires and bodies—far more than the guest count for the main part of the ball. It seemed that all the kingdom's people still awake at that ungodly hour of the early morning had been invited, with what had to be every one of the crown's watch to guard them.

Before they'd made it ten paces in, one of the wealthy arrivals wrapped an arm around Lorenz's shoulder, pulling him into a conversation. His fingers slipped from Cin's. He seemed to be trying to catch Cin's eye over his shoulder, but a drunk couple stumbled between them, laughing as they bumped into each other. Beyond them, he swore he could see the top of Floy's hat. It seemed like a sign that the moment he were back in the public eye, Cin would always be losing Lorenz to the people who disliked Cin most. His heart felt too light and small, a sick knot in his gut.

The outer wall of the castle was so close. He could just leave. Leave and never look back; that might be easier on his heart. Get free before the full weight of the pain set in. Walk into the sunset with himself. It should have been enough.

Yet the top of Lorenz's head still bobbed, now a few more people between them, lifting and turning like he was searching for Cin in the crowd. At some point, Cin would have to leave, but a part of him needed to know how the announcement went.

He pushed through the crowding guests, muttering apologies as he went, but as he focused on one gaggle of party-goers in front of him, he paused. Was that... *Dorthe?*

It took Cin a moment to recognize her out of her dark mourning dress, now clothed in her finest outfit, a pretty yellow dress with ruffles on the ends of the long sleeves, her bodice sweeping low across her luscious chest in a way that made Cin smile. She would have her pick of new partners sooner rather than later. When she noticed Cin, she smiled too, playing with the long silver chain of the necklace that fell between her breasts.

The charm at the end jiggled just a little higher, revealing three feathers, stained in a ruddy brown.

Cin felt equally flattered and bothered by the sight, and that should have been the extent of his emotions, the feathers just another small reminder of the complicated chaos between the blood of his victims and the joy their deaths brought.

Except it wasn't.

Because as the token of Aldous Earhart's death slipped free of its bondage between fabric and flesh, someone else pressed in from the crowd around them—someone Cin recognized far quicker, their eyes just as wide with shock as Cin's. Cin's stomach lurched.

Floy was moving before he could even step forward, their hat falling from their head as they sprang at Dorthe. Dorthe took a flailing step back, but Floy latched around the chain of her necklace and yanked. It came free, feathers and all.

Cin finally managed to lunge then, his hand reaching instinctively for the blade at his back as he moved. But he couldn't—this was *Floy*—at the royals' ball—surrounded by the crown's watch—

He stalled, and it gave Floy just enough time for their fingers to connect with the edge of his cloak. The feathers came free in their hand as they pulled, pressed against the ones from Dorthe's necklace. Floy's look of pleasure sent a chill down Cin's spine. He felt frozen to the garden stonework, the knife still tucked harmlessly at his back screaming at him.

As he stood there, Floy ducked back into the crowd.

Cin's heart pounded in his chest, and he didn't know—couldn't be sure—whether they had enough to prove his identity as the Menace, but he felt it in his gut. Floy knew. Somehow, they'd put all the pieces together.

They'd seen him for who he really was.

But Floy was not someone Cin wanted to be seen *by*.

Dorthe tried to speak, but Cin patted her shoulder insistently, pressing her toward the path that led, eventually, to the castle's front gate. "Go! Don't talk to anyone, just—"

There were already crown's watch moving toward them to investigate the commotion, but Cin worried more for what they'd do once they knew what Floy had done. He avoided the watchers, sliding his way towards the outer castle wall and Cin scrambled up the side of a planter, peeking out over the heads of the guests. It took him another few moments to spot Floy: weaving their way through the opposite edge of the party, coming up on the main patio where the space had been cleared for Queen Idonia and King Warner.

Cin's head felt light as one of the royal guards lifted a hand to stop Floy from approaching the queen and king. It was enough to get the queen's attention, though. She motioned Floy closer. The frantic way Floy spoke was accentuated by their clear certainty. They lifted the Dorthe's bloody charm, then the torn feathers of Cin's cloak, and the queen's eyes lit on them like a fire.

That the feathers looked identical meant nothing, Cin told himself—they were pigeon feathers—but he also knew that if there was a way to prove their origin, whoever did so would find them just as indistinguishable in that as in their appearance. The crown needed only to hold him long enough to do so.

Cin's world swayed.

"My dove!" Lorenz's voice sounded so small in the thunder behind Cin's ears. Larger hands closed around his.

He took a breath, and turned.

Lorenz stood on the garden path, low enough that Cin seemed

to be the taller of them now. His eyes were moist. He gave Cin's fingers a squeeze. "I thought you'd—"

There was no time for that. "Floy is telling your parents about me," Cin hissed, trying to put the full force of his meaning behind the words.

Lorenz must have gotten it, because his face paled. "You're certain?" His voice cracked with panic. "I can't convince them of your innocence a second time."

"I know—"

At that moment though, a guard—flushed face and damp behind the ears, as though they'd been one of those traipsing through the castle in search for the last hour—pushed into their midst, bowing slightly before barking, "Prince Lorenz, your parents request your immediate presence!"

"One moment—" He turned back to Cin, desperation and despair written in equal parts across his face, but the guard snapped again.

"They were very clear—"

"My God," Lorenz countered, "I am marrying someone under their duress, they can give me one final minute of freedom, *please*!"

The guard's face grew redder still. They bowed their head again, taking a single step back. "If you'd hurry..."

Cin glanced back across the garden, and locked eyes with Queen Idonia across the distance. She did not look happy. The queen nodded to Floy and with a wave, three of her personal watch rushed off the patio. Towards Cin.

The parts of the crowd nearest the guards seemed to notice, but they were quickly distracted by a blast from the trumpets that had

first announced the queen and king's entrance. The party went silent after, letting Queen Idonia's strong voice ring out across the
garden as she spoke with a warmth and confidence her expression
had been completely lacking just moment before.

"Welcome, my esteemed friends! As you well know, our dear
Prince Lorenz has spent the last six weeks courting the most eligible
young people in the kingdom in search of a partner who will support him as he begins his role as your some-day king. My husband
and I are honored by each gracious and..." The queen continued,
but Cin could no longer focus on the words, as the watch members
she'd sent out continued to wind their way through the crowd towards him, acquiring more help with each watcher they passed.

"You must go," Lorenz said, yet he seemed incapable of releasing
Cin's hand. He held it tighter. "Flee immediately to Falchovari, or
beyond. Don't look back."

Don't look back. It was what Cin had been half-dreaming of all
day. But now that it was time, the thought sunk like a rock in his
stomach. "I can't leave you—"

It was more than the Frog Prince's command: it was the truth.
Cin couldn't walk joyously into his future without Lorenz at his
side. Without his prince, he'd always be looking back.

"I'll find you, wherever you are. I'll follow your feathers," Lorenz
promised, squeezing Cin's fingers. "I won't forget my affection for
you."

"I know you won't," Cin said, and he wanted, so desperately, to
believe it.

"You told me the magic means your shoes fit only you?" Lorenz
asked. It was such an abrupt question that Cin nodded on instinct.

He had not managed to add a verbal affirmative before his prince continued, "Give me one of them, quick."

The royal guards were almost upon them, yet Cin found himself stripping one elfin-made shoe off and handing it to Lorenz as though that were the most natural thing imaginable.

Lorenz took it with both hands, holding it against his chest. "I'll make enough chaos to cover you. Now go!"

Cin leaped from the planter, scrambling through the last few throngs of people between himself and the castle's outer wall. His heart pounded in his ears, but he could just make out the pushing of the guards behind him as people exclaimed softly. He was smaller and lighter than them, though, no armor or heavy weapons to weigh him down. When he reached the wall, he launched himself up, using the magic of his remaining shoe to hold himself there as he found the cracks and irregularities he needed to pull himself up, once, then twice, then he was out of the guards' range.

He kept moving, up and onto the top of the wall. Cin dropped his body over the other side, his single shoe bracing him to the stone. Freedom called, but the moment his gaze found the garden's patio, he could no longer force himself to move. Queen Idonia continued her announcement, her husband behind her.

"And so, without adding further anticipation to the matter, we are pleased to announce our son's upcoming engagement," the queen declared, and Cin felt like he was falling, "to—"

Before Queen Idonia could bless one of the select few standing behind her with the future sovereignty, Lorenz burst into the cleared patio space, hurling himself in front of his mother with a hand raised high.

"My engagement will be to the gentlest and fairest of the land, as decided by the lightest of magics," he shouted, and in his fist he displayed Cin's magical shoe. "My hand in marriage will go to the person whose foot herein fits!"

The garden erupted into chaotic applause, confusion and delight tearing through the crowd as the queen and king watched on in shock.

Cin dropped to the ground outside the castle walls, the first of a show of fireworks blasting off above him.

Twenty-Nine

It was a shame Cin couldn't have flaunted his way down to the stage, just to see the reaction of the crowd as the magic of his shoe fit it perfectly to his foot. A shame, because each step away from the prince hurt like barbs being yanked from deep within his soul. A shame, because now that he'd dropped away from Lorenz's side, he might as well have dropped out of his life entirely, if the cage around his heart had anything to do with it.

He should have at least kissed Lorenz goodbye.

Cin could focus on little else as his flock-creature carried him out of the city, the fireworks popping in swells of light and color behind him. It would have taken a single second. One final kiss, in case it was their last. A memory to hold onto. As though the hundred they'd shared already weren't enough.

But they *weren't*.

They never would be.

Cin wiped a hand over his blurring eyes and kept riding. He could barely see the road before him, yet his mount carried him towards home with long, steady strides. Perdition was still there, with what little he owned. If he was to start a new life without Lorenz, Cin at least needed her.

Before Cin had time to process everything that had happened, much less all that he would have to do in the coming hours, days, and weeks to restart a full life in a new place—no home, no skills, no money—he was standing before the Reinholzes' dark, empty estate, his magical glamor still cloaking his outfit, and his mount beside him.

It had been a beautiful house once, he thought. In many ways it still was, with its impressive silhouette, vines overgrowing its edges. It wasn't his, though, no matter what grave lay in the garden, or how many times he'd lit those hearths. His own family had never made it into a home for him, only a place to work.

With a shaky breath, he walked up the front steps for the last time.

The chill seemed to permeate everything inside the house, deeper and more treacherous than the cold night beyond its walls. Cin tucked his arms around himself as he passed from the foyer into the first parlor. From the shadows, something lunged for him.

He hissed a sound almost like a scream as he grabbed for the knife strapped to the back of his belt. Too quick for him, frail hands gripped his arms, then wrapped around his back. Not an attack, but a *hug*.

"Cinder-Szule," Emma sobbed quietly, clinging to him.

"Emma?" Gently as he could, Cin detached her hold on him so that he could see her better, his eyes fighting with the darkness. Her ball dress felt grimy, her hair half-fallen from the delicate wraps Cin had put in for her that morning.

She had not once looked at him through that entire process, no "thank you" at the end, no smile or laugh. Now, at least, came the emotions. Though not the ones Cin wished.

His heart ached as he held her, cupping her face with his hand. "Are you all right?"

"Yes," Emma sniffled out. "I left the ball."

Despite himself, Cin almost laughed. "I can see that. But why? How did you get back?"

"I walked." Emma leaned a little too hard against Cin's hold as she said it, and he nearly stumbled as she did. Carefully, he settled her down on the nearest chair. In the back of his mind, he knew he had little time to waste.

But he could hardly focus on that when Emma was here, dirty and crying. "*Why* did you come back, Emma? What's wrong?"

She sniffled again, and began anxiously twisting her hair in one of her hands. "We got into the city and I just—I didn't *want* to be there anymore. Not without you. It was the last night, and you were supposed to get to go—Mother had *promised* me. So I—I left."

Cin's heart ached. She hadn't even known he'd left; hadn't heard his fight with their family or seen him storm out the door. And no one had bothered to tell her. He put his fingers over hers, gently stopping her frantic motion before she could add any new knots to the mess already tumbling halfway off her head. "Oh, Emma."

"You weren't *here,* though." She sounded sullen—not accusatory, simply *sad*.

Cin felt sad, too—sad, just for a moment, not to live in the world where he'd never loved Prince Lorenz, and had instead been sitting in the parlor with a roaring fire in the hearth, ready to sweep his little sister into his arms the moment she arrived. Maybe in that world, it would have been her love that propelled him toward a brighter fu-ture; they could have planned to flee together, hand in hand, with both of their family's horses and all the money they could filch over the course of months.

Maybe.

"I'm sorry," Cin said. As he knelt there in front of her, he could feel the small shivers beneath her cold skin. "Here, this will help." He rose, pressing his lips to Emma's forehead before moving to light the hearth. The logs smoked and went out, and he was forced to add more kindling to help them catch.

By the time he'd finished, Emma's gaze was on him, sharp and bright. "You... have an outfit?"

"It's magic. I've been to all the balls, in this, riding a horse made of my pigeons." It sounded absurd even with the mention of magic, but Emma only nodded as Cin continued, "I just couldn't let Mother know, until now."

"I'm not Mother." She looked so tragic as she said it, like she was realizing why that didn't make a difference, and hoping desperately that Cin would correct her.

He couldn't. "It's not that I don't trust you..."

"But you *don't* trust me," she said, then sniffled again, "Because I'm *irresponsible* and *incompetent*." She said them the way that Louise did, a little flare on *-sponse* and *-comp*, like those parts of the words were offending her. The little hiccup that followed cut the intimation short, though.

"No, Emma," Cin said, even though he wanted to say *yes Emma, get a fucking grip*. But for all the things he should have said a long time ago, he didn't think that was one of them. "You're inexperienced, but that's not your fault. It's Mother's, and Floy's, and Manfred's, and even our goddamn father's for all putting every responsibility on me and never finding you the things that you can learn to be good at. You're capable of so much—you just proved that, for fuck's sake! You walked all the way back from the capital in the dark, alone, wearing—Oh God, your poor *feet*."

Now that the logs had caught, Cin could see Emma's state properly, her dress torn and ragged and her hands and face dirty. But worst of all were her feet: scraped and cut, cracked with blood and dirt covering the sides. He could see each red-brown place she'd stepped since arriving.

Cin wanted to protect her all the more for it, but somehow, he got the sense that this was a sign of the opposite: Emma was more capable than he'd imagined.

"There were wolves," she said, oddly timid about it. "My heels were caught in the dirt, so I took them off."

"You walked here alone, in the dark, with the *wolves*." Cin laughed. *"Emma!"*

"Sorry?" Emma said meekly. A little tug came into the edge of her lips though.

Cin sighed and gave her hair a ruffle. "Stay put. I'll get some water and wrappings for them."

He could almost hear the back of his mind screaming now: *you have to leave. They'll be on to you soon. Caring for her is not worth your future.*

Still, Cin shot the voice down. He had time. "Keep watch out the front for me, won't you?" he said as he left the room. "Let me know if anyone is coming down the lane."

"Okay," Emma chimed. "Are you waiting for someone?"

It made more sense to lie, but... hadn't he done that enough? He'd just told her that it wasn't her fault that no one had given her the opportunity to grow. She, who had run from wolves on bloody feet. "The palace guards," Cin called down the hall. "They think I'm the Plumed Menace."

He listened closely to the silence from the parlor as his heart beat, then Emma said with genuine confusion, "But you *are* the Plumed Menace, aren't you?"

Cin froze, the water pail from the kitchen halfway to his hip. "What do you mean?"

"Well, you have the pigeons." Emma shouted slightly to reach him down the hall, and it felt like each echoing word was imprinting into the foundations of the house. "And you're so quiet, and you hate it when anyone is mistreated."

By the end of her explanation, Cin had made it back to the parlor, his heartbeat only a little out of time with the rest of him. She had known, all this time—and kept his secret, so thoroughly that even he hadn't realized. He didn't know why that should come as a shock.

Of course she would know, and still love him, and still protect him. She was his Emma.

"I can't deny any of that," Cin said, kneeling in front of her. He took one of her bloody feet, sliding it into the water. "Why didn't you tell someone?"

Emma's brow tightened. "Because the palace wants to lock you away," she replied, as though maybe Cin had forgotten. She flinched as Cin began to scrub gently at her wounds. Then things seemed to sink in a little more fully. "If the guards are after you now, where are you going to hide?"

"I'm not hiding." Cin switched to her other foot. "I'm leaving."

"For how long?" She sounded miserable at the thought, but like she was trying to hold herself together for his sake.

He couldn't bear to look up at her as he replied. "Forever, Emma. I'm going to Falchovari, or beyond. To start a new life."

It didn't sound like him. Not his future. Not yet.

Emma, at least, looked like she could see it.

Her eyes welled and she sniffled as she brushed at them. "You're leaving me?"

Cin took a breath, drawing Emma's second, cleaned foot from the water to dry it off, and forced himself to look up. "You can come, too, if you'd like that."

"Oh," Emma said. A fresh set of tears followed, larger and uglier than the last. "And we couldn't take Mother? Or Floy or Manfred? Or Father, even?" She seemed impossibly, stupidly hopeful.

"No, Emma." Cin had to swallow down the lump that left in the back of his throat. He began wrapping Emma's feet in careful, tight folds of bandage. "They haven't been good to you. Or to me."

"I know, but..." Emma gave a tiny sob. "I still love them."

Cin had thought his heart could break no further after the night he'd left behind—the prince he'd left with it—but he could feel whatever remained shatter afresh. "I know," Cin whispered. He had too, once.

He turned his head to wipe at the moisture gathering at the edge of his eye, and his gaze slid to the front windows. Out across the yard, the darkness of the night sky was giving way to the deep blue of impending morning. Below it came the silhouettes of a dozen riders.

Cin's heart launched into his throat, and he scrambled up so fast that he nearly stumbled over Emma's bandaged feet.

She twisted around to look. Her face paled. "I forgot to watch!"

"It's fine," Cin lied. He grabbed her shoulders. "Pretend— No, don't bother. Tell them I was here, and I fled. I'll come back for you in a month or two, when things are safer, okay?"

"Yes. Okay." Emma nodded, looking nervous, but determined.

Through the front windows, Cin could see the approaching soldiers dismounting, setting towards the house at a jog. He ran for the back.

As he reached the kitchen, though, the knob of the back door rattled. Someone cursed and banged against it. Someone who sounded an awful lot like Floy.

Cin's fingers twitched toward the knife at his back. Floy was no less malevolent than any of the bastards he'd killed before, no less willing to hurt their own family if there was something in it for them. But as he tried to grab for the hilt, his hand shook. His breath shuddered. He turned away.

If they were at the back, and the front—

He could hear the door to the entry hall opening. Emma shouted "I don't know, I don't know!" at whatever question was hurled her way, and Cin took the only course he could think of. He dove for the giant kitchen hearth.

It was dark and cold, and he slipped over the piled wood as quietly as he could, lifting the edge of his cloak to his mouth as he wedged himself up and into the chimney, grateful for his remaining magic shoe. He barely fit, his shoulders crammed on both sides. The soot from fires past swirled around his face, clumps of it dropping each time he moved. Somewhere above, he could hear the coo of pigeons.

He couldn't risk trying to reach them, though, as footsteps and the guards' voices resounded through the kitchen. With each breath, he feared he was dislodging too much soot already. Lantern light flickered across the logs.

"I don't know," Emma repeated, sobbing again. "I think he went out the back?"

"Useless idiot," Floy snapped. They sounded too close for comfort.

Cin risked a glance down. He could see the tips of Floy's shoes at the edge of the hearth. Part of the group seemed to move back out, charging through the house in a clatter of heavy boots and doors thrown open. But Floy didn't budge.

So neither did Cin. He focused on counting the seconds as he inhaled, then exhaled, slow but steady. His back ached from the pressure of the chimney. Soon his arms and legs would join it, he knew. But he could not risk trying to leave—not up nor down the chimney—until everyone was gone from the kitchen.

And Floy seemed determined not to move.

From above Cin, something shifted. Soot spilled down, showering his eyelashes and settling across his shoulders as two birds landed on him. He knew them instantly: Lacey and Ragimund. Of course they'd come. He wanted to laugh and cry all at once. The bob of his chest shifted his weight slightly and he cringed as a large mote of soot fell like a shadowy snowflake through his legs.

"What..." Floy muttered. They shifted back, and the top of their head appeared.

At that same moment, both of Cin's pigeons dove down, wings flapping and small, clawed feet raised as they collided with Floy's face.

Floy stumbled out of view, cursing and gasping. "Fucking *birds*! The hell does that Cinder-whore even *like* you?" They rattled something, shouting, "You come back down here and I'll crack your tiny skulls open!"

Cin felt every nerve in his body turn to fire and ice at Floy's threat, but it was quickly drowned out as chaos erupted from the front of the house. The noise and motion seemed to catch Floy's attention instead. Finally, Cin was almost certain the room was empty.

He began to shift, slowly, carefully upward, inch by inch. The sounds of the rest of his family echoed from the direction of the parlors—whether they'd come back with Floy, or on their own, Cin couldn't tell. The voice that responded to them made him stop short.

"I have the shoe with me." Lorenz sounded as confident and controlled as Cin had ever heard him, but there was a barrier to that tone—a hidden depth that Cin was all too familiar with from their early time together.

What was he *doing* here? *Here?*

Cin's home should have been the last place he'd go. But as Cin wavered between his confusion and resuming his climb toward the insistent coos of his pigeons above, another person spoke.

"We regret the informality of this visit," Queen Idonia said, "but my son insisted we go home to home for this." There was an unhappy sharpness to her voice.

Cin's heart pounded so hard that it hurt. If she was here too, was this her idea or Lorenz's? Surely not the individual shoe fittings, but perhaps when her son had demanded they visit the suitors at their homes, she'd taken advantage of it to come here. By the sounds of it, though, neither Louise nor the royal family were going to acknowledge the rush of the guards still scurrying throughout the house. Cin could hear two of them in the yard now as well. So much for climbing out onto the roof.

He wiggled one shoulder, trying to avoid a cramp rising in his arm.

"We are honored by your presence," Louise cooed. "Please, please sit! We can bring—"

"That won't be necessary," Prince Lorenz said. "There are many suitors to attend, and we mustn't stay long." Just hearing his voice so close, yet so far, made Cin ache inside.

"But the day is so young," his mother chided. "We can spare a few moments after the ride here."

"A few *moments*," Lorenz replied, soft enough that Cin could barely hear him.

"Excellent!" Louise clapped. "Floy and I will prepare the tea."

Cin tried not to panic.

Thirty

Cin could see an infinite number of ways this could go, and none of them were worth being trapped there to witness, stuck between the guards seeking his head on a platter and the prince who could not love him no matter how much they both wished for it, but the knowledge that his magic shoe wouldn't fit Floy was darkly satisfying.

They clearly knew it too, as Floy stormed into the kitchen, saying, "You saw its size! I can not fit into that. If that is truly Cin's shoe, it's a wonder *he* has managed it."

"His feet aren't that much smaller than yours," Louise objected, her voice equally low. "We'll make room."

The distinct metal-on-wood sound that followed was eerily like the thrum that the largest of their cooking knives made when pulled from its mount. Cin's stomach turned at the thought. But they couldn't—they wouldn't—

"Mother!" Floy snapped, and beneath their anger Cin caught their fear, stark and rising.

"It'll only be one foot," Louise replied. "Hurry! They'll grow suspicious."

"I don't—"

The scoff Louise gave made Cin feel like a child again, soot smeared across his face and not sure what he'd done, but certain he must have ruined things for all of them. "Would you not give a part of your heel to be Queen?! You will have the very best slippers, servants to carry you, a stable of horses—your foot need only *fit*."

Floy's voice, when it came again, was smaller than Cin had ever heard it, tight and terrified. "Fine."

Cin's nausea grew, and he curled his toes against the inside of the single shoe he still wore, telling himself it wasn't his feet, it wasn't *his* feet. His heels hurt. They felt too large suddenly, two protuding knobs that might fall off if he twisted his ankle the wrong way.

Floy and Louise shuffled about, and a chair slid loudly across the floor. Then the noise stopped. In the silence, the carving of the knife through flesh sounded thick and ragged. Floy's suppressed groan turned to a sob as it happened again. And a third time.

Something flopped wetly onto the ground.

Bile rose in the back of Cin's throat and he nearly slipped. His head felt light. He'd seen blood, seen death—slid knives into backs and throats and bellies—but not seeing was worse somehow. The thing was no longer out there, external, untouched, but inside him, his mind building weight and pain to the echo of that meaty thud.

Floy's sniffles lessened as Louise barked at them to quiet themselves. Cin swore he could hear the blood as it seeped into the bandages Louise applied with none of the care or love that Cin had given Emma's. When they were done, Louise left on steady feet, and Floy at a lopsided shuffle.

Louise's voice sounded as cordial and unaffected as ever as she greeted the party back in the parlor. "It seems we need to send for water to make the tea, but in the meantime, my dear Floy would be honored to try on that royal shoe of yours."

Cin knew the magic in his elvish-made shoes would not let Floy's feet fit, heel or not, yet the fear of it was still suffocating; whatever his head told him, his heart could not stop believing there was a chance—a chance that Floy would be the one at the prince's side for the rest of their life, Cin forever hearing news of their exploits in papers and cross-kingdom gossip.

Stranger things had happened so far that day. Lorenz was there, in Cin's parlor, after all; for some stupid, haphazardous reason, he'd wound up a hall away from Cin, talking amicably with Louise and Floy. Cin could imagine the scene in visceral detail: Lorenz's smile masking his fear and loathing, Louise's calm gentleness pinching to anticipation around the edges, Floy holding back the pain with a stony expression.

"Here, if I may?" Lorenz asked, and he could only have been kneeling.

"Please, yes!" Louise exclaimed, and Floy said something softer.

Lorenz would be picking up their foot then, the bandage hidden beneath a pristine stocking. Cin hoped his fingers brushed the place Floy's heel had been. Hoped they bit their cheek open to stifle their cry, pink lacing their teeth when next they tried to smile.

Envisioning that was the only thing that kept him from panic.

The shoe would be going on now, in the silence and the tension. The moment seemed to drag on forever. Cin's arms shook. Flecks of soot rained from where his feet braced.

"Does it fit?" Queen Idonia asked, and for the life of Cin, he couldn't determine the emotion behind the question.

Lorenz answered impatiently. "It's nearly…"

Through the moment of quiet, Floy cried out in pain.

"My god!" Lorenz's voice lifting above an onslaught of shuffling and whispers. "Are you *bleeding*? I'm terribly sorry."

"It's nothing—" Louise interrupted him.

"Clearly not!" Lorenz snapped. "The back of their heel is *red*."

Cin tried to smile, but he could hear the *hack-hack-hack-flop* of that heel falling to the floor once again and his body gagged against the joy he wished he could find in the situation. There was no future with Lorenz for Floy. Heel or no heel.

Louise seemed to be arguing against that very obvious fact, but Queen Idonia cut her off with a solemn determination. "Clearly, the shoe does not fit."

And Cin thought she sounded just the tiniest bit disgusted.

"My— Floy is not my only eligible child," Louise said, almost begging now. "Please, let me get my eldest."

"If you will," Queen Idonia said, yet she did not sound particularity interested.

Cin caught the sound of a guard's voice, too low to make out the words, then the queen gave an equally soft response. The guard moved through the house once more—clearly not ready to give up quite yet—though it seemed most of their group had already moved outside.

The sounds of the search party were lost under Manfred and Louise's footsteps as they burst into the kitchen.

"But my feet are bigger than Floy's!" Manfred protested.

"We trimmed Floy's heel and they nearly fit," Louise said. "Without your toes…"

"My *toes*? Fucking hell!"

"I have let you sleep in my home and gamble my money while you contribute little to this household." Louise's voice was a hiss, so imposing it seemed to snake into Cin's very bones. "I need not sustain your slothful habits, you understand me?"

An image flashed through Cin's mind of Manfred's sneer turning to a scowl as he curled one fist. Louise was no fighter, and though tall as her children, she was wiry and brittle. She'd crumble under a single punch from Manfred.

Yet the next sound that came was not the clap of skin on skin, but the soft struggle of their Father's voice. "Louise is right, son."

Cin hadn't even known he was there—had he watched Floy's heel come off, too? Silent, uncaring. Or hiding it all inside, telling himself that it was for the best.

Manfred growled, "Fucking do it already."

Cin did not want to be there. As much as he hated Manfred, he did not want to listen to this again. The sickening slice, the muffled cry, the visions that would accompany it.

Cin breathed in a little too fast and deep, his cloak slipping from around his mouth. Soot burned in his lungs. He held in his breath as best he could, choking as his body fought to cough.

The first *thwack* came wet and fast, and Manfred breathed like he was fighting through tears. The second cracked against bone. Manfred moaned, a long, low noise like a dying animal, his voice blending into the sound of sawing that came next. Then it cut out entirely. The sawing continued.

Soot stung up the back of Cin's throat. One of his arms slipped. He moved his foot to adjust for it.

He closed his eyes at the final slap of Manfred's fallen toes onto the floor. The world swayed around him, and he couldn't bear to listen as Manfred was helped out of the kitchen, the rumblings from the parlor repeating what he'd already heard from Floy's presentation. It didn't matter—Cin knew the outcome.

Now was his time to leave. He bit back nausea as he prepared himself to climb once more. From the parlor, Lorenz seemed to be wrapping up another unsuccessful shoe testing, his voice quickly losing its mask of grace and charm.

"I have a final child," Louise was pleading, and some bitter part of Cin was satisfied that he was not included among that count, until his stepmother called out of the parlor, "Emma!"

Cin's blood ran cold.

Emma's clumsy footsteps echoed down the hall as she answered dutifully, but when she was pulled around the kitchen corner, with what sounded like the whole family in her wake, she begged under her breath. "But I don't want—"

"Your feet are just a little small," Louise was saying, like the crown was somehow still one brilliant mutilation away. "We only need to stretch them out…"

Panic snapped through Cin's mind, blotting out all fear of the crown's watch hearing him. He would not see Emma brutally used for their mother's mad scheme first.

Cin tried to drop from the chimney with care, but the moment his remaining magical shoe left the brick, his whole body slid. His feet hit the logs piled in the hearth, and they twisted, dumping him forward. He gasped in pain as his ankles twisted, and soot rained around him, sweeping into his lungs.

Cin hacked it back out, stars dancing across his vision.

"My God!" Louise proclaimed.

Cin lurched out of the hearth as he coughed, reaching behind him for his knife, but something hard and metallic slammed into the side of his head. The world spun and flashed, time sliding forward as though not all moments were equal. He could see the blur of Louise's ankles, a poker in her hands.

Behind her, Emma burst forward so quickly that Floy and Manfred had to scramble on their mutilated feet to grab her.

"What are you doing to Cinder-Szule?" she shrieked, struggled against her sibling's grips. "Stop!"

Something moved at Cin's side as his world nearly turned dark again as he tried to look over his shoulder. A hand brushed gently against his head. Cin's heart caught in his throat as his father spoke.

"Your mother would have been so ashamed."

The back of Cin's eyes burned. It was not sadness he felt, though; it was righteousness. Perhaps he was not good or pious, but neither were the rest of his God-forsaken family. Cin, at least, knew how to turn his villainy on those who deserved it.

As his father stepped away, Cin shoved his elbows under himself, scrambling to his feet. He only made it halfway before the poker slammed across the side of his head. He hit the floor again, his vision wavering. This time, he smelled blood.

A pair of sharp pigeon screeches filled the air, echoing through Cin's head. They were followed by Louise's screams.

Her arms swung, the poker swinging with them.

Cin's consciousness slipped out entirely, but into the darkness carried a thwack. Like a knife in flesh. Like fist on bone. Like a tiny body, being struck to the floor. Again.

And again.

And again.

Thirty-One

Cin felt the sick terror in his stomach before he could form a coherent thought. He didn't have to force his eyes open to know the cooling bodies of his pigeons were splayed beside him: one silky and gray, one splotched brown and white. If they were alive, he would not have felt the snap in his chest, like a cord between them had been cut short.

A cord of magic, withdrawing from their tiny bodies, and returning to Cin's.

The magic they'd been using: it was never truly his flock's, Cin realized. It was always his own magic, only he'd given it away, unknowingly spreading it around in little hopeful pieces until he hadn't even known he was the origin. Amongst his birds. To the only living creatures who'd cared for him after his birth mother passed.

The only creatures, except Emma.

She sobbed for Cin now, and as he forced his eyes back open, he could blearily see her, struggling against their siblings. Manfred wrenched her back so hard that she spilled into the counter, toppling to her knees.

"Stop!" Emma gasped.

Manfred grabbed her again, clamping a hand over her mouth as she tried to scream.

A fire lit in Cin's chest, seeming to burn through his grief and turn it to anger, to rage. Something rattled in the chimney, but no one else seemed to notice. Cin heard it, though, the first clatter, and the second one. Hisses and flaps echoed with it.

Manfred wrenched Emma onto the table, Floy holding her legs while Louise searched for a kitchen tool that would achieve her desired foot-stretching, however pointless and unwanted that might be. Emma locked eyes with Cin. Tears streamed down her cheeks. Their father stood over her shoulder, patting her head while she struggled.

"Listen to your mother, Emma," he said, soft and dead-eyed.

Cin hated him most of all.

He didn't try to run at his family again, though. As much as he wanted to plunge his knife into their flesh and see the world turn right for once, that was not the way. Because justice should not have had to be a thing that slipped quietly into backs.

It deserved to be loud.

Behind and above him, the chimney sang like a storm, and Cin's flock poured out of it.

Dozens upon dozens of birds—pigeons, doves, songbirds, even a few crows—flooded through the chimney in a shrieking, sooty cloud. They descended on Cin's family, too dense and violent for Cin to make out more than the screams, but he could feel their actions like they were extensions of himself, hearts and minds linked through his magic. From amidst their fury, Emma scrambled out on all fours.

She hugged Cin's leg, shaking as she she held onto him. A single scratch ran the length of her jaw to her forehead, a trickle of blood running like a tear from one eye. But she was safe.

She would be the only one.

Cin's flock swelled and raged around him as he swept up Lacey and Rags' small bodies into his arms, Emma still clinging to him fiercely as he cradled his lost pigeons, their unbeating hearts warm against his chest. Tears slid down his cheeks, but he held his chin up, letting the shrieks of his family echo through him. Slowly, the sounds of torment died to whimpers.

His flock began to pull back, still swirling and dancing through the kitchen like a feathered storm. The paths vacated by their claws and beaks revealed a terrible scene.

Manfred moaned where he slumped across the table, the flesh of his hands picked down to the bone. Shiny tendon strings from his partially intact wrists and streaks of blood crisscrossed the wood beneath him, but each finger had been stripped to sparkling whiteness. Beside him, Floy shuddered, their jaw hanging open. Cin could see every one of their teeth, from gum to tip, where their lips had been stripped away in jagged chunks, what remained of the flesh there flopping against their chin. A fresh drizzle of blood slid free with each of their ragged breaths. A whisper came from Cin's father where he sat on the floor, two deep, bloody holes where his eyes had been, blood welling in the pits and dripping down the long ridges of the gashes that extended into his cheeks.

What Cin could see of his stepmother seemed whole in comparison—her eyes dull from pain, her mouth open in her gasping, her fingers clenching the edge of the table. But as she pulled herself up,

Cin could see where the front of her gown was gone, her under-dress hanging in tatters across strips of muscle and fat where the birds had ripped away the front of her chest. The bone of her sternum gleamed where it met ribs. Beneath them sat the erratic pump-pump of a heart. Each beat came slower than the last.

Cin held Rags and Lacey's bodies all the tighter.

He wanted to finish this.

He wanted this to end.

He *wanted*...

Louise's exposed heart went still, and Cin didn't know *what* he wanted.

Through the chaos of his flock, a shadow shot toward him.

Arms wrapped around Cin, Lorenz's hands grasping at him, pulling him close. Not a spot of blood was on him, but the front of his shirt had been ripped open by the claws of birds, his crown lopsided upon his tussled hair and stray feathers caught in his clothing. Cin could see the faint impression of the bonds around his heart. The prince ignored the carnage, holding onto Cin so tightly that Cin could feel the press of the metal in his chest, the subtle thrum of a heartbeat beyond.

"You've done it, my Menace," he whispered. "You're free."

The breath Cin took then felt like his first in ages. It cracked in a sob at the end.

Around them, his birds barreled outward. They shot through the windows, glass shattering outward in a crystalline rain, and the back door tore open under their weight, peeling back with such a fury that it was dragged off its upper hinges. Cin sobbed again, clutching Lorenz's shirt.

His family's moans still whispered through the space, but the weight of his wrath felt lighter. Emma sniffled, burying her face into the side of Cin's leg, clearly terrified, but safe. Free. They were, both of them, free.

Almost, anyway.

From the hall to the parlor rushed the final member of the original watch team, the one who'd been continuing through the house even as the others had all turned their searches outside. Behind him, Cin could just make out the queen, her face pale as she stared at the scene in horror, three of her personal watch members surrounding her. When her gaze landed on her son, the bonds of his chest on full display, a new terror appeared, followed by fury.

Cin tensed. His flock careened by the windows, birds flying through the open back door to fill the space behind him like a deadly throne, a weapon prepared to launch. Those before him weren't villains, though—and Cin wasn't a victim in this. He'd made his choices, and he had no regrets.

As the watch member lifted his sword point for the charge, Cin held his ground, his flock alert but unmoving behind him. It was Lorenz who stepped forward.

"You will not touch him!" The desperation in his voice made Cin's heart lurch, Lorenz growing hoarse as his shouting continued, thick and painful with emotion. "You will not touch the man I l-l—"

The word cut off in a cry. Between the strands of his ripped shirt, the serrated bonds that locked his heart pulsed with darkness as they writhed deeper into him. He grabbed for them, blood welling between his fingers, and Cin grabbed with him. Lorenz's eyes met

Cin's, endless and open, no longer a pool but the completeness of the night sky, brimming with something so precious Cin did not have to guess at it.

"I love—" Lorenz managed, crying out in pain at the final word.

And Cin whispered back, "I love you, too."

With everything within him and everything outside himself, every feather of his flock and sparkling drop of their shared magic, he pulled. He could feel his will collide with that of the monstrous dark thing. His mind went numb, like a mile of water lay above him, murky and muggy. A heartbeat pounded in his ears. He could sense more than see: the forest, a fight, a splatter of blood and a scream of agony. But the heartbeat remained, through the shimmer of golden sun on green. The croaking of frogs bubbled in the distance. Hope and fear caught in Cin's throat. He tightened his grip.

He could sense his flock around him again, their strength flooding his veins. He shoved against the vile magic once more, and its darkness broke for him. It moved like a living thing beneath his fingers. It left gaps of bloody flesh in its wake as it peeled itself off Lorenz's chest, coming free into Cin's hands.

With one final shove of power, he hurled it across the kitchen. The dying metal collided with the kitchen hearth. Sparks flared through the chimney and rolled across the stone, unfurling like vines until they met wood. The wall caught fire.

Cin grabbed Emma's hand in one of his and Lorenz's shoulder in the other and pulled them toward the back door. The queen and her guard followed on their heels, a flood of birds pushing them all toward safety. Behind them, Louise's corpse already smelled of burning fat and seared muscle as the magic-sparked fire spread in a rampage. Floy and Manfred whimpered and wailed as they scrambled away, their father catching flame silently behind them.

Cin ignored them all. He dragged Lorenz and Emma far enough into the garden that he couldn't feel the fire as it curled up the kitchen walls and ascended through the house's too-many rooms. Carried, Cin hoped, by the draft in his own room. He could feel Perdition's small body as she slipped through that very gap, fleeing the fire in a burst of magic.

As they came to a stop, he could not help but smile at his prince. Lorenz swayed, and his hand came away from his chest. Red.

Fear turned Cin's body cold. Lorenz collapsed away from him, crumbling onto his back in the garden grass. Blood pooled in the open gashes where his bonds had been, spilling in streams across his skin.

Cin's whole world seemed to sway. He was atop Lorenz in a moment, his flock a distant crackle in his ears as they poured around him protectively. He shoved his palms against the wounds he'd left when he'd torn Lorenz's bonds free. Wounds, deep as blade-marks. Cin choked on the thought. He could hear the queen screaming somewhere, everywhere—or maybe that was him, crying Lorenz's name as he tried frantically to stop the bleeding.

Through the cloud of birds around him, a single pigeon descended on to his shoulder.

He knew her by touch, by song, and by the way she pressed into the crook of his neck, her soft back ruffling against his skin. Amidst the din of his terror, her weight sparked something in the back of Cin's mind; she was heavy. Far heavier than Lacey and Ragimund's bodies now were, tucked into one arm as he used his hands against

Lorenz's chest. No bones, no blood, no flesh remained of them—only feathers, shimmering with a final hint of magic.

Cin moved on instinct. He pressed the feathers into Lorenz's wounds. Wherever they entered, fresh skin spilled into place, modeled in Lacey's gray and Hap's white and brown, as though knit from the very souls of Cin's precious companions. As the final gash sealed over, he could feel a spark of them settle into Lorenz, gracious and arrogant, kind and brave.

Lorenz gagged in a breath and coughed it out. A shimmer ran through his new flesh, the tangled lines crisscrossing his chest. It held in place, healthy and strong as the magic that flowed through it.

Cin wasn't sure whether he was laughing or crying as he leaned over Lorenz, pulling him into his arms. His prince clung to him in return, echoing his sentiments until slowly their sounds turned to soft, giddy cackles. Lorenz cupped the side of Cin's face, grinning up at him.

"I love you," he whispered, and the magic flesh over his heart shimmered as though in agreement. He said it again, then a third time, and with each repetition, Cin's smile widened. If they had been the only people on earth, he would have been happy to stay like that forever.

But even with Lorenz's love, Cin was still the Menace, and his prince the future king, and a whole different justice was coming to call for them both.

Thirty-Two

Cin was growing increasingly aware of the crowd circling him and Lorenz. A ring of Cin's flock—now even larger than it had been in the kitchen—guarded them as the crown's watch members waited beyond, weapons drawn. Edging closest was the queen. Her husband had a hand on her shoulder, like he might try to pull her into the protection of his arms if the birds descended, though his eyes were locked on Lorenz.

"Ren..." Queen Idonia's voice was desperate, and she inched forward as if Cin were a wild beast who'd pounced upon her son only to miraculously set him free.

Lorenz did not smile at her, his expression dipping toward sadness. Cin squeezed his hand.

The queen's gaze flickered between them, and for all her obvious doubts, she seemed to interpret one thing clearly. "Is this who you've chosen to lead our kingdom with you, my son? A killer?"

"No Mother," Lorenz said, rising slowly to his feet. He pulled Cin up with him. "This man whom I've chosen as my partner is not a killer—he's a *good* man, a man of integrity and justice, who has struggled to fill the gaps we left in our kingdom when we allowed our grief and fear to keep us from caring properly for our people..."

He took a breath, and Cin could feel his prince's—his *partner's*—confidence waver, then return, brighter and more certain. Cin caught his previous smile sparkling deep in his eyes, his hair fluttering, for once, in a very real breeze. Somehow, that same wind sent smoke billowing around the house without spreading it toward any of them, as Lorenz continued, "My dearest dove and I will not be leading anyone. Neither of us is going to be Hallin's next king."

Despite all of Cin's hope and yearning for a future where Lorenz sought his own happiness, his own life, he still faltered from shock. Under the light of this announcement, the world felt ethereal. Lorenz's parents looked less thrilled by the idea, however.

"What will happen when your father and I are gone, Ren?" Queen Idonia floundered. "There is no one in the direct line but you—"

"We will find someone else," Lorenz said. "You may have claimed you were looking for a partner to *help* me rule, but we all know you were hoping to entrust the kingdom primarily to them, not to me. I am not the son who was meant for that."

The queen took a step toward him, seeming no longer to notice the horde of watchful birds still circling. She held out her palms pleadingly to her son. "You could be! With practice—"

"I don't wish for practice!" Lorenz shouted. There was no cruelty in his voice, but his expression stayed firm as he met his mother halfway, taking her hands in his. "I want to travel our kingdom, without a crown or a watch. I want to see and learn all that I've missed keeping myself away in the castle. I want to know our people, as a fellow person, not as sovereign. And perhaps, there may be a time, long after that, when it means the crown feels the correct weight for my head, but I can make no promises. I can only serve our people in the way that feels right for me now, and let the future come when it may."

Queen Idonia seemed to be taking this explanation like it was a raw lemon, her face contorted and her eyes watering, but she inhaled deeply, and her gaze shifted to Cin. "And you wish to do all this with him?"

"Yes, Mother." Lorenz looked at her sternly, the expression only slightly marred by the upward quirk of one lip. "Throwing my love in the dungeons won't stop it, you know. Even I can't seem to properly cage my own heart." His voice grew more solemn as he added, "I believe there is a great good that the Plumed Menace can do for Hallin. We need someone who understands the suffering of the least fortunate in our kingdom and has fought, if crudely, to alleviate that. You had Father for your council in that, once—he spurred you to create the watch in the first place, did he not? But now you are both far too isolated to fully realize what must be done next."

The queen flinched at that, diverting her gaze. Slowly, though, she looked behind her, locking her eyes with her husband. Her voice was barely a whisper as she asked, "Would *you* pardon him?"

Cin's heart seemed to stutter, a thousand eyes still peering down around him as though waiting to know whether they'd need to sweep him up and whisk him and Lorenz into a new life or not.

"Should he agree to Ren's ideas, then I certainly would," the king confirmed, placing a hand on his wife's shoulder. "But I only want you to agree to this because you believe in it."

It was fascinating to watch a man so soft and quiet as Lorenz's father speak with such reassuring confidence. He would not have burned beside his wife, Cin thought. King Warner would have, just as calmly and gently, found her corpse, and carried her out.

Queen Idonia sighed. "Ren loves him, and if I am being truthful, I have known you and he to be a finer judge of character than myself." She looked to her son as she said it, giving him a small, proud smile. "If he cares for Lorenz as much as he ought, then I'm certain we can reach a consensus."

"I do," Cin said. He found there was no hesitation in him, no circles he needed to run around the thought of giving up the Plumed Menace—not when there was other change, broader change, he could instill. He had never needed the Menace, he found. What he had needed was justice. If the crown was open to seeing that through, then he'd take the opportunity and run with it.

"See," King Warner said, and kissed his wife's temple. "You are a fine enough judge. You picked me, after all."

"Oh, stop," the queen grumbled, but it was with the softest smile Cin had ever seen. Her face fell into a weary despair in moments though, her gaze returning to Lorenz and Cin. "If you are truly so committed to giving up the crown, then in the coming months we may begin to discuss—all of us—who we might train up in your place."

As she said it, Cin's body was flooded by the sensations he'd first felt from Lorenz's bonds: the sense of life, of pain, of transformation, and then...

Cin shuddered. It fit so well with everything he'd already wondered at, it almost scared him. But those bonds were not just the cage around Lorenz's heart—they'd been more, too, once. They'd been Adalwin's crown. They'd witnessed his death, if death was what it had been. Cin wasn't so sure.

He had no desire to give Lorenz or his parents false hope, but it all seemed too much of a coincidence to not at least warrant attention. Before he could let his worries convince him otherwise, Cin spoke up. "We may already know who the best person for the kingdom is." He waited as the queen and king's attention fixed on him, searching for the balance between reason and desire. "When I drew Prince Adalwin's mangled crown from Ren's chest, I felt the memory of the dark magic that imbued it when Adalwin was attacked."

Lorenz had believed he cast the dark magic on himself, but Cin thought otherwise. It seemed to have been in the crown already, placed there by the villain who'd attacked Adalwin's party. Perhaps it had been intended to take over the heart of its victim, or maybe Lorenz had simply pulled it forth with his grief, but it had existed there before Lorenz's journey into the forest, and through it, Cin knew he'd sensed the truth.

"I don't believe Adalwin was killed with his party," Cin continued. "Whoever attacked him was a skilled sorcerer who might have inflicted him with all manner of curses. He may still be out there somewhere, unable to return to you."

Lorenz nearly stumbled, his pupils so wide that the sparkle of brilliant green in them was nearly overtaken. His voice came out hoarse. "My brother is alive?"

"I can't promise anything," Cin admitted. "But I think we should look for him."

"Alwin..." the queen whispered. A single tear slipped down her cheek, but her expression was pure hope.

Lorenz laughed, a deep, sobbing sound, and threw himself at his parents, all three of them wrapped in each other's arms as they cried. "He could be out there—"

King Warner stuttered, "But we've looked—"

"We'll look again!" Queen Idonia exclaimed. "If there's even the smallest chance we missed him…"

The sight of their little family together, sharing their joy and grief so openly, made Cin's heart ache. He could never have had that with Louise and Penrod, not even over the lives of his own siblings. But there was still someone he loved enough to mourn with, even if they hadn't yet discovered how to rejoice together.

Leaving the royal family to their joy, Cin walked awkwardly back through the garden, noticing his missing shoe far more now that all eminent danger had passed. Those of the watch who remained parted for him. Whether it was from the crown's promise of a pardon, or their fear of the birds that still circled Cin from a distance, he wasn't sure.

Most of the watch members had moved on, though, a few preparing Floy and Manfred for transport—to the nearest doctor, Cin assumed, though he wasn't sure how much good it would do them—while the rest attempted to fight back the fire that still raged within the Reinholzes' estate. It seemed to have no desire to burn beyond the house, not even to the tree growing from the grave of Cin's birth-mother, no matter how many sparks rained through its branches.

Father was still in there, burning along with Louise's corpse, but Cin only felt the slightest grief for that. He had been given his chances, to stay or to leave, to make a difference, to be kinder, even if he couldn't be stronger. He'd chosen to stand silently by instead, the same in life as he was in death. A part of Cin would miss him—would miss Louise, even, and Floy and Manfred too, if they didn't survive the shock of their wounds—but that feeling was so tiny compared to the satisfied beast of his hatred, now curled contentedly around his chest, purring like a cat.

Cin found Emma sitting at the edge of the garden, her knees to her chest and her arms wrapped around them. She barely looked up as he settled on the ground beside her, the heat close enough to leave a glow on Cin's exposed skin. What a pair they must have made: Cin covered in soot, and Emma in her torn and dirty church-best, bare feet bloody—though gratefully un-stretched—and the deep cut on her cheek closing over in an angry red scab. Her eye seemed all right but for a single red line in the white.

Cin said nothing, just sat with her, waiting. It felt good to simply feel. To ache. To want. So much had been taken from them in such a short time, and so much offered up, yet untouched. He barely even noticed when Manfred and Floy were finally taken away, one of them still moaning.

"Did I deserve that?" Emma whispered, so sudden that Cin almost didn't register the words. He nearly thought she meant the scratch on her cheek, but then she lifted her finger to the fire instead.

Cin cupped his hand around hers, lowering it. "No," he assured her.

And, he thought, perhaps neither did their parents—not all of what had come for them, anyway. If he were going to be helping his kingdom find a new method of justice, one that didn't rely on his birds or his blade, he had to grant his family that grace, too, if only in retrospect. That hardly meant he regretted the present outcome, though. Earning and deserving were two different things, and his family had certainly earned this.

Cin wrapped his arm around Emma's shoulder and pulled her nearer, resting his chin on her head. It felt like it had been ages since he'd last held her so close in such quiet.

Too long, at least.

Emma glanced up, her brow tight despite the hope in her voice. "Will I get to visit you at the castle?"

Cin hesitated, brushing back the stray hairs that had fallen from her lopsided styling. "I don't know where I'll live, whether it will be the castle or someplace else, but wherever it is, you can always come too."

Emma hugged onto him. Into his chest, she whispered, "What if I keep ruining things?"

"You have never ruined anything, Emma," Cin said. And he found he meant that.

He held her like that, the fire uncomfortably close as it raged, then dimmed, the wood of their family home crumbling in on itself, until Lorenz and the queen finally approached with their horses alongside both of the Reinholzes', Cin's flock-creature already forming into its equine shape behind them. Cin stood, offering Emma help onto one of their family steeds. After a tiny sniffle, she took it.

All those times he'd dreamed of the hearth flame twirling out and up, searing into wood and taking them all with it. He'd always

anticipated it would feel good, but this was nothing like the sancti-
fication he'd imagined. This was hope. It was a future, unfolding in
front of him with each crackle and split of the Reinholz estate's ag-
ing wood.

And whether under the smile of God or a sullen frown, Cin
could not wait to step into it.

Thirty-Three

The ride away from the Reinholz estate was a blur for Cin. No one questioned Emma's inclusion, for which he was grateful. As more and more people joined the edges of their procession, her presence became one oddity of many. The growing crowd seemed to make the queen nervous, but she kept a barrier of watch members between her own little party and the rest of the world as she put on her best smile. Some changes, Cin figured, would come slowly.

By the time they'd reached the main square of Darmburg, it seemed as though the whole of the town had emerged to see them. The excited villagers packed so thoroughly into the streets on either side of the square that it stalled the royal party at the center. Through the dispersing morning gloom, Cin caught the gleam of the castle towers. With Lorenz beside him, they did not feel quite so distant anymore.

The prince's horse danced on its hooves as Cin's flock-creature rubbed up against it. Cin leaned close enough to whisper, "I think you may need to abandon your dream of a bare-chested statue in this particular village. Now that they've seen your own sculpted musculature, no metal or stone will live up to it."

Lorenz laughed, adjusting the torn fragments of cloth that still hung off his shoulders. For all that he claimed his rakishness was a front, he *had* denied the watch's offer of a jacket, though he'd played it off as chivalry. Cin suspected it had more to do with the fresh skin over his newly freed heart though, with the way Lorenz's fingertips kept tracing the magical flesh absentmindedly. It shimmered in response to his touch, alive with Lacey and Rags' spirits.

Cin had caught himself smiling at the feather-like shine every time.

Now though, his attention was taken in by the still-growing crowd. Cin recognized the better half of them, and for once, it seemed some even noticed him in turn. Echoes of the same conversation traveled through the amassing villagers—"Is that one of the Reinholz children? The quiet one? Oh, what is his name?"—but more and more, those confused whispers turned to excited shouts.

"Is he the one?" called the miller's daughter, pulling herself onto her tiptoes to wave at Lorenz.

From the other side of the square, the old man who lived two houses down from Dorthe cried, "Tell us, does the shoe fit?"

"Show us the shoe!" someone nearer demanded, the desire echoing in a wave throughout the crowd.

Beneath Queen Idonia's regal poise, she seemed hesitant, all the bravado she'd had while within her castle walls clearly strained by the uncontrollable anticipation around them. Lorenz seemed almost to buckle with her, but Cin slipped his hand into his prince's and squeezed. The light returned to Lorenz's face tenfold.

He raised Cin's hand above their heads, shouting back to the crowd, "Shall we find out?"

A cheer sprang up at that. The queen and king nodded their approval. From her spot on her mount off to the side of the party, even Emma gave her own call of encouragement.

The crown's watch cleared space for Lorenz to dismount, and Cin allowed his own steed to vanish into a flock of spiraling pigeons that made the crowd cry out in shock and delight. Talk of magic spread through them, until it seemed like the whole village was debating whether they knew that Cin could control the birds—every person who claimed they'd known was certainly a liar—and Cin swore he heard the words Plumed and Menace together, though no one seemed to take it seriously.

This was the man their prince had chosen, after all.

He could only be good and gentle and pious, surely.

A happy flutter spread through Cin's stomach as Lorenz settled onto one knee in front of him, drawing Cin's other shoe from the small bag at his waist. Blood still stained the heel and toe, but the leather shimmered gently, dark yet sparkling, as though its magic were coming alive especially for Cin.

He didn't extend the shoe to Cin, though, his voice low as he asked, "You do know that while my love for you is as deep as any love could be, I am still not one to feel the dreamy passions of romance?" Lorenz looked nervous, but hopeful, his brow tight and his eyes pleading. "The bonds on my heart are gone, but who I am hasn't changed. I would cross kingdoms to be at your side, and without you any future of mine would be empty and unbearable, but my affection is still a steady beast, committed, but, I'm afraid, a bit unexciting if you're looking for a love with the same giddy passion as our physical intimacy. Are you certain you'll be happy with that?"

"*I* am a little giddy for *you*, I think." It had been slow in coming, and it was a sensation so firmly tied to who the prince was at his core, in the corners of his soul that only time and attention had revealed, but the feeling was there. Cin brushed his thumb over his own heart. "But if you say your love for me is so deep as this, regardless of the ways in which you feel it, it's enough. The giddiness of a new romance fades, anyway. We're simply ahead of the curve."

Relief and joy spread across Lorenz's face. "Then what do you say, my dove?" He raised his voice, its charming arrogance only outmatched by the tender kindness Cin had grown to love him for. "Would you marry me?"

"I suppose." A giddy smile pulled across Cin's face. Carefully, he lifted his bare foot, giving his toes a little wiggle. "You *do* owe me a shoe, after all."

Lorenz laughed, wiping at the corner of his eye before sliding the shoe onto Cin's foot. It fit perfectly. The whole village seemed to erupt in revelry, but their joy faded in comparison to the peace that settled over Cin. He knew in that instant, if he hadn't known all the moments before, that this was the future he'd always been heading for: one where this man, this prince, was beaming up at him with awe and pride and wonder.

Lorenz laughed again, fuller this time. "I think this means you have to tell me your preferred name."

This time it felt easy, simple: "It's Cin. Not like the misdeed, but the ashes. Cin like a cinder hot enough that when wrongfully stoked it will light the world ablaze."

"You *are* covered in the stuff." Lorenz grinned, brushing his hand through Cin's hair a few times, each sweep dislodging more gray clumps. Perdition cooed at him for it, and the tangle of new flesh over Lorenz's heart shimmered in response.

"Don't you start," Cin grumbled, but he found he didn't mind the thought of his old nickname, if it was Lorenz laying claim to it. He was Cin, but he could be Cinder, too, and a thousand other things, some more bloody than others. Though, he thought, not a king.

And that was all right. He and Lorenz would serve Hallin in other ways, just as valuable but far more suitable.

Cin's prince looked as though he was already serving his kingdom then, as he lifted Cin's hand into the air once more, grinning his wide, satisfied smile as he announced, "Behold, my fiancé: Cin Reinholz, the Pigeon Prince!"

Cin's flock responded to the call, encircling them both in a rush of feathers before most veered off into the sky where the cheers of the crowd still echoed. Perdition stayed behind, landing—not on Cin, for once—but atop Emma's messy head, picking free tangled strands of her hair as she laughed. *Pigeon Prince.* Cin felt his smile ache in his cheeks, beaming out of him in ways he couldn't understand, much less contain. It felt like... like being seen, for the first time. Pigeon Prince.

He squeezed Lorenz's hand and it felt as though he might never, ever have to let go again.

His prince leaned in to whisper to him, his warm breath tickling Cin's ear. "How do we make them part for us?"

Cin glanced toward the sky. He had always been connected to his flock, but now they seemed to share one heart as the simple look brought them down again. The birds flew through the crowd, their magic sweeping the villagers harmlessly to the side to carve a way forward for the royal party. When part of the flock returned to form back into Cin's mount, he pulled Lorenz up behind him. His partner wrapped both arms around him, hugging close against his back, no gap this time for the cage of his heart, just flesh on flesh, love against love. It felt righter than it ever had—like with Rags and Lacey's magic in his chest, Lorenz, Cin, and their flock were all made from the same stuff now.

In a way, Cin suspected they were.

He leaned his head back, settling it against Lorenz's shoulder as they meandered their way out of the village, waving to the crowd as it finally dispersed. "Now that we're engaged, does this mean that we get to have sex in your bed?"

Lorenz gave a tiny nibble on Cin's jawline. "Only if we still get to have it everywhere else, too."

Cin grinned. "Everywhere, and then some."

They'd need to be on the move anyway, if they were going to find Adalwin. While Cin still worried he'd given the royal family false hope, he was more and more certain of himself by the minute. Right now, Lorenz's brother was out there somewhere, as green as the frogs that croaked around him, trying to be content in the knowledge that at least Lorenz was loved. If they could find him again, perhaps they could figure out how to break whatever curse had been placed over him, the same way Cin had broken the dark magic in Lorenz's bonds.

Despite the ease with which Cin's flock had led him there last time, he could already feel it would be a harder journey now. But a worthwhile one. Anything was worth bringing Lorenz back his brother.

And all the while, Cin would have Lorenz at his side: a man who didn't need him, but wanted him all the same, wanted him for everything he was, bloody hands and all. Riding toward the palace, under the light of the noon sun and the shadows of his flock's wings, Emma's tired giggles before him and the dwindling smoke of his family home behind, Cin knew he might not have been as pious as his mother had hoped. But he felt that what he'd done was good. And that was enough.

Epilogue

Cin raised his head from the bared skin of Lorenz's chest, lifting his brow cheekily. "Should we get up or do you have more such wonders in store for me?"

They were still partway undressed—as undressed as either of them had made it, anyway, before tumbling into the tent they were meant to be taking down, as desperate for each other after the three straight weeks they'd spent together as they'd been when their time had been limited to a few stolen hours at the ball. Lorenz's hair was mussed on one side, sticking out at odd angles beneath the crown Cin still requested he wear. It made Lorenz's parents happy too, as an outward display that their son was still the prince of the country they loved so dearly, even if he was never going to be its next king.

Cin still hoped he and Lorenz would right the dilemma of an heir soon, though with each failed search he was fearing more and more that he'd led them out on false hope.

They'd decided—with the queen and king's agreement—to tell very few people of the purpose of their quest, taking only a handful of trusted castle staff with them. Among those were two of Lorenz's personal watch, Lieselotte and Mildred, one of whom had been reassigned to Cin, as well as Conrad from the cooking staff, Roza from the stables, and Berit, who filled in their little party by attending to everything else. At that very moment, Cin could hear Berit distantly bickering with Mildred over something that seemed, based on the little he could pick up, to be about the stacking of the cooking supplies. Both he and Lorenz had grumbled last night that the two needed to get over themselves and fuck already.

As much as Cin was growing to adore their small party of kind and dedicated members—even enjoying the drama that sprung up from time to time, which was always resolved with a care and compassion he'd never experienced at home—he missed his familiar haunts, his town, and most especially Emma. She was happier back in the city, though, where she'd joined the crown's newly reconstructed watch, working alongside the common folk to decide how best to incorporate a benevolent system of justice throughout the kingdom. When she had the peace of mind to focus, it seemed she could be incredibly perceptive, even if she still had not mastered a proper braid.

They all had their own path in life, though, Cin knew. He was proud of Emma for seeking out her own, just as he and Lorenz were doing. Though at the moment, all theirs seemed to entail was traipsing uselessly through the forest and fucking.

From beneath Cin, Lorenz groaned dramatically. "I think I may lie here a moment and contemplate the weary state of my poor bones." He shifted, pressing his lips tenderly to top of Cin's head. "But you go on. I can feel you're restless."

Cin couldn't deny that. His magic had been useless at finding Adalwin thus far, but for the last few days a worrying little tug in Cin's chest had appeared, pulling at him with something nearing aggression. He could sense a twinge of it reflected in Lorenz where the shimmer of Ragimund and Lacey still gleamed in his chest.

Lately, out of the corner of his eye he'd been catching Lorenz tenderly cuddling a pair of ghostly pigeons against his shoulder, but the forms always vanished when Cin looked at his partner head-on, and Lorenz only smiled and waved after. Cin gave one last kiss to the magical flesh above Lorenz's heart all the same, praying a soft thanks to the birds who had made this future with his lover possible. The warmth that overtook his chest after seemed to come from somewhere outside himself, and he could not help but smile through the sheen of moisture that still formed over his eyes whenever he thought of Rags and Lacey.

Cin slid back on his trousers and buttoned himself up, leaving Lorenz to his last few minutes of rest before their trek would begin anew. A little shiver ran through him as he exited the warmth of the tent. With a spark from his magic, his feather cloak slid down from around his shoulders. He meandered through their little camp, exchanging short greetings with the other members of their small group. All the while, he could feel the protective gazes of the birds resting in the half-bare winter trees around them.

His flock had only grown since he'd realized the magic of his pigeons came from deep within himself, each small nurturing of that power allowing him to divvy it out to new members of their growing protectorate. Most of his flock were still pigeons, but while they traveled the forest, Cin had found owls and vultures and the occasional hawk to be more comfortable within the trees than his usual town-birds, many of whom were currently awaiting him in the closest of the villages. If he closed his eyes and focused, he could sense them in a nebulous way, like distant extensions of himself.

There was, of course, one pigeon from his flock who, regardless of the forest's depths and horrors, still never left Cin's side. She landed on his shoulder as he neared the edge of their small camp, puffing up her chest as though she was the queen of their flock. He gave Perdition's neck a scratch, which she tried, obstinately, to dodge.

She latched around his earlobe instead and tugged.

"How rude!" Cin protested, trying to shift her away from his ear. She moved to nipping at his fingers instead.

The tug of magic in Cin's chest suddenly strengthened. The babble of frog-song echoed through his head, and for a single breath, the air felt thick and muggy despite the early winter chill. Hope rushed through Cin. He dashed through the camp, shouting as he went.

His excitement seemed contagious, hoots and hollers echoing between the group's members. Their joy only made the smile spreading across Cin's face grow. They trusted him, without hesitation or question. It was such an incredible feeling to be surrounded by people who understood and respected him for his place in their lives. Cin didn't think he'd ever quite get used to it, at least not for months or years yet.

Lorenz's expression was a bit different from the rest, though, as he stumbled out of the tent still working through the buttons of his shirt. His eyes were so wide they seemed mostly whites, his face slack with worry. He grabbed Cin's hands, holding them in a death grip.

"You really think— Could this be— If it's really him—" He didn't seem to know how to finish his own sentences, babbling them through shallow breaths.

Cin squeezed his hands in turn and pulled him close. "I hope so, yes," he said, but he could see the real question on Lorenz's face, one that had slipped out in bits and pieces over the course of their travels. "He still loves you. He's your brother. He always will."

"But there were so many years where I couldn't love him," Lorenz whispered, tucking his face against the side of Cin's.

"He'll understand." Cin believed that, but he knew it might take Lorenz meeting his brother again—talking to him, hearing of his life, and letting Adalwin hear of his—for it to truly sink in. He squeezed his prince's hands again. "We need to get going. I don't know how long I'll feel this pull."

Lorenz swallowed, but he nodded, putting on a brave face. "All right. Let us find my brother, then!"

Sometimes, it turned out, God smiled on those who'd thrown aside piety, so long as they'd done it for the sake of goodness.

Hallin would have its crowned prince after all, and Lorenz would have his brother, and Cin—Cin would have them all: a family, a partner, a future. If Cin had anything to say on the matter, they were all going to live happily ever after.

Cin smiled. "Let's go find Adalwin."

T hank you for sharing Cinder's adventure with me! As always, if you enjoyed this story, you can show your appreciation by reviewing it at your favorite book review site or book seller. If you have a local library card, you can also request they purchase Cinder so that other readers might find and enjoy it there.

If you'd like more of the Brother's Grimm inspired achillean romance, check out the rest of the GriMM Tales series...

Red Riding Hood by TJ Rose
Zel by Amanda Meuwissen
Hansel and Gerhardt by W.H. Lockwood
The Elves and the Shoemaker by Emory Winters
Cinder by D.N. Bryn
The Frog Prince by A.M. Rose
Rumpelstilzchen by Sam Northman
Snow White and the Seven Little Miners by Kit Barrie

LOOKING FOR MORE BY D. N. BRYN?

For more M/M yearning, check out *Guides For Dating Vampires*, a series of loosely connected standalones following soft vampires and the humans who would kill for them.

For more magic and mayhem, try the *These Treacherous Tides* series, a fantasy universe with a dash of steampunk and scientifically reimagined mythological creatures, and a variety of queer main characters.

Learn more through the QR code below: